Elsewhere....

ELSEWHERE

EDITED BY TERRI WINDLING &
MARK ALAN ARNOLD

Interior Illustrations
by T. Windling

ELSEWHERE

The editors would like to thank the following for their help, suggestions, and/or moral
support:
Susan Allison, James Patrick Baen, Nicholas Crome, "Rabbi" Richard Freeman, Linda
Goldfarb, Lisa Hauck, Allan Jones, Tappan King, Ellen Kushner, Robin McKinley, Beth
Meachem, Mimi Panitch, Kenneth Peck, Leesa Stanion, Reg Wells, Jane Yolen, and
The Lithuanian Service of Voice of America.

An Ace Book

First Ace printing: September 1981
Published Simultaneously in Canada
2 4 6 8 0 9 7 5 3 1

Manufactured in the United States of America

Acknowledgements. . . .

Tatuana's Tale by Miguel Angèl Asturias first appeared in *Leyendas de Guatemala*; American translation copyright © 1973 by Barbara Howes and reprinted here with her kind permission from *The Eye of the Heart*.

Sea Change copyright © 1981 by C. J. Cherryh.

Ku Mei Li copyright © 1981 by M. Lucie Chin.

The Green Child copyright © 1981 by John Crowley.

Pooka's Bridge copyright © 1981 by Gil FitzGerald.

Queen Louisa copyright © 1972 by John Gardner, reprinted from *The King's Indian*, Alfred A. Knopf, Publishers, a division of Random House, Inc.

Song of Amergin by Robert Graves reprinted by permission of Farrar, Strauss, & Giroux, Inc. from *The White Goddess* by Robert Graves, copyright © 1949.

The Thunder Cat copyright © 1956 by Nicholas Stuart Gray; reprinted by permission of Faber & Faber Ltd from *Mainly in Moonlight* by Nicholas Stuart Gray.

Viriconium Knights copyright © 1981 by M. John Harrison.

The Magician copyright © 1971 by William Kotzwinkle; reprinted by permission of Pantheon Books, a division of Random House, Inc., from *Elephant Bangs Train* by William Kotzwinkle.

The Unicorn Masque copyright © 1981 by Ellen Kushner.

The Song of the Dragon's Daughter copyright © 19 77 by Ursula K. Le Guin; reprinted by permission of the author and her agent, Virginia Kidd.

The Last Voyage of the Ghost Ship copyright © 1972 by Gabriel García Márquez; translated by Gregory Rabassa; reprinted from *The Leaf Storm and Other Stories* by permission of Harper & Row, Publishers, Inc.

Overheard on a Saltmarsh by Harold Monro is reprinted from *The Silent Pool* by permission of Gerald Duckworth & Co. Ltd.

Elric at the End of Time copyright © 1981 by Michael Moorcock.

Sweetly the Waves Call to Me copyright © 1981 by Pat Murphy.

Little Boy Waiting at the Edge of the Darkwood copyright © 1981 by Andrew J. Offutt.

Tales of Houdini copyright © 1981 by Rudy Rucker.

The Prodigal Daughter copyright © 1981 by Jessica Amanda Salmonson

Pale Horse by Masao Takiguchi copyright © 1969 by Nicholas Crome; reprinted with his kind permission from "TransPacific Magazine" No. 2, 1969.

The Succubus by John Alfred Taylor copyright © 1971 by Nicholas Crome; reprinted here with the permission of Nicholas Crome and the author from "TransPacific Magazine" No. 6, 1971.

The Golden Slipper by Antanas Vaiciulaitis is reprinted by permission of the author from *Selected Lithuanian Short Stories*, edited by Stepas Zobarskas, copyright © 1959, 1960, 1963.

The Judgement of St. Ives copyright © 1981 by Evangeline Walton.

The Renders copyright © 1981 by Janny Wurts.

The Story of Alwina, from *Islandia: History and Description* [by Jean Perrier, translated by John Lang] by Austin Tappan Wright copyright © 1981 William Wright, Phyllis Wright, Benjamin Wright and Paul J. Mitarachi

The Tree's Wife by Jane Yolen copyright © 1978 by Mercury Press, Inc. from "The Magazine of Fantasy & Science Fiction"; reprinted by permission of Edward L. Ferman and the author. Merman in Love: copyright by Jane Yolen.

"It's never wise to steal from the Faeries...."

Table of Contents

Introduction

Fantasy is as old as literature; the fantastic tale as ancient as the spoken word. Storytellers ancient and modern have swept their audiences—young and old alike—away from the world we live in to far lands where magic dwells and the extraordinary is commonplace—beyond the light of the campfire, beyond the edges of the sea or the borders of the galaxy, over the next hill to that mysterious, alluring place that always lies elsewhere, that has been the landscape of fantastic fiction for thousands of years.

Fantasy tales can be traced back through time to the clay tablets of the oldest written epics, and still further back in the oral tradition of bards, shamans, ollaves, wisewomen. Despite the dominance of naturalism and social realism in nineteenth and twentieth century fiction, fantasy has survived, and even flourished, in the literary marketplace of the last two decades, albeit segregated into genre categories: horror, "sword-&-sorcery", magical or "high" fantasy, contemporary fairy tales and fable (often segregated further into a "juvenile" classification), and that modern, technological extension of fantasy: science fiction. Although generally dismissed by modern American critics as a less than serious form of writing fit only for children and the childlike, there is quite a bit of successful fantasy to be found disguised as "post-realist", "idiosyncratic", "visionary" works of the mainstream: John Barth's *Chimera*, John Gardner's *Grendel*, Gabriel García Márquez' *One Hundred Years of Solitude*, Robert Nye's *Merlin*, Tom Robbins' *Another Roadside Attraction*, Richard Adams' *Watership Down*, R. M. Koster's *Mandragon*, Joyce Carol Oates' *Bellefleur*, Angela Carter's *War of Dreams*, Sylvia Townsend Warner's *Kingdoms of Elfin*, John Crowley's *Little, Big*, represent a very few examples. We can hope these works suggest that the borders between genre and mainstream fantasy may be crossed more regularly, that each camp might stop regarding the other with suspicion or disdain. The elegant flights of controlled imagination that grace good genre fantasy can enrich and enliven the whole of literature in an age where wonder is rare indeed; in turn, the literary challenge of excellence can, must, be applied to genre fiction to return fantasy to a vital place in our literary culture.

Fantasy and realism are not, perhaps, approaches to fiction as antagonistic as they might seem. The most stark and austere street portrait still grows as a creative fantasia from the singular mind of its author (a Jungian would contend that the same creativity draws from a fantastic wellspring indeed); while fantastic fiction draws its substance and life from reality. Without that grounding in the real, the most lavishly constructed fantasy world caves in on itself and turns into nonsense, like fairy gold turning back into the dead leaves from which it was made. Good fantasy has the ring of truth.

To my mind, the best fantasy occurs in the intersection of the wondrous with the ordinary, at the moment when the threshold between the weird and familiar is crossed. There is a Swahili word, *svaha,* that means *the moment between the lightning and the thunder,* that time of electricity infused stillness when the doors between worlds open, when strange creatures stand suddenly revealed and disappear again in the blink of an eye. *Twilight* is artist Brian Froud's title for an eerily beautiful canvas of shimmering, transparent fey folk—twilight, "the Faery Time, as Hallowe'en is the twilight of the year when all the spirits come abroad . . . the moment of stepping between this world and the faery world; it is a time charged with possibilities". Paul Klee, defining his art, discusses the *surnaturel,* which is not something different from reality but the reality normally hidden from view. Rene Magritte's bland and mundane landscapes are transformed, shattered by the unknown mystery of some impossible element. Fantasy is that which lurks at the edges of reality, half seen and turned invisible again in the instant of recognition; fantasy is what occurs when dreams enter the world, and worlds turn into dream.

In this collection you will find stories that range the spectrum of fantastic literature, a variety generated by two editors of diverging tastes and a common love for the field. Some of the stories are set in contemporary worlds only slightly apart from our daily norm; others sweep into far distant realms where reality is only the shadow of a shadow of our own.

In collecting these tales, Mark and I followed no rigid theme or aesthetic ideology—we simply gathered fantasy stories wherever they were to be found, seeking those which best evoke a sense of wonder, wonder being the soul of fantasy. Thus original works by new and veteran fantacists mix with tales culled from less familiar collections and foreign works in translation. This volume, the first in a three-volume anthology, is presented neither as a definitive work or historical survey—readers looking along those lines are commended to try Robert K. Boyer & Kenneth J. Zahorski's *Fantastic Imagination*, Terry Carr & Martin Greenberg's *A Treasury of Modern Fantasy*, and Jane Mobley's *Phantasmagoria*.

The following tales were chosen to delight, to set you off on the road to those mysterious lands that lie forever over the horizon, elsewhere.

T.W.

*   *   *

Magic dwells in lands of boundless dimension, lands not always apparent. Faerie, for one, is often invisible and often beside us. The vistas and images of fantasy describe an endless atlas of invented worlds, planes, pastures, castles and cities; oceans and heavens of myth and dream; veiled corridors of the past; shadowed corners next door, up the attic, in the kitchen; distant hills and tors and redoubts stretching in all directions to the beginnings and ends of time. Anything can happen.

The range of magical fantasy stories and ways in which fantasies are told are also lands of boundless dimension, not always apparent. Fantasy can mingle fairy tale, legendry, adventure, dream, reflection, desire, fable, parable—and has done so, around the world, since earliest civilization. Fantasy has never been absent from music and balladry, art, games, dance, drama, or literature. The lands of magic are equally open to writers of escapist entertainment, of best-selling novels, and of Nobel prize winning fiction. Spellbinding sorcerous visions are narrated by inventive children, oral yarnspinners, plain and straightforward storytellers, finely disciplined stylists, and experimentalists of a hundred schools. Works derived from every culture, every language. Humor, idyll, tragedy. New faces for heros familiar to some, outlandish glimpses of countries unknown to most. From the simple beauty of an old tale told real well to the complex reinvestiture of myth, to challenging apperceptions of illusion and reality. Stories relentlessly phantasmic, and stories magical only in their giddy, convincing impossibility.

This is a sampler of lands.

M.A.

Terri Windling &
Mark Alan Arnold
St. George, New York
Summer, 1981

Elsewhere....

Windling 1981

The Green Child

John Crowley

This story is recorded by Ralph of Coggeshall and by
William of Newbridge, both of whom say that it took place
in their own time, about the middle of the twelfth century,
in West Suffolk.

At a place called the Wolf-pits, a woman of the village
came upon two children at the entrance to one of the pits, a
girl and a younger boy. The Wolf-pits, though everyone
knew about them, had never been explored, as they were
considered dangerous and unlucky, and no one knew how
deep they were or where they led. The two children stood
blinking in the sunlight, their pale eyes blank as though
they had just opened them on this world. They were quite
small for what seemed their age, and their skin was green,
the pale, luminous green of the verges of a twilight sky in
summer.

The woman dropped the ball of wool she had been
gathering, crossed herself, made other signs against the
Evil Eye and the good people; the children watched her,
but made no response, as though they didn't understand
these gestures to be directed at them. The woman, feeling
that despite their green color, the color of fairies, they
might be just lost children after all, approached them,
asking their names and where they came from. They drew
back from her, the boy attempting to run into the pit's
mouth; the girl caught him, and held him back, and spoke
words to him the woman couldn't understand. Pulling
away from her, the boy shook his head and shouted, as
though not believing what the girl told him; she pulled him
roughly away from the pit's entrance, and spoke sharply to
him. The boy began to weep then, a storm of tears, and his
sister—it seemed to the woman they must be brother and
sister—held him tightly as though to smother his tears, all
the while looking with her large pale eyes at the woman,

for help, or from fear, or both.

Pity overcame the woman's wonder, and she came to them, telling them not to be afraid, asking if they were lost.

"Yes," the girl said, and her speech, though in form different from common human speech, was intelligible. "Yes. Lost."

The woman took them to her own house. The boy, still weeping, refused to enter it, but with her rough yet protective manner his sister drew him in. The darkness within seemed to calm them both, though the boy still whimpered. The woman offered them food, good bread, a bowl of milk, but they refused them with revulsion. The woman decided to get help and advice. Making gestures and speaking softly, she told them to stay, rest, she would be back soon; she put the food nearby in case they should want it, and hurried out to call her neighbors and the priest, wondering if when she returned the green children would not have disappeared, or her belongings, or the house itself.

She brought back with her a weaver known to be a fairy doctor, who could cure the stroke, and his wife, and several others whom she met, though not the priest, who was asleep; and they all went to see the green children, the village dogs barking behind them.

They were as she had left them, sitting on the bed, their arms around each other and their bare green feet hanging down. The fairy doctor lit a bit of blessed candle he had brought, but they didn't start at it; they only looked with silent trepidation, like shy wild things, at the faces peering in the door and window at them. In the darkness of the house they seemed to glow faintly, like honey.

"They won't eat," the woman said.

"Give them beans," the fairy doctor said. "Beans are the fairy food."

They were fairies to this extent, at least; when the woman gave them beans, they devoured them hungrily, though they still refused all other food.

They would answer no questions about the place they had come from, or how they had come to the Wolf-pits;

when asked if they could return to where they came from, they only wept, the boy loudly, the girl almost grudgingly, her face set and her fists clenched and the tears trembling on the lashes of her luminous eyes. But later, at twilight, when the people had all gone away, and the boy had fallen asleep exhausted by grief, the woman by kindly questions did learn their story, holding the girl's cool green hand in hers.

They came from a land below the earth, she said. There it is always twilight, "like this," she said, gesturing to include the dimness of the house, the crepuscular fast-darkening blue of the doorway and the window, perhaps also the birds sleepily speaking and the hush of evening wind in the leaves outside. It was cool there; the rushing cool breath the villagers had noticed coming even in high summer from the Wolf-pits was the exhalation of her country. Everyone there was the same hue as herself; she had been as much frightened, she said, by the woman's odd color as by the unbearable brilliance of the sun.

She and her brother were shepherd's children, and had gone in search of a lost lamb. They had got lost themselves, and after a long fearful time had heard, far off, a bell ringing. They had followed the sound of the bell, and had found the exit of the pit.

Would they go home again? the woman asked.

No, they could not. Whatever is an exit from that country, the girl said, is not an entrance; she was sure of that, though why this should be so she couldn't explain. They couldn't go back that way again. Her brother, she said, wouldn't believe this; but it was so.

Night had come, and the woman again offered the girl the bowl of sweet milk. She took it now, with a kind of reverent fear, and as carefully as though it were mass-wine, she drank some. She gave the bowl back to the woman, wiping her mouth with the back of her hand, her face frightened yet resolute, as though she had drunk poison on purpose. The woman put her to sleep on the bed with her brother, and curled up herself on the floor. In the night she heard the boy more than once awake and cry; but the girl cried no more. Years later the woman would look back and try to remember if the girl had ever cried again; and did not remember that she ever had.

In the morning the priest came. He questioned the children closely. The boy hid himself behind his sister and was silent, but the girl, less tongue-tied now, told in her strange accents what she had told the woman the previous evening, shyly insisting this was the truth, though the priest tried subtly to trap her into an admission that they were of the devil, either minor demons themselves or figments created by the devil to lead mortals into error. They had no fear of his cross or of the saints' relics he had brought in a glass vial; yet the girl could not answer any questions he put to her about their Savior, the Church, heaven or hell. At last the priest slapped his knees and rose, saying that he couldn't tell who or what they might be, but they must at least be baptized. And so they were.

The boy remained inconsolable. He would not eat any food but beans, which he gorged on ravenously, without seeming to gain nourishment from them; he spoke only to his sister, in words no one else understood. He wasted rapidly. His sister would let no one else nurse him, not the woman, especially not the fairy doctor, though it was clear the boy declined; soon he even ceased to weep. In the middle of one night, the girl woke the woman and, dry-eyed, told her that her brother was dead. After some thought and prayer, the priest determined that he might be buried on consecrated ground.

The girl continued to live with the woman, who was childless and a widow. She came to eat human food without difficulty, and in time lost most of her green color, though her eyes remained large and strangely golden, like a cat's, and she never grew to proper size, but remained always tiny, thin, and somewhat insubstantial. She helped the woman about the house; she herded the village sheep, she heard mass on Sundays and holy-days, she went to processions and festivals in the village. The priest, still alert for devilish signs, heard stories that she was wanton and had no modesty and that any boy who asked her in the right way might have her in the pasture; but she was perhaps not the only one in the village of whom that might be said.

The woman, grateful that she had stayed and had not sickened like her brother, ceased asking her about her far country and what went on there; but many others wanted to hear her story, and came from some distance away to question her. She received them all, sitting in the chimney corner in her best dress, and rehearsed the tale for them; and over time it grew a little longer. She said that the name of her country was St. Martin's Land, because St. Martin was its patron. The green people there were Christian, she said, and worshipped our Savior, but on Saturdays like the Jews. She said that at the border of her country was a wide river, and beyond that river was a bright country where she had always longed to travel but could never reach. When she talked of this bright land, her pale eyes sometimes grew tears. The woman, old now, hearing her tell these things, and remembering how before the priest she had been ignorant of religion, wondered if these stories were not substitutes for true memories of her far dark country, which she had lost over time as she had lost her twilight color.

Eventually, it is recorded, the green child married a man at Lenna, and there "survived many years." It's not recorded what sort of man he was, or what sort of wife she made; nor if there were children of this union, and, if so, whether the blood in them of the land their mother called St. Martin's Land made them different from other children. If there were children, and children of those children, so that in some way that green land elsewhere and also the distant bright country glimpsed across the wide river entered our plain human race, it must surely be so diluted now, so bound up and drowned in daylight and red blood, as not to be present in us at all.

William of Newbridge says these events took place in the reign of King Stephen, and that at first he didn't believe the story, but that later the general testimony compelled him to believe it to be true.

IT WAS A WILD, DARK PLACE...

WINDLING

Pooka's Bridge

Gillian FitzGerald

There was an old lord named Niall MacMahon O'Farrell who saw all of his sons die in battle, leaving him without an heir to his great riches. He knew he had but a handful of years left on earth, and he had no wish to see his land go to his cousin Cathal, who was a hard man. So he looked about for a wife, and his eyes fell upon Mairi Ni Rory, a woman whose temper was as sweet as her warm, green eyes. He'd not hoped to love his new wife, for he had thought his heart buried with Maeve, the woman who'd given him four fine sons and twenty years of her life. After the fierce passion of his love for Maeve, he felt he had no right to ask for more, but he could not help loving Mairi: she had the way about her. She was as gay and pretty as a bird, with long, dark hair falling like a river about a petal-pale face, and tilting green eyes that smiled as gaily as her wide, soft mouth. She sang often as she moved about his house, and her gentle ways won the hearts of everyone in the hall from the youngest kitchen-maid to the gruffest of Niall's soldiers. For all her soft answers, though, no one thought her weak; they knew her for a brave woman, as well as a sweet one.

She bore Niall a son, and three years later, a daughter, and their joy was complete. But the happiness was not to last, for Cathal grew angry at the news that he had lost the hall to a babe in arms. He kept hoping that the boy would die of some childhood illness, but instead Garrett grew strong. So, seeing no other chance, he led a troop against his cousin. Niall heard, and made his plans carefully, for he knew that his few men could not hope to win against the hired soldiers bought by Cathal's gold. He took Mairi aside, and told her to flee with their children. She protested that she had no wish to leave him, but he was firm.

"Mairi, my wife, you have given me more happiness

these last years than I had any right to expect. I do not desire to be the cause of your death, and if you stay with me, you and our children will most surely die. So you must go, so that you can raise our son to manhood, and when he is grown he can reclaim what is his." He took her in his arms and kissed her tenderly, then smiled. "Now go to the stables, Mairi. You'll find Seumas waiting for you, and he will see you safe away."

She flung her arms around him, kissed him one last time, for she knew she would not see him again, but she did not allow her tears to fall for that was not her way. She found her children, packed a small bundle of clothes and food, then took them to the yard where old Seumas, Niall's trusted lieutenant, sat waiting with two horses. He took seven-year-old Garrett in front of him, and she held little Megeen in her arms as they rode out under the cover of darkness. Two hour's ride away they came to a forest, but to enter the wood they had to cross a deep stream. There was a bridge across it, and as they rode over Seumas said, "You and the little ones will be safe enough here, lady. They say the bridge is the haunt of a Pooka, and Cathal is one to stay clear of such things, so his men will not bother you."

They followed a narrow path deep into the dark and silent wood until they reached a clearing. There was a small cottage with a thatched roof, the kind that poor farmers lived in, and it was here that Seumas reined his horse to a halt. "This will be your home, lady. You will find food and turf for the fire, and all that you need. The people will know where to find you, and they will see to your needs. As for me, I go back to the hall. I have lived at Niall's side, and I will die there." He gave her a brief salute, then wheeled about and was lost in the darkness.

She found the cottage as he said it would be, and set about making a fire from the turf piled on the hearth, and when it had blazed high, she had a look about. It was a small place, with two small rooms. The main room, with a fireplace, was a kitchen, holding a rough table and a cupboard and some chairs. The other room was a bedchamber with a large bed for her and Megeen, and a little trundle bed that pulled out from it for Garrett. There was a chest for their clothes, and another small one with blankets against the cold of winter.

She put the children to sleep, then went back to the kitchen to kneel before the fire. She saw that someone had provided her with a spindle and a small loom, that she might spin thread and weave cloth for their needs, and there was a large sack of wool beside the spindle. It was Niall's doing, she thought, for he knew how much she hated idleness. And then she stared long and sadly into the fire, too unhappy for tears at the thought that she would never again see the good old man who had been her husband. Though he had not been the hero of a young girl's dreams, still he had been a kind companion and the father of her children, and his death left an empty place that ached and could not be filled. She fell asleep like that, and when she woke to the first light of dawn, she put aside her sorrow and began to live her new life.

Her days took on a sameness. She fed and cared for the children and kept the little house sparkling, and sometimes she gathered herbs and plants that she could use for healing, for she knew much about curing the sick. As the days grew colder, she spun her wool into thread, and then wove woolen cloth from it so that they might have warm clothes for the winter. It was a simple life, and a pleasant one. She had few cares, for her husband's people took it upon themselves to see that she and her little ones were fed; they would leave her cheese or milk or a slab of bacon. In return, she did what she could for their sick, but she felt ashamed that she could give back so little to her people who gave her so much.

There was little love lost for Cathal, for he was what Niall had called him: a hard man. He showed no mercy for a peasant whose rent was a day or two late, or who could not meet the rents because of sickness or misfortune. Those who could not pay he turned out homeless, with no care for their families. Mairi heard the stories from those who came to see her in the evenings, and she remembered her promise to her husband. But how could a little boy like Garrett gain back his land? That was a job for a soldier, not a lad of seven years.

Garrett was growing into a fine boy, with his mother's dark hair and his father's grey eyes, and the courage of them both. He had a high heart, did the boy, and the curiosity of a cat. He loved best to be exploring the woods, and though his mother bade him stay close by, if the truth be told, he did not always obey. And so it was that one day he wandered away as far as the Pooka's bridge, and when it grew late he still had not come home. Mairi was nearly wild with worry, but she could not leave the house and Megeen all alone so that she could search for him.

When one of her husband's men came to leave her some food, she begged him, weeping (and she did not cry often), to find her son for her, and he promised to do what he could. He returned the next night, and his lined face was grave.

"Lady, the news is not good. I've asked about, and this is what I've heard: It seems some of Cathal's men came down to the pub for a drink or two, and they spoke long of what they'd seen. They were down at the bridge—the Pooka's bridge. They came upon young Garrett, and thought to make sport of him, for they thought he'd a look of the old lord about him—that he might be one of his one of his by-blows—begging your pardon, lady, but they judge all by Cathal. When they went to cross the bridge to grab him and carry him to the hall, a huge, grey horse came out of the woods, and bent down to let the boy mount. And then the horse disappeared into the woods, and they could find no trace of it, not even a hoofprint in the dirt." He shook his head. "It must have been the Pooka, lady, that came for your son, and I don't know which could be worse, the Pooka taking him or Cathal."

"I've a better chance of getting Garrett back from the Sidhe, than from Cathal O'Farrell, for if he'd gotten his hands on my son, there'd be no hope at all. Cathal would know him for Niall's son as soon as he laid eyes upon him." She got to her feet and pulled her grey cloak from the hook by the door and wrapped it round her. "And if you will stay with Megeen, I will go fetch my son."

And though she sounded quite calm and unafraid, her heart was thudding quickly in her breast, for she was sorely troubled for Garrett. She hid her fear, however, and spoke calmly, for that was the way she was. "I shall return as soon as I have found him," she said, and told him where to find a loaf of bread, and the makings of the breakfast porridge and tea, in case she should not get back before Megeen woke.

Wrapped in her drab cloak, she made her way through the forest. She no longer feared the woods. All the creatures knew her, and would not have harmed her, and the night-noises were as reassuring to her as the soft sound of Megeen breathing in her sleep. But when she reached the bridge she no longer felt at ease. It was a wild, dark place, a stone bridge built so long ago that it was easy to believe that the Sidhe themselves had made it, and it glittered darkly in the wan light of the moon.

She crossed the bridge, till she stood in its exact center. Then she called softly in her clear, sweet voice, "Pooka! I have come for the boy you took yester night. Pooka!"

All was silent.

"Pooka! I have come for my son, the boy you carried away last night! Pooka, come to me."

There was no sound but her own breathing to disturb the quiet.

Shivering in the cold, more frightened by the silence than if she'd heard a banshee keening, Mairi tried a third time. "Pooka, it's tired of waiting for you I am. You've taken my son, and I've come for him. Show yourself to me now, or I'll think you a coward."

Then from the woods she heard a sound like distant thunder, and she trembled, for she knew it must be the Pooka coming in answer to her challenge. She was not a coward to tremble, for anyone with sense would think twice before angering a Pooka. They were said to be fiery of temper, wild spirits that could not be tamed, and with little love for humankind. They were shape-shifters, taking many forms, but most often that of a horse or an ass, and leading travellers astray.

The dim crashing of hoofbeats grew louder and louder as the Pooka came closer and closer. At last it stood at the edge of the wood, a great grey horse with eyes that shone like flame and a mane and tail of silver, and silver hooves. It looked at her and spoke.

"Who is it who calls me so late at night?" It had a wild, fearsome voice, like the wind, but there was an undertone of sweetness in it, like the clean quiet after a summer storm, and the huge, glowing eyes had the warmth of flame as well as its brightness.

"'Tis Mairi O'Farrell, and I've come to fetch my son. He's the boy you stole last night," she said boldly.

"And what use would I have for a boy, silly mortal woman? Why should I steal a boy?"

"As for that, I'm sure I don't know, but the old tales say the Sidhe sometimes do so, and it's you that Cathal's men saw carry off my boy last night."

"Oh, is it the dark-haired lad you're after? I did not steal him at all, I just carried him away to safety before that villain's men did harm to him. That will teach you not to heed the gossip of old women," he said reproachfully.

"Then I thank you for saving my son, for Cathal would have had him killed, and I'll thank you doubly for bringing the boy back to me."

Then the Pooka pawed the ground three times with his silver hoof, and shook his silver-maned head. "That I cannot do, mortal woman, for he dwells with the Sidhe now, and only our king, Finvarra, can let him go."

At that Mairi threw back her hood and raised her pale face to the sky, and whispered, "God in heaven, what's to become of me? I've lost my husband, and now I must lose my son as well." Her white cheeks were wet with tears that shone like diamonds in the moonlight, and even in her sorrow she was beautiful.

"If you ask Finvarra, it is possible that he will send the boy back to you," said the Pooka.

"But how shall I find him?"

"In his sid, under the earth."

"And how should I know where that is?" asked Mairi. "It is not marked on any map I've ever seen."

"And why should it be? Such maps are for men, and what have men to do with the Good Folk? But I can carry you there on my back, as I carried your son."

Then he stood quietly so that she might climb onto his back. "Catch hold of my mane, for the ride will be long and swift, and you must not fall off for I will not be able to save you if you do."

"Pooka," said Mairi, clutching tightly around his neck, "what can I give you for this favor?"

"You have given me your tears, and that's more than any other human has done. Now hold fast, for we go!"

It seemed to Mairi that they took to the air, though the Pooka had no wings. The only sounds were the rushing whoosh of the wind, the distant roaring of the sea, and the occasional hoot of an owl. At first she kept her face buried in the Pooka's mane, which was soft as silk against her cheek, so that she could see nothing, but at last she looked about her and saw that the ground seemed very far away, the trees and road and houses like a toy village. Then the mist swirled up around them, and the dark night clouds enwrapped them like a cloak of black velvet and there was nothing but the wind and the darkness.

"Pooka," whispered Mairi, "if the Sidhe do not steal children, why are the stories told?"

"And how would I know that, Mairi O'Farrell? Who tells these stories?"

"The minstrels sing them, and the seannachies tell them at the hearth. One of the old stories says that the Good Folk pay a tax to hell of a living man," said Mairi.

"Not the Sidhe!" roared the Pooka. "We are the children of Danu, who came to Ireland long before your race thought of it, and we owe allegiance only to our king, and to no other—not even Hell would dare to stand against us. So if you hear this story again, tell them the truth of it."

"Well," conceded Mairi, "they say it happened over the sea, and not in Ireland."

The mists of darkness began to thin, and once more Mairi could see the earth spread out below her, but it was not the countryside she knew. It was a strange and wondrous place, an island set in the middle of a lake like a jewel, and on the island was a great castle all of shining glass. Through the crystal walls she could see the light of torches and richly-garbed figures moving gracefully through the halls.

"You see the castle of Finvarra."

And the Pooka glided down to the smooth grass. Then he stamped his silver hooves three times, and suddenly there stood in the place of the great grey horse, a man.

He was tall and slim, garbed in shimmering grey velvet and silk, embroidered all over with silver thread. His hair, falling to his shoulder, was so pale that it had a silver sheen to it, and his light grey eyes sparkled with silver lights. He had the merry face of one who has never known fear or pain, only joy, with a wide, mischievous mouth made for laughter. He bowed to her with an elegant grace.

"My lady, shall I bring you to the king?"

"Are you my Pooka?" asked Mairi, a little breathless from the swiftness of it all.

"And who else should I be? But this is my real shape, if any shape is real. Now come, you must see to your son." He took her hand and led her through the crystal doors and into the great hall of the palace.

The crowd of dancers, all beautiful, all richly dressed, parted before them, and they walked straight from the door to the dais on which sat Finvarra and his lady on two thrones of silver and gold. Behind them hung tapestries shining with gems, and the torches burned bright in jeweled holders. The floors were marble, whiter than new snow, but the dais on which the two thrones rested was of pure gold. Finvarra, the King of the Sidhe, was a man as golden as the sun, and his flame-haired queen was as glorious as a summer sunset.

The Pooka bowed low before them. "My lord and lady, I ask your pardon for this, but I have brought a mortal to your hall."

"This is the second time you have done so," said the King sternly. "Do you plan to make a habit of it?"

"You told me I had done well to bring the boy, and now I come with his mother, who would speak to you about her son."

Mairi curtsied. "I am most grateful for what you have done for my son, but I have come to fetch him home."

Finvarra said, "No one leaves this land once they have come."

"My son is mortal, and he belongs at home, not here. He and his sister are all I have left, and I promised his dead father I would raise him to claim his heritage that Cathal O'Farrell stole."

Then the queen spoke. "The Pooka told us he saved the boy from those who would do him harm. Would you take the boy away from here, where he is safe and will never grow old—would you take him from this, back to the world, where he will know toil and pain and death, where an enemy waits who might kill him if he had the chance?"

Mairi shut her eyes against the magnificence of it all, for what mother could wish her child to trade such beauty for a poor cottage and the hope of gaining back a timbered hall? But at last she met the king's gaze squarely, and this was her answer: "My lord king, it is not my choice to make. I made a vow to my dead husband Niall, and I must keep that vow. Now where is my son?"

The king made a gesture, and one of his lords came forward, leading Garrett by the hand. He ran to his mother and put his arms about her, and she held him tight for a moment, then said over his shoulder, "Thank you, my lord, for what you have done for me."

"Mairi O'Farrell, you are no ordinary woman. Not since the days of Finn and the Fianna has one of your kind come freely to this land, seeking nothing from us. You have the heart of Emer when she came to Tir N'an Og searching for Cuchulain, and for your courage I grant you this: if ever you have great need, you have only to send us word by the Pooka and we will aid you. Go now, and take your son with you."

So Mairi and her son left the castle with the Pooka, and when they reached the lawn, the Pooka resumed his horse shape. Mairi mounted him, with Garrett before her.

"The trip back will go easier—it's easier to go than to come," said the Pooka.

"Why is that?" asked Mairi.

"And how would I know that? I only know that it is."

The ride was swift as a bird's flight, and it seemed scarcely a moment before Mairi stood again on the old stone bridge, with the pale moonlight glinting silver on the Pooka's mane.

"I have done what you asked, woman," said the Pooka. "I hope you are satisfied."

"I am that, Pooka. Is there nothing I can do to show you my thanks?"

"Nothing."

Then, as quickly as the moon vanishing behind a cloud, she bent and kissed the Pooka on his forehead, between his great, glowing eyes. "My thanks for your help, then."

And she took Garrett home to the little cottage where Megeen slept peacefully, guarded by the old soldier.

For a time all went well for the three of them. They did not grow rich, but they did not want for much either. Mairi's fine weaving and needlework brought them a little money, and she used this to pay back the people who had helped her. Winter came, and on most days she and the children huddled around the warm fire, while she sang and told them stories of the old days. Garrett especially loved to hear of the Sidhe, and he would often talk of the wonders he had seen in Finvarra's land—and Mairi would remember how the Pooka looked in human form, with those large grey eyes smiling down at her.

Then one day, a young farmer came to Mairi and begged her to help his wife, who was having their first child, and the midwife could not come because of the snow. Mairi had no wish to leave her children alone, but she saw the fear in the young husband's face, and so she told Garrett to stay with his sister and let no one in. Then she drew on her cloak and went out. The birth was a long, hard one, but at last the mother lay with her new babe in her arms, and Mairi could go home.

As she walked through the woods at the young man's side, she was suddenly overcome by foreboding. The woods were too quiet, as if all the animals were hiding, and the snow looked as if many feet had trampled it flat. When she saw smoke, she broke into a run, and although she half-expected what she saw, it was still a shock.

The little cottage was only a smoking ruin. Her children were nowhere to be seen, and there was no sign of them, though she searched the charred remains of her home.

"It is Cathal who has done this, may the devil take his black heart," she whispered. "He has killed my husband, and now he has taken my children. I will have him for this. I will have him."

"Lady!" The young man caught her arm, but she shook free of him.

"I go to seek my vengeance for this. Go, and bring together all of my husband's men who still live. We will meet together at the Pooka's bridge at dawn."

She strode away from him, and made her way to the bridge.

"Pooka!" she called. "Pooka, I have come to claim my boon from Finvarra."

With a thudding of hooves, the Pooka came galloping, then stopped stock-still before her. "What do you want of me, Mairi O'Farrell?"

"Vengeance," she said.

"For what?"

"For my husband, who is slain, and my children who will die at Cathal's hands. He came this night, and burned my house and carried away my children. I have called together my husband's men, and we will attack at dawn.''

"And what do you want me to do?"

"Bear my message to Finvarra, and tell him that I ask his aid in my trouble. He will know what is the best way to help me. I have faith in his wisdom."

He bent his head, as if to bow. "I am gone, my lady."

She waited through the night at the bridge, and one by one the men gathered there. When the first light of dawn lit the sky, there were only a score of men with her, all that remained of her husband's once-proud troops. When the sun began to rise in the sky against the crimson clouds, the Pooka appeared.

"What news from Finvarra?"

"He bids you climb on my back, and ride against Cathal. His aid will come when you most need it."

So she did as Finvarra bade her, and led her men against Cathal's troops at the hall. And as the dawn flamed brightly, they charged forward across the snow.

"And what do you think to do with those old men at your back, woman? Surely you don't mean to do battle? If so we'll have to arm ourselves with brooms, for fear we'll break their aged bones."

She ignored the taunts of the sentries. "Tell Cathal I've come for my children, and to reclaim the hall in my son's name."

The sentries laughed, but a moment or two later Cathal himself appeared on the walls. "Go away, woman. Your children will be safe with me."

"As safe as their father, Cathal MacRory?"

But what answer he might have made to that the world will never know, for at that moment, as the sun glowed golden in the dawn sky, turning the icicles to diamonds, a cloud of glimmering gold and silver and bronze appeared on the horizon, and thunder was heard, and lightning flashed, though there was not a storm cloud in the sky. And as the great, shining mass moved closer, it could be seen to be a host of riders in armor of silver and bronze, and at their head was a rider all in gold, holding aloft a golden spear, and he was Finvarra himself.

"Do you dare to stand before the host of the Sidhe?" cried the Pooka. "Can a mortal man hope to withstand the might and glory of the Tuatha de Danann? Surrender, Cathal, if you've a grain of sense."

It was not up to Cathal to order his men to do anything, for they were so terrified at the sight of the great troop that they dropped their weapons and fell to their knees, too afraid to lift their heads. Then Finvarra threw his golden spear, and it struck Cathal in the breast, killing him instantly. When its work was done, the spear returned to his hand.

"Take warning, mortal men, that you do not interfere again with those I have chosen to protect, for I may not spare the rest of you next time."

Then the host left as swiftly as they had come, and there was not even a hoofprint left behind to show that they had ever been there.

The men went in to set the hall to rights, and Mairi turned to thank the Pooka, and found that he had taken human form again.

"Mairi O'Farrell, you have done as you promised your husband. The hall belongs to your son, to rule when he comes of age. Your life is your own now. Spend it with me in Finvarra's land."

She leaned her head against his shoulder. "Would that I could, but I am not yet free, Pooka. I have still to raise my son to manhood, before my vow is fulfilled."

"And how long will that take, woman?"

"When he takes a wife, my duty will be over. Then I will be mistress of my own life again."

"When that day comes, you need only call for me, and I will be there."

"Pooka, Pooka, how can I thank you for your kindness?"

He bent his head and kissed her lips. "You have given me your tears, and you have given me your kiss. For now that is enough."

Then he was gone as well, leaving her alone.

She whispered softly, so that no one would hear, "I give

you my love, Pooka, and my heart."

The years passed, and Garrett grew into a handsome young man. He ruled wisely and well with Mairi's advice, and never acted rashly or harshly, remembering how his people had cared for the three of them after his father's death. Megeen found a kind and handsome husband, and Garrett saw her wed with great ceremony and joy. At last his own eyes fell upon the lovely daughter of a lord of the West, and so they were married. Mairi, still lovely though her long, dark braids now glinted with silver, smiled as she saw her son lead his new wife to the place of honor.

While the hall feasted, she dressed herself in her finest gown of green silk sewn with a design of leaves and knotwork, and donned a cloak of white wool bordered in green and embroidered all over with green and gold, so that she looked like a bride herself. Then she crept out of the hall and rode to the bridge, where she called in her clear, sweet voice, "Pooka!"

This time, when she heard the sound like distant thunder, she still trembled, but not from fear. As the dim crashing of hoofbeats grew louder and louder, her heart thudded in her breast. At last the Pooka stood before her, a great grey horse with eyes that shone like flame and a mane and tail of silver and silver hooves.

"Who is it that calls me so late at night?" And its voice was wild and fearsome like the wind, but with an undertone of sweetness like the clean quiet after a summer storm.

"Tis I, Mairi O'Farrell."

"And what do you want of me?"

Before her eyes, he changed into the smiling young lord with pale hair that shone like silver, and she turned away from him, suddenly seeing herself as he must see her. Her dark hair was streaked with gray, her pale skin lined, her green eyes set about with wrinkles. She had grown old, old, while he, through the magic of Finvarra's land, was still young. How could she ask for his love?

"There is nothing I want from you, Pooka," she said

dully, her heart aching with sadness.

"Then I will tell you what I will give you, Mairi, my heart's treasure. You have my love, for as long as you want it."

"You can look at me and say that? Pooka, do not mock me. I know I have grown old. Do not laugh at me."

"I look at you and see the fairest of women, with hair as dark as the night sky, and cheeks smooth as rose petals and whiter than seafoam, and a heart brave enough to dare to tame a wild thing like a Pooka. You have tamed me, Mairi. Will you leave me alone to grieve for all my days?"

He turned her about and took her in his two arms and kissed her gently as a summer rain. "See yourself through my eyes, lady."

And when she looked down she saw that her thick braids were indeed dark as the night sky, with no silver at all, and when she reached up a hand to her cheek, her skin was soft as a girl's.

And they went away together to Finvarra's land, and there they may be living still, for no one ever dies or grows old there. And that is how a lady once tamed a Pooka, with nothing but a brave and loving heart.

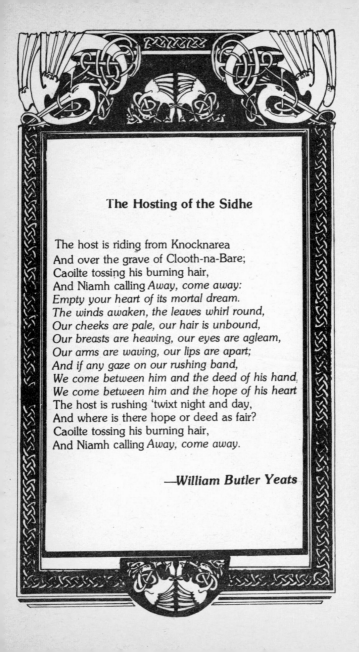

The Hosting of the Sidhe

The host is riding from Knocknarea
And over the grave of Clooth-na-Bare;
Caoilte tossing his burning hair,
And Niamh calling *Away, come away:*
Empty your heart of its mortal dream.
The winds awaken, the leaves whirl round,
Our cheeks are pale, our hair is unbound,
Our breasts are heaving, our eyes are agleam,
Our arms are waving, our lips are apart;
And if any gaze on our rushing band,
We come between him and the deed of his hand,
We come between him and the hope of his heart
The host is rushing 'twixt night and day,
And where is there hope or deed as fair?
Caoilte tossing his burning hair,
And Niamh calling *Away, come away.*

—*William Butler Yeats*

The Judgment of St. Yves

Evangeline Walton

I had this story from old Yaouank Ar Guenn, that aged
fisherman whose years must number nearly a hundred
now. During my last visit to Brittany, when I called on him
to gather material for a projected book of folk-lore, the talk
gradually turned to the cult of Yves le Veridique. I asked
Yaouank if he himself had ever witnessed any instance of
this last strange survival of the mediaeval Judgment of
God.

"Yes, Madame," he answered, "when I had not yet ten
years, there were a man and woman in my own village that
asked St. Yves to judge between them."

"A man and a woman," I said, laughing. "Two between
whom there was no love lost, *n'est-ce-pas?*"

"Ah, but Madame does not know," he answered.
"They did love each other."

I pricked up my ears at that. Lovers who would invoke a
judgment that within the year must bring death upon one
or the other! I had heard often of the cult of Yves le
Veridique—that grim old belief which even a generation
ago still held the Breton peasants in implicit thrall. In those
days any who considered themselves wrongfully accused
could send a hired pilgrim to the statue of the great St.
Yves to pray the saint to judge between the traduced and
the traducers: that the guilty might wither and die within a
year. But lovers. What strange and terrible mystery of the
human heart was here?

"But how could they, Yaouank? What was it?"
And then he told the tale that follows.

It began with Jenovefa Le Bonniec, once the greatest of
the ballad-singers, whose name was known from one end
of the Basse Bretague to the other. They used to say the
sound of her singing would make homesick for Brittany

even one whom the good St. Peter had admitted to Paradise. . . . But that was long ago, a hundred years ago. . . .

It was she, Madame, who reared the boy Yann, that was grandson to some cousin of hers, and her own little orphaned grandchild, Azou, so named for the mother of our good St. Yves. People used to say old Jeno had ancestors among the fairy folk, and whoever looked upon those two children could of a surety believe it. They were both very slim and fair, not dark and healthy-bodied, like our people; and like, more alike than brother and sister, so that none thought it strange that they did not marry even when they were grown and all could see their great fondness for each other. And ill was usually spoken of any girl's fondness for Yann. He became one of our wandering Breton poets, of whom, alas, there are none any more, and went from town to town, making poems, which was well, and love, which was not so well. There was a charm upon him in both matters, Madame, so that the most honest wife and the purest maid must follow where his green eyes beckoned. . . . It may be that he was really of the fairy race, and had their magic and their wickedness, for they are not of the children of God.

Azou had the same charm. She had also a kind of wild shining beauty that was not like flesh and blood, and her hair was fine, so very fine that when she combed it, it was a wonder to see the soft gold of it showering through her fingers and sparkling in the sun.

She married Tremeur Le Goffic, and the women, who never loved her, said it was because he had a larger farm than any other unmarried young man in Plouarzel, but I did not think that true. Why should it have been? For Tremeur was tall and dark and good to look upon, and there was not a better wrestler in the Basse Bretagne. Why should she not have loved him? And I know that on the wedding day her face was like a song.

They were very happy until the time came for the fishing fleet to set out for the northern seas and the banks of Iceland. It had been the habit of Tremeur to go with the

fleet, although he had so good a farm, for he loved the sea.
But now that he was married he would not have gone had
not Azou urged him, a thing which gave even her friends
wonder. Madame knows that many of our men do not
come back from that summer-long voyage.

Some of them even spoke openly to her of it, the last
Sunday before the sailing, when she came out of church. I
mind how she laughed at them, with Tremeur's arm about
her.

"I am a wife, not a nursemaid. Does he look as if he
needed a *bonne,* my great strong Tremeur? Besides," and
her white teeth flashed, "*I* am not like you, my good
friends. I have no fear of the mermaid who kisses sailors to
death. I am much, much younger than she, and my blood
is warmer, for I have not lived in the cold sea. She will think
twice before she bothers my man!"

But I remember my own mother snorted, and some of
the others looked aghast at this brazen mocking of the sea
that all our women fear so much. One of them said darkly,
"You may live to regret those words, Azou!"

She only laughed as if at a jest, and looked up over her
shoulder at Tremeur, with a smile that was like a spell.
"You will be true to me, will you not, my Tremeur, no
matter how many pretty daughters of the sea entice you?"

And he answered, laughing, "There is not one of them
that could not learn a trick or two from you, little witch!"

She did not go down to see him off the day the fleet
sailed. But early that morning my mother sent me up to the
Le Goffic farm on an errand, and I saw them standing
together on a rocky ridge near the house, the sun turning
her streaming hair to light. She was clinging to him so
tightly that they were but one figure there, and I heard him
say:

"Why will you not watch the boats sail? If you really
have fear, Azou—"

But she threw back her head, and though it seemed to
me a mist sparkled on her eyelashes, her laugh was its old
fairy self.

"Anyone would have fear under all those women's

eyes! The sea is in your blood, and even love irks if it come between a man and what is in his blood. I would not have your love for me become like a load on a donkey's back. Go, and good fortune with you! Better a short happiness than a long and dull life!''

When he had gone, she stood looking after him with her face very white and strange; and I heard her moan, calling upon Ste. Anne, the Virgin's mother, the protectress of Breton sailors against the cruel and lustful sea sprite Ahes, or Dahut. Her voice broke in a wailing sob, and she slipped down and hid her face among the stones, while long shudders shook her body. And though I longed to help her I ran away, for there was that about her that gave me fear. . . .

Yet she never showed anxiety again. Old Jeno, whom everyone loved, refused to leave her cave and live with her granddaughter during Tremeur's absence, but Yann was not so unreasonable when his wanderings brought him back our way. Azou welcomed him with both arms, and it was said he spent as many nights in the Le Goffic house as in his old aunt's cave. It deepened the old women's distrust of Azou's beauty and waywardness. And it is true that after Yann's return they were one again, united beings in a secret elf-world of their own, as in the days of their wild childhood. But they were no longer children; tongues were wagging now. Many a time have I been to the Le Goffic farm, and have heard them laughing together elvishly, slim golden men and slim golden woman, in their delicious, intimate comradeship, while old Gabik, who had been Tremeur's father's man before him, watched them with sullen, angry eyes. But they never heeded him. They were twin to each other in beauty and strangeness, and, many said, in wickedness.

Not a week before the fishing-fleet was first sighted, Yann kissed Azou and old Jeno, and was off again on his travels, as all had said he would take care to be. When Tremeur Le Goffic came up from the sea his wife was alone, and she welcomed him as if she had pined him

through all those months. He went home from the quay
with his arm about her, their two faces lit as though by a
torch.

There was a *pardon* a few days later. I am old, and
Madame will forgive me that I cannot recall of which saint it
was the *pardon*. All the village attended, the women full of
thanksgiving for their men's return, the men still full of joy
to see their women again. . . . Ah, what a sight that was!
The dancing under the trees, the line of white-robed girls
with candles in their hands, the wild cries of "Iou, iou!"
when the rector lit the ceremonial fire and the red flames
surged up. That was a night to live!

But I, who loved Azou even when my thoughts of her
were worst, I had fear when I saw old Gabik lay his gnarled
hand on Tremeur's arm, and draw him off under the
shadow of a tree. His wrinkled parchment face was working, and his eyes were horribly eager, eager as the fire.

Then I heard Azou humming a song under her breath,
and went to her. It is said, and I myself believe, that her
voice was as beautiful as old Jeno's, but none can know.
She never sang aloud.

Then, of a sudden, Tremeur came striding to her
through the crowd. His face was dark, dark and hard as
one of those old stones of ours you say the heathen priests
used to worship, and old Gabik's was still eager, like a
wolf's when it sees a lamb.

Tremeur halted before her. "Azou, tell this man he lies,"
he said. "He says he saw you among the old stones in the
middle of the night, laughing and running from your
cousin Yann. And that when Yann caught you he kissed
you, not once but many times, and you went into the
house still laughing, your arms about each other."

His voice was calm, calm as the sea the minute before
the black storm clouds break. All there shivered, but
perhaps her flesh and blood were really not like ours.
Those wonderful eyes of hers were steady when she faced
him, unafraid.

"I cannot say he lies, Tremeur. It is only that his mind is

unclean, and would soil me. I did those very things with my cousin Yann, who has always been as my brother. The night was too beautiful for sleep, so we played together as we used to do in childhood. Surely you have not jealousy of children's kisses, Tremeur?"

This seemed too silly, too foolish a tale for belief. He stood there looking at her, his great brown hands knotting and unknotting.

"You—" I will not give the name he called her, Madame. It was harder than a blow. It blisters the ear that hears it. Her face went white as death.

"You lie," she said.

He came so close as almost to touch her. His face was as black as a storm; it had the fire of a storm, but she did not shrink.

"I lie, do I? You dare to say that, you brazen ——! If I killed you, it would be too little!"

"I had rather be dead than live to remember I have given myself to a man whose thoughts of me could be so vile. Your love, Tremeur—ah, God, a beast's would never have shamed me so!" Her voice, that had been as hard as his, broke in a wail of pain. "I thought we loved each other so much, so much. . . ."

He caught her outflung hands. "Will you admit it?" he asked harshly. "I warn you, you had better. I will not be mocked."

I do not see how any could have failed to shrink before his face then, but she did not. She cried out with answering fire: "No! Before I will do that, I will see your burned in hell—you and your sneaking, spying dog there. I will swear by Christ and by our Lady that you lie, though St. Yves himself were to be the judge between us!"

He freed her then. He tossed her aside with a savage laugh, as though the madness within him had at last found outlet.

"Annik! Annik!" he called, and a stoop-shouldered old woman with a frightened look hobbled out of the crowd. No wonder she had fear, old Annik. More than once she had been sent to St. Yves' shrine in Tredarzec; more than once death had followed her going; yet never had the matter been such as this.

But it was to Azou that Tremeur spoke. "So you would have St. Yves to judge between us, my good wife," he said, and his face was cruel, like a cat's when it has the mouse between its paws. "You could not please me more, if you have the courage to abide by it. I shall give you your wish."

She did not look afraid, though a shade passed over her face. She said wonderingly, "You could truly do that, Tremeur, though you know that one of us must die? You would be willing to doom me —"

His face was hard and fierce and eager. There was an almost gloating savagery in his voice.

"I could. I will. Yves le Veridique shall judge between us, and the liar shall pay the price. If you are so good you need have no fear, but if you are not. . . ."

She was smiling back at him, smiling dreadfully, and suddenly her eyes were green and awful, more awful than the wildest sea. Ninety years ago it will soon have been, yet I can still shut my eyes and see hers as they were then.

"Then let him judge," she said, folding her arms over her breast. "And make your peace with God, Tremeur. I am not afraid."

He turned to old Annik then. His voice rang out in a great cry.

"You shall have three hundred francs, Annik, if you start for St. Yves's shrine tonight! And when you stand there, bid him judge between this woman and myself—that the liar may wither and rot before a year has passed!"

He looked at Azou as he ended. No doubt he thought to see her break then; God knows I hope he would have preferred that to her death. But her face still wore that soft dreadful smiling, like that of some beautiful demon out of the sea. She laughed at him, and I have heard the sea laugh with that same silky, purring sound.

"It should be very amusing, Tremeur, to see such a great strong man as yourself wither and die. It does seem quite impossible that even the greatest saint could do it in a single year."

There was a silence then, I can tell you, Madame. We felt as if in truth she were no woman, who could thus defy our great St. Yves and certain death. And then all eyes were turned from her, for Tremeur called "Go!" and his great voice seemed to fill all the night. Old Annik turned, and sped, for all her years, like an arrow from the bow. We watched her disappear into the darkness; there was the chill of death in all our hearts. For we knew whose shadow must follow her home. . . .

Then there was a cry from Azou, and she ran forward, and clutched at Tremeur. "Call her back, Tremeur! Ah, God forgive me . . . Call her back. Oh, Tremeur, surely you love life. I will say whatever you choose. Only call her back. I was angry; I forgot! O, Tremeur, Tremeur. . . ."

She was sobbing pitifully, and the tears were running over her white face like beads. He loosened her clinging hands and flung her off. His voice was loud, whether with rage or pain. "It is too late now. You will get what you have earned!"

She was very white as she stepped back, and there was a strange dignity about her. "That I do not doubt, Tremeur," she said in a voice dead and dull as ashes. Then she turned and went from us, with her head up. Her face was the face of a dead woman, but her eyes had a distended look as if she saw some horrible thing far off, something we could not see.

She went back to old Jeno that night, and for months none saw her except when she came to the church to pray. She would kneel for hours before the statue of St. Yves, that awful white look always upon her face. Ah, none could doubt she was fading, day by day. . . . You say such superstition itself was enough to kill, that the good saint would never do it? You are wrong, Madame; you do not know the power of our great St. Yves.

As for Tremeur, he went about his farm with his jaw set like some great rock, and his skin growing grayer and grayer under the brown. He drove his men as they had never before been driven, and he had no laughter, and scarcely a word to his lips.

Then Azou was brought to bed of a child. She had suffered hard for a whole day before old Jeno brought the priest, and all thought St. Yves had spoken, and this was the end. But they say that when Father Jean came to her, her tortured bitten lips curved into her old soft eerie laughter, and she said, "There is no need to shrive me this year, Father. I may be my husband's murderess, but God and St. Yves know this body of mine was true to him."

She bore her son before midnight, and both lived. When Tremeur heard of it, he said nothing but went and paced the cliffs until dawn, his face so gray that all brown had fled from it. . . . Folk began to wonder after that. For she bloomed again after her baby's birth, a white and tragic blooming. But Tremeur grew ever grayer, and men said his arms were not so strong as they used to be. So the last month of the dreadful year came. That month Yann the bard came back to Plouarzel.

Azou was praying in church the day the end came; kneeling before the pillars with the baby kicking and crowing on the stones beside her. I was watching from the shadow of the pillars, thinking how one could almost see the light through her, when the door opened, and Tremeur came in. There was a storm rising, and the shrieking menace of the wind entered with him, both of them dark and grim. With a cry she rose and turned to him.

"I have come to look at my son, Azou, for the first and the last time," he said quietly, and then his eyes went to the baby that lay on the floor, laughing and reaching up to them. But she said nothing, and I could not see what was in his face.

It was like a stone when he turned to her. "I am going out to sea. No one man could get a boat past the reefs in this weather, and I will not die tamely in my bed!"

I heard her moan: "Oh, Mother of all pity! How could I do it, how could I give your life——"

He shrugged. "Was I unwilling to give yours then? Better to die knowing the truth than to live believing what I believed." Suddenly the hardness went out of his voice. "Do not cry, my beautiful one. Forgive me, Azou, and God keep you and cherish you as I did not, my sweetest love!"

He had her in his arms, kissing her wildly, passionately, though with a great tenderness. Then he put her down and was gone, and the doors of the church were crashed to behind him.

It was her cousin Yann that caught her as, reeling and breathless, heedless of the gaping folk, she followed Tremeur to the wharves. She twisted in his arms, and her voice came back to her. I heard her cry out, "It is Tremeur, Yann! He is going to his death, and all this long year I have prayed to St. Yves——"

Yann stepped back, still holding her wrists firmly, and it seemed to me something like contempt was in his eyes.

"How tamed you are, sweet sister! And I had always fancied there was truth in the tale of our fairy blood, for only that could explain such hearts as ours! Ah, well, they say even fairy women will grow tame when they love a mortal." He bent and kissed her, then stepped back, his face colorless, a strange sparkle kindling in his eyes.

And then he was off, light as a bird, over those rocks that all others must climb so carefully. . . . Tremeur's boat was already free, already forging into the surf, but Yann leaped down into it as it passed beneath him. We saw the gray-green waves boil up; we saw all that happened, but we could not hear. Yet afterwards we learned what was said.

"Have a care, cousin Tremeur! You have a wife and child."

Tremeur did not answer. They were being swept toward the sea's cruel teeth that gape at the entrance of our bay, and the waters boiled all about them. Only Yann's clear poet's voice could have pierced the tumult.

"Have no fear of St. Yves, Tremeur. *She* has prayed for you so long that I, who never prayed to Yves or any other friend of the Church's God, cannot but think Him gentleman enough to send you escape as the sign of his mercy.

And if *I* do not escape—why then I shall go the sea-fairy and see if she can hold my heart longer than other women—I who never loved but one woman truly, and that with a brother's love!"

It was then that the great wave came, then that the breakers rose, and before the gray-green waters entombed the boat we saw Yann thrust Tremeur backwards. It is incredible that mortal man could have been so quick; small wonder that he had not time left to leap himself. For when the green waters cleared, Tremeur was alone there, drenched and bruised, clinging to the rocks.

They say, Madame, that if one walks on the cliffs on a moonlight night one may hear Yann below there, singing among the waters. . . . It may be that in the sea-fairy he found a mate at last.

"But Azou and Tremeur?" I asked. "Was Yann right? Had he really won their release from the judgment of St. Yves?"

I thought he nodded, but it was of the sweet singing in the waters that he mumbled, and I could get no more out of him. He is old, and for the time he had forgotten the lovers who proved each other's love so strangely in his memories of Yann the poet, Yann whom no earth born woman could ever hold.

Sweetly The Waves Call To Me

Pat Murphy

The harbor seal lay just beyond the reach of the waves—its dark eyes open in death. The surf had rolled and battered the body; the mottled gray fur was dusted with white sand. Gulls had been pecking at a wound in the animal's head.

Kate shifted her weight uneasily as she stared down at the body. She was alone; Michael, her lover, was still asleep at the cottage. Kate had come walking on the beach to escape the restless feeling left by a melancholy dream. She could not remember the dream; it had retreated like a wave on the beach, leaving behind feelings of loneliness and abandonment.

She raised one hand to touch the ivory pendant that dangled from a chain around her neck, a circle etched with the likeness of a seal. Michael had given her the pendant the night before—as a peace offering, she thought.

Michael had come to visit for the weekend to apologize and to forgive her—managing the seemingly contradictory acts with the competence that he brought to every task. Kate had left Santa Cruz and Michael to live for a summer in her parents' old cottage; she had needed the solitude to finish her thesis on the folklore of the sea. Michael had brought her the scrimshaw pendant to apologize for accusing her of using her thesis as an excuse for leaving him.

She did not think that she was using the thesis as an excuse. But sometimes, in the dim light of early morning when the gulls cried overhead, she was not sure. She knew that sometimes she needed him. She knew that he was solid and he was strong.

She could hear the distant roar of a truck traveling down Highway One. The cottage was halfway between Davenport and Pescadero—south of nowhere in particular, north of no place special. A lonely place.

Looking down at the dead body of the seal, Kate had the uneasy feeling that she was being watched. She looked up at the cliff face, then out to sea where the waves crashed. Just past the breakers, a dark head bobbed in the water—a curious harbor seal. As she stared back, he ducked beneath a wave.

She hurried back to the cottage, scrambling up the sandstone slope, following the narrow path that was little better than a wash erroded by the last rain.

The cottage was perched at the top of the bluff. The waves that pounded against the cliff threatened to claim the ramshackle building someday. The sea fog had begun a slow offensive against the cottage: the white paint was chipped and weathered; the porch sagged at one corner where a supporting post had rotted through; the windchimes that hung from the low eaves were tarnished green.

"Bad news," Kate said as she stepped in the kitchen door. "There's a dead seal on the beach."

The kitchen was warm and bright. Michael was making coffee. "Why's that bad news?"

"Bad luck for the person who shot it," she said. "It could have been a silkie, a seal person who could change shape and become human on land. If a person kills a silkie, the sea turns against him."

Michael was watching her with an expression that had become familiar during the time that they had lived together—he did not know how seriously to take her. "You've been working on that thesis too long," he said, and poured her a cup of coffee.

She laughed and slipped an arm around his waist, leaning up against him and feeling the warmth of his body. Almost like old times. "Huh," she said, "There speaks the scientist."

"It'll be simple enough to get rid of any bad luck," he added. "I'll call the University at Santa Cruz. There's a class that recovers stranded marine mammals for dissection."

Kate released him, and sat down in one of the two

wooden kitchen chairs. The cup of coffee warmed her hands, still cold from the fog. "They don't need to get it. It'll wash out to sea at high tide tonight."

Michael frowned. "They'll want it. This is the only way that they can get specimens."

"Oh." She sipped the hot coffee. Far out at sea, over the crash of the waves, she could hear a sea lion barking. "It doesn't feel right," she said. "It seems like the body should go back to sea." Then, before he could laugh or call her foolish, she shrugged. "But I suppose it doesn't matter. In the interest of science and all."

Michael called the University and arranged to have a crew of students come to pick up the seal that afternoon, explaining that Kate would meet them, that he would be gone.

He looked at her when he hung up the phone and said, inexplicably, "Is that all right?"

"Of course, of course, it's all right," she said irritably. And when he came around the table to hug her, she realized that he had meant that he was leaving, and was that all right? She had been thinking of the seal.

When Kate stood alone on the porch, waving goodbye, she felt uneasy again, unsettled. The fog smelled of salt spray and dying kelp. Michael lifted a hand in farewell and she listened to the crunch of wheels on gravel and watched the sedan until it vanished into the fog. The engine changed in pitch when he stopped at the end of the drive, turned onto the highway, and picked up speed.

Kate realized that one hand was clinging to the pendant around her neck, and she released it. A gull shrieked in the fog and she retreated into the kitchen to work.

The papers that she spread on the kitchen table were the result of months of collecting the stories told in the Santa Cruz fishing community. There were so many stories— and so many warnings—about how one should behave around the sea.

She remembered sitting in the sun on the fishing dock while an old man mended a net and advised her: "If you cut yourself near the the sea, never let the blood touch the water. Blood calls to blood. If the sea has your blood, you belong to the sea." She remembered a Scottish fisherman's widow, a sturdy old woman with bright blue eyes, had served her tea and warned: "You must not take the sea lightly. Those who take from the sea lay themselves open to the powers of the sea. And many dark creatures dwell beneath the waves."

The sea dwellers of legend were tricky. The kelpies or water horses could take human form to entice mortals into the water to drown. Mermaids and mermen could raise storms to sink ships.

But the silkies, the seal people that Kate's thoughts kept returning to, were a gentle folk. Kate leafed through one of her notebooks and found the widow's account of a young salmon fisherman who had shot a seal feeding near his boat, and had died in a storm the next month. The old widow had said that the silkies were tolerant of humans and angered only by the death of their own kind. They came ashore on moonlit nights to dance on the beach in human form. Fishermen had captured silkie maidens for wives by stealing the skin they used in their seal form; silkie men had been known to take human lovers.

Kate began listing the elements that the widow's tale had in common with traditional tales of silkies. Just before lunch, she was interrupted by the sound of tires on the gravel drive. She picked up her sweatshirt and stepped onto the porch.

Three students—two men and a woman—climbed down from the cab of the ancient pickup truck parked in the drive. "I guess you came to pick up the seal," Kate said hesitantly. With Michael gone, her uneasiness about the seal had returned. But she could not turn the students away. "I'll take you down," she said.

The day was still overcast and the wind from the sea was cold. Kate hauled her sweatshirt over her head. The cloth caught on the chain of her pendant and she yanked at the sweatshirt impatiently—too hard. The chain broke and she caught the pendant as it fell. "Damn," she muttered. Aware of the eyes of the students upon her, she stuffed the pendant and chain into her pocket. "I'll take you right down," she repeated.

The students unloaded a stretcher from the back of the truck and followed Kate down the narrow path. They had to scramble over the jumble of rocks that extended from the base of the cliff to the water. At high tide, the waves crashed against the cliff, making the broad beach where the seal lay inaccessible from the path. When the moon was full and the tides reached full height, the sea swallowed both the tiny beach at the bottom of the path and the broad beach to the north.

Kate felt ill at ease with the students, unwilling to introduce herself or ask their names. These people did not belong on her beach. She stood several yards away as the two men squatted by the seal and positioned the stretcher so that they could roll the seal onto it. The woman stood at the animal's head. She shifted her weight uneasily, glanced out to sea, then back at the seal. Kate crossed her arms and hugged her sweatshirt tighter around her, suddenly cold. The woman shivered, though she was dressed more warmly than Kate.

She stepped toward Kate and caught her eye. "You must be half seal yourself to go in swimming this time of year."

Kate frowned. "Why do you figure I've been in swimming?"

The woman pointed to a set of footprints, left by bare feet, leading along the edge of the sea toward the body. The prints were almost obscured by bird tracks and boot prints.

"Not me," Kate said. "But that's odd. Those weren't here this morning. And I'm the only one who lives near here."

The woman shrugged. "Probably just a hitchhiker who stopped off the highway to walk on the beach." She looked out to sea, where the grey waves crashed against the rocks.

Kate nodded. "I suppose so." She squatted beside the footprints and peered at them closely. Just footprints in the sand; nothing unusual.

"Come on," one of the men called. The two men had picked up the stretcher and started back in the direction of the path. Kate and the woman walked in silence. Over the sound of the surf, they could hear the men talking and laughing.

"I don't see how those guys can joke about picking up bodies," the woman said. "I always feel like a grave robber."

"Yeah?" Kate glanced at the woman's face. "That's how I feel. My boyfriend called the University. I would have just as soon let the body wash back out to sea. I don't know why."

The woman nodded sympathetically. "It must be something about the ocean. And the fog. And the time of year—we're almost to the shortest day."

"The winter solstice," Kate murmured. "A bad time to mess with the ocean."

"Yeah?" The woman shot Kate a curious glance. "Why's that?"

Kate shrugged. "According to folk stories, the winter solstice is when the powers of darkness are at their strongest. It's a dangerous time."

The woman hugged her jacket closer around her, hunching her shoulders against the cold wind that blew from the sea. "You almost sound serious about that."

"I'm studying folklore and the old stories kind of get to you after a while." Kate hesitated. "It's not that I believe them. It's more like I respect them. This is old stuff. Strong stuff." She shrugged again, then fell silent.

The men lifted the stretcher into the back of the truck and the dead eyes of the seal gazed mournfully at the rusty metal of the tailgate. The woman paused before she climbed after the men into the cab. She laid a hand on Kate's arm. "Take care of yourself," she said. She hesitated as if she wanted to say more, then climbed into the cab.

The tires crunched on the gravel drive; Kate lifted a hand in farewell. She turned her back on the highway and listened to the truck shift gears when it reached the end of the drive, but she did not watch it drive away.

The fog had lifted but the sky was overcast. The horizon was marked by an almost imperceptible difference in shading between the grey-blue of the ocean and the blue-grey of the sky. The ocean was calm. A grey beast waiting at the foot of the cliff, not impatient for an end, but certain that an end would come. The setting sun was a hazy circle behind the clouds on the horizon.

Kate shifted her feet and the gravel made grinding noises. To reach the beach, a hitchhiker would have had to follow the drive to the path. If anyone had passed the cottage, she would have heard him walking in the gravel. But there had been footprints on the beach.

The sun sank out of sight. A night breeze ruffled Kate's hair and she shivered, then retreated to the cottage.

After dinner, when the warmth of the cottage had chased away thoughts of silkies and solitude, she stepped out on the porch to watch the moon rise. The lights of the kitchen glowed cheerfully through the curtains behind her. The moon would be full the following night, full and round like the ivory circle of her pendant.

She dug in her pocket to touch the smooth ivory. Her pocket was empty. Her fingers found a hole in the cloth and she cursed herself for carelessness. She must have dropped it on the path or on the beach.

No gleam of ivory rewarded her search of the path. She walked toward the broad beach, searching the sand with no luck. The tide was rising. A breaking wave washed among the rocks at the base of the cliff. When the wave retreated, she hurried across.

The dry sand of the broad beach just above where the wave had reached was marked by footprints. Bare feet. The prints led away from the path, toward the spot where she had found the seal's body.

"Hello," Kate shouted. "Is anyone out there?" No answer.

She looked back toward the jumble of rocks that separated her from the footpath. The tide was rising and the water lapped higher with each wave. Kate broke into a run, following the footprints. She took long strides and when the waves hissed under her feet she ignored the spray that splashed up to wet her jeans. Beside the rocky outcropping where she had found the seal, she stopped and scanned the beach.

There. In the shadow of the cliff at the end of the beach she saw a flickering light and a moving shadow. The light was too pale and too bright to be a campfire. A flashlight beam, perhaps.

"Hey!" Kate called. "The tide's coming in. Hey, you!"

The light remained where it was. Kate raced toward it, shouting, then saved her breath for running. When the light moved, she could see the outline of the person holding it.

She was a hundred feet away when a wave crashed against the cliff and sent an arc of spray over the flickering light. The shadowy figure moved, a darting movement too quick and graceful to be human. Like a cat. Like a sea otter. Like a seal in the water. And the light vanished.

Kate's momentum carried her three more steps. She stared at the cliff, which suddenly seemed clearly lit by moonlight. There was no one standing beneath the cliff. There was no flashlight beam. There was no nook, no cranny, no crevice where a person could hide. Just moonlight and water and a tall black cliff. Just a vanishing light and a fleet shadow.

Over the hiss of a retreating wave, Kate thought she heard a sound—a long sigh like a seal taking a breath of air after a long dive. The moonlight gleamed on a white circle on the sand before her. Her pendant. Here, far from where she had walked. She stepped forward and reached for it, aware of eyes upon her. A wave rushed in to snatch the circle of ivory away before she could touch it. She groped after it in the surf, but it slipped away, lost in the foam and the moonlight.

Kate turned and ran for the path. She passed the rocky crag—her heart pounding, her breath rasping through a dry throat. The waves splashed high against the cliff and even in retreat left no dry rocks. Moonlight glistened on the swells.

A wave washed among the rocks and Kate plunged into the water, hoping to cross before another broke. The icy water sucked at her legs, dragging on her jeans. Beneath her boots, the rocks were slick with kelp and eel grass. The water was knee-deep, waist-deep. The ocean tugged at her legs, another wave broke, and a rock shifted beneath her boot. She slipped and floundered in the water, her ankle caught between two rocks. She wrenched the foot free and stood, sputtering through a curtain of wet hair. She struggled forward, hampered by wet jeans, crippled by an ankle that gave beneath her. Stumbling again, but recovering. She limped through water that was waist-deep, knee-deep. Onto a sandy bottom. Onto a tiny beach.

She collapsed on the dry sand and drew in a long shuddering breath. And another. Only when she lifted her right hand to brush the wet hair from her face did she realize that she was bleeding from a ragged gash across her palm. Cut on a rock. She staggered to her feet, and her ankle throbbed with dull persistent pain. The waves hissed in the sand, leaving an innocent line of foam.

Droplets of blood fell from her clenched fist to stain the foam.

A shadow moved beyond the breakers. A flicker of pale white light. A will o' the wisp. The eyes were still upon her; she could feel them. And the loneliness that had touched her that morning had returned.

"Not me," she called hoarsely to the light. "I didn't kill her. Not me." The light dipped out of sight beneath the crest of a wave.

Kate turned away to stagger home to the sanity of a warm kitchen, a cup of tea, a hot shower. But the rush of water from the showerhead rattling against the metal walls of the shower did not cover the sound of the surf. Even as Kate washed sand from the cut on her hand, she could hear the rhythmic crashing of the waves, gentle and steady. While she was heating water for tea, a storm began with the soft touch of rain against the windows, a persistent whispering like many soft voices speaking so quietly that she could not understand them. When she caught herself listening for words in the soft rainfall, she turned on the radio.

The storm picked up in force, competing with the wailing of pop rock. The wind howled across the chimneytop. The rain lashed against the windows and blew in through the bathroom window, which was warped partly open. Kate stuffed newspaper into the gap and the paper soaked up the rain. Once soaked, the paper dripped on the floor, beating a steady counterpoint to the pealing of the wind chimes—high and furious—outside the window.

Kate paced within the kitchen, trapped but unable to sit still. Once, when the wind rattled the door, Kate thought she felt the cottage shake and she thought of mudslides and collapsing cliffs. The silkies, like the mermaids, could raise storms to shatter ships. A storm could also shatter the timbers of an old beach cottage.

The cut on her hand throbbed; her ankle ached, but she paced. She picked up the phone to call Michael, but the phone was dead. No doubt the lines were down on the highway. And if she had been able to get through, what could she have told him? That she feared for her life in a storm that the silkies had raised.

So she paced, reminding herself that the seal people were a gentle folk—not like the mermaids, not like the kelpie. She had done nothing to harm the silkies, really.

At midnight, the wind lessened and the rain eased to a gentle rhythm. As Kate lay in bed, trying to ignore the twin pains in her ankle and hand, she heard a sea lion barking from the rocks below the cliffs. It sounded much closer.

She slept uneasily and woke shivering when the wind chimes rang lightly. The rain had stopped and the sea fog had crept up the cliff to wrap itself around the cottage. She had dreamed again, though the memory of the dream was not clear. She remembered an overpowering loneliness, a fierce yearning, a hunger for something unattainable.

Kate hugged the blanket closer around her, but the chill of the fog had seeped into the cottage and into her bones. Reluctantly, she left her bed to get another blanket, crossing the cold kitchen floor to the linen cupboard and pulling a quilted comforter from the stack on the shelf.

The wind chimes jingled again, and Kate thought she heard another sound—a long sigh that could have been the wind. But it did not sound quite like the wind. The floorboards creaked beneath her as she stepped toward the door. She hesitated with her hand on the doorknob.

What did she fear, she wondered. Her mind formed an image in answer: she feared a slender manshape, standing on the porch with the fog swirling around his waist and hiding his webbed feet. The fingers of the hand that she imagined to be resting on the porch rail were joined by a thin skin. From his other hand, her pendant dangled. He smelled of the sea and a strand of eel grass clung to his shoulder. When she reached out to take the pendant, she touched his hand. It was cold—as cold as the sea.

Kate stopped with her hand on the doorknob, only half aware that she was listening for the sound of breathing. Then she twisted the knob and jerked the door open.

Shadows of the fenceposts shifted and moved in the moonlight and drifting fog. The posts teetered this way and that, barely supporting the single strand of rusty wire that was all that remained of the fence. Nothing to hold back the sea.

The porch was empty. No webbed hand rested on the porch rail, but at the spot where she had imagined his hand lay a circle of white. With fingers that were suddenly as cold as the fog, she picked up the pendant by the chain and held it in her bandaged hand. The breeze stirred the mist and the wind chimes jingled faintly. She backed away, retreating into the kitchen, and from the doorway, she noticed a single strand of eel grass trailing across the top step. She locked the door behind her.

She did not sleep after that. With the kitchen lights blazing, she wrapped herself in the comforter and made hot chocolate. She worked on her paper and tried to ignore the ringing of the wind chimes and the crash of the waves.

In the light of dawn, with a cup of coffee in her hand, she opened the door and peered out onto the porch. The strand of eel grass still lay on the top step, and she told herself that it must have fallen from her boot when she staggered into the cottage. Just as she must have put the pendant on the railing when she broke the chain rather than into her pocket.

She called Michael from a pay phone at a gas station, saying only that she had twisted her ankle and was coming to town to see a doctor. She arranged to meet him for dinner.

In the restaurant that evening, the traffic noises ebbed and surged like the sound of the waves. The sound distracted Kate and disrupted her thoughts as she told Michael of the storm. She did not mention her vision of the silkie, but talked of mudslides and her feeling that the cottage could collapse into the sea. Even so, she felt like a fool. In the warm cafe that smelled of coffee and pastry, the crashing terror of the storm seemed far away.

He gently took her bandaged hand in his hand. "Something really has you worried, doesn't it?" he asked.

She shrugged. "The ocean gets to me when I'm out at the cottage, that's all," she said. "The fog and the waves and the sea lions barking . . ." And the madness that lingers at the ocean's edge, she thought.

"I told you it was a lonely spot," he said.

"Not lonely so much as . . ." She hesitated. "I never feel quite alone anymore. And I get to imagining things. The other night, I thought I saw a light, dancing on the waves just beyond the breakers. I don't know; I guess my eyes were just playing tricks."

Michael grinned and stroked her hand. "Don't worry about your eyes," he said. "You probably did see a light. Have you ever heard of bio-luminescence? There are micro-organisms that glow . . ."

Michael explained it all—talking about red tides and marine chemistry. Kate let the reassuring words wash over her. Michael never had time for the vague, ill-defined feelings that plagued her. She listened to him, and when he was done, she managed a smile.

"You've been working on that project much too hard," he said. "Why don't you just stay in town tonight and spend the night with me?"

She stared at her coffee in silence.

"Don't be afraid to come back to me," he said softly. "You can if you want to."

She did not know what she wanted. "I have to go back tonight," she said. "I have work to do."

"Why tonight?" he asked. "Why not wait until tomorrow?"

The answer came to her mind, but she did not voice it: the moon would be full that night.

She freed her hand from Michael's grasp and held her coffee cup between her palms. "I have work to do," she repeated.

She drove back that night, speeding around the curves in the twisting road that led from Santa Cruz to her little patch of nowhere. The old Beatles song on the tape deck drowned out the whisper of the waves: "I'd like to be under the sea in an octopus's garden with you."

The full moon hung in the sky over the cottage as she rolled up the drive. She turned her key. The music stopped. And the crash of the surf filled the car.

Kate walked to the edge of the cliff. Below her, the sea shimmered in the moonlight, the swells rising and falling in a rhythm as steady as breathing. She felt eyes watching her from the ocean below.

She slipped three times as she descended the path. The third time she caught herself with her wounded hand and the cut flared with a bright new pain. Her ankle throbbed but she continued to pick her way down the slope.

The waves had not yet reached the bottom of the path. The tiny beach was a silver thread in the moonlight, extending away in either direction in a shimmering line. She stood on the silver strand and gazed out to sea.

A light danced on the wave. Loneliness swept over her

as a wave swept over the sand, touching the toes of her boots with foam. Involuntarily, she took a step to follow the retreating water. The next wave lapped around her ankles and a fierce pain touched her wounded hand so that she longed to sooth it by touching it to the cold water. Somewhere in the back of her mind, she heard the echo of a voice saying: "Blood calls to blood." She took another step forward and the water lapped at her knees, dragging on the legs of her jeans.

The light danced—out of reach. The water was cold against her ankle. It eased the pain. The water could ease the stinging in her hand. If only she waded out further.

With her bandaged hand, she gripped the pendant that hung around her neck. Michael would not believe that there was a watcher in the water. But the light was there. And the loneliness was with her. She watched the dancing light and thought about the glowing micro-organisms that Michael had described. The water tugged at her legs.

"No," she said softly to the water and the light. Then louder, "No." The water tugged at her, urging, insisting. "No."

She could feel eyes on her as she trudged up the path. Turning her back on wonder. No, turning her back on cold gray waters that would beat her against the rocks.

There was no storm that night. But she heard the sound of the waves against the cliffs—calling, calling. She slept uneasily and she dreamed of a lover: a salt-sea lover with hands like ice and the face of a prince. Between his fingers, webbing stretched; his teeth were pointed; he carried with him the scent of the sea. He loved her with a steady rocking as rhythmic as the sea, and he held her when she cried out—was it in pleasure or pain?—at the chill of his touch. She stroked his dark hair, sleek as the fur of a seal. He came to her for comfort, this silent lover whose kisses tasted of salt. He came to her to make a truce.

She woke to the scent of the sea and the sound of a gentle thumping. Half-awake, she fumbled uselessly for the pendant at her neck. It was not there, though she could not remember taking it off the night before. She left her bed, wrapping the quilt around her and stepping into the kitchen.

The door to the porch swung wide open, moving slightly in the breeze and bumping gently against the kitchen wall. She picked up her pendant from where it lay on the porch railing. She did not put it on. She did not need it. No fear was left in her.

The single wire of the old fence was strung with drops of dew, one drop on each rusty barb. The old fence should come down, she thought. It served no purpose anymore.

The waves washed against the base of the cliff; the ocean moved in its endless rhythm. Drops of her blood ebbed and surged with those waters. And the strength of the sea surged in her.

Far away, a sea lion barked. And the bright sunlight of early morning glinted on the two strands of eel grass that lay across the steps.

The Merman In Love

Overhead a boat sails by,
the ripples in its wake
as quick and white
as the under-wings of a gull.
Somewhere the sperm whale sings
his lonely lowings
along the current.
I am not deaf,
do not think I am deaf
to the music he makes.
But the songs
her fingers croon
and the bubbled melodies
from her mouth
are more beautiful to me
than whale songs,
than the call of gulls
skimming low over the waves,
than the mournful mating
of the foghorn
as it cries its love
to the sea.

—Jane Yolen

The Renders

Janny Wurts

Stars flecked the sky when Jaiddon reached the headland that sheltered the town of Fisherman's Cove from the sea. Every turn in the deserted road showed the Pattern which secured all Shape on the Isle of Circadie against the Void. Delicate as knotted gilt thread in the failing light, its interlocking tracery of force was visible in the veins of the leaves, the curve of the hills, even the dry sand of the shoreline which stood against the tireless rush of the sea.

Beyond the headland lay a scene of devastation. As though smashed by a fallen sky, the town lay splintered in ruins. The sight struck the breath from Jaiddon's lungs. Not even the boats in the harbor had been spared. The beach glittered with the silvery, crescent corpses of a skipjack's dismembered hold. Smooth sand lay sundered by a ragged gap that passed clean through the shore. Ocean swells rolled through the breach, unimpeded by shallows or shoreline, and on the other side, the land where people had once raised homes lay twisted beyond memory of patterned Shape.

Jaiddon could count the bodies. Trained since childhood, he could see the snarled remains of the patterns that held their spirits in life.

Air sobbed into his throat. Renders had undone an entire town as though its existence was no more solid than morning mist. Jaiddon hardly felt the path beneath his feet as he stumbled over the dunes. The Renders had gone on into the hills. Their trail would not be hard to follow, marked as it was with wreckage.

Anger and hatred gripped Jaiddon in the shadow of that levelled town. Would all of Circadie be undone, as Fisherman's Cove, until her tortured rings lost power and slumped into the sea? Jaiddon bunched the hands whose promise had set him against the Renders into fists. Perhaps if he released the solidity of the ground where the cursed beings stood, he could drop them into the deep. Certainly, that had never been tried. The Masters, all, were bound by oath to preserve the Pattern.

Jaiddon showed his teeth in an expression not quite a smile. He might wear a Master's Colors, but he had sworn no such oath.

Over and over, he was impressed by Circadie's vulnerability until, half blinded by tears of frustration, he was sorry he had not refused the Master's request.

He still found it difficult to believe the bedridden cripple he had faced that afternoon was the Master Shaper of Circadie. The Master whom Jaiddon had always known was a tall, ruddy man, black haired and full of humor. His hands had been strong and capable, nothing like the warped, skeletal claws Jaiddon had seen trembling on the coverlet. And the face! Jaiddon flinched with horror at the memory of features deformed beyond all recognition.

Yet the eyes in the deep, crumpled sockets had opened. They were still yellow, not yet devoid of the life that once shaped the cycles of Circadie with such enviable confidence.

"I am blind, Jaiddon, though within, I can still Shape your memory," the Master said. The light eyes closed. The ruined face smoothed as an image of a white robed, barefoot novice with sparely muscled bones and hair the color of brass formed behind seamed lids. "Jaiddon, there are Renders in the land."

The Master's words drove a sharp spike of fear through Jaiddon's thoughts. Few could stand against the power of Renders, outsiders whose disbelief could unravel Shape like a tear in knitted wool. Not even the Pattern of Solidity, foundation of all Circadie, was secure against the destruction such a mind could unleash. Blind and deaf to all but Reality, two of them had once blundered through an entire forest without perceiving the fragile power that held its existence against the Void. Everything they touched was destroyed, reduced in a moment to the flotsam from which it had been created.

"The Renders number three," the Master Shaper said, snapping Jaiddon's paralysed shock. "They are shipwreck victims, dazed and delirious with thirst. Megallie thinks they are mad. Certainly, they are strong, stronger than any Render who has ever challenged the Solidity of Circadie. We are desperate, Jaiddon. That is why you have been summoned."

"But my Lord!" Jaiddon stared with fresh horror. "I barely passed my apprenticeship a fortnight ago!"

A nightmarish parody of a smile touched the Master's withered lips. Jaiddon felt his heart twist in response.

"Years and experience have proven useless against these Renders." The Master Shaper spoke with difficulty. "Varna, Loremistress of the Pattern, lies dead. Myself, they have broken. I can no longer Shape even a child's toy. Circadie is dying. I place her last hope in your hands."

Tears spilled sudden and hot down Jaiddon's cheeks. He was glad they could not be seen by the man in the bed. "What can I do that you could not?"

The Master was silent for a long while. "I do not know," he said at last. "You are young. Your training is incomplete. But you are talented beyond all that have gone before, so is it inscribed in the Pattern of your hands. It is my hope, all of Circadie's hope, that you, with your untried, unchannelled power, might find means your forebears missed by the wayside. I realize I am probably asking your death. Yet, I ask. Will you face the Renders, and challenge their Reality with Shape?"

Jaiddon stood like a statue. Sunlight spilled through the window and branded a square of warmth in the sweat that chilled his back. He was afraid. Once as a child he'd had a cut that would not stop bleeding. It had been Shaped to health, but the man, the Master whose hands had wrought against the Void, lay dying of a Render's touch. Jaiddon swallowed again, and spoke.

"My Lord, the Renders will have me anyway. I may as well meet the Void in their path."

But the blue tunic and white shirt of Mastery given him

after his audience did nothing to ease his self-doubt. For all his alleged talent, Jaiddon could not even read his own lifepath. His peers had laughed often over that.

Black as oblivion, the Renders' path ran northward. Jaiddon could sense its presence without sight by the utter lack of resonance beneath his feet. Here and there, his step struck solidity, and he recognized the harmonics that answered. They were Megallie's. Newly appointed Loremistress in Varna's stead, she had been mending, perhaps after seeing the Master Shaper comfortable.

Her work had been cursory, her touch, unerring. Gazing downward through the darkness beneath his soles, Jaiddon saw where a Grand Axis of the Pattern was laid bare. Megallie had fused it, perfectly. He could not repeat her work. Years of training lay ahead before he dared attune to a major ring, far less forge one complete.

Jaiddon cursed. His earlier plan was no better than a foolish dream. Having seen the original Pattern of Solidity after which all others were formed, he knew himself incapable of breaking even its simplest curve.

Jaiddon moved on. Anger drained away and left a rocky bed of despair.

The Renders lay in a hollow beneath a tangle of scrub thorn, asleep. Jaiddon came upon them so suddenly he nearly fell into the ditch their unbelief had torn through the fabric of the ground. There were three, as the Master had said, opaque bodies dark as blight against the Patterned perfection of grasses fired like crystal by starlight. Even passive, the Renders' Reality radiated threat like a breath of cold.

Jaiddon shivered and fought revulsion. His ancestors had once been formed of substance, as these Renders were, but generations of Shaping had transformed them gradually away from Reality. Cast upon the sea as exiles, they had delved among the mysteries of the mind and the illusory laws of sorcery, and in their fusion, developed the art of Shaping. Circadie was raised above the waves through generations of effort. Ring upon ring of power, joined and interlaced, held its soil dry above the tide. From that framework, the Shapers of Circadie forced tiny allotments of wood, metal, and stone to serve the needs of many.

The Pattern and the Shape that was Jaiddon would not be visible to the Renders when they wakened, just as the grass, the trees, and the soil did not exist through their senses.

Jaiddon groped through despair for an action, any action, that might halt the Renders' terrible course. He knew from memory each passage from the ballads that described past encounters with their kind. But such facts were useless. The Master Shaper had charged him to abandon precedents. Jaiddon pressed damp palms to his temples. If Circadie and the people who inhabited it could be made visible to the Renders, their disbelief might weaken, diminishing their ruinous effect upon the Pattern.

The simple act of enforcing the shape that surrounded them would not suffice. That had been attempted already without success. Jaiddon decided instead to inscribe the Pattern directly upon the minds of the Renders. Surely even Reality's logic could acknowledge and accept the laws of solidity and allow Circadie existence.

Jaiddon took a last breath, unmindful of the thornbranch that hooked his sleeve. Substance never yielded its Reality easily, and a Render was a living entity, self-aware, and defended against intrusion. Prepared for struggle, Jaiddon closed his eyes and reached out for the thoughts of the Render who lay nearest. Had his training been complete, he would have known the Pattern of Solidity represented the framework of madness to the mind he sought to Shape, but he had barely won his novitiate, and in ignorance, he touched.

Contact opened a blind abyss of unreason. Jaiddon broke into sweat, strove to hold firm against a Reality whose nature commanded Shape to go molten and flow formless into the Void. It seemed as though his Pattern of existence would be crushed to powder beneath the weight of the Render's mind. As the first tremor of dissolution crept through the fibres of his body, Jaiddon cried out. So this was what happened to the Master! Panic thundered through the gaps in his being, twisting reason into a hard knot of terror. Jaiddon tore free.

He was drenched, shaking, and the echo of his scream seemed reflected in the quivering stars. Shocked by the enormity of failure, Jaiddon did not pause to review the nature of what he opposed. Instead, he flung himself recklessly into a second attempt. This time, he shaped fear into a bastion of support.

The Render flinched beneath his touch. He stirred and moaned softly as Jaiddon began to inscribe the primary axis of the Pattern behind his thoughts. As the secondary axis was begun, his protest became louder. Jaiddon tasted sweat on his lips. If he slipped, he would die. With remorseless determination, he bent the will that opposed him and fused the first of the seven rings of power.

The Render shot bolt upright and yelled. His companions roused at once, and the force of their waking thoughts threw Jaiddon from his feet.

"Sweet Jesus, Alaric, what ails you?" said one of the Renders sharply.

Alaric shook his head and shivered. "I dreamed. Mary Mother, I dreamed I saw grass and trees, land."

"Ye're mad, man," his companion said. "There's nothin' here but ocean, and this silly boat afloat on it." He thumped his hand. Circadie shuddered in recoil. Bushes, soil, and a nearby boulder frayed like overstressed fabric, and vanished.

Jaiddon dragged himself to his knees, numbed beyond thought by the heaving dark that bloomed at the Renders' touch. He had failed. Though the effort left him weakened, he had to move clear of the Render's blundering presence and think of something else. Slowly, he rose.

The motion caused Alaric to whirl, eyes widened in panic. The incomplete Pattern within his mind allowed him partial sight of the Shape surrounding him, and he yelled hoarsely. "Almighty God, there's a ghost!"

"Alaric, ye fool! Ye'll have yerself overboard!" A companion jerked him back by the shoulder, then fixed a flat gaze upon the spot where Jaiddon stood. "No ghost there, man. Nothin' but sharks 'n' salt water."

Unbelief struck Circadie like a stormwave. Shape shattered to fragments before it, land and the life it harbored flung piecemeal into the yawning dark of the Void. Jaiddon cried out as the ground under his feet came unbound. Every skill he possessed fought to hold his being complete against a rushing tide of ruin. Loose pebbles and soil slipped like lost hopes through his fingers as he tumbled between debris toward the restless ocean beneath.

His fall was broken by unyielding blue light; a bar of the Pattern itself laid bare. Deformed like wax touched by flame, it had not yet parted beneath the stress of the Renders' unbelief. Jaiddon groped for handholds in the riven earth, dragged himself upright. Dizzied and confused, he forgot caution, and the moment his head appeared above ground level, Alaric screamed again.

The other Renders restrained him with difficulty. "'Tis the devil's work, surely," said one. "A clear case of possession."

Jaiddon dragged himself clear of the ruinous gap. The word devil meant nothing to him, and with uncomprehending eyes, he watched the Render who had spoken kneel over Alaric.

"Christ deliver us," he said. "I never thought I'd perform an exorcism for a soul in an open boat."

More strange words, and the chant that followed was in an unfamiliar language, as well. But its effect upon the Pattern was instant annihilation.

Half a hill exploded soundlessly into oblivion. Jaiddon screamed. The Void rose to engulf him. He felt light, insubstantial as ash. The breeze off the sea blew through the rifts as the Render's strange ritual unbound the force that held him complete. Trapped in a rushing vortex of wind and dark, Jaiddon suddenly longed to see the disbelief that was destroying him take Shape. Shape could be opposed, and on the heels of thought came insight.

He had always been ridiculed as a dreamer, unable to master his own imagery. What if he broke precedent, abandoned control and coupled the result with his lifelong training as Shaper? Jaiddon cursed and laughed. Poised on the edge of dissolution, he threw his wild imagination free rein. It seized upon the darkness that gnawed him and clothed it with pictures. Though they reflected unrelenting nightmare, Jaiddon patterned them and gave them Shape.

Circadie flowed and changed at his bidding. Plant, soil, and twig mirrored the fabric of his images. Fast as thought could unreel, Jaiddon found himself in an alien place of red haze. The ground turned to ash beneath his feet, littered with the Shaped symbols of the Renders' disbelief, among them every desire, hope, and motivation that founded it.

Jaiddon stepped carefully between the glancing sparkle of gem stones, jewelled goblets, and the dirt-gray bones which were his reshaping of the Renders' dead senses. He had no understanding for much of what he patterned, nor was he given time to seek it. Jaiddon waited to see which form would seek his death.

They came as demons, three of them, savage and thoughtless as the unbelieving minds they represented. Starved, naked, and crowned by bleached shocks of hair, they moved through the shadowed haze of imagery, eyes sultry as candleflame, and forked tongues tasting the air. Jaiddon knew immediate fear at the sight of them. But their Shape was comprehensible. It could be opposed.

Bending, Jaiddon scooped up a fistful of ash and placed his will upon it. Form broke and ran fluid at his touch as he repatterned Shape to match desire. Controlled, that which seconds ago had been ash assumed the outline of a longsword. Jaiddon tested the balance, then grimly inflected the pattern of tempered steel.

The weapon in his hand warmed. Its rough surface acquired the glassy bluish sheen of the forge. Jaiddon shivered with impatience. The change would take too long. The demons had sensed his presence, and with a hiss like a water kettle, two of them charged. The patterning was not yet complete, but Jaiddon had no choice. He raised his blade to meet them.

The demon that rushed at his throat was impaled. It screamed and wrenched. The half finished sword snapped off near the hilt. Jaiddon fended the second one away with his forearm. Teeth and nails tore like knives through cloth, then flesh.

Jaiddon bashed himself clear with his knee and thrust the demon back with the jagged remnant of his blade. It sidestepped and spat. Jaiddon turned with it. The fallen one writhed underfoot, treacherously close. Nearby, the third crouched, watching with a baleful yellow eye.

"Render!" Jaiddon forced the word around the terror that gripped his tongue.

Nimbly avoiding the steel, the demon attacked, slashed, and twisted clear of Jaiddon's riposte. Thin furrows opened in Jaiddon's arm as it struck. Blood soaked through shredded silk shirt. Fear made the breath rattle in his throat. Circling, feinting, he survived two more rushes. Sweat stung his eyes. The demon was still unmarked. The third crouched, still, to one side. Jaiddon knew he was finished when it chose to fight.

Raising his free hand, Jaiddon shaped in glowing lines that portion of the Pattern that sealed its final Solidity. The demon hissed in fury and sprang for Jaiddon. Patterning broke with an aching flare of light. The creature bore him down. Hot breath scalded his skin. Fangs mashed his shoulder, and the demon's nails gashed at his side and back. Jaiddon battered unsuccessfully with his hands. Dizziness whirled his head. All would be lost in a matter of seconds. Aware of nothing but the final darkness that closed over thick as water to drown him, Jaiddon threw himself into a last, desperate attempt to Shape.

He wakened, choking. Water and blood had soaked his hair and clothing. Callused hands shook him.

"Death, 'e looks like the sharks been at 'im," said a voice from above.

Jaiddon opened his eyes, blinked. He lay in a boat. Two strangers stood over him with faces bearded, gaunt, and peeling from overexposure to the sun. He struggled, craned his neck, and tried to see over the gunwale.

"Easy, lad," said the man. His fingers tightened on Jaiddon's shoulders, making dizziness flood back. "Ye come near to drownin'. Best stay still a bit an' catch yer breath."

Jaiddon closed his eyes and wrestled despair. He had fallen into the hands of the Renders. Why was he not dead? Where was Circadie?

"Let me be," he said softly as soon as he could speak. The hands fell away.

Jaiddon sat up, gripping the boat with bloody fingers. His body burned like fire, it was cut in so many places. When he stared outward, a triple image assaulted his eyes. If he looked with a Shaper's perception, the hills of Circadie appeared, churned and distorted where the Renders' thoughts had warped its form. The Pattern of Solidity glowed through, serene and blue where it remained whole, black and gapped where the Renders had broken through. Over top, pale and insubstantial as a ghost's drawing, moved the heaving, restless shoulders of ocean swells that stretched in endless ranks to the far horizon.

Jaiddon fell back, suddenly weak. In his last moment of awareness, he had sought to Shape himself a form beyond the Void. He should have died. Instead, his dying act had transformed him close enough to Reality that the Renders could perceive him. When the sun rose, his flesh would cast shadow, as did all Substance.

Jaiddon dared a look at the Renders. Two stared at him with eyes that bore the haggard stamp of hardship. The third lay grotesquely sprawled and still in the stern. Jaiddon recognized the Render he had inflicted with a fragment of the Pattern. Remembering, also, the demon that had fallen beneath his sword, Jaiddon drew a painful breath and spoke.

"What happened to Alaric?"

The Renders started. One of them blanched with fright.

"Dead," said the larger of the two. " 'E woke up raving an' died. It was madness that done for him, but how did ye know his name?"

The other Render started forward and shouted. "He knew because Satan sent him! Didn't he appear at the moment of Alaric's exorcism?" He pointed an accusing finger at Jaiddon. "You come from Hell, your purpose to tempt us from faith. God will punish us for bringing you aboard."

The large Render spat. "The devil, Chaplain? Do ye smell brimstone?" Laughter followed, but it was forced.

Jaiddon raised himself onto the seat in the bow. Dizzy, sick, and weak as he was, it was evident the Renders distrusted his Reality. They might kill him, in their misunderstanding. Jaiddon thought quickly. Though he knew nothing of Hell, the devil, or exorcism, they were obviously powerful images to the Renders. Perhaps even these might be Shaped to advantage.

"I did not come from Hell." His voice startled both men. "I would help, but if you have no faith, I am powerless."

"Christ have mercy," said the Chaplain.

Jaiddon ignored him. "You suffer greatly from hunger and thirst." Both men stared, speechless. Jaiddon plunged ahead and hoped their confusion would last long enough to weaken their disbelief. "Fetch me a container. I will provide you with food and drink. Then give me your oarshaft, and I will Shape you a sail to carry wind, that you may return to the land you desire."

The larger Render laughed. "Would ye make miracles, lad?" He rummaged among the floorboards, and after a moment, extended a wineskin. "Ye've got my faith, what there is of it."

"Fill it with seawater." Jaiddon's eye fell on the Chaplain. "Do you have faith?"

The Chaplain swallowed and crossed himself uneasily. "I pray four times daily."

"Pray, then." Jaiddon accepted the dripping wineskin. Its rough leather stung his torn flesh unpleasantly, but that

did not deter him. Every kitchen drudge in Circadie knew
how to pattern the salt from the water they drew to wash
their pots. This was the simplest form of Shaping, and it
took Jaiddon the space of seconds. He copied the Chaplain's motion over the wineskin for effect, and offered it to
the Renders. "Drink. If you have faith, you will be re-
freshed."

The larger Render pulled the stopper, peeling features
stiffly expressionless. He raised the wineskin to his lips,
filled his mouth, then swallowed greedily. When his thirst
was eased, he knelt before Jaiddon in awestruck silence
while the Chaplain, also, drank his fill . . . .

The tale is still told, in dockside taverns, of how a chaplain and a deckhand survived the wreck of the ship *Saint
Helena* by saving a holy man from the teeth of a shark. In
turn, he rewarded them, changing seawater into cheese,
bread, and wine by miracle. There were witnesses who
observed the two tacking into the harbor, their sail the bare
shaft of an oar. The holy man was not with them. He was
said to have left the boat by walking on the face of the sea.

Somewhere, over the horizon on the isle of Circadie,
Jaiddon's ballad is still sung. It tells of a young novice who
took a Master's Colors to defend the Pattern of Solidity
from Renders, and how he accomplished his purpose and
returned, bleeding and weary, the only Shaper since the
Founders to cast a shadow.

The Golden Slipper

Antanas Vaičiulaitis

Translated by Kate Pendleton

Once upon a time there were three brothers who went out
to sea to cast their fish nets. When they were far from shore
a violent storm broke out. The wind roared and blew so
hard that the gulls were almost beaten down onto the
surface of the water. They were so frightened that they
sought refuge on the sides of the boat. The waves rose
higher and higher. More and more the storm ran riot,
carrying the helpless craft along with it. Finally, after many
weary hours, the fishermen rejoiced to see the shore, a
sharp and rocky cliff atop which they saw a maiden seated.

"What is she doing here?" asked the astonished men.
"In the midst of the winds and storm, at the edge of a
raging sea?"

The youngest said, "I am going to ask her what she is
waiting for."

But the others rebuked him and tried to dissuade him.

"Do you not see that the slope is very steep? A falcon
could not fly over it, nor could a squirrel climb up. Why
attempt the impossible?"

Nevertheless the youth did not heed his brothers' advice
and leapt toward the edge of the cliff, which was so high
that one almost had to turn one's head upside down to see
the top.

The young fisherman clung to the rocks and climbed
higher and higher. The wind blew so fiercely that the birds,
blown from the sea, struck themselves against the sides of
the cliff and fell dead in the foaming whirlpools below. But
the young man hung onto the jutting rocks and climbed
from one to another. He felt pain in his hands and feet, but
the peak was already near at hand and across the tempest
he heard the maiden sobbing bitterly. Below in the deep,
the boat floated like a little shaving, and his brothers
appeared scarcely larger than needles.

The youth made a last leap and found himself at the side of the beautiful stranger.

"Why are you crying?" he asked her.

"I was walking in my garden when a sorcerer appeared. He seized me and carried me to this rock; then he threw my golden slipper into the sea. How can I return with a bare foot? The entire city would mock me, for my father is the king and my mother the queen. The servants would point their fingers at me and make fun of me." And the princess, thinking of her golden slipper, abandoned herself to sobs while her shoulders shook convulsively.

The fisherman said to her: "Where did the slipper fall? I will retrieve it from the water."

"Do you see that reef?" she pointed. "The reef near the dashing whirlpools of water? It is there that the sorcerer has thrown my golden slipper. How it glittered in the sun as it fell!"

The young man descended to rejoin his brothers and they rowed toward the little island. There they waited three days and three nights in their boat, but could find nothing. Yet when the fourth morning came they saw something that shimmered at the bottom of the sea.

The youngest dived into the water. There the fish looked at him with goggly eyes, wiggling their tails and gaping as if waiting to swallow him. But the young man was brave and dived without fear until he felt the floor of the sea underfoot. Little sea animals were pushing the golden slipper around with their noses. The young fisherman seized it and returned to the surface.

The brothers rowed him to the shore and he began to ascend, but this time without feeling the least pain in either his hands or feet.

When the princess saw him, she began to smile and allowed him to place the shoe on her foot. While fitting it, he did not stop admiring her beauty. He did not hurry and when he was finished he was not anxious to return to his brothers.

"Come down, come down! The storm is over; we have cast our nets and, when we have fish enough, we can go home untroubled," they cried to him.

But the princess arose moaning: "Something has happened to my leg. How unfortunate! Could you help me as far as the city?"

"I will carry you," he answered.

She rewarded him with a happy smile.

Turning toward his brothers he called to them: "Row home to our parents and tell them their youngest son is carrying a princess to the city. If he is delayed in coming home, a little bird will fly there and perch near the window. If the messenger has a little branch of linden in his beak, that will tell them that their son is happy. If he is not happy, the bird will carry a branch of nettles, and if he is no more of this world, the bird will bear a needle of spruce."

He picked the princess up in his arms and carried her away across the dunes. The maiden rested her head on his shoulder, her lovely hair caressing his face.

The day waned, nevertheless they saw no travellers, passed no hamlets, so far had the evil sorcerer carried her. Night fell. They stopped in the middle of a forest before a small abandoned hut. The young fisherman made a bed of leaves and put down moss for her. He went into the thicket, picked fruit and gave it to the princess. When the light of day was completely extinguished, when the stars came out, the princess retired on the moss and her dreams were full of golden slippers.

But the young man could not sleep. He sat ouside near the door and told himself that the princess was truly beautiful.

Then the beasts of the forest, awakening from their sleep, one after the other assembled around the little cottage. The squirrel came first hopping from branch to branch. Then came the marten running beside a wolf. Ending the procession was a bear advancing waveringly. There was also a ferret and a deer—in short, a marvelous multitude of inhabitants of the forest.

All of them surrounded the hut and greeted the fisherman: "We were sound asleep and we have dreamed that a princess has come through forest and thicket. We wish to see her."

"No, she is sleeping now and you should not wake her," he answered.

The animals beseeched him: "At least tell us if she is as beautiful as they say."

"Ah, big and little animals, she is so beautiful that the fish of the sea frisk to the shore when they see her; the eagle, high in the sky, pauses and listens to her voice when she speaks; and when she touches you, the most serious wounds cease to cause you pain."

The squirrel spoke up: "While leaping in the fir trees, I pricked my nose and I'm suffering terribly."

The bear growled: "Your little nose will heal up. Such a hurt has no need of being touched, but I, oh how happy I would be just to look at her."

The fisherman pitied those poor animals. He opened the door a little and permitted them all, one after the other, to look at the princess.

The animals approached the hut on tiptoe. They shook their heads and clucked their tongues in wonder at seeing her hair as bright and shining as the rays of the sun. After that, all, the bear as well as the deer, lay down around the little cottage to watch over the princess. When the sun came up, they went into the forest. One came back with nuts, another with combs of honey, another with roots, and since they believed she might be afraid, they hid behind the bushes and trees and watched through the branches for the time when she arose from sleep.

On awakening the princess spoke: "I have been dreaming that I slept in the castle of my father and that a hundred soldiers stood guard over me."

The fisherman replied: "They were not soldiers, but all the animals of the forest that guarded you last night."

As he spoke, the wolf and the marten, the squirrel and the deer, the big as well as the little, all the children of the forest came out of their hiding places. Very discreetly they appeared, too shy to approach closer; they marvelled from afar and nudged each other saying: "Look, she eats the nuts I gathered, the honey I found, the berries that I picked."

The bear said to her: "Mount my back princess, I wish to carry you to the city."

She got onto his back and clung to his fur and put her feet in the golden slippers against his ears.

So they began their journey through thicket and heather. The fisherman came on beside the princess. The squirrel leaped ahead and the wolf and marten formed the rear guard. Only the deer disturbed the order of procession. Overcome with joy, it could not contain itself and leaped unceasingly over raspberry bush and under hazelnut trees, while the grouse, balanced on branches, turned their necks, as if asking: "What is going past here?"

Toward evening, they entered open country and saw a tower in the distance.

The bear let the princess down from his shoulders, saying: "We are afraid of the soldiers and their guns; we will go no further."

All the animals returned to the forest to hide in their dens.

The princess and the fisherman went on to the city and, thanks to her golden slippers, the people recognized her. They threw their hats into the air and acclaimed her so loudly that the roofs shook.

And when the king heard the news, he mounted his white steed and had a coach follow him to bring his daughter home. Everybody sang from dusk to dawn without forgetting to eat and drink, bringing out casks of mead from the wine-cellars of the monarch.

The fisherman was seated in a place of honor and when the feast was at an end, the king called him and said: "I will give you a bag of gold, so that you will return home a rich man with shining boots and an ermine coat. You will not have to work any more and you will be able to lie in bed late and drink good wine."

"Your gold and treasures are of little importance to me if I must leave. Give me work to do and I will be happy at your court."

The king employed him as gardener. He pruned the trees, dug the ground and that year the apple blossoms were so fragrant that they put to shame all those of former springs. The princess liked nothing better than to walk among the trees.

One day the fisherman said to her: "When you come here among the jasmine and the cherry trees, all the bees hum more sweetly."

And he spoke of the sea, the golden slipper and the animals of the forest.

But the king stopped their meetings under the blossoming fruit trees. He sent the young man to the stables to care for the many royal chargers. Then the coats of the chargers became bright. The young man curried the prancing horses until they shone. The princess took great pleasure in her carriage.

The young fisherman, while hitching up her chestnut horses, said gallantly: "I hope you are more comfortable in the carriage than on the back of the bear."

Then the king gave him orders to mount the top of the tower to see if the enemy was coming. Seven days and seven nights he watched there. At the dawn of the eighth day, he saw a troop of knights approaching the city. At their head rode a man with a red cloak and golden crown. His armor shone so in the sun as to dazzle the eyes of all.

The fisherman told the king: "I have seen a troop of knights. Is this the enemy?"

"No," said the king. "It is my neighbor who comes to ask the hand of my daughter."

The poor fisherman went to the garden and walked among the blooming pear trees. He saw the princess coming to him.

He spoke to her: "I have found you beautiful and neither the waves of the sea, nor its black depths have frightened me. I mounted the sharp edges of the cliff and left my parents and brothers and carried you in my arms through the forest and protected you against the wild animals and permitted them to serve you."

She was silent.

He spoke again: "What must I do to have you speak? Must I bring you a bird that sings differently? Must I go to the isle of the far seas to shear the sheep with the golden fleece?"

She did not answer. She listened to the trumpets which sounded at the city gate. Then she returned to the castle. The sad, young fisherman sat down by the fountain. Later he walked into the orchard and bade goodby to the blossoming trees. Then he made his way to the stables to bid farewell to the chestnut horses.

He began his journey across fields and through swamps. The brambles tore his coat. The pebbles wounded his feet. The birds fluttered around and asked him why he looked so unhappy. In the forest, the bear looked at him with surprise and the squirrel was at a loss as to what to think, finally deciding to stand on his hind legs with his tail raised in a question mark.

The youth travelled on until he came to the seashore, where he remained all day and all night. When the morn came, it was stormy. The waves were high, leaping like wild steeds, casting their white foam against the rocky shore.

The gaze of the young fisherman followed the swirling sea until, suddenly, he caught a fleeting glimpse of a golden slipper gleaming at the bottom.

He leaped over the boulders into the waves and dived down and down, farther and farther. A little bird, a swallow, darted out. It circled bravely above the waters, breasting the gale over the spot where he had gone down.

It flew over the forest, stopping to pluck a needle from the spruce tree. When it reached the home of the young fisherman, it perched on the hedge near the window and waited. The brothers passed by and did not see it, the father saw it and did not understand, but when the mother, seated at her spinning wheel, saw the swallow with the green needle in its beak, she wept bitterly.

A Spell for Sleeping

Sweet william, silverweed, sally-my-handsome
Dimity darkens the pittering water
On gloomed lawns wanders a king's daughter
Curtains are clouding the casement windows
A moon-glade smurrs the lake with light
Doves cover the tower with quiet

Three owls whit-whit in the withies
Seven fish in a deep pool shimmer
The princess moves to the spiral stair

Slowly the sickle moon mounts up
Frogs hump under moss and mushroom
The princess climbs to her high hushed room
Step by step to her shadowed tower
Water laps the white lake shore
A ghost opens the princess' door

Seven fish in the sway of the water
Six candles for a king's daughter
Fives sighs for a drooping head
Four ghosts to gentle her bed
Three owls in the dusk falling
Two tales to be telling
One spell for sleeping

Tamarisk, trefoil, tormentil
Sleep rolls down from the clouded hill
A princess dreams of a silver pool
The moonlight spreads, the soft ferns flitter
Stilled in a shimmering drift of water
Seven fish dream of a lost king's daughter.

—Alastair Reid

The Last Voyage of the Ghost Ship

Gabriel García Márquez

Translated by Gregory Rabassa

Now they're going to see who I am, he said to himself in his strong new man's voice, many years after he had first seen the huge ocean liner without lights and without any sound which passed by the village one night like a great uninhabited palace, longer than the whole village and much taller than the steeple of the church, and it sailed by in the darkness toward the colonial city on the other side of the bay that had been fortified against buccaneers, with its old slave port and the rotating light, whose gloomy beams transfigured the village into a lunar encampment of glowing houses and streets of volcanic deserts every fifteen seconds, and even though at that time he'd been a boy without a man's strong voice but with his mother's permission to stay very late on the beach to listen to the wind's night harps, he could still remember, as if still seeing it, how the liner would disappear when the light of the beacon struck its side and how it would reappear when the light had passed, so that it was an intermittent ship sailing along, appearing and disappearing, toward the mouth of the bay, groping its way like a sleepwalker for the buoys that marked the harbor channel until something must have gone wrong with the compass needle, because it headed toward the shoals, ran aground, broke up, and sank without out a single sound, even though a collision against the reefs like that should have produced a crash of metal and the explosion of engines that would have frozen with fright the soundest-sleeping dragons in the prehistoric jungle that began with the last streets of the village and ended on the other side of the world, so that he himself thought it was a dream, especially the next day, when he saw the radiant fishbowl of the bay, the disorder of colors of the Negro shacks on the hills above the harbor, the schooners of the smugglers from the Guianas loading their cargoes of innocent parrots whose craws were full of diamonds, he thought, I fell asleep counting the stars and I dreamed about that huge ship, of course, he was so convinced that he didn't tell anyone nor did he remember the vision again until the same night on the following March when he was looking for the flash of dolphins in the sea and what he found was the illusory liner, gloomy, intermittent, with the same mistaken direction as the first time, except that then he was so sure he was awake that he ran to tell his mother and she spent three weeks moaning with disappointment, because your brain's rotting away from doing so many things backward, sleeping during the day and going out at night like a criminal, and since she had to go to the city around that time to get something comfortable where she could sit and think about her dead husband, because the rockers on her chair had worn out after eleven years of widowhood, she took advantage of the occasion and had the boatman go near the shoals so that her son could see what he really saw in the glass of the sea, the lovemaking of manta rays in a spring-time of sponges, pink snappers and blue corvinas diving into the other wells of softer waters that were there among the waters, and even the wandering hairs of victims of drowning in some colonial shipwreck, no trace of sunken liners or anything like it, and yet he was so pigheaded that his mother promised to watch with him the next March, absolutely, not knowing that the only thing absolute in her future now was an easy chair from the days of Sir Francis Drake which she had bought at an auction in a Turk's store, in which she sat down to rest that same night, sighing, oh, my poor Olofernos, if you could only see how nice it is to think about you on this velvet lining and this brocade from the casket of a queen, but the more she brought back the memory of her dead husband, the more the blood in her heart bubbled up and turned to chocolate, as if instead of sitting down she were running, soaked from chills and fevers and her breathing full of earth, until he returned at dawn and found her dead in the easy chair, still warm, but half rotted away as after a snakebite, the same as happened afterward to four other

women before the murderous chair was thrown into the
sea, far away where it wouldn't bring evil to anyone,
because it had been used so much over the centuries that
its faculty for giving rest had been used up, and so he had
to grow accustomed to his miserable routine of an orphan
who was pointed out by everyone as the son of the widow
who had brought the throne of misfortune into the village,
living not so much from public charity as from the fish he
stole out of boats, while his voice was becoming a roar,
and not remembering his visions of past times anymore
until another night in March when he chanced to look
seaward and suddenly, good Lord, there it is, the huge
asbestos whale, the behemoth beast, come see it, he
shouted madly, come see it, raising such an uproar of
dogs' barking and women's panic that even the oldest
men remembered the frights of their great-grandfathers
and crawled under their beds, thinking that William Dam-
pier had come back, but those who ran into the street
didn't make the effort to see the unlikely apparatus which
at that instant was lost again in the east and raised up in its
annual disaster, but they covered him with blows and left
him so twisted that it was then he said to himself, drooling
with rage, now they're going to see who I am, but he took
care not to share his determination with anyone, but spent
the whole year with the fixed idea, now they're going to
see who I am, waiting for it to be the eve of the apparition
once more in order to do what he did, which was steal a
boat, cross the bay, and spend the evening waiting for his
great moment in the inlets of the slave port, in the human
brine of the Caribbean, but so absorbed in his adventure
that he didn't stop as he always did in front of the Hindu
shops to look at the ivory mandarins carved from the
whole tusk of an elephant, nor did he make fun of the
Dutch Negroes in their orthopedic velocipedes, nor was he
frightened as at other times of the copper-skinned
Malayans, who had gone around the world enthralled by
the chimera of a secret tavern where they sold roast filets of
Brazilian women, because he wasn't aware of anything
until night came over him with all the weight of the stars

and the jungle exhaled a sweet fragrance of gardenias and rotten salamanders, and there he was, rowing in the stolen boat toward the mouth of the bay, with the lantern out so as not to alert the customs police, idealized every fifteen seconds by the green wing flap of the beacon and turned human once more by the darkness, knowing that he was getting close to the buoys that marked the harbor channel, not only because its oppressive glow was getting more intense, but because the breathing of the water was becoming sad, and he rowed like that, so wrapped up in himself, that he didn't know where the fearful shark's breath that suddenly reached him came from or why the night became dense, as if the stars had suddenly died, and it was because the liner was there, with all of its inconceivable size, Lord, bigger than any other big thing in the world and darker than any other dark thing on land or sea, three hundred thousand tons of shark smell passing so close to the boat that he could see the seams of the steel precipice, without a single light in the infinite portholes, without a sigh from the engines, without a soul, and carrying its own circle of silence with it, its own dead air, its halted time, its errant sea in which a whole world of drowned animals floated, and suddenly it all disappeared with the flash of the beacon and for an instant it was the diaphanous Caribbean once more, the March night, the everyday air of the pelicans, so he stayed alone among the buoys, not knowing what to do, asking himself, startled, if perhaps he wasn't dreaming while he was awake, not just now but the other times too, but no sooner had he asked himself than a breath of mystery snuffed out the buoys, from the first to the last, so that when the light of the beacon passed by the liner appeared again and now its compasses were out of order, perhaps not even knowing what part of the ocean sea it was in, groping for the invisible channel but actually heading for the shoals, until he got the overwhelming revelation that that misfortune of the buoys was the last key to the enchantment and he lighted the lantern in the boat, a tiny red light that had no reason to alarm anyone in the watchtowers but which would be like a guiding sun for

the pilot, because, thanks to it, the liner corrected its course
and passed into the main gate of the channel in a ma-
neuver of lucky resurrection, and then all the lights went
on at the same time so that the boilers wheezed again, the
stars were fixed in their places, and the animal corpses
went to the bottom, and there was a clatter of plates and a
fragrance of laurel sauce in the kitchens, and one could
hear the pulsing of the orchestra on the moon decks and
the throbbing of the arteries of high-sea lovers in the
shadows of the staterooms, but he still carried so much
leftover rage in him that he would not let himself be
confused by emotion or be frightened by the miracle, but
said to himself with more decision than ever, now they're
going to see who I am, the cowards, now they're going to
see, and instead of turning aside so that the colossal
machine would not charge into him, he began to row in
front of it, because now they really are going to see who I
am, and he continued guiding the ship with the lantern
until he was so sure of its obedience that he made it change
course from the direction of the docks once more, took it
out of the invisible channel, and led it by the halter as if it
were a sea lamb toward the lights of the sleeping village, a
living ship, invulnerable to the torches of the beacon, that
no longer made it invisible but made it aluminum every
fifteen seconds, and the crosses of the church, the misery
of the houses, the illusion began to stand out, and still the
ocean liner followed behind him, following his will inside of
it, the captain asleep on his heart side, the fighting bulls in
the snow of their pantries, the solitary patient in the infirmary, the orphan water of its cisterns, the unredeemed
pilot who must have mistaken the cliffs for the docks,
because at that instant the great roar of the whistle burst
forth, once, and he was soaked with the downpour of
steam that fell on him, again, and the boat belonging to
someone else was on the point of capsizing, and again, but
it was too late, because there were the shells of the
shoreline, the stones of the streets, the doors of the disbelievers, the whole village illuminated by the lights of the
fearsome liner itself, and he barely had time to get out of

the way to make room for the cataclysm, shouting in the midst of the confusion, there it is, you cowards, a second before the huge steel cask shattered the ground and one could hear the neat destruction of ninety thousand five hundred champagne glasses breaking, one after the other, from stem to stern, and then the light came out and it was no longer a March dawn but the noon of a radiant Wednesday, and he was able to give himself the pleasure of watching the disbelievers as with open mouths they contemplated the largest ocean liner in this world and the other aground in front of the church, whiter than anything, twenty times taller than the steeple and some ninety-seven times longer than the village, with its name engraved in iron letters, *Halalcsillag,* and the ancient and languid waters of the seas of death dripping down its sides.

Pale Horse

Translated by Hisakazu Kaneko

Smothered murmurs come from the depths of the sea.
They come from a horse faintly visible through the water,
a pale, blind horse walking over the bottom of the sea.
Its memory of once carrying man
on its back is getting dimmer and dimmer.
When did the horse begin to live under the sea?
Is the blood stain on its back his or someone else's?
The horse walks on, brushing off
all the sea-weed coiled around his legs.
Its blind eyes are bluer than the blue of the sea
—the blue of a lonely distant sea.
The blood oozing from the wounded side,
washed in the sea, drifts away.

In Autumn,
a cold mist rises from the surface of the sea,
then the lonely horse crouches, its legs tucked away,
behind the sea-bottom rocks,
patiently bearing the cold,
patiently waiting.

—*Masao Takiguchi*

The Thunder Cat

Nicholas Stuart Gray

Once there lived a king who hoped he was a good one. He really did his best. He made sensible laws and kept them. He ruled well, for he liked and respected his people. He went to war only if the matter was forced on him, and when he did, he won. He then arranged fair and wise treaties, which somehow satisfied both sides. Everyone was devoted to him. His name was Jerrard. By the time he was thirty-six years old, his small kingdom basked in peace and contentment. Life seemed very calm and happy.

It took him completely by surprise when, one evening, all the happiness and peace shattered around him.

Sitting by a great fireplace, surrounded by friends, with a loved hound lying heavily across his feet, he heard a disturbance and an outcry at the door, and the voice of a page saying in shocked tones, "You cannot just walk in so! You must ask permission, use a little courtesy—"

Another, deeper voice was raised in desperate urgency:

"We have to see the king *now!*"

"Let them come in," said Jerrard.

The small group of men that entered seemed composed of the leaders and elders of some country village. There were seven of them. One was very old, a frail, dim-sighted man, who yet had a forceful and determined look about him. The others were burly, middle-aged, weather-beaten farmers. All were dressed, with functional respectability, in rough, woolen shirts and breeches, knitted stockings, and leather or sheepskin jackets. Their hats were in their hands. As soon as they came in through the doorway, they bowed to the king. And the old man moved forward from the rest and bowed again. Then he said, "Sir, I pray you excuse our haste and lack of formality. We are in great need of help. May I tell?"

"I wish to hear," said Jerrard.

He gestured toward a nearby stool, but the old man did not avail himself of the courtesy. He merely came a little closer. But he stopped twisting his hat between his fingers, and his set look relaxed somewhat. The other men's faces cleared, too, and some of the nervous tension left them. Their confidence in the king's good will had been confirmed. Yet for a moment or two, no one spoke.

"Will you not tell me what is troubling you?" said Jerrard.

"Fear, sir."

The king stared at the thin lined face of the old farmer.

There was a sharp and indrawn breath among those who listened. But the king's face did not change. He said, very quietly, "What do you fear?"

"The Thunder Cat."

Silence fell. Everyone was very still. The old man took a step nearer to the king's chair.

"The Thunder Cat that runs among the mountains and spits the lightning," said he.

Jerrard looked at him with thoughtful eyes. After a moment he said, "I have not heard of this creature. Tell me about it."

The spokesman glanced over his shoulder toward the other farmers, and a murmur rose from them.

"Tell the king—"

"Go on and speak—"

And a look of strain had returned to their faces, as though their thoughts had become shadowed with something horrible.

"We had never heard of it either, sir, until we were told. And at first we did not believe what we heard. We laughed, sir," said the old man, and his voice quavered slightly. "It seemed too strange, too improbable. And yet, in time we knew it was true."

"I think you must tell me just what you heard," said the king. "And who told you. And why you believe the tale."

He glanced around at his court, as his counselors, his soldiers, his friends. They were shaking their heads in bewilderment and incomprehension. It was obviously the first time they had heard of such a creature. And the old man saw their faces and threw out one hand as though in entreaty.

"You will think us foolish, perhaps," he cried. "But you do not live, as we do, right under the towering heights of the mountainsn under the sound and sight of the great storms that rage across their peaks! Do you know how terrible they can be?"

"Yes," said Jerrard gently, "we all know the mountain storms. But they are only storms, and they die out up in the heights where they are born. They do little harm to the lands below."

"Not yet," said the spokesman in despairing tones. "They have not harmed us yet. Because the Thunder Cat has not noticed us, yet!"

And he went on quickly, as though he must say what he had to say while he had the courage to mention it at all. He said, "Careless and wild it plays among the storms. White as a cloud—swift and thoughtless as the wind! Its purring is the thunder, it spits the lightning, and the avalanches fall away under its padding feet. Oh, it has not harmed us, sir, that is true. But our fear of it grows and grows! We hear it, we see it, but we have no knowledge of its nature or its will. One day, one night, soon or late, it will notice us and spring! We are afraid. The terror is growing. We no longer have the courage to plow our fields and tend our beasts. There is no singing and no dancing in our village. Not anymore. Only, we whisper to ourselves the terrible legend of the Thunder Cat."

Silence fell again. The king was frowning, his thick brows dark across his angry eyes.

"Who first told you this legend?" said he.

"We have brought him."

The old man nodded toward the other farmers, and one went to the doorway and said a few words to someone else outside.

Two younger men came in. They had another gripped tightly between them, and they brought him to the king.

He was not struggling, though from the look of him he

had been doing so. His head was down so that nothing of his face showed beneath his bronze hair. His custodians released his arms abruptly, and one gave him a hard shove so that he stumbled forward and fell before the king's chair in an untidy sprawl.

Jerrard watched all this in silence, still frowning. He said nothing. And the stillness in the room became charged with a sort of uneasy menace. No one moved. No one seemed to breathe. Everyone was waiting to see what the king would do, and he did absolutely nothing. It was the young man on the floor who moved first.

He lifted his head and looked at Jerrard with eyes the color of his hair. And his look was cold and calm and perfectly self-possessed.

"What have you done to my people?" said the king at last.

The old farmer answered the question:

"He told us of the Thunder Cat. This is Corvin, son of Caspar the singer. He learned many legends from his father, while he lived, and many strange things. And he frightens his hearers to make amusement for himself."

"Why, Corvin?" said the king.

The troubadour's son shrugged his shoulders.

"I don't know what they're talking about," said he lightly. "I tell them tales, and they shake with silly fear. I sing to them, and they tremble when the thunder rolls in the hills. Who knows why? Now they have dragged me here and treated me with roughness and anger. Fools!" he snapped. "My father was rewarded and admired when he sang for them."

"Your father," said one of the farmers angrily, "sang only good songs. We were glad when he came to our village. He told no tales of terror nor left a shadow of fear in his wake when he passed by."

Corvin was sitting back easily on his heels on the hearth in front of the king's chair. He looked at the last speaker, opening wide eyes in an expression of mock surprise. He said, "Now, how would I guess you were all so childish? How would I know you'd take fright at a few fairy tales?"

He glanced sideways at the king very quickly. Then he put his hand on the head of the great black hound that was lying near, and it waved its tail and blinked sleepily at him. The king watched this performance bleakly.

"Were they fairy tales?" he said with an edge in his voice.

"What else, sir?" said the minstrel.

"Untrue ones?"

"Just legends, sir. Everyone tells legends. If fools choose to believe all that they hear . . ."

Corvin laughed, quick and high and gay. And the king frowned down at him. The old spokesman shook his head.

"He is making a mockery of us, sir," said he, "so that you will scorn us and dismiss us and leave us in our misery."

"I'll not do any of those things," Jerrard told him. "Yet you heard what he said? That he told you lies."

"We heard what he said. But who knows to whom he is lying? To us or to your Highness?"

The son of the minstrel laughed again.

"Be quiet, you," said the king.

He looked broodingly at him for a moment or two and then across at the villagers.

"What can I do?" he asked them. "What do you want me to do? I am at your service, always. But what assurance can I give you that these legends are only legends? That the storms are just the old storms that have never harmed us? How can I prove the untruth of these malicious tales?"

The villagers shifted uneasy feet, and their eyes moved one to another. There was a long pause. Outside the castle the wind went suddenly around the walls like an echo of the minstrel's laughter. The king's friends and servants looked over their shoulders with sudden nervousness and came closer to the king. And the king leaned his elbow on the arm of his chair, a hand half-covering his mouth, and he stared at Corvin. That young man went on petting the hound. But at last even he became aware of the silence and tension—or decided to become aware. He gave Jerrard a slightly comical grimace.

"They want you to go and look for the Thunder Cat," he said. "They told me. But they are too cowardly to ask, for fear you're angry with their stupid impudence."

"No!" exclaimed the old man. "We are not afraid—not of our king. I was only trying to find the proper words."

"Is that your wish?" said Jerrard. "That I should go and seek a legend in the mountains?"

He spoke very quietly, and the voice of the old farmer was equally low when he replied:

"It is what we wish, sir. You are our ruler. Who else can be wholly trusted to look after us? If this is a lying tale and the storms are only storms, we will believe you if you tell us—if you have been there and seen the storms rise and die away. And if the Thunder Cat is stalking the crests of the mountains, spitting the lightning while it waits to spring—tell us that, and we will be resigned. What must be will be. But we must know. It's far worse to fear the unknown than to know the worst."

"Very well," said the king. "You are perfectly right. And I'll go to the mountains for you. And bring back the truth."

He caught an interested flash of russet eyes in the firelight, and he said, "You will come with me, Corvin. It will be a long journey. You can tell your legends and sing your songs, to me."

High among the crags straggled a rough goat path; there was a cold wind howling dismally; snow was starting to fall and gathering on the icy white heaps that lay already at the foot of rocks and precipices. Against the wind, two men went with difficulty, heads down and eyes narrowed against the gusts.

Jerrard had wrapped his great scarlet cloak tightly about him. His boots were already scratched and discolored with hard climbing. He was finding it hard to breathe and was angry with himself for being out of condition after years of ease and comfort. He was angry because Corvin went so lightly beside him, with his long hair blowing wildly around his bright eyes and uncovered head. The minstrel was in the middle of a long and unnerving tale.

". . . it falls on your neck like a wet and blood-hot toadstool," he finished with some glee.

"Entrancing," said the king coldly.

Corvin fell back a pace. He kicked a stone so that it fell clattering into the gorge nearby.

"I'll tell you no more of my warning tales," said he. "You never heed them."

"I am not afraid of your petty goblins, fellow," said the king.

There was silence for a while.

"All right," said the minstrel suddenly. "This I will tell you, which I've never told anyone else—and this, I swear, is true."

"Huh!" said Jerrard.

He went forward more quickly, but Corvin kept pace with him and lowered his pleasant easy voice that yet had power to carry through the wind and snow.

"Not far from this spot, on a jagged spar of rock, lives a thing named Ower. It has eleven hands, and they are flabby, sticky, shaped like the toes of a hen. If ever you feel a faint breath of wind on the back of your neck, it is most likely Ower who is following you. Two white eyes searching for you. All its horrible hands groping and stretching for you. Its five teeth, mildewed and spongy, are opening for you! Whenever you feel a breath of warm wind . . ."

He had fallen back a little, and now he moved close behind Jerrard and blew against the back of his neck. Then he gave a wild yell and clutched at the two hands that spun him around and propelled him toward the near precipice.

"I have warned you," said Jerrard between his teeth, "that I will not endure your tomfool tricks! You amused yourself with the villagers, who trusted you, but you will not amuse yourself with me."

Corvin looked into the king's eyes and blinked. He was very near the brink of the chasm. He said, in a breathless whisper, "Let me go! I give you my word, I'll sing only pleasant songs, and . . ."

He bit his lip. The look on the king's face was not pleasant to see. But the anger slowly drained from it, and

Jerrard drew a long breath and pulled the other back onto the track and released him. He looked at Corvin for a moment, in a baffled sort of way, and then turned abruptly and walked away.

The minstrel followed in silence for a while, his eyes on the tall figure of the king. When he spoke at last, it was hesitantly and without a good deal of his customary lightness and mockery.

"Let us go back, sir," he said. "You can tell the people that you have seen the Thunder Cat and spoken with it, and that it means no harms and is powerless to trouble them. I will back you up. It will content them," he said.

But the king's answer was bitter and remote.

"An excellent solution—if you could be trusted."

No one spoke again, and the night came down about them.

They were still silent while they lighted a fire in the partial shelter of some tall rocks. It raised an ineffectual glow against the frost-bright stars and the new moon. The meal of bread and cheese was soon eaten, but the silence between the two men still endured. Even to Corvin it was obvious that the king had something on his mind, for he sat wrapped in his cloak, staring at his hands and frowning and thinking. And his thoughts were not happy, to judge by his dark look and set mouth. He was like a powerful statue of stone, carved to show a man with a terrible problem in his mind and a weight on his heart.

Corvin lay by the fire, propped on one elbow, humming softly under his breath and watching the starlight on the snow all around and the swirling mists in the depths of a great crevice nearby. Only a few feet away from the fire, the mountainside opened into this fearful drop. And two paces behind Corvin and the king, the mountainside went soaring up in overhanging cliffs and jagged spurs and crannies. Some thin clouds blew overhead, and the wind rose and screamed thinly. One of the sudden mountain storms rose from nowhere and turned the night black and noisy. Corvin gave a small laugh.

Against the darkness, the king's face showed like granite

in the glow of the fire, as he turned.

"Listen to that," said he. "It is one of the storms that are now frightening my people. And still I find it hard to kill you."

"Kill? Me?" said Corvin blankly.

He made a startled move, but the king's hand shot out and caught his arm.

"Keep still," said Jerrard. "Now is the time that I must make my decision. And I warn you not to sway me one jot against you. There's little enough on your side as it is."

The king rose to his full height, still holding Corvin in a grip of iron. He stood for a while without further movement, his head lifted to watch the storm mounting to its wild climax, with the snow blowing in it and the wind shrieking. And the minstrel was deeply afraid, as he had never been before in all his life, too much afraid to struggle, too afraid to plead. He did not even raise his eyes to look at Jerrard's face and what might be written on it. He just stared at the precipice, so close by, and tried not to tremble lest so small a movement might swing the balance toward his ending.

The lines around Jerrard's mouth were graven like furrows as the muscles tightened there. His hands clenched on the minstrel, and he made one jerky and compulsive stride toward the chasm. There was a glazed and horrified look in his eyes, but slowly it became one of determination. He said tautly, as though each single word hurt him, "I brought you here to kill you—did you not think of that? There is no other way out of this business. For you cannot be trusted at all. The harm you've done can only be remedied by your death. And I will make my people believe that you confessed your lies and died of regret—"

The minstrel's tongue had failed him completely. His quick and facile mind could find nothing to say. Jerrard had brought them both to the very edge of the abyss. It was a thin cleft, with mists coiling and pulsating in its deeps, lighted by the sudden white lightnings that flickered among the peaks of the mountain. Only the strength of the king's hands held Corvin from falling, for one of the young man's knees was already over the brink, and his back was curved like a bow.

"Here is the end of your singing," said the king.

He slackened his grip, and the storm came shrieking down the mountainside and struck against the two men in all its frenzy and uproar. And in the wind and flying snow, in the tumult and flurry, in firelight and lightning-light, went the Thunder Cat. With outstretched paws it went; with streaming tail, widemouthed, slit-eyed, it shot overhead and down into the depths of the chasm. And with it fell the king and Corvin.

It was a good deal later when Jerrard stirred and groaned. He put out his hands and felt the piles of snow that cushioned him about. He was lying in a great drift that slanted from the towering cliff above. His fall had scored the loose surface and banked it before him until it had brought him to a halt. The king ached all over, and his head was spinning, but he managed after a while to sit up and rub his hands over his face. He had lost his cloak; his hair and his clothes were icily soaked; and he groaned again, wondering just what sort of nightmare had him in its claws. For the events of the night could not be true. He shook his head. This hurt but cleared it a little . . . and remembrance came clearly and painfully back to him.

With difficulty, being so wet and stiff, and with the unsteady steps of an old man, Jerrard began to search.

The storm had gone, blown quite away, after the sudden habit of these storms, and the stars were clear again and the fragile curve of the moon. The crevice was too deep and narrow to allow more than a glimmer of light to drift down and reflect back from the snowdrifts. A great many broken rocks and stones lay all about, covered thickly with ice and snow. And Jerrard passed and repassed it many times before he saw the body of Corvin. The king went to him. The minstrel was lying in an untidy heap, half hidden under a blanket of snow that was no whiter than his face. His eyes were shut. Yet he lived. As Jerrard touched him, he turned his head away, and said in a whisper, "You saw?"

"I saw," said the king.

And he waited. And after some minutes had gone by in silence, the other turned his head again on its pillow of snow and looked at him and said, "I made it up—I thought I made it up. A tale to frighten simple people. I never had my father's gift of song and I wanted some sort of power over them . . ."

Corvin's face had changed. There was solemnity in it and the dawning grace of humility. He stayed quite still, one shoulder buried in the snowbank and his hair plastered with wet white clusters of it. The king continued to watch him without speaking. Corvin drew a shaken breath and said, "Now that I know it's real, I'll never speak of it again. Can you trust me, sir?"

He got no reply. He struggled up a little onto one elbow.

"Then I will never leave this place," said he. "Go back to them, king, and tell the people whatever version of my death you think best."

Jerrard pulled him to his feet. Then, turning away, said grimly over his shoulder, "Whether either of us will leave this place still remains to be seen."

And Corvin noticed for the first time just where they were and how hopelessly placed.

On three sides of them, the walls of the crevice stretched upward like solid walls of ice, without foothold and overhanging slightly. No man could have climbed them. On the fourth side, the narrow cleft wound away from them, only a few paces wide and strewn with rocks and boulders, all deep in snow. Fifty feet away a sharp twist hid its farther direction. There was no way out of the place. It was like a trap.

"Where did it go?" said the minstrel. "Did it leap out again—or is it still somewhere down here?"

"Let us go and see," said Jerrard.

Without another glance at his companion, the king began to make his way along the difficult path, scrambling over piles of fallen stones and scraping through narrow places where the sides of the fissure almost touched one another.

The king was thinking again.

"What shall I tell my people? That the Thunder Cat is real and terrible?"

And then . . . "Did some instinct guide the minstrel's son toward the truth, even in his light-minded malice? Is the Thunder Cat the menace of which he spoke? Or is it a harmless spirit of the storm? Can it be placated? Will it destroy?"

While stumbling and groping toward what might at any moment prove to be another blank wall of rock—or some place where the track might end in a yet deeper chasm—the king's thoughts went round and round in turmoil.

"Perhaps the Cat is a god. A mighty force that cannot be known or controlled by plea or prayer. Or does the Cat lie beneath the hand of a greater power that gives it the storms for its playthings—a flung white screw of paper that it can chase and worry? Will it be content with such a toy and have no wish to destroy people? Does it indeed know anything about the existence of humans, of their fears and nightmares?"

"Look, sir," said the minstrel, laying a hand timidly on his sleeve.

The king started. And saw what he had not before noticed in his deep abstraction.

The gully had made a sharp bend to the left, which the two men had just rounded. And there was the end of the path, only a pace or two ahead. It was a great, smooth wall of rock, as Jearrard had feared—but with a jagged arched opening in it, like a high doorway into darkness.

Jerrard caught his breath. Just beside the arch was a ladder of ice, strongly and evenly formed. It stretched up and up, out of the chasm into the moonlight, to the world beyond. It was the way of escape. The king looked at it thoughtfully. Then he said, "I will take your word, Corvin, if you swear you'll go into another country and breathe no hint of what has happened here. That is your way."

"Where are you going?" said the other.

Jerrard smiled faintly, and without saying anything

more, he went through the archway into the dark unknown.

Corvin followed him.

They went slowly, treading a smooth floor, their outstretched hands touching nothing. It was not easy to tell if
they were going straight forward or turning in a circle, for
the darkness was so intense that it was like something solid
muffling them.

Then there came a faint glow of light in the far distance.
And the king hastened toward it. Though he feared what
he might find, he thought of his people, of their fears and
their hopes, their deep reliance and trust in him.

And they came to the Thunder Cat.

Its paws were folded, their enormous claws half-hidden
in the snowy fur. The eyes that had blazed in the storm
were closed now. And only a small echo of thunder purred
through the cavern where the Thunder Cat was sleeping.

The king stood tall and powerful but quite dwarfed by
the huge creature that lay ignoring his outstretched hands.

"Spare my people," prayed the king. "Do not destroy
their little farms and towns, their little lives. What are they
to you, great one? Be satisfied with your storms and your
lightnings."

The Cat stirred no whisker.

"Are you a god?" said Jerrard. "Are you a god that
claims the craven homage of men as a tribute to your
power? Do you demand sacrifice? I am here. Will my life
content you?"

The Thunder Cat made no sign.

At the king's shoulder a quiet voice said clearly, "Two
lives are here at the mercy of your claws, but mine is the
one to take. Let the king go back to his palace and tell the
people you have collected your tribute and are satisfied.
Be again what you were, before I set your fearful image in
their minds. Be again the thunder that is only thunder and
not your purring voice, the lightning that is not spat from
your mouth. Be the spirit of storm but of the storms they
know and fear not."

The Cat's eyes stayed shut. The faint glow that came

from the sweep of its white fur was like starlight reflected on snow.

The king touched Corvin on the shoulder.

"Come away," said Jerrard hopelessly. "We will never know what it is or what it means to do. We shall never know if anything in the universe can hold it, or curb it."

They turned and saw the misty light of the arched opening in the distance, as though, somewhere outside, the dawn was breaking. They went back through the cavern that was so huge that no sign of wall or roof could be seen. And at the archway itself, the king stopped and turned.

He looked back, and he gave a gasp and a breathless cry of wonder and relief.

With eyes grown accustomed to the midnight of the hidden heart of the mountain, he saw what he had not seen before.

In the vastness of the cavern sat a god. And the Thunder Cat was sleeping on his knees.

Queen Louisa

John Gardner

1

Mad Queen Louisa awakened feeling worried and irritable. That was by no means unusual for her. It had been happening since she was a little girl, or, as she sometimes clearly remembered, a lizard. She fanned herself with the fingers of one hand, anxiously searching, as she always did for the first few minutes, for the deeply buried secret of her soul's unrest. She was not afraid of rape or poverty or death. She'd established these facts beyond a shadow of a doubt many years ago—she'd long since forgotten precisely how, but one cannot keep plowing the same old ground. As for lesser fears, suffice it to say that she'd read all the books in the royal palace—not only those in Slavonic and Latin, but those in German and French as well, and one in English, sometimes reading in her character as queen, sometimes as a huge and sleepy-eyed toad in spectacles—and she'd systematically crossed off all possible causes of distress from anorexy to zygomatic fever. Despite that, she always woke up worried and irritable. Her solution, which was simple and brilliantly effective, once she was awake to remember it, was to find little nothings to attach her deep, vague worry to. The lady-in-waiting seemed peaked, out of sorts; some trouble with her husband? Or the castle's north wall had moss on it. Do moss roots run deep? Could they loosen the stones?

She opened the curtains of her huge gold bed. (The king always slept alone these days. He said it was the wars. Had he taken some mistress?) Already the chamber was alive with light—the chambermaid always threw the windows wide open at six o'clock. Orderly details make orderly days, Queen Louisa believed. Also, toads like the early morning damp. Every surface, every plane or flange or lozenge of the furniture gleamed, almost sang, with light. The combs and brushes on her dressing table were so bright she had to blink.

Carefully, she slipped her toes into the cold, then her shins and knees. The floor, when she reached it, was deliciously icy. She'd catch her death of pneumonia, she realized, and hurriedly felt left and right for her slippers.

The door flew open, and the chambermaid rushed in. She was supposed to be here when the queen awakened. Queen Louisa felt a catch and thoughtfully narrowed her large and luminous (she knew) eyes. What had the chambermaid been up to? she wondered. The girl looked flushed. She was fourteen, no older. She looked—the queen touched her bosom in alarm—she looked pregnant!

At Queen Louisa's moan, the child rushed to her and seized her hands.

"Are you ill, your majesty?" On her cheeks, two bright roses. Her eyes were gray.

"*I'm* well enough," the queen said very cautiously. Her mind raced over whom it might be. Not the page, certainly. He was fat as a pig and reeked of old cider. She did hope not one of those trumpet players! It couldn't be one of the knights, of course, because of the wars—unless perhaps one of the wounded ones. Her mind fixed with horrible and vaguely pleasurable fascination on the thought of the chambermaid creeping to the infirmary, slipping into bed with some great gored creature with a six-month beard. She secretly whispered a prayer to protect her from salacious thoughts.

"I just stepped out for a minute, your majesty," the chambermaid said.

Queen Louisa was sick with worry now. Perhaps it was no one from the castle at all. Perhaps the girl's father, some peasant from the village.

"Help me with my dressing-gown," the queen said weakly.

"Of course, your majesty!" She bowed very low and went pale for an instant. A sign of pregnancy if ever there was one! But the queen said nothing. Mad she might be—so everyone maintained, though they did not seem so all right themselves, in her opinion—but she was not a person who poked into other people's business. A little cry escaped her. The lady-in-waiting who'd been fighting with her husband should be here now too. Was she off with the great dog, the chambermaid's father? The girl was studying her, alarmed by the cry. Queen Louisa smiled gently, and the girl was reassured. Queen Louisa extended her arms for the golden sleeves.

"Is his majesty at breakfast?" Queen Louisa asked. It was important to keep one's servants at ease, keep their minds occupied.

"He left in the middle of the night, my lady. The wars, you know." The child's voice sounded so apologetic you'd have thought the wars were all her fault.

"Well, no matter, my dear," Queen Louisa said. "I'm sure we'll manage."

"I do *hope* so, your majesty!"

Queen Louisa froze. There was no mistaking the distress in the voice of her chambermaid. It was something beyond any personal distress. (Mad Queen Louisa had a sense about these things.) She moved toward her gold and ivory mirror, lacing up the front of her dressing gown. Very casually, she said, "Is something wrong, my dear?"

Suddenly, touched off by the tender concern in her majesty's voice, the chambermaid burst into tears. "Oh, my lady, my lady, how dare I reveal it?"

Queen Louisa frowned, profoundly worried, then hurriedly smiled, for fear she might shake the child's foundations, and lightly patted the chambermaid's hand. "Tell me everything," she said, "and Queen Louisa will fix it."

The child required no further encouragement. Clinging to her majesty's hand, she said, "A witch has appeared on the mountain and put all the hermits to flight. The peasants are so frightened they can hardly speak for shuddering. What are we to do? Oh, your majesty, your majesty! The king and his knights are a hundred miles away!"

Queen Louisa sighed but refused to tremble. She put her arm gently around the poor girl and sadly gazed into the mirror. Her great heavy-lidded eyes gazed back at her,

and her wide, sad toad's mouth. The golden dressing-
gown clung tightly to her thick, rough, swampgreen torso,
though the sleeves were loose and a little too long. "Never
mind," she said. "Queen Louisa will fix it." And she
would. No question. All the same, it was inconsiderate and
irrational of the king to leave his kingdom in the hands of a
queen who was insane. Fleetingly, she wondered who his
mistress might be. *Not* her own lady-in-waiting, surely! But
the moment the thought occurred to her, she was certain
she was right. (These hunches of hers were infallible.)
But if so, then his majesty was the chambermaid's
fat peasant father, who was sleeping with the lady-in-waiting
because of her troubles with her husband; and the peasant's child, that is, the king's, her little chambermaid, could
be only—her own lost daughter! Queen Louisa smiled,
feeling wildly happy, but said nothing for the moment,
biding her time. She felt warm all over, and strangely
majestic. She was soon to be a grandmother.

2

"The Court is now in session," Queen Louisa said.
   The judges looked befuddled and a trifle annoyed,
which she could well understand. But the facts were simple, and nothing makes a trial run more smoothly than
simple facts. It was not, of course, the business of royalty to
explain itself to mere judges of the realm. ("Never complain, never explain" was Queen Louisa's motto.) And the
facts were these: that the king and his knights were all far
away, except for the knights in the infirmary, and there was
no one at home to deal with the troubles but the Royal
Court. Therefore Queen Louisa had assembled the Court.
   The chief justice looked over the tops of his spectacles,
holding his wig away with the backs of the fingers of his
hands, partly for the sake of seeing better, partly for the
sake of hearing. He looked from the empty defendant's
chair to the empty benches where the various lawyers and
their witnesses should be. It was a tense moment, and the
chambermaid glanced in alarm at the queen. The lower

justices, one on each side of the chief justice, pretended to study their copious notes and copy them over more legibly, though the queen suspected they had nothing written down in the first place. Queen Louisa could easily forgive them, however. Indeed, she'd have done the same herself. Surely they'd never encountered a case quite like this before.

Timidly, but with a hint of irritation, the chief justice said, "Where is the defendant?"

The lower justices smiled as they always smiled at every question he asked, as if saying to themselves, "Very shrewdly put!" Their smiles emboldened him to ask it again, even letting out a little smile himself: *"Your majesty, where is the defendant?"*

Queen Louisa smiled too, though she pitied them, really: dependent as children, hopelessly shackled in rules and procedures, wholly unprepared for the rich and strange. In their long white wigs they looked like sheep. In fact, when she saw how they held their pencils—poked between their pointed hooves—she became half-convinced that they *were* sheep. With the greatest possible dignity—to set a good example for the chambermaid, since a kingdom where the honor of courts is forgotten is a kingdom in trouble, and also because sheep are people, too, whose feelings can be hurt—but mainly because she had a vague suspicion that only by speaking with the greatest possible dignity could she prevent her words from seeming ridiculous, even to a sheep—Queen Louisa said: "You ask me where the defendant is. *That,* my lord justices"—she paused dramatically—"I leave to the wisdom of this Court."

They looked at each other, and the chief of the justices paled a little and glanced at the clock. Again he peered down at the empty benches where the defendant, witnesses, and lawyers should be. He cleaned his spectacles. "Your majesty," he said at last, like a creature completely baffled . . . but he let his words trail off.

Queen Louisa said nothing, merely patted the chambermaid's knee to show that all was well. The child, of course, never having been in a court before, had no idea how long these things took. She too kept glancing anxiously at the clock, wringing her hands, and pulling at her kerchief till it was so twisted around one could hardly see her face.

Meekly, the justices began to make guesses. "Is the defendant somewhere else?" asked the one on the left.

Queen Louisa pursed her lips and thought. "You're warm," she said at last. She exchanged winks with the chambermaid.

"Somewhere outside the castle?" asked the one on the right.

"Warmer!" said the queen, and squeezed her hands together.

"He's having his coffee!" the chief justice cried.

"Cold," snapped the queen.

"Poor devil!" they moaned. They had no real understanding of trials, she saw, or else they weren't really trying.

"In my opinion," the chambermaid whispered, "this Court's getting *nowhere*."

"Trials are like that, my dear," said Queen Louisa. "But if you insist, I'll give their honors a hint."

"Would you?" begged the girl.

Queen Louisa rose and extended her long-sleeved arms for silence. "My lord justices," she said, "let me give you a hint."

They accepted eagerly, all three of them waiting with their pencils poised.

"Our business, I think you'll agree," said the queen, "is justice."

The justices furtively glanced at each other, as self-conscious and timid as newts. For no clear reason, she was suddenly filled with a profound sadness. Still the justices waited, hoping for something more and scratching their foreheads with their chewed-down eraser ends. ("Justice," the chief justice kept mumbling, picking at his lip. He wrote down: "Just Ice?")

Queen Louisa continued, watching them carefully for a

sign they'd got it: "You've perhaps heard that our hermits have been frightened from the mountain by an alleged witch." She paused, startled, rather pleased that she'd thought to say *alleged*. It was the first real clue. The witch was perhaps in fact *not* a witch, in which case, of course, the whole trial . . . She glanced suspiciously at the chambermaid, then remembered, in confusion, that the child was her daughter. The child glanced suspiciously back at her. But still the judges' faces were blank. Queen Louisa sighed and worried that she might be spoiling everything by revealing too much. She continued, however: "Since the king and his knights are all away, it seems to me our bounden duty to investigate this matter. I therefore suggest that we ride to the mountain and investigate."

"Hear, hear!" the judges cried wildly, all three of them at once, and glanced at each other.

That must have been the answer (though Queen Louisa had to admit she'd gotten lost somewhere); because the poor little chambermaid was trembling all over and clapping her hands and weeping.

3

There was some difficulty with the queen's horse. In the end, they all rode in the royal carriage. The chambermaid huddled in the shadow of the queen, contributing nothing to the conversation, no doubt partly because, sitting with the queen, she was wedged in tight.

"I was born of simple, honest stock," the queen narrated. The chambermaid looked up at her eagerly, from the seat beside her. Outside, the landscape was glittering white. On the castle wall, now far in the distance, the gored knights from the infirmary were all waving colored banners and shouting. The three old sheep sat leaning far forward, for Queen Louisa was speaking very softly, harkening back. All three had their thin hooves folded on their knees and their bowlers in their laps, for the ceiling of the carriage was strangely low. She was reminded, and spoke of, the ceiling of the cottage at the edge of the forest where her parents lived. (She sat with her knees pulled tightly together, despite cramp and discomfort, but even so she could give no more room to the chambermaid. As she spoke, Queen Louisa kept her hands carefully in front of her great green wattles, merely as a kindness to the others. Personally, she rather enjoyed her appearance. ("A queen with a *difference*," she liked to say, winking coyly.)

"It was a marriage no one believed would work. Mother was Irish, and Father was a dragon. Except for a very few dear friends, they were cut off by both communities. But the cruelty of people who had supposedly loved them served only to intensify their love and deep respect for one another. I was the youngest of the children, of whom there were sometimes seven and sometimes four, depending."

"Depending on what?" the chief justice broke in, not at all urgently—in fact tears were streaming from his large, pink eyes.

"Depending on our parents," Queen Louisa explained, and realized now for perhaps the first time how profoundly true that was. "We were poor but extremely proud, you see. Of course it was difficult for Father to get work." She remembered with a pang how he'd sit by the fireplace pretending to read the evening paper, though in fact, as everyone in the family knew, it was a paper from last year. A tear ran down the side of Queen Louisa's nose. "It was difficult," she said once more—merely to find her place again—"for father to get work."

"It would be, yes," said the sheep on the left, "being married to a Catholic."

Queen Louisa brightened. "But poor as we were, we had each other!"

"Perhaps that's why sometimes there were only four," the chief justice said.

She had a curious feeling, which she couldn't in the least explain to herself, that the conversation was losing direction. She decided to leap forward. "When I was nine, there was a fire in the old wooden church in the nearby village. Naturally, Father was blamed for it." She paused, frowning, though she was secretly flattered. "Excuse me," she said to the chief justice, "are you writing all this down?"

He looked up, startled, still weeping profusely, then immediately blushed. He held the paper toward her, on which he'd been writing, in large block letters, with the greatest imaginable concentration. The paper said: JUSTICE ST. JUICE CUTE JEST [crossed off] SUITE SITE TIE IS US USE

Queen Louisa mused, the chambermaid peeking around past her elbow. "IST!" Queen Louisa said suddenly in German.

"TU ES," cried the chambermaid in French.

"JE SUIS," cried the sheep on the left.

They merely looked at him.

Queen Louisa sighed. "Well," she said, "they took Father away. I remember his parting words to us. He was a poet at heart, I've always felt. It was a wintry morning very like this one." She gazed sadly out the window. "He gazed sadly out the window, a policeman standing at each side of him—he had only his old singed overcoat on, and I remember the tears were coursing down his cheeks—and he said:

" *'My loves, do not blame the authorities for this. Who can swear that his own apprehension of reality is valid? There are certain insects—*
I forget which ones—that have no apparatus for determining that other insects of their own same kind exist. Such is our lot. Have faith! Love even those who bring sorrow to you!' "

"Hexameters—loosely," the chief justice said.

She looked at him with new respect.

There, unfortunately, she was forced to discontinue her narrative. They'd arrived at their destination.

4

The monastery gates were open wide. Queen Louisa discovered, descending from the carriage and keeping the

chambermaid's hand in hers to give the poor child courage, that in the monastery yard there was no one at all, not
even a footprint in the snow to suggest that possibly someone had been there, or at least someone's shoe. She
tiptoed softly to the monastery door, leading the child, and
the three old sheep came audiculously behind her, huddled close together and holding their bowlers on with both
hands, as people would do in a windstorm. There was, of
course, not a breath of wind, but logic was not their strong
point (she thought fondly) and, also, the bowlers were
new. The inside of the monastery was also empty. She
tried the back door.

"I'm frightened," said the chambermaid.

"Call me Mother, if you like," Queen Louisa said.

The chambermaid looked at her, then looked away,
sucked in her lower lip, and seemed to think about it.

Queen Louisa laughed gently. "You young people!"
she said.

In the snowy back garden they encountered a truly
amazing sight.

The garden's stone walls were encased in ice, as was
every tree and shrub and leftover flower stalk. But in the
center of the garden there was a glorious rosebush in
triumphant bloom, such bloom as would hardly be natural
on even the warmest summer day. And beside the bush
there was a horrible ugly old witchlike person who was
trying to cut down the rosebush with an axe. With every
swipe she took, the trunk of the bush grew wider and
stronger, and the roses bloomed more brightly. At the feet
of the ugly witchlike person, an old red hound lay whim-
pering and whining.

Queen Louisa stared in astonishment, believing for an
instant that her whole life had been a terrible mistake. But
somehow or other she collected her wits and called out in a
stern and commanding voice, "Stop!"—for she was capable of such things, if driven too far.

At once both the witchlike person and the dog looked
up at her. For an instant the witchlike person was thrown,
but only for an instant. "Never!" she cried, her lean lips

trembling and her eyes so ferociously green with evil that Queen Louisa was fearful that the chambermaid might faint. Immediately the witchlike person began swinging the axe like someone in a drunken rage, and the old dog whimpered and whined in such awful and unspeakable misery that even the Royal Court was moved to tears. The rosebush, of course, grew stronger by leaps and bounds.

"Stop her! Do something!" the chambermaid hissed, clinging to Queen Louisa with trembling hands.

But Queen Louisa thoughtfully narrowed her eyes, pursed her lips, and calmed the chambermaid by patting her hand. "Be quiet, Muriel," she said very softly. "I don't think we've quite understood this situation."

"Muriel?" said the chambermaid.

"My dear," said Queen Louisa in a stern but not unfriendly voice, signifying by a look that she was addressing the person swinging the axe, "every stroke you strike makes the rosebush stronger."

"Good point!" said the judges, frantically searching through their trouser pockets for their notebooks.

"Get away! Be gone!" said the witchlike person.

Queen Louisa smiled. She said, "Dog, come here."

With an awful groan, the old red hound got up and came timidly toward her. It settled at her feet and closed its eyes like a creature enormously embarrassed.

"Muriel," Queen Louisa said out of the side of her mouth, "meet your ridiculous father."

The chambermaid looked at the dog, touching her chin with three fingers. "How do you do," she said at last.

The witchlike person was perspiring now. Her black robe clung to her armpits and back, and her nose and chin (which were as blue and as pointed as icicles) dripped. She stopped swinging and leaned on her axe, panting. "I'm not beaten," she whispered.

Immediately, as if at a signal, a hundred wolves in the robes of pious monks came bounding over the garden wall and crouched, growling, with their ghastly fangs bared, in a semicircle around Queen Louisa and her friends.

The witchlike person laughed. "You see, my ancient

enemy," she cried, "your whole life has been a terrible mistake! The forces of evil do exist! Ha ha!" Words cannot describe the unearthly horror of that final "Ha ha!" She raised the axe in one hand and brandished it. "We're cosmic accidents!" cried the witchlike person. "Life is gratuitous, it has no meaning till we make one up by our intensity. That is why these gentle monks have joined me in seeking to wreak havoc on the kingdom. Not for personal gain. Ha ha! Ha ha! But to end the boredom! To end all those mornings of waking up vaguely irritable! Ha ha!" She sidled toward the queen. "I have seduced your husband. What do you think of that? I have filled him with the feeling that life is meaningful, if only because it can be thrown away. I have—"

Suddenly Queen Louisa heard, behind her in the formerly empty monastery, a thrilling crashing and clanking of armor. The witchlike person went pale with fear. "Strike now!" she exclaimed to the wolves. "Strike now, and quickly, before it's too late!"

But the wolves stood trembling and wringing their paws, too terrified to move an inch. And before you could say Jack Robinson, the door behind Queen Louisa opened and a thousand gory wounded knights came out, pushing into every available space in the garden, saying "Excuse me" as they passed Queen Louisa and her friends, and they raised their swords to execute the wolves.

"Stop!" cried Queen Louisa.

Everybody stopped.

Queen Louisa walked with great dignity and calm to the miraculous rosebush, her webbed hands gracefully crossed across her wattles.

"You've all misunderstood everything," she said. "Or else I have. But no matter, since I'm the queen." She could have explained, if she wanted to, how sorry she felt for the wicked of this world, who couldn't even cut a rosebush down. Though she'd admit, in all fairness, that perhaps the rosebush *was* cut down, since she was insane and could never know anything for sure, and perhaps the whole story was taking place in a hotel in Philadelphia.

"Watch!" said Queen Louisa. She closed her large and luminous eyes and concentrated. A gasp went through the monastery garden, for behold, Queen Louisa had changed from an enormous toad to a magnificently beautiful redheaded woman with a pale, freckled nose. Her white, white arms were so delicately dimpled at the elbows that neither knight nor wolf could refrain from licking his lips with desire. "Mother!" cried the chambermaid. "My beloved!" cried the king—changed that same instant from the dog he was before. The witchlike person was reduced in a flash to the lady-in-waiting. She sat weeping and groaning at her monstrous betrayal of everybody, and especially her husband. The leader of the wolves said, "Let us pray." The rosebush, being of no further use, withered to an ice-clad stick.

Queen Louisa extended her soft white arm to the chambermaid. "My sweet," she said, "it's natural that youth should be rebellious. I was rebellious myself. But I want you to know that if you want to come home, your father and I agree, you're welcome."

Neither demanding nor expecting that the others would follow her, lovely Queen Louisa turned, with a gentle bow, and went back into the monastery and through it to the yard and on to the carriage. She got in and, with a thoughtful frown, turned back into a toad. Immediately the three sheep got in, and after them Queen Louisa's daughter, Muriel, and then His Majesty the King and Her Majesty's lady-in-waiting. The wounded knights lined up behind the carriage to follow it home. With two extra people beside them now, the three sheep were so crowded they could hardly breathe. Yet they smiled like madmen in their joy at the king's proximity.

Queen Louisa said—the child looked up at her with admiration like a gasp—"Don't blame yourself, my sweet. It's true, of course, that your dramatic leaving gave your father ideas. The poor old fool was in his forties then, and, I'm sorry to say, all people in their thirties and early forties have this awful lust—this ridiculous hunger for experience, so to speak. And the pretty way you mocked him, of course, and flirted with him—''

"*I* did all this?" the chambermaid said.

Queen Louisa smiled sadly at the look of dismay and bafflement in little Muriel's eyes. Then, with the carriage gently swaying and the snow falling softly from the pitch-dark sky, Mad Queen Louisa told her beautiful newfound daughter the story of her life.

The boy beside the coachman said: "Isn't this a marvelous tale to be in?"

The coachman, who was silver-haired and wise, gave his nephew a wink. "You barely made it, laddie!"

The Song of the Dragon's Daughter

I am the dragon's daughter
smokeborn of broken shell
I am the winged the broken child
I fly and do not fall.

Teeth talons sworded spine and jagged armor
I tear the air I sear
the edges of the wind I soar
burning in the hard fire I wear.

I will eat you, hero,
I will eat your heart
seek me for I seek you
to do you hurt.

I seek the sword to kill me
to pass my test
death is my test: o seek me
free me at last.

defenseless and unarmored, cool and bright
as water, holy, whole:
deliver me, deliver her,
your bride, my child, our soul.

—*Ursula K. Le Guin*

The Prodigal Daughter

Jessica Amanda Salmonson

Four centuries agone the Castle Green had been raised on its round stone morro overlooking Morsk Valley. It held its age well. In time of war it had proven an ideal vantage-point and fortress against siege and foe. If times were not yet wholly peaceful, quarrels at least were things to settle privately, not with the aid of mobilized forces. So the Castle Green's site, in the generation of Dame Unise of Morska-on-the-Tarn, was esteemed chiefly for its scenic quality.

Unise had not returned to the Castle Green in many years. Now she stood on an elevated stone terrace, admiring the panoramic vista spread out before her. She experienced a nostalgia of lost innocence and childhood. Had she never ridden from these comfortable confines in pursuit of adventure, she might still retain a degree of her lamented innocence—or ignorance. But never her childhood; no one is gifted the choice of retaining that. So she would sing no monodies for past decisions. Had she never left the land of her birth, she would still take it all for granted: the present sight would not seem so much a wonder, nor awaken these grand emotions—nor ease her secret fears . . .

In all her travels surely she had seen valleys as quiet and verdantly beautiful as this; but the scent and sight and sounds, even the texture of this one stone wall and the feeling of this very terrace beneath her feet—it all came together in a fashion both remarkable and unique to her senses. She could put no name to it. She knew only that the little city of Morska far below was, to her, more charmingly dignified than the richest of great capitols the world over. The mirror-smooth lakes around it were purer and more serene than the most isolated waters in which she had bathed, far from peopled lands. The lazy river itself—winding twixt the hills like someone's lazy pet serpent—was as majestic as the vast mountain tributaries with their rushing falls. And the wilderness all around was no less magnificent than game-rich, fruit-laden jungles in the South.

She had wandered far to find this place.

Yet she should not have come. Her presence would attract danger. The thought reminded her of the desperation which drove her home.

"My Lady." The voice of a woman-child interrupted her reverie. A cousin: Miranna. She had been little more than a newborn when Unise left—they were strangers to one another, though reared beneath the same roofs.

"A message, Miranna?" The girl would never have spoken without that much permission—the rules and etiquette of a noble house had not much appealed to Unise at that age either. It would be nice even now to drop the barriers of propriety and embrace this beautiful child for no reason beyond her being kin.

"Grandpapa is informed of your arrival," she said formally. "He will see you in his chamber."

Miranna led the way (as if Unise did not know it!) up small steps and through narrow, dark corridors lit intermittently by misty whiteness through thick, translucent, quartz windows. Unise felt Miranna's tension as her own; no one ascended to the patriarch's chamber without vacillation. Unise felt small as the child before her, again in awe of a gnarled codger who had seemed, not so long ago, the supreme vessel of wisdom and power.

"Was he angry to hear I have come?" Unise asked softly. Wide eyes peered back at her, betraying awe here too; what had people told her of this woman knight-errant? How overbearing must seem a child's world, impinged upon by cantankerous venerables and women clad in chainmail and breeches.

Miranna obviously did not know a proper way to answer the question. She said carefully, "He said bring you at once. He did not smile."

Of course. He would not.

They continued up the winding, stepped corridor at the child's pace—a pace made slow by reluctance. To change the unsettling mood, Unise asked, "You would do a weary knight a favor, Miranna?"

She did not look back again, but answered quietly, with reverence, "Anything, Lady."

"First, call me Unise. For my name is not Lady."

Miranna swallowed, replied, "I will try, Lady."

Unise chuckled. Then she said, "The favor is this: the stablemistress was absent when I left my horse. Could you find her and tell her that the Lady of the Castle Green has returned a knight?"

"Oh, yes, Lady! I like her!"

" 'Unise,' Miranna. Try it."

"U-Unise."

"Is it easy?"

"It is easy," she said. "But not before company. I would be scolded."

"All right. Shh!"

They came to the familiar door.

Inside the patriarch's study, Miranna waited nervously for permission, or command, to go. Receiving it, she darted back into the dark hallway like a tadpole into murky water: pleased to be on her errand, and happier to return to the courtyard to play or study or await the midday meal than to stand under the hard glare of the man none called gentle.

Lord Arlburrow was a man of morbid tastes. His study was a musty, fearful place lit by a few thick candles and sometimes by sun or moonlight through a paneless window. It was presently shuttered from within. The walls were lined with rows of ancient leather and iron-bound books, arcane yellowed scrolls, and stacks of clay tablets of a tongue older than the Castle Green by far, older than civilization; and no one but Arlburrow had deciphered their secret knowledge.

What portions of the wall were not hidden by books were disguised instead with astrological charts and cryptic diagrams. In one corner, on a pedestal, stood a blue globe of the heavens; in the opposite corner sat a slender one-eyed deity, patron of star-gazers, its head cocked back.

The old man's furniture was squat, ordinary, sturdy, made of unpadded hardwood. Upon his desk were strewn various minor implements: quill, inkwell, compass, blotter, rule; and stretched across the length of it lay a grey lynx with tufted ears and no hint of tail. From its lazy repose, the cat transfixed the woman with a cautious yellow gaze.

The lynx had been Unise's parting gift—a kitten then; it had grown tremendously. She had wondered at the time if he would keep it.

Her grandfather ceased stroking his pet, rose from a chair behind the desk, and approached Unise. He leaned heavily on a short oak staff; he had not carried one before, Unise remembered. His lips were a hard line barely distinguishable from other lines on his face. His eyes were unreadable, and grey as the cat's fur. Unise knelt before the patriarch and presented her sword.

"I am in your service, Lord Arlburrow."

Her eyes watched the floor, and she spied a cricket moving along at the base of the desk; the lynx dropped silently at the corner and waited patiently. Unise swallowed hard and felt herself beneath her grandfather's cold, silent scrutiny. She dared not rise without permission—a paw reached out and caught the cricket, teasing it, undamaged.

Unise knew her discomfort was no greater than her grandfather's. For all his aloofness and mystery, he was a kind man deep inside, the living cornerstone of an ancient clan. His was a terrible responsibility, and traditions more than wisdom helped him cope at hardest moments. Before him now bowed an insult to traditions he valued more than blood.

That emotionless visage began to harden into something more clearly definable. He knocked the sword from the woman's outstretched hands, marring his carved cane on the weapon's keen edge. The lynx hissed and backed beneath the star-globe, its hackles raised.

"Damn you, woman!" he cursed. "To kneel before me like a man! Stand, damn, I say! Stand and curtsy as all proper women must!"

It was said this man once shared laughter that shook rafters. If so, that deep and throaty merriment had passed into legend. Unise remembered him as an omniscient extension of the Castle Green, perhaps the personification of the Castle itself, made of the same hard stone and grey throughout. But in his private way, she knew, he had always loved her, as he had all the children his long life had witnessed come into the family; and he had never hurt her.

How cruel her presence must be to him now—he who had lost a frail and lovely wife with his own life not half done, and by the portraits in the mainroom Unise shared her features in a weathered fashion. Her grandfather had endured so many hardships through the years, borne so many burdens. His wife had left a rebellious, brazen, and somewhat selfish daughter, who in turn raised a daughter with twice the courage. That alone made Unise black sheep enough—daughter of a woman who laughed at authority. But worse, now, she was knighted, and was known to have fought in battle. When she had left, they had called her hussy; what could they call her now? Their clan had contended with whores by making them outcast, speaking of them never. But a woman lean and muscled, with reddish blonde hair cut scandalously close and sword at hip—*who* was she now?

She stood from her kneeling posture, biting her tongue, her face flushed and angry. She had hurt him; he was old; anger often covered other feelings—his, and hers. His wounds were the more bitter to know she was as much like him as his own once-despised daughter. Unise understood that she was, after all, a symbol of his guilt, and he knew this, and he fought.

"My Lord and grandfather," she addressed, cordial between mutual hostility. "I am knighted Dame Unise of Morska-on-the-Tarn, by my king and yours, for whom I led a battle. Yet if you command me twice, I will curtsy for your favor—though in all my travels I have seen it done but once, and that before a Lord who was later proved a bastard and usurped by the knight who was true Lord."

Arlburrow glowered. By his own breech of etiquette he had earned return insult. And hers was the more grievous blow. Already Unise regretted her words. She was demanding respect by denying it to another—the while hiding behind figurative skirts. No man would dare challenge Lord Arlburrow in this manner, be he kin or Mountain Lord. She had seen the wizened patriarch bring Mountain Lords to their knees for smaller crimes. But it was not for fear of him, but for love of him, that Unise quaked.

Possibly because it was a private affair, a family dispute, the old man relented; and he would never give in if he truly believed himself right. He stepped backward, lowering himself into a broad, hard seat.

"I will not dishonor the knighted," he said. "But if you would serve me, it must be as granddaughter and not as soldier." He looked very tired.

Unise unbuckled her sheath and, placing the sword within it, set it out of sight. Then she bent to her grandfather's cheek and left a kiss.

"Did your stars tell you I would come?" she queried.

His eyes turned up to her suddenly. "They did not," he admitted sharply. She did not understand his tone.

"But they have told you something," she said wisely. "Of a coming danger. You must look at my chart, grandfather. That danger, and I, do come together. Something stalks me—something I chanced to release from a tomb sealed in a far, past millenium. I have not yet seen it, but I know when it is near; for it instills so great an instinctual dread that there is no mistaking it. I cannot begin to describe! I am haunted, grandfather. Already others have died for it."

The tailless cat leapt silently into Arlburrow's lap and beneath his fingers. The oldster seemed to be watching the flame of a candle which reflected in those cold, grey eyes.

"I have known, since before you were born, that the Castle Green would one day come to peril. I have outlived my time awaiting it. I did not know the nature of that foe, or the outcome of the battle. I had supposed a plague, an earthquake, a return to arms. Never did I suspect a grand-daughter."

He meant no belittlement, but guilt was in her mind and she replied softly, "I will go. The danger will go with me."

"It will not!" He pulled himself out of the chair, spilling the rumbling cat. "You will not! I have prepared. I have been preparing for a long time. You came to me for help; you will have it."

"I came home," she corrected. "I think to die."

Returning to the livery, Unise saw that her steed had been unbridled and washed down. Boys scurried around, hard at their labors—but the woman called Jonathon was not to be seen. Unise was severely disappointed. If Miranna had gotten the message to her, the stablemistress ought to be waiting with open arms—unless, as Unise feared, even Jonathon would be unpleased to see her.

From the loft above, Jonathon leapt, startling the knight and scaring off insecurities. "Ho!" laughed Jonathon, "and Ho! What a strapping strong thing you are!" The livery woman had landed with feline grace, and stood with fists on hip, looking her old friend up and down. "Devils but you are good to see!"

Unise's heart raced at the sight of this physically power-ful woman. Jonathon's hair was a good deal longer than Unise's, cropped straight along the shoulders and giving the impression of a horse's great shaggy mane. Unise said, "Embrace me, my droll friend."

They hugged. "Droll is it? Droll?"

"Aye." They held each other at arms' length and looked far into one another's soul. "If not you would have come with me. Look at you, Jonathon. You were a swashbuckler born, more than I. Why do you choose to clean stables?"

"*I* do not clean them!" she protested. "I am *master* here!" She reached over a stall and pulled a peeping stableboy up by the ear. "Scat!" she told him, and he scurried off to more useful industry. "Adventures are for the discontent, my darling. I am comfortable; no *man* could want for more. Nor offer it. I am good at what I do—as you are at what you do, I surmise from stories told 'round supper tables. And horses do make better friends than people. With rare exception."

"You were content in my absence?" The idea hurt Unise, who had never been content. Never. She stood by as Jonathon took up curry and began to brush a mare.

"I missed you every night, if you mean that," she said. "But I was no less content. To be without you was no more painful than to wait in my loft at the call of my mistress, like some king's poor catamite. You are of noble blood—I, a common worker. And that, my love, kept us further apart than shame." She grinned at that jest.

Unise was unamused. "My love for you is no burden, Jonathon. But my responsibilities were."

"My love for you, and yours for me, Unise, would have dishonored your clan. Well I know that."

The knight fell to one knee before the stablemistress, and took one hand to hold near her cheek. And she said, "Never dishonor, Jony. No greater honor was ever mine."

Jonathon pulled Unise to her feet, then turned away, to place the mare in her stall and set the brush aside. Her humor was only for the moment broken, and she said, "I have caused you hurt! Forgive? Now that I see you I say, 'Jonathon-girl! You erred in staying here!' Come, let me show you a sight familiar!"

Jonathon patted the mare's rump and leapt out of the stall, taking Unise by the hand and tugging her along. Unise followed, up a ladder, to a loft, to a small room at the far side. It was a retreat, Jonathon's retreat from a house of many kin—a house unlike a castle, where the numbers of residents could manage not to see each other at all. It had also been a retreat for Unise, for a while, and not so long ago as it seemed.

There, on a shelf, among many odds and ends, sat a blown-glass bear with its arms held out. It was so fragile a thing, Unise was surprised it had not been broken these past years. There were other rememberances about . . .

The room looked still-used, and Unise felt a pang of jealousy. The mattress covering the big wooden box was thick with straw; she remembered being poked by the stuffing, laughing and rolling and touching and sharing the sounds of one another's sighs. The place was unchanged. The smell of it, the sight of it—it was like the feeling she had found upon the terrace looking over all the majesty of Morsk valley . . . all that majesty compressed into a room no bigger than a stall: no bigger than the warmest, happiest corner of her best memories.

"Have you had other lovers?" Jonathon asked, with a gleeful curiosity.

"Many. Men as well. You?"

"Not many. Never so good. My duties suffice." Her eyes glistened. "I cannot abide men, I fear; and the hunting ladies who come here are not like you—prim, with their riding sticks and caps. They rarely notice me, except in snide fashion. Men make better friends, I will give them that. And regret it. I have few opportunities—but I carry no torch, Unise. Good will come."

Unise could scarcely comprehend a human being so devoid of bitterness. Jonathon was a jewel—a beautiful, unbreakable gem. She took Unise firmly by the arm, and drew her toward the bed.

"No, Jon-girl; not now!" They shared laughter. "By broad of day? With urchins underneath?"

"Ho! And is that new?"

Unise looked dour and spoiled the mood. "I do not feel it. My mind is preoccupied. I am afraid, Jonathon. Afraid to die."

"We all will die, beloved Unise. What is upon you that leaves your mind so drear?"

Their eyes matched for a long time of silence. Unise saw concern, love—what did Jonathon see? Not rejection, certainly not that. A fearful reluctance to be bound, perhaps—or unrelated preoccupations. The scent of straw and horses was all around, and the musk of two women. Unise said at last, "It is nothing. Comfort me Jonathon. I need it."

They sat upon the straw mattress, Jonathon unbuckling the leather straps of the chainmail. Beneath this, a blouse, which Unise pulled over her head—the muscles of her back rippling soft and mighty. Unise put long fingers through Jonathon's shaggy mane.

Yellow sun struck the floor, the floor covered with yellower straw. The wind was cool through the uncovered windows above; it kept them from overheating in their passions. It took her back, this lovemaking; it gave her the illusion of safety and satisfaction. It made her wonder why she ever left this, only to bring danger upon herself and all she loved. Remembering this, she could not climax—but Jonathon would forgive her that.

After a long while of careful play, Jonathon arched her back as Unise moved her hand steadily, skillfully, between the kiss of the stable woman's mons. Jonathon crooned, almost rolled to one side, gripped Unise's ankle almost too hard and said, Ah, my love, Ah. Ah.

Time had passed quickly; clouds had closed over the sun, and as they lay together in each other's arms, their bodies cooled, and they hugged closer, after a while speaking:

"When I first saw you," Unise said, "I knew this would happen."

"We were children. You knew nothing of nothing."

"Well, I suspected. Your pa the stablemaster then, and you his best hand."

Jonathon smiled, remembering her father in the best way. He was a flawed man, but the years since his death had smoothed the corners of him in Jonathon's mind. She and Unise had shared death then—for Unise's mother died the same month of the same contagion. "When I was born," Jonathon said, "he was almost disappointed. He had wanted a son—and I did not disappoint him after all. My, but I was a rough-and-tumble. Pa had three more sons, and more daughters, but I was eldest, and his pride. Mother looks at me sometimes now, and I suspect she sees him. She is proud of me. I had more support for my strength than you."

They clung in the growing chill, and Unise remembered running naked through meadows and flinging themselves in brooks or clear lakes. They were children—swiftly knowledgeable children. They had pleased each other well. If anyone noticed, they may have thought it was something that would pass. They were never forced apart.

"You told me," Unise said, "or you boasted—that you were your pa's oldest son and strongest fighter."

"And you told me, 'You're a woman-child like me—and someday I'll make you glad of that.' I had no idea what you meant."

"See. I *did* know!"

"Ho! You did not know what you meant yourself! But I remembered the promise, and it was not long—it was not long. I lay at your side, still babes were we, and I said, 'I am glad. I am glad.' For you were right. No longer my father's son—I was your woman then. And there was sorrow in that. I wished to be neither boy, nor another's woman; not even yours. I wished to be my *own* woman, and that, dearest Unise, is why I did not go with you. I was your slave! I was glad to be free, for all the pain of it."

Unise pushed away, took up her blouse from the floor. "And now I have come back."

Jonathon touched her carefully, and they were unmoving for the moment. "You are too sensitive. I would not tell you that, if it were still true. I am stronger now. That, or I know my limitation. You were no less slave to the Castle. You were no more free than I. Did you cry on leaving?"

"No."

"There, then. It did not lessen our love."

"It will be different now," Unise said, but then stopped herself from promises. She might not live to ease old burdens, and the clouds gathering outside reminded her of that. They had appeared too swiftly, each curling nimbus. They were not entirely natural.

She recognized the signs. Now was the time to run. Flee! Upon her horse, to the next town or country. But this time she would face it, whatever it was that followed her.

"Unise!" Jonathan shook her. "What is this look on

you?"

Unise whispered. "Terror, Jonathon. Terror."

Fire roared in the hearth of the big mainroom. Servants
busied themselves at the Castle's multitude of shutters,
and stoked fire into the myriad smaller hearths in various
rooms, arming against the ensuing storm. The evening
repast was done; the day had been more hectic than
average. Children wrastled, shouting beneath the scrutiny
of old, old portraits, tumbling about the center of the vast
tiled floor. The mainroom was the evening gathering
place, the warmest place on a day that grows unexpectedly
cold. Aunts and nannies and cousins and middle-sons and
daughters and what few guests currently resided at the
Castle Green broke into factions and groups, dividing
themselves among the sets of ornate furniture scattered
against the high, tapestried walls. Idle talk commenced,
and whisperings—largely about the tall woman in their
midst, rightful Lady of the Castle, a stranger in her own
home.

She stood before the fire, the hearth's maw gaping
higher than her head. With hands locked behind her back,
she peered into the reds and oranges and blues which
danced and coruscated over the burning logs. She was
clad now, after bath, in a blouse with fluffed sleeves, lace at
wrists, a tightly buttoned velvet vestcoat over this. Her
figure, her womanhood, was less in doubt thus clad—but
even without sword and mail, she remained an anomaly in
the mainroom, the only woman with breeches tucked in
leather boots.

Older men were still absent from the gathering. Some
might be gone on long missions, a few to the King's navy,
some to employment or businesses in nearby Morska, or
to the dens of a further City that catered to those rich who
gambled and drank, an equal number merely at their
various duties outside the Castle itself—not to be driven
indoors until the broiling weather could no longer be ignored.

Among the other fracasing children, Miranna played.

She had made a sword, binding twig to limb to form hilt and blade, tacking a blouse-button to the hilt as pommel. It was poor match, the boys thought, for their own wooden swords, exquisitely carved by toymakers for the express purpose. Miranna challenged one who teased her without warrant. He chided her and shared a belittling joke with a friend. Miranna stomped her foot and challenged them both, then stood in a swordstance so threatening that the two boys agreed among themselves to teach her a lesson. But she was good. Her limber branch went swishing among them like a foil. They and their stiff, overlight balsas were no match for the agility of the mock weapon or its maker. The two boys were hard pressed in the game.

Unise turned from the fire and her own unspirited musings to watch the lithe youngster; it was pleasing to see. Knight strode to children, and coached the girl.

"Yes, parry my darling—that's it: thrust. Ha. Watch! They are wiser now; they're splitting up. Do not let one behind you. Again! Again! Guard the left! Thrust! Aha: Good!"

Both boys sweated under Miranna's zealous assault. When she broke the guard of the tallest—pressing her harmless creation to his chest so that the leaf at its end bent—the boy began to cry. He cried for the sake of lost face, which grown men call honor. Defeated by a girl! The other boy refused to continue, not wishing to risk the same fate; he defended his companion saying it was unfair sport. "You cheated," he said to Miranna. "You were aided!" Then he glowered at the knight as though his small manliness more than weighted his favor against her height.

The other boy continued to wail, deeming a show of genuine injury less effacing than honestly admitted defeat. Aunts and elder sisters gathered around, coddling the boy, comforting him with reinforcements until he ceased to whimper. At the same time, they railed against Miranna: you've hurt him, you naughty thing; what sort of game is this for a girl; come now, apologize to Edor; that's a good girl—now, throw that nasty stick into the fire!

The scolding levied against her strength, the forgiveness

that came with cowering—Unise watched Miranna caught up in the mesmeric insistencies of wives and spinsters, until even the knight felt the dizzying affect: dance for them right, dance for them left. She remembered her own girl-hood, which within these many walls had upon occasion seemed hideous after her mother's death. She remembered the powerlessness she felt in frills and petticoats while boys leapt in tights. Miranna would not cry, but Unise almost cried for her. The squealing jabber of these . . . these *hens* roiled in her system until she could not hold back the shout, "No! She will *not* throw her sword into the fire!"

The room was suddenly and remarkably quiet, with only the crackle of fire and the thump of a half-burnt log to break the still. Miranna's eyes looked out from the hems of giants, as if to say, Unise, Lady, No: It will do no good.

A puffy old woman who was Unise's great-aunt and her nemesis since childhood came forward with strides as long as the knight's; and Unise wondered for a moment: what kind of human being *might* you have been? The old woman said sharply, as though Unise were still a girl to be scolded and sent off to her room: "And what kind of example do you think you are for little girls? This is your doing, with your swagger and your pants!" She turned from Unise in a swirl of long cloth, and said, "Come, Miranna. Show the Lady of the Castle Green—" did she recite the title vindictively?—"that you are not a horrible little girl."

Miranna allowed herself to be led by the puffy woman to the hearth. The child stood as before the gate of hell, and threw her makeshift toy within.

So many eyes were upon Unise, with too many accusations. Children were scudded away, lest they share Miranna's admiration. The knight stormed within herself, frustrated deep inside with an intensity that drove her thoughts to madness: she envisioned herself with sword to hand, hacking down foes—old ladies and their smug daughters—until the mainroom was astrew with piles of fancy clothes bloodied by the folded corpses within. And

after that by God, she would await the husbands and old
uncles and slay *them* one by twos by threes as they came
home; for they, somehow, were the true cause of all this,
though Unise could not fathom how, in their eager absence!

All this madness passed like a cloud, leaving in its wake a
dampness and depression. There was a certain hopeless-
ness in her now, but perhaps it was the doing of the restless
dark outside the Castle Green—the storm rising fast, and
no one but Unise and the codger in the tower aware that it
was of supernatural source.

Her great-aunt approached anew, and said with a
haughty fine grace which hypocritically belied hostility:
"The servants have battened the Castle, and been otherwise preoccupied so that your room has not been readied.
I shall see to it personally then." She started off toward a
stair that led to master quarters, a room of which had once
been Unise's.

Unise stopped her, saying, "Please. Do not trouble
yourself. I have a place in the livery." Jonathon would
applaud this statement, for the honesty of it if not the
discourtesy. The face of the clucking hen before her grew
puffier in wroth, revealing in this manner her knowing and
disgust. But the old nemesis minded her tongue lest *others*
understand so fully.

The great-aunt had little power and no authority beyond
her reign over house-servants and kin. She might wish it,
but she could not make it go hard for Jonathon once Unise
were gone, or dead. Unise did not mean to flout; but
neither could she find cause to respect the sensibilities of
those who made no concern of *her* feelings. She took a
mild delight in her great-aunt's deduction and disapproval.

None else understood the full meaning of Unise's stated
intent; still, all remained silent, and they were yet appalled.
They had other reasons: little as they understood her,
much as they feared her, she was nonetheless Lady of the
Castle Green. To sleep with horses! It was unthinkable—as
unthinkable as the Lady's knighthood; as unthinkable as,
as, well: what if Lord Arlburrow slept in stables? It would be

the same thing. No one liked him either; but they knew his place, and they knew theirs.

Unise turned from hen to gaping others, with a flourish of her arm. She addressed them:

"If I am not fit company for these children, then I am not fit beneath these roofs! No matter that I am Arlburrow's heir—so long as he or I live, *your* stations are secure. You need not fear my vengeance, whether or not I ever rule this estate. But consider: you are too small before my eyes to merit my dying anger and my welling sorrow. I pity you more greatly than you do me, and for better cause. You would beat the heart out of your bravest girls and shame them for being bold. You would tear the spirit of the mightiest, to make all women like yourselves. But fear you this: some of us survive!"

By their eyes she saw that it had all passed by their heads. They could not count her hero, or wise—for some of them had known her as a helpless babe, then mischief-maker demanding a constance of scolds. It is said, a hero will always be unheralded in her home. Nonetheless, for all their lacked respect or understanding, they held her in awe. Any eloquence she might spare for them could not help but be lost on the small minds of nobility. Whatever she said, they would discount it as proof and parcel of her awesome, perverse, and begrudgingly admirable nature. With sinking despair, Unise left them, taking the narrow stair to the Lord's loft. Miranna ran to the foot of that passage and called up the gloomy well in proud rebellion: "I love you Unise."

Behind, pointless chatter had resumed.

Big as it was, Arlburrow's cat stepped with dainty purpose, along the narrow ledge of a bookshelf, halting stone-still whenever the shelf creaked beneath the weight. Not a book or an artifact was upset by the stalking animal. At length it was positioned above Unise's head, for she sat in the hard chair in front of Arlburrow's desk—and the lynx counted that seat its own.

Arlburrow peered through a glass at the tiny script of an

old, clay tablet he had placed upon the scatter of star-charts and measures. He had queried Unise until her head was sore; and he had quested the day long through his mystic library. From what she was able to remember about the tomb—location, design within and without, precise nature of the contents, glyphs on the sarcophagus—Arlburrow had been able to date its millenium, and, eventually, find the occupant's name. He had not yet said the name aloud; no doubt he would tell her in his own time, though Unise did not truly care to know whose ghost she had released. She had no need of a name for it, but, rather, its poltice. Whoever it had been, man or woman, it was an evil thing—and mighty, to have survived imprisoned aeons. She regretted her soul to hell that it was her hand which broke the ancient seals of sorcery against the fiend. Let Arlburrow keep its name—forever if he wished, for the sake of his beloved secrecies. Only, tell her of its bane.

Storm battered at Arlburrow's window, behind him and his desk, as though aware that within sat potential foe.

Unise felt old as Arlburrow, heavy and shrunken in her seat; and like Arlburrow, she found, oddly, a degree of comfort among the tomes and arcana of a library others perceived as foreboding. The dimness of light nurtured her mood. The smell of antiquity—leather, clay, papyrus, char—eased her own sense of fleeting mortality and pending doom.

The lynx hissed and set its ears far back, tensed to leap upon the head of the usurper of its seat. It was a wild beast after all, for all its gentleness with Arlburrow—and a territorial beast. Unise said with impatience and not much voice. "You cannot frighten me, Mite. You are big. But I have wrestled cats twice your size and bigger."

The lynx leapt—into the lap of the uncowed woman. She patted the animal, static tickling her fingers as lightning cracked outside.

"It follows you," Arlburrow said, looking up from studious concentration, "because it is bound to your service. You freed it: it is yours."

Unise considered the point. "If this is so," she said, "I could command it back to its grave."

As she feared, the answer was too simple to be useful. Arlburrow said, "It is your servant as much out of gratitude as by the magic of its long-dust captors. That gratitude should not last beyond such a command. In one manner, it is fortunate the monster tracks you, granddaughter; for there was reason and intent behind each aspect of the sorceries which bound it before, and bind it yet. I shudder to consider what havoc it would bring upon the land were it free to go its way. It cannot be free until it has served its liberator—and its only service is murder."

The lynx rumbled in her lap, and kneaded her with its large, furry feet, never quite breaking flesh with its retracting, razored claws. Arlburrow had broken it of that.

What Arlburrow had told her did not relieve Unise's intense dread. Indeed, if everything he said were irrevocably true, the very act of freeing herself from the devil would endanger all of humanity the more.

"What am I to do," she said, and again, "What am I to do." It seemed she spoke only to herself, or to the lynx who raised its tailless rear to her.

"By the stars I have calculated, the beast will not fully enclose the Castle Green until midday tomorrow—though by then, midday will be as dark as this night, in the shadow of the thing! It will crush the mortar from these walls to get to you, its master, unless we prepare through the night. I have already sent riders to gather in all who reside around the Castle Green. They will wonder at that, for it has been many years since siege—but by the time all realize the true danger, I will have seen to the Castle's defense. Fetch me that case!"

He pointed to what might have been a shipping crate for a company of swords—that, or a child's coffin. It was plane, and pegged shut. Unise unsettled the cat, and took up the container. It was heavier than she had thought it would be. With barely a sound and leaving nary a scratch, she set it upon the desk. Arlburrow watched her with an odd compassion, and might have been disguising a reluctant pride over the ease with which she hefted the heavy box. He worked at the pegs; she helped. Within, five elongate objects were wrapped in oiled cloth. Arlburrow slowly unwrapped all but one: four thick rods of argent material, like silver, shone in the chamber's candlelight.

Behind Arlburrow, the window shutters rattled with a kind of desperation, as though an imp clung to the tower wall and strove for entry. Then: the wind screamed . . . what? an obscenity? Trick of the mind and ear . . . Unise, like Arlburrow, pretended not to hear.

"What can these do?" she asked.

"Protect the Castle, I believe. You will take one to each of the high, corner watchtowers. Set them carefully facing respectively: north, east, south, west." He pointed to specific ones. "Do not confuse them! Like magnets, set wrong end together, they will fight one another rather than unite to form a covering matrix over all the Castle Green. No one and nothing, save the supernatural being that fills the nighted sky, will see or feel that barrier. The monster's wrath will no doubt increase—and it will be only penned out, not defeated. For victory against it, I fear you will have to prove yourself a knight to me after all." It was a hard thing for him to say. "The old magicks still upon it have provided many safeguards. If I understand the spells defined in the ancient scripts, the monster can be reduced to a semblance of its living form, and may then be defeated. But not at leisure. I confess I think it beyond you, granddaughter; but there is no other tested warrior in this county, and in any event, only its master can call it down to size. How good a fighter are you, Dame Unise?"

It was the first time he had used her title. The acknowledgment made her shoulders square, her back straighten, and she said, "How good need I be?"

"Better, I fear, than any warrior known to those antique sorcery-makers, or they would have had this demon slain rather than imprisoned. Yet it must be tried. It will face, in mortal combat, none but the woman who unleashed it, the one to whom it is bound. For no other would it make itself vulnerable."

Without further statement, Unise took up the four rods, not querying about the fifth, and went after her task. The lynx, Mite, followed her, running up and down staircases and spatting at any servant they chanced to pass. The cat was a terror to all.

Unise's task was not swiftly completed. The Castle was huge, and it felt as though she had gone up and down every staircase within those vast confines. There were shorter routes, but mostly leading through the central mainroom. The women might be off to their varied chambers at this hour, but the men of the Castle would be in now, telling stories and imbiding small sports. And soon, the cotters and families and even the squatters on the estate would be gathering below—including Jonathon's clan—and the half-sleeping Castle would buzz with life and curiosity. Unise did not feel up to confrontations with all those puzzled folk, who soon enough would learn the danger.

She took the longer ways, the first of which brought her out into the storm. With her weighty bundle, she walked alongside the battlements of the Castle's wall, and felt the gloom pressing down from above. There was an almost beckoning sweetness to the icy terror that flooded through her veins. Sanguine promises of greatness and power impinged upon her brain: *we can rule the world as one* . . . She ignored the seductions of the dark and came to the first of four high towers.

The crenelated lookout was rarely visited in these times of comparative peace. She ascended the spiral stair. In the circular room above, she leaned over a sill to mount the first argent rod in a setting intended for the Banner of the Castle Green, facing its proper end North. As she did this, Mite licked at wetted fur and paws. Sudden pellets of hail struck the back of her neck—vindictive stingings which she ignored until the job was done. The verse of a warrior bard passed through her thoughts unbidden:

Death by hammer, death by spear
these things would I face

One thing only do I fear
mere courage can't erase.
And that? The specter at my back
That unseen, unknown wraith's attack.

Death by tulwar, death by lance
no dirk frightens me
Only ghostly circumstance
incites my plaintive plea.
Nameless fear creeps up my spine—
That beating heart! Is it mine?

Death in battle, by the axe
near to Death I fell
But the Scythe again grew lax
and Fortune bore me well.
But what would mortal weapons do
to stay a foe the wind blows through?

Descending to an interior floor, she proceeded to the next tower, and the next, and lastly the westernmost keep. When the final rod was in position, the gloom did seem pressed back, though for the moment Unise detected no other difference.

When she turned from the uncovered window through which she had attended the banner-mount, she saw Mite with back arched and fur standing—the cat saw something human eyes could not, and was terrorized beyond recount. A moment later, lightning webbed the whole of heaven, branching from horizon to horizon as though the dome of the universe were cracking into flaming bits. Almost immediately there followed a clangor so incredible in pitch that it nearly knocked Unise to the flagstone floor.

Mite vanished down the stairwell, and would be beneath the starry globe of Arlburrow's lair long before Unise's feet had carried her there.

The terrible rage of the storm would alert all the Castle now. None would mistake that hateful roar for a natural torrent. As Unise strode quietly through halls, she heard whisperings of fear and wakening comprehension, filtering from the various private and family cells. She heard also the complaints regarding the number of rabble invited into the lower floors. Some of Unise's kin would rather huddle with small, frightened groups in dark quarters than contend the presence of serfs in larger, supportive gatherings. Hearing their talk, she regretted less that she brought them all to danger.

Servants were all about the place, lighting candles in the corridors and chandeliers in the rooms. Their faces were ashen and troubled; Arlburrow must have told them much earlier in the day to be prepared for an arduous night.

But as Arlburrow promised, they would be safe. The preternatural deluge could only fall as rain upon the Castle Green; the thing that haunted the firmament was, itself, held at bay.

By her grandfather's earlier command, Unise went briefly to the room which had not been readied for her. There, she took up her chainmail, sword and leather armor from the closet in which she had stored them against Arlburrow's sight.

She regretted that she could not attend Jonathon, who would be downstairs with the rest by now. At least her dear stablemistress would not be waiting in her loft for someone who unexpectedly did not come, reminding her of those other times of similarly unfilled expectations.

Glum of spirit, Unise took her armor to Arlburrow's chamber, where on the morrow he would, remarkably, serve as her squire. There, she piled the armor and weaponry in a corner, and fell back into the chair near Arlburrow, who seemed not to have moved in her absence. His attention did not raise from the compassing of his charts. Mite, dignity regained, lay on a small, worn carpet of intricate design, a few feet from the globe.

Unise, hair and breeches still damp, felt the ache of a long battle, though the battle was yet to begin. Weariness enfolded her limbs, her neck, her body. She longed for Jonathon's strong hands to loosen the muscles along her spine. Heavily, her head fell back, her eyes closed. Slumped uncomfortably, she slept out that horrible night.

* * *

Horses screaming in the distance awoke the knight.

She was instantly on her feet, looking left and right to regain her bearings. Kneading the crick in her neck with her palm, she strode from the chair that had served as unlikely bed to Arlburrow's single window. She unlatched it, pulled it open. The storm was gone. It ought to be well into day, but only crimson night greeted her. The horror which haunted the sky filtered the morning's sun, blocking all but a faint red from the spectrum, giving the world not the look of morning, but of bloody dark. By the grim light, she could tell the heavy clouds still hung above the castle in a gigantic sworl—yet they seemed to have played themselves dry during the long, torrential night. She could also see the whole of the countryside, showing like a faded painting in carmine and grays.

Unise's face warmed with momentary embarrassed surprise: she had never realized her grandfather had so perfect a view of the livery. She reminded herself it no longer mattered who suspected or knew about her and Jonathon. Let it be an open secret, at least! Still, it was disconcerting to think Arlburrow might have known for as long as she knew herself.

Below, Jonathon moved with swift grace, cracking a long bow whip. She never allowed it to actually lick a horse's flesh; it was used merely to herd them by its noise, back toward the stables. Something was astir, and the horses knew it. Perhaps only the red dark frightened them, as would fire, urging them to break from their enclosures. Or they may have sensed things people could not, as Mite had done. In either case, nothing could confine a horse confirmed to escape.

Donning chainmail, Unise intended to hurry to Jonathon's aid. No one person, not even Jonathon, could handle all those horses at once. But the chamber door opened, and Arlburrow entered. He was returning from some errand. His boots and the point of his walking stick were muddy. Unise wondered if he ever slept. She had wondered that when she was little, too; for even then he seemed to retire long after everyone else, and rise before.

"Not yet," he said simply.

"Jonathon is outside the protection of the Castle," she protested.

"She is in no danger. Trust me that."

"Even so. She needs help gathering the frightened horses."

"Better that she struggle with them alone," Arlburrow said, no hint of antipathy in his tone. "You have a more important task." He bent to pick up a leather breastplate. "This piece first?" he asked.

She directed him in binding her armor, piece by piece, to her tall, powerful body.

"If it kills you," Arlburrow said, "it will be free of its geas. It will still be unable to penetrate the Castle's shield, but certainly it will lower itself into the valley and level Morska-on-the-Tarn. From then, it will be a free agent, to torment all the world."

Unise's armor seemed heavier than ever before. "A terrible burden," she whispered, and he looked up into her face sharply to say, "The greatest you will ever bear, granddaughter."

He turned to his desk, where the case still sat with one rod left in its oilcloth. Arlburrow unwrapped the object . . . it was no mere rod after all. It was a sword made of the same argent material. She took it from him by the hilt, asking nothing of its strength.

She descended to the mainroom with Arlburrow at her side. The folk gathered there looked up from the beds made on floors and couches; children peered from their curled positions in large chairs. They were a weary, frightened lot. Servants had already begun to devide morning-cakes among them, and those awake enough ate without tasting. The few whisperings left after the long night died quickly when Arlburrow and the knight appeared. There were a hundred questions in each mind, but the sight of this formidable pair silenced them all. Arlburrow, who was rarely seen by folk outside the Castle itself, and Unise McKensie, his heir, the most notorious and unlikely soldier ever to hail from Morsk Valley . . . they watched these two pass through their midst, and Unise felt their stares.

At the farther entrance, Arlburrow turned and said, "It will be safe to watch from the battlements. Go!"

They did not move for a moment.

"Go!" he barked, shooing them with a gesture from his cane.

Parents snatched up babes, and they scurried with un-disguised curiosity and bared excitement up the stairways toward the upper walls of the Castle Green. When the mainroom was empty, Arlburrow said, "You go on from here alone. It will meet you in Danden's Field—" the meadow was named after a ferocious battle eight generations before—"when you call it down from heaven."

"Its name, grandfather." The servants had opened the gates; her eyes looked out into gloom.

"Hophaetus."

The woman breathed deeply. Tears welled but did not fall.

"God of Iron," she said, softly, to herself.

"He was that, yes, to pagans. To us, granddaughter, he is only the ghost of a man turned devil."

She stood now at the gate and turned to face her grand-father, left behind. Red sky outlined her. She said, "Why not call him god, my Lord Arlburrow? If he slays me—and you think he will—his angry spirit will haunt the lands with a more horrendous appetite than any mortal tyrant."

"I did not say I thought he would slay you, granddaugh-ter. He may. But the stars bode your favor, though one great tragedy is outlined by the charts. I do not know what; only, no battle is won at no cost. Remember this: Hophaetus favored his left leg in life—"

"Hurt, it is said, in his fall from paradise. . ."

"Or twisted in a common fashion!" he responded hotly. "His supernatural spirit was born of earth, Unise. It will die of earth, at long, long last. He may even be grateful for that. Remember the leg, that is all. He was mighty in the bronze age, when he alone wielded iron. But your sword is stronger than the bronze knives he faced before."

"He may not take the form of a man," Unise said lowly. She was afraid. Afraid. "You said a semblance. Only a semblance of his former self. . ."

"It is time, granddaughter."

A man stood outside with Unise's horse, bridled and shielded with its own leather garb. When Unise saw that her grandfather had seen to this, she realized also how the horses had escaped: he knew Jonathon would never watch safely from the battlements. She had to be gotten out of the way, for her own sake as well as Unise's. Unise turned back once more, and raised a gauntleted hand to him.

"Farewell, grandfather."

"Fare thee well, Dame Unise of the Castle Green."

She rode to Danden's Field.

The grass was high about her mount's legs. Unise reined the beast up short. Looking skyward, she saw the eye of the stilled hurricane, a circle of blue amidst the slowly sworling red. Sunlight poured through the opening in the sky, and lit the dell like a stage. How magnificent the scene must look from the view on the battlements!

She did not hesitate. Her horse reeled around and around at her command, as she cried, "Hophaetus! Come to me Hophaetus! We will dance the dance of death! We will embrace like lovers until one of us is broken!"

The eye above her narrowed with malevolence. The sworls of red darkness gained speed, turning like a celestial whirlpool trying to draw her into heaven. Unise laughed, hysterical or resigned. The bloody sky began to funnel down, down, until it touched the ground in front of knight and steed. The circle of blue was sealed. Before her stood a transparent column of red mist, shining and turning. The funnel circled her like a weird, living tornado inspecting its object before smashing her.

"Let me see you, Hophaetus! Let me see your myth-praised sword of doom!"

The pillar broke loose of the sky above, shrank down-ward until it was consolidated into a ball of thick, soupy

mist. It glowed from within. It throbbed with light. It grew
more and more tangibly a shape, loosely the form of a
man. For a moment, it seemed to reverse its progress, to
lose substance again—but Unise screamed its name, over
and over, compelling the being to materialize; until . . .
almost in anger, with remarkable speed and a blast of hot,
lake-hued light: Hophaetus stood before her.

He appeared unmounted. She had that advantage.

A prejudice perhaps: she had expected him to be ugly.
He was not. She had never seen a man with a more
beautiful face. His perfection was marred only by the
redness of his skin, hair, armor, sword. He was a demon
out of hell, she could not doubt that, made of fire or molten
iron. But he was lovely to behold.

And there was no malice on his face. Rather, she saw in
him a kind of compassion, agony, sorrow. She knew these
things were feigned.

She spurred her steed to charge. The demon raised his
shield against the argent sword Unise bore. The horse
carried her past him; she reined about to see what affect
she had had.

He had not even staggered under the blow.

His shield began to spin in his outstretched hand. It
became a ball of fire and he unleashed it. The horse reared
and took the fire ball full in the chest, then dropped in a
heap, killed. Unise had rolled away and came to her feet
prepared—prepared to die. It was clear that she could not
hope to defeat this being.

There was distance between them for the moment.
Hophaetus approached her slowly, the grasses shriveling
into ash with every step he made. He opened his mouth. A
tongue licked out like flame. Now his eyes burned her with
hatred, all pain and sorrow gone. Unise raised her sword,
though it now seemed a feeble gesture. He raised his
sword in kind—and between these swords danced lightning.

Unise felt electricity course through her body. She felt
herself glowing with some terrible power. She saw her

arms, her hands, her entire body, her sword, turning a brilliant, glimmering blue. She thought: *I am a demon too.* As he was red throughout, so had she become as purely blue as sapphire. She no longer waited for Hophaetus to close the distance: she leapt for him, her lips peeled back in a gargoyle's grimace, showing him her cobalt teeth.

The battle was engaged. Unise felt herself a supernatural force. Whether this power was invested in her by her foe, to even the match, or wrought by the magic of a charmed sword . . . she never knew, did not care. She lived only for the fight. Broadsword struck broadsword, and the sound was not like the clash of steel. It was like the roaring of a forest fire covering half the wooded earth; or glacier ice rushing from the poles with tremulous power.

Weariness did not invade her limbs. She beat Hophaetus back. Then he beat her back. Back and forth this went until it was clear that they were evenly matched. Eternity might have passed. Unise was free of all terror, except for a moment when she envisioned herself locked in ceaseless combat on Danden's Field, to the end of time, neither warrior able to defeat the other. At least then the world she had endangered would be safe. And her aunty could charge tokens for townfolk to watch from the battlements of Castle Green.

So enrapt had she become in her battle, Unise did not see the mounted woman charge across the dell. Jonathon's whip lashed out, caught Hophaetus about the neck. The whip instantly burst into flame, and Jonathon's horse stumbled, in terror of the flame or in a pot hole, it hardly mattered. Unise remembered Arlburrow's prognostication: the battle would not be won at no cost. Was Jonathon to die?

Unise could not help the dazed woman to rise: she knew that to touch Jonathon would freeze her to the spot, just as the touch of Hophaetus would burn her to charcoal. Jonathon, raging and foolish with courage, staggered to her feet, scrambled blindly toward the fray. Unise could not speak; like Hophaetus, she no longer had a voice. She could not warn Jonathon off.

Over the dell, as from a dream, an old man came slowly, cane in hand, cat lumbering beside. He was shouting: "Get back, Jon-girl! Can you not see you are making it worse?"

The battle went unabated. But Unise had lost much ground fretting for Jonathon and now Arlburrow. Hophaetus pressed the attack. Unise stumbled backward, fell, and Hophaetus' most powerful blow knocked sword from hand. The demon stood with all his malice revealed, but he did not deliver the killing blow. He turned instead on Jonathon, knowing in his devil's manner that this would be a more painful death to Unise. And Unise remembered those sweet, dark promises Hophaetus had made to her before they had even met, haunting her dreams from the very night she chanced to free him from a tomb. She knew, now, that jealousy turned Hophaetus' wrath upon the other woman.

Mite had leapt between Jonathon and Hophaetus. The cat's hackles raised from neck to haunches, back arched high: he spat and snarled at the evil killer. Hophaetus slowed for one moment only, perhaps pondering the import of other cats he had seen—an old warlock's familiar.

Arlburrow was at the devil's back. Unise saw that the old man did not have his cane with him after all. He had removed one of the argent rods from the tower keep, no doubt weakening the defenses of the Castle itself in favor of one last and chancy gambit. It would be like Arlburrow, Unise reasoned, to sacrifice himself, to make sure he, and not Jonathon, was the price read in the stars. It was not purely heroic kindness: it was manipulative in its way. He was old. He would die soon anyway. Unise might pine unto death without Jonathon; and then the Castle Green would have no capable overseer. With Arlburrow's death, Unise knew she would be bound to the Castle, all adventure past.

The oldster raised the argent rod and, before the demon could strike either Jonathon or Mite, Arlburrow had stricken the demon's spine. A flash of white light sent Arlburrow reeling backward, to fall, unmoving. Mite meowed monstrously, and even Unise freed her voice from some icy prison to wail a terrible lament. The cry carried its horrid message of agony and loss throughout the boundaries of Morsk Valley, and beyond—unto paradise itself.

A black stripe had appeared along the spine of the otherwise uniformly scarlet being. Before Unise's own cry had faded from the valley and hills, she had reclaimed her sword, lunged toward the demon, swung the weapon not overhand, but under. She raked upward along the inside of Hophaetus' left leg. He fell to one knee, hurt, and looked up with his nefarious nature again disguised. His eyes begged mercy. But she did not hesitate. Her own sorrow had become an addition to her strength. It tipped the balance. She thrust the icy blade into the fiery heart of Hophaetus. She left the weapon there and lurched back.

Hophaetus made no sound even then. He did not move. He did not fall from foot and knee. He began to cool, his redness fading into black. He had become an iron statue of fey, masculine beauty, bent to one knee, looking up pitiably. The blue sword had returned to argent white, protruding from the devil's bloodless heart.

Red sky faded too. Sunlight flooded the site with a cheeriness that mocked. There should be rain. Tears should fall in mourning. Unise stood tall, her flesh and garb still blue, and she wondered: Am I forever like this? Mite pawed at Arlburrow's body until—god witness—the old man moved! Unise felt drained of all power. She tried to shout again, for Jonathon to keep away: Don't touch me, I will kill you. But she could not speak, and as Jonathon reached for her, Unise fell into darkness.

Arlburrow was blind. It seemed a terrible price indeed, as the stars forwarned, for the codger's life revolved around his library. Yet he seemed to think it small enough price. He tapped the floor with his cane as he neared Unise's sick bed. She gazed out of her weariness, saw his eyes, burnt black by the light that streaked Hophaetus' spine. "I had read all those old books anyway," he said, reaching out a hand that Unise took, to draw him near her bed. "The only things left are some old clay tablets even I had not yet been able to decipher. I can feel that writing with my fingers!"

His spirits were high enough for both of them. She had heard him laugh, as folk said he had done when he was a young man. Unise, then, could repose in continued despair, leaving her portion of gladness to Arlburrow. The horror he had lived these years to defeat was gone—and whatever days were left him, he could live them at leisure, though in darkness. Unise's future was equally certain: the day would yet come when she would be bound to Castle Green. Arlburrow had survived the battle well, giving her respite from responsibility. But how much longer could he live? Perhaps he never slept—but eventually, the longer sleep would catch him.

These were selfish thoughts Unise had, to begrudge an old man a peaceful death. She did not want to master a castle. She was not sure *what* she wanted. At present, she felt she had had her fill of adventure.

Miranna brought tea to Unise's room. The girl seemed distraught less by what had transpired on Danden's Field than by the fact that Unise lay now in bed like a sick old nanny. Most of the women Miranna had known had fallen ill at one time or another, without visible cause; she had thought Unise above this.

There was a disturbance in the hall. Arlburrow stepped aside, cocked an ear. Unise's great-aunt's voice was complaining of horse smells and rabble. She sounded shrill and angry. Jonathon's unperturbable nature was for once perturbed: "Put it up your arse, biddy!" She burst into Unise's room, the puffy woman storming behind, insisting stable workers did not belong in the master quarter of the Castle, or in any part. Seeing Arlburrow silenced the old aunt, but Jonathon swept by the blind man and the child without explanation or apology. She tore the covers off Unise's bed, and demanded. "Up with you, lazy wench! Beds never cured melancholy! You need sun!" She forced Unise up, helped her to dress, slapped her behind. She even drank Unise's tea. The great-aunt stewed in her place, but Arlburrow laughed encouragement. Miranna went with the women into the gardens while, at Arlburrow's request, one puffier and puffier aunt saw that the Castle coffers were deeply plumbed so that a royal feast might be prepared for all the silly rabble who had spent the night in Castle Green.

But one serious matter remained. Before nightfall, Arlburrow told Unise to be certain the iron god was carted to the long unused, deepest dungeons of Castle Green. There, Hophaetus was locked away, a hauntingly lifelike statue of fey and sorrowful beauty, to await some other hapless hero who might draw the argent sword from his chest.

Little Boy Waiting at the Edge of the Darkwood

I wish I didn't have to wait here this way. Those gnarly trees cast wavery shadows and the owls are scary. But I always have to wait while Grandpa goes into the forest, hunting. Sometimes he's gone for hours. Sometimes he comes back while the moon's still up, and there's still hair on his face and palms. I wish I could hunt with him. Maybe when I'm older.

Andrew J. Offutt

The Tree's Wife

Jane Yolen

There was once a young woman named Drusilla who had been widowed longer than she was wed. She had been married at fifteen to a rich old man who beat her. She had flowered despite his ill treatment, and it was he who died, within the year, leaving her all alone in the great house.

Once the old man was dead, his young widow was courted by many, for she was now quite wealthy. The young men came together, and all claimed that she needed a husband to help her.

But Drusilla would have none of them. "When I was poor," she said, "not one of you courted me. When I was ill treated, not one of you stood by me. I never asked for more than a gentle word, yet I never received one. So now that you ask, I will have none of you."

She turned her back on them, then stopped. She looked around at the grove of birch trees by her house. "Why, I would sooner wed this tree," she said, touching a sturdy birch that stood to one side. "A tree would know when to bend and when to stand. I would sooner wed this tree than marry another man."

At that very moment, a passing wind caused the top branches of the birch to sway.

The rejected suitors laughed at Drusilla. "See," they jeered, "the tree has accepted your offer."

And so she was known from that day as the Tree's Wife.

To keep the jest from hurting, Drusilla entered into it with a will. If someone came to the house, she would put her arms around the birch, caressing its bark and stroking its limbs.

"I have all I need or want with my tree," she would say. And her laugh was a silent one back at the stares. She knew that nothing confounds jokers as much as madness, so she made herself seem very mad for them.

But madness also makes folk uneasy; they fear contagion. And soon Drusilla found herself quite alone. Since it was not of her choosing, the aloneness began to gnaw at her. It was true that what she really wanted was just a kind word, but soon she was so lonely almost any word would have done.

So it happened one night, when the moon hung in the sky like a ripe yellow apple, that a wind blew fiercely from the north. It made the trees bow and bend and knock their branches against Drusilla's house. Hearing them knock, she looked out of the windows and saw the trees dancing wildly in the wind.

They seemed to beckon and call, and she was suddenly caught up in their rhythm. She swayed with them, but it was not enough. She longed for the touch of the wind on her skin, so she ran outside, leaving the door ajar. She raised her hands above her head and danced with the trees.

In the darkness, surrounded by the shadow of its brothers, one tree seemed to shine. It was her tree, the one she had chosen. It was touched with a phosphorescent glow, and the vein of each leaf was a streak of pale fire.

Drusilla danced over to the tree and held her hands toward it. "Oh, if only you *were* a man, or I a tree," she said out loud. "If you were a man tall and straight and gentle and strong then—yes—then I would be happy."

The wind died as suddenly as it had begun, and the trees stood still. Drusilla dropped her hands, feeling foolish and shamed, but a movement in the white birch stayed her. As she watched, it seemed to her that first two legs, then a body, then a head and arms emerged from the bark; a shadowy image pulling itself painfully free of the trunk. The image shimmered for a moment, trembled, and then became clear. Before her stood a man.

He was tall and slim, with skin as white as the bark of the birch and hair as black as the birch bark patches. His legs were strong yet supple, and his feet were knotty and tapered like roots. His hands were thin and veined with green, and the second and third fingers grew together, slotted like a leaf. He smiled at her and held out his arms, an echo of her earlier plea, and his arms swayed up and down as if touched by a passing breeze.

Drusilla stood without movement, without breath. Then he nodded his head, and she went into his arms. When his mouth came down on hers, she smelled the damp woody odor of his breath.

They lay together all night below his tree, cradled in its roots. But when the sun began its climb against the furthest hills, the man pulled himself reluctantly from Drusilla's arms and disappeared back into the tree.

Call as she might, Drusilla could not bring him out again, but one of the tree branches reached down and stroked her arm in a lover's farewell.

She spent the next days under the tree, reading and weaving and playing her lute. And the tree itself seemed to listen and respond. The branches touched and turned the pages of her book. The whole tree moved to the beauty of her songs.

Yet it was not until the next full moon that the man could pull himself from the tree and sleep away the dark in her arms.

Still Drusilla was content. For as she grew in her love for the man of the tree, her love for all nature grew, a quiet pullulation. She felt kin to every flower and leaf. She heard the silent speech of the green world and, under the bark, the beating of each heart.

One day, when she ventured into the village, Drusilla's neighbors observed that she was growing more beautiful in her madness. The boldest of them, an old woman, asked, "If you have no man, how is it you bloom?"

Drusilla turned to look at the old woman and smiled. It was a slow smile. "I am the tree's wife," she said, "in truth. And he is man enough for me." It was all the answer she would return.

But in the seventh month since the night of the apple moon, Drusilla knew she carried a child, the tree's child, below her heart. And when she told the tree of it, its branches bent around her and touched her hair. And when she told the man of it, he smiled and held her gently.

Drusilla wondered what the child would be that rooted in her. She wondered if it would burgeon into a human child or emerge some great wooden beast. Perhaps it would be both, with arms and legs as strong as the birch and leaves for hair. She feared her heart would burst with the questions. But on the next full moon, the tree man held her and whispered in her ear such soft, caressing sounds, she grew calm. And at last she knew that however the child grew, she would love it. And with that knowledge she was once again content.

Soon it was evident, even to the townsfolk, that she blossomed with child. They looked for the father among themselves—for where else *could* they look—but no one admitted to the deed. And Drusilla herself would name no one but the tree to midwife, priest, or mayor.

And so, where at first the villagers had jested at her and joked with her and felt themselves plagued by her madness, now they turned wicked and cruel. They could accept a widow's madness but not a mother unwed.

The young men, the late suitors, pressed on by the town elders, came to Drusilla one night. In the darkness, they would have pulled her from her house and beaten her. But Drusilla heard them come and climbed through the window and fled to the top of the birch.

The wind raged so that night that the branches of the tree flailed like whips, and not one of the young men dared come close enough to climb the tree and take Drusilla down. All they could do was try and wound her with with their words. They shouted up at her where she sat near the top of the birch, cradled in its branches. But she did not hear their shouts. She was lulled instead by the great rustling voices of the grove.

In the morning the young men were gone. They did not return.

And Drusilla did not go back into the town. As the days passed, she was fed by the forest and the field. Fruits and berries and sweep sap found their way to her doorstep. Each morning she had enough for the day. She did not ask where it all came from, but still she knew.

At last it was time for the child to be born. On this night of a full moon, Drusilla's pains began. Holding her sides with slender fingers, she went out to the base of the birch, sat down, and leaned her back against the tree, straining to let the child out. As she pushed, the birch man pulled himself silently from the tree, knelt by her, and breathed encouragements into her face. He stroked her hair and whispered her name to the wind.

She did not smile up at him but said at last, "Go." Her breath was ragged and her voice on the edge of despair. "I beg you. Get the midwife. This does not go well."

The tree man held her close, but he did not rise.

"Go," she begged. "Tell her my name. It is time."

He took her face in his hands and stared long into it with his woods-green eyes. He pursed his lips as if to speak, then stood up and was gone.

He went down the path towards the town, though each step away from the tree drew his strength from him. Patches of skin peeled off as he moved, and the sores beneath were dark and viscous. His limbs grew more brittle with each step, and he moved haltingly. By the time he reached the midwife's house, he looked an aged and broken thing. He knocked upon the door, yet he was so weak, it was only a light tapping, a scraping, the scratching of a branch across a window pane.

As if she had been waiting for his call, the midwife came at once. She opened the door and stared at what stood before her. Tall and thin and naked and white, with black patches of scabrous skin and hair as dark as rotting leaves, the tree man held up his grotesque, slotted hand. The gash of his mouth was hollow and tongueless, a sap-filled wound. He made no sound, but the midwife screamed and screamed, and screaming still, slammed the door.

She did not see him fall.

In the morning the townsfolk came to Drusilla's great house. They came armed with clubs and cudgels and forks. The old midwife was in the rear, calling the way.

Beneath a dead white tree they found Drusilla, pale and barely moving, a child cradled in her arms. At the townsfolk's coming, the child opened its eyes. They were the color of winter pine.

"Poor thing," said the midwife, stepping in front of the men. "I knew no good would come of this." She bent to take the child from Drusilla's arms but leaped up again with a cry. For the child had uncurled one tiny fist, and its hand was veined with green and the second and third fingers grew together, slotted like a leaf.

At the midwife's cry, the birches in the grove began to move and sway, though there was not a breath of breeze. And before any weapon could be raised, the nearest birch stretched its branches far out and lifted the child and Drusilla up, up towards the top of the tree.

As the townsfolk watched, Drusilla disappeared. The child seemed to linger for a moment longer, its unclothed body gleaming in the sun. Then slowly the child faded, like melting snow on pine needles, like the last white star of morning, into the heart of the tree.

There was a soughing as of wind through branches, a tremble of leaves, and one sharp cry of an unsuckled child. Then the trees in the grove were still.

Introduction
Tappan Wright King

For those who have not yet visited Islandia, the story of Alwina provides an oblique, if fascinating, introduction to the country, rather like discovering England through reading an excerpt from Holinshed's Chronicles. Most readers know it from my grandfather Austin Wright's novel Islandia, first published by Farrar & Rinehart in 1942, a decade after his death, and currently available in an NAL/Plume trade paperback edition.

Set at the turn of the century, Islandia is the story of John Lang, a young American who falls in love with Islandia's older, more agrarian way of life, and takes its part against the threat of exploitation by Western powers. The novel, however, represents only a fraction of Austin Wright's creation. There is also a complete unpublished history with maps and appendices, attributed to Jean Perrier, French Consul to Islandia, a character in the novel. It is from that history that Alwina's story has been excerpted.

A Harvard law professor, Wright created Islandia for his own pleasure, with little thought of publication. Like Professor Tolkein's Silmarillion, the History is the original work, out of which a novel of adventure grew. The History itself is beyond summary, so detailed is Wright's invented world. Islandia is a country inhabited by a light-skinned race of uncertain origin, which occupies the southern tip of the Karain subcontinent in the Southern Hemisphere. By way of background, the incidents here take place in the early 1300's, after the death of King Alwin XIX, whose only heir was a daughter, Alwina. In addition to bringing to life one of Islandia's most colorful and capable rulers, the chronicle also illuminates a turning point in Islandian history, when its borders were secured, its great naval fleet was built, and the seafaring provinces of Winder and Storn annexed.*

Not intended as fiction, the History reads like all good histories: straightforward, concise, and as accurate as sources permit. The text here is taken from the first English language edition (Islandia: The City, 1909). The translation by John Lang removes a few of M. Perrier's Gallic excesses, while preserving his preference for affairs of the heart over affairs of state.

**Please note that this excerpt from The History has been severely condensed to fit the space requirements of this anthology and edited for continuity. —T.W. & M.A.*

An Islandian Tale

Austin Tappan Wright

The Story of Alwina

(Excerpted from *Islandia: History and Description* by Jean
Perrier, first French Consul to Islandia—Translated by
John Lang, first American Consul.)

Alwina, on her father's death, was a girl of twenty in a
singularly hard situation. No woman had ever before ascended the throne of Islandia. Not for merely personal
reasons did she aspire to that honor—the next in order of
succession beside herself was her cousin, grandson of
Alwin The Lazy, a man of thirty, and a vicious character,
but with certain pleasing characteristics. There were greater problems yet: there was the unfortunate breach with the
province of Winder to be closed, a question of particular
moment because of the growing danger to the nation
through the recent development by the Karain of a sea-
going force. There was the mystery of the Demiji invasions
to be cleared up, and the ever present threat of the unde-
stroyed armies of Kilikash.

Even before the death of her father, trouble began over
her succession. It was opposed by Dom XI and by most of
the council on the grounds of her youth and sex, though
she had staunch supporters in Mora X and Cabing, a man
of great power. Over the opposition of those last two and
several others, the council, acting for the National Assembly, had passed a resolution that no woman should succeed. When Alwin died, however, the council was not in
session. Alwina's position was bettered thereby, but was
still a perilous one. Her first act was a rather doubtful one.
At her insistence, Cabing appointed a number of lieutenants sufficient to turn the scale in the council. Cabing's
authority theoretically ended with the death of the king
who appointed him, but he asserted his right to hold office
till a successor was appointed. Alwina by "definite act"
reappointed him. The council hastily met, and was at once
in an uproar. After a stormy session a vote was passed
declaring Alwina's right to succeed. The adherents of Lord
Dorn protested against the presence of Cabing and his

lieutenants, but without avail. The army certainly backed their leader and queen, and the threat of force therein doubtless limited the Dorn party, for the time being at any rate, to threats. Alwina was declared queen with pomp and circumstance.

Her next step, though perilous, showed her wisdom. Stating that the action of the council, in not being unanimous, filled her with dismay, she called the National Assembly—taking the decision directly to the people of Islandia.

The Assembly met at Reeves in the early summer. There were known to be many who were opposed to Alwina, but twelve thousand came—many to see her, doubtless, because of her famous beauty. Let us remember that they were men unaccustomed to a woman's rule, stern and independent, and that she was but a girl of twenty, whom many graybeards knew as a child under the strict rule of a parent. She must have seemed not unlike their own daughters. But Alwina was mistress of the occasion; she appeared before them not only with the fire of her loveliness and the aegis cast upon her by her beloved father, but with things to say for herself. It is reported that she called attention to Cabing's deeds and his needed reappointment; and adroitly to Dorn's opposition. She then spoke of her father's dying directions to protect the country from the Demiji, to prepare to meet the coming fleets of Karain, and to accomplish reconciliation with Winder. She said she would do this last first and thereby secure a fleet to meet that of Karain. If it was their will that she be queen, she would go at once to Winder. Her directness and activity after her father's well-known procrastination carried the day. With scarcely a dissenting voice she was again declared queen. Though the Dorn party still voiced protests, her position was now unassailable, and soon in the light of what she did dissentient voices died out.

News of the building of ships in Mobono came to Islandia before the sack of Miltain. They appeared off the coast in 1308, but the Karain were still timid at sea and merely landed and took a few prisoners and then departed. Again in 1312, 1316, and 1319, vessels appeared,

more bold. And meanwhile, rumors of the construction of
a great fleet to capture The City continued to come over
the border. It is no wonder that far-seeing eyes in Islandia
viewed these developments with fear, and saw in the
defection of the people of Winder the possibilities of disaster.

Doubtless with these thoughts in mind more than anything else, Alwina, true to her promise, set out for Winder
as soon as her reign received the sanction of the Assembly.
A girl of twenty, but full of energy and determination, and
with a clear head, she made Cabing and Mora of her train
and rode through the fertile spring plains of Bostia,
through Loria and Inerria, and from the travellers' hostel at
the upper waters of the Cannan River sent word to Tor, at
Winder, that she was about to enter his land.

No reply was received. The queen's entourage advised
her to turn back and gather men to punish the insult, but
she sent a characteristic message: "Alwina is angry at your
discourtesy, but the queen of Islandia grieves for the safety
of your people and her own." She followed it with herself,
and Tor, with decided bad grace, prepared to receive her.
She crossed the high pass between Blyth and Tor's city,
and rode down, timing her arrival at noon. It is a scene
frequently painted: Tor, sullen and angry, receiving with a
few followers the amazingly beautiful queen. She dismounted from her horse, advanced on foot, and without a
word embraced and kissed him, saying: "In these times the
people of Islandia must love their brothers." The kiss was
thus made an international political event—but still it was a
kiss, and Tor a young man, the queen a beautiful woman.
Alwina stayed but a very few days at Winder. The welcome
to her, grudgingly begun, ended in enthusiasm. She made
a great impression on the people of Winder by the fire of
her personality, her earnestness and her beauty. When she
left, she arranged for the support of the Winder fleet in any
eventuality and for the dispatch of vessels later in the
season to the East coast, pledging in return a renewal of
ship money. Returning to Islandia, she convinced the
council of the necessity of this step. As the chronicler says:

"She had the appearance of a child, but words of wisdom came from her mouth." This active young woman then hastened to Miltain and Carran travelling without stop, and roused the people there to the danger threatening them and informed them of the promised coming of ships. The hostility to Winder was strongest in the east, but she smoothed the ruffled emotions of the lords and people there so that a cordial reception to, and harmonious action with, the coming squadron was assured. This task done, and leaving Cabing and Mora behind, she sped south by Dean, Manry, and Searles to Stom, there to meet Tor and his fleet. It was then the month of Austus, and the south west winds were blowing strong. The queen waited a full month, with a small retinue chafing at the delay. News was coming from the south that Karain corsairs were off the coast. Eventually Tor appeared with only half the ships he promised. Alwina and he quarrelled, and finally, in a fury, he made her a prisoner. No doubt he was already enamoured of her, and her position was by no means a safe one. But she was indomitable—she eventually persuaded Tor to release her and proceed on his way. There were larger factors to be considered than her own pride.

In the middle of the month of Septen, Tor set out, with the example of his ancestor to lead him on. There was almost a mutiny, which doubtless roused his nature. While Alwina by rough roads crossed the Ardan hills, Tor rounded Stornsea, and reached Ardan not long after the queen. The quarrel was patched up, and she herself accompanied the fleet on its week's voyage south against head winds to the port of Tire. This journey is the great episode of the Islandian poem on Tor and Alwina. One is tempted to follow the poet and consider them as in the long hours together they reconciled their differences under the force of a growing love. On the other hand, common sense and historical evidence seem to indicate that the queen's whole relation with this man, whom in the end she so completely dominated, was the result of a cold, keen mind, considering only politics.

Karain ships were supposed to be in the Beldon River,

and the queen landed; Tor went north again, but success
eluded him. By reason of their oars the Karain escaped
down the coast. Tor kept on faithfully and eventually
surprised four Karain ships plundering farms just north of
the forest of Balian. It was first blood for the Islandians.
Tor, after his easy victory, sailed on to Carran, and then to
Madly Bay, where he refitted with the materials and
supplies forwarded by Cabing. No more Karain appeared
that season, and no incursion being feared in the season of
Windorn, Tor returned home. The indefatigable queen
travelled into the far west to investigate conditions there
and reconcile herself with the family of her cousins, the
Doms, who had opposed her accession.

Her spies on the border told her that in the next year,
some definite move might be expected from Kilikash.
During the season called "Leaves", Kilikash endeavored
to open negotiations for the cession to him of Carran and
northern Miltain, but Alwina returned his ambassadors
without hearing them.

The campaigns of the second year of this war were
much the same. Kilikash had the advantage of a base
south of the mountains, but he was unable to break the
lines along the Balian.

The attitude of Tor had been most unsatisfactory—he
sent fewer ships than promised, and did not come himself
to lead them. In Windorn, Alwina made him another visit,
and stayed several months. Queens are not above criti-
cism; many accused Alwina of being his mistress. But the
opposite seems nearer the truth—Alwina knew she must
marry as a duty she owed her country, but marriage with
Tor was not politically desirable unless it achieved a desirable result. Her position as wife of a man hostile to her
people would be impossible; until Tor threw his whole
strength in her support, it would be folly to unite with him.
The worst that she can be accused of is of dangling herself
as bait.

The German historian Schlauter has chosen to misread
a letter of hers to Mora X, a man of fifty-six then, her most

trusted adviser, and one to whom she showed almost a daughterly love: "This man (Tor) breaks my heart," she wrote from Winder in Febor 1323. "He will and he won't. He loves me and hates the queen. He talks of marriage and I say no. . . . But we are building ships." The last sentence tells a great deal.

Though news of their betrothal was expected, none came, and Alwina left Winder in early Avrilis for Miltain, and arrived there to learn that Kilikash had broken through, and that his fleet, larger than ever before, was moving up the coast in a compact body. To make matters worse, the Demiji appeared in force in northern Islandia, and on the Matwin opposite Brome. The campaign was well coordinated, all forces being directed towards the unfortunate city of Miltain.

The Karain army kept together until the Beldon was crossed, and then with the fertile plain of Miltain before them spread out far and wide. The fleet passed through the Stanes unopposed and took possession of Endly. The Winder fleet sailed south into Toobey Harbor after picking off a few stragglers of the vastly superior force.

It was a time of trouble for Islandia that cast the thoughts of men back a hundred years. The Karain were better armed with their coats of mail, their ships were less dependent on wind, and the horses of the Demiji were fleeter than those of Islandia. The whole country was not sufficiently roused. Aid was slow in coming to Cabing's hard pressed force, and Tor with his fleet was in no hurry to run into a noose. He rounded Stornsea and put into Ardan bay—and waited.

Kilikash reassembled his troops. An attack was made at Dole, which was only a feint to draw off the Islandians. It was followed by an attempt to storm Miltain, which failed. The Karain fleet was working up the river and had it arrived the city might have fallen—with it the queen. A siege began, and on the arrival of the ships the city was wholly surrounded; Alwina remained, perhaps foolishly, perhaps wisely, and news of her presence came to Kilikash. His demands were even more arrogant: all of Miltain and her person for his harem. The siege was well conducted, but the besieged were indomitable.

So things remained till Windorn of the next year. The queen made a daring escape from Miltain and returned to the capital; the season was spent in preparations. Ship-building went ahead everywhere, and as soon as weather permitted a stream of vessels began to round Stornsea and gather at Ardan.

The queen went then to Ardan to put courage and daring into the hearts of all, crying that the Karain would never be defeated until their own city was destroyed and that only a well-prepared fleet could do so. This was too long a look for most.

Kilikash meanwhile began determined efforts to capture Miltain. Against the advice of everyone, Alwina went back to Miltain, and her coming raised a flame in the hard-pressed defenders. It also had another effect, upon which she perhaps counted—news of her plight came to the hesitant, dour, but amorous Tor. A personal call was needed to move that dweller in a land still largely of clans. He set sail when news came to him, with no other intent than to destroy every Karain ship he could find, but the later were too wary. Their whole fleet withdrew into the mouth of the Haly River, and Tor, being no fool, did not venture to attack them there but watched them from his base at Toobey Harbor. There was no decisive action that year, but the queen had accomplished her task: the Win-der fleet was brought into use to its full extent at last.

Matters became darker. Large parts of the city of Miltain were captured. The Demiji irrupted again into Islandia. Troops crossed the river and raided Deen and Brome. Worst of all, Cabing was killed in a skirmish and there seemed no one fit to take his place. Kilikash made a reasonable offer: the cession of Miltain, which he oc-cupied in fact, parts of Brome and Deen, and the dispersal of the Winder fleet, which was a thorn in his side. In fact he made separate offers to Tor, who dallied with them. The

Islandians lost heart—all but their queen and Mora, who undertook the command of the army. There was a deadlock. Another winter came. The war had now lasted four years and seemingly the Karain were firmly the masters of Miltain. The Demiji were more of a curse every year. The Winder fleet, fearing the bad weather, sailed north to the better harbor of Ardan. The queen was not idle. She escaped a second time from the beleagered city and she travelled all over her realm, seeking to stir her people to a great effort in the coming year. She visited the fleet at Ardan, where Tor for the first time had remained. Her conquest of him progressed.

In spring the perennial siege of Miltain was renewed, but this was not Kilikash's main objective. A great fleet set sail from Mobono with the Sultan himself in charge. The ships in the Haly joined him and the whole force set out for the south with the object of rounding Stornsea and falling upon The City [the capital of Islandia] itself. Delayed by baffling winds, they put in at Beal, captured and sacked the town. Tor, learning of their advance, quitted Ardan, not to be caught in a trap. The weather grew more favorable as day by day the southeast winds lessened and Kilikash started on his way, his ships blackening the ocean for miles with Bant slaves at the oars. The Winder fleet boldly went out to sea for room to manoevre. Unwilling to attack so vast a force, they kept to windward and harried the wing. Nevertheless Kilikash progressed steadily. Off the rocks of Stornsea there was something of a fight, but the advance was not checked. The cape was rounded. Terror spread through Islandia. The army was concentrated at Miltain. Hordes of Dimiji were sweeping through the center. To withdraw to protect the City meant laying open Deen and Brome.

Then abruptly the balance swung.

There came up a gale from the southeast on the fifth of Maya. The Karain became terrified. Tor seized this opportunity and his ships sailed before the wind into the heart of the Karain fleet; the whole great force was scattered in a few hours. Weatherly handled, Tor's ships suffered little

danger, while many of the Karain vessels were sunk.
Others were rendered prey to the wind and were blown on
the unhospitable shores of Niven and Alban. Discouraged,
the Karain were defeated in several battles before Miltain,
and their hold on that province became insecure. The
Islandians, however, had not strength enough to route
them on land, and towards the end of Sorn the scales
turned the other way again. The Demiji were never more
ferocious or bold. They burned the unwalled town of
Bostia to the ground, and invested Reeves.

The queen had her problems that winter. An ill-timed
exultation possessed her people. The sea victory was
magnified far beyond its real significance. There was a
slackening of energy that promised evil results. Alwina,
now a woman of twenty-five, showed her true greatness:
The four years of war had convinced her that the way to
victory lay not upon land but upon the sea; her policy of
building ships was beginning to bear fruit. Hitherto the
Winder fleet had been indispensable; now, without recourse to Tor, she could send to sea a substantial fleet of
larger vessels than those he commanded. She had not
been wholly pleased with his behaviour after his relief of
The City. He had not kept his ships together and returned,
as she wished, to the East coast. She could not afford to
disregard him entirely, but she was in a position to treat
him with a higher hand. She had before her four great
tasks: the defeat of the Karain, the solution of the Demiji
riddle, the annexation of Winder and Storn, and the con-
tinuation of her line. So far she had not perceptibly advanced to the solution of any. She might well have been
discouraged, but if she was she did not show it. In this
momentous year, in many ways as dark as any, she set in
train the forces that solved all four.

So far, Alwina had shown no particular aptitude in the
choice of leaders. Cabing was an inheritance and he was
gone. Names shifted across her record not worthy of mention. The gentle Mora X was not a leader, though he was a

trusted friend to whom she unburdened herself. Tor, the unruly, was not yet in her control. Most of the provincial nobles were men of little mark; Dorn XI still sulked over his defeat as to her succession. In this year she found the first of her three great followers—a young man from Hoe Bay, of an old Winder family that had long been at odds with the reigning dynasty of Tors. He had been employed in connection with the building of ships, and was largely responsible for the excellence of the growing Islandian fleet. The queen imposed more and more trust in him and in 1326 made him "Marriner", commander in chief of all Islandian vessels. Tor protested, but the queen retorted with his failure to follow up his victory. It was a dangerous game for her to play, but she risked it, reading her man well. The controversy spread dread through Islandia—coming after Tor's victory it boded ill in the eyes of most people. In Winder the adherents of Tor suspected that Alwina was scheming to supplant him. A great deal of discontent spread over the two nations, and her old opponents came to the fore again.

Then the queen electrified everyone. When the snow was still crisp and frozen she went to Reeves, and visiting Ingo, its lord and lord of the most ancient province of Islandia, shamed him publicly for allowing the Demiji to overrun his land year after year. Were the Demiji superhuman? she asked. They were men and must come by human paths. She pointed to the mountains, saying "You fear these barrier friends, and they return your fear with contempt and punish you. Let us not dread the mountain but treat him as our brother. He will reveal his secrets if we seek them, and if we aid ourselves he will aid us." Gathering a small retinue, she set out up the Islandia River, following its West Fork, and on foot crossed over into the frozen valley of the Upper Doring. No one ever ventured into these regions in winter! The queen showed that it was not impossible. Guided by instinct, or perhaps by knowledge she professed not to have in order to make her discovery more striking, she went straight to the hitherto unknown Lor pass, singularly concealed from the

Doring valley. It was ascended, and for the first time Islandians looked down from their own mountains on the vast Karain basin, and below them, visible to their eyes, were the piedmont lands occupied by the Karain and Demiji, whose settlements were visible. The secret was explained; the answer was to seize and fortify the pass. The queen had shown the way. A later party, ascending the Doring, discovered the Doring pass, and both were strongly held in Spring. The Demiji were bloodily repulsed when their hordes advanced, confident that they would find the back door into Islandia open as usual.

The queen's daring or good fortune or intelligence had its reward—when the story of her courageous venturing into unknown and terrifying places spread over the country she regained most of her lost ground. Her people prepared for the coming season of fighting with confidence in her, and trusted her to be successful with her new fleet, even without the aid of Tor. On land things went much as before, there was the inevitable deadlock, but at sea Alwina had reason to be proud of herself. Marriner kept the coast clear. The Islandians showed that they could fight at sea without the aid of Winder. There were no decisive battles, but there were many engagements and when Windom came again, no Karain ship dared venture as far north as Tire Island.

Alwina returned to her capital, the idol of her people. Perhaps her successes turned her head a little; she showed signs of a certain wildness of character that later manifested itself more strongly. Politically she took no pains to conceal her attitude towards Tor and Winder. She had called them to her aid, and they had not come. She talked openly of divesting them of everything they had gotten from Islandia, and to a certain extent she was justified, but it seems to us now a path of folly from which she was extricated by marvellous good fortune rather than the intelligent course of a wise queen. Winder could do Islandia incalculable harm, and she apparently widened the breach deliberately. Her ships would be no match for

Tor's, and without him no match for the new fleet she must have known that Kilikash would have ready the next year. But perhaps she knew better than this outer semblance— the end ultimately justified her.

If she was not guilty of political indiscretion, it is less easy to absolve her for her private conduct. She attracted to herself a group of young men, including Marriner, a popular hero, and another, Strale, a young officer in her army. It seems hardly safe, not only on what historical evidence we have but also on our knowledge of her character, to assume that she was deliberately reckless with these lovers—for such they were. It seems unwarranted to call her their mistress. The sounder view seems to be that after all she was a young and beautiful woman as well as a queen, indulging in dangerous but innocent amusements.

The end of Windorn found her on the alert again, and adopting a less haughty mood towards Tor. Her letters to him are not those of an enemy, but rather of a woman who has quarrelled with her lover. She feels wronged, but she needs his aid, and she writes to him anxiously and is generously willing to forgive, somewhat repentant, and herself in love. Tor, in his answers, showed an inclination to bargain. The advancement of Marriner rankled bitterly. But he, too, showed the lover in his jealousy, the anger of the man obscuring the fear of the leader. There is an insistent personal note in the relations of these two. Whether or not Alwina ever loved Tor is a question—she pretended that she did, and perhaps persuaded herself that her pretense was the truth. That he was a man in love is unmistakable, but he was also a wily chief who was not going to marry without securing something for himself and his people. In their correspondence we see the very first signs on his part of a willingness to give without getting; he professed not to be satisfied but he promised to have his fleet in readiness.

Spring found Marriner prepared for the onrush of the Karain fleet with Tor still hesitating. Kilikash was once more at sea, once more ambitious to sweep it clean. Cir-

cumstances were in his favor. The forces of his enemy
were separated. This was a year of sea fighting—it was also
the year of greatest effort on the part of the Karain. Their
armies swept up to the Haly River and crossed the Miltain
near Dole. Marriner avoided being shut up in the River and
sailed south pursued by Kilikash. There was a running fight
all along the coast. News came to Tor, and still he hesitated. Kilikash, intent on crushing the Islandians before he
arrived, pressed harder and harder. Then happened one
of the finest actions in Islandian history: Marriner, realizing
that Kilikash was so hot that he would follow regardless of
danger, put to sea in terrible weather off Ailsea, with
shortened sail so as to draw Kilikash among his vessels.
There was a desperate engagement with more losses from
marine perils than from the perils of war. Both fleets were
badly depleted, but it was an Islandian victory. The queen
was wild with delight. Many supposed that she meant to
marry the hero.

Though the year's campaigning was not over, Alwina
left the front, contrary to her usual custom, and went to
The City, sending for Tor. He came grudgingly. Their roles
were reversed. His own people were angry at him for
suffering the Islandians to win all the glory with the inevitable menace to themselves. Here he and the queen stayed
during the summer in negotiation broken by quarrels but
steadily tending to an agreement. The year ended with
new glory for Marriner, and very nearly with defeat for the
Islandian army, though late in Austus the Karain were
driven back across the Haly at Branly where they had
forced a crossing, in a bloody fight which established Strale
as the coming man on land.

The agreement which Alwina and Tor reached eventually was not generally known until the next year, but it bore
fruit as soon as the snows melted. Kilikash made yet
another attempt, and again it was by sea. His fleet, greatly
augmented, rendezvoused at Carran but by the time it was
ready to sail, Tor, with the full force of Winder ships, was at
Ardan, and Marriner was ready to slip cables from Raisby
at a moment's notice. Tor and Marriner, who hated each

other passionately, temporarily settled their differences in the face of a desperate situation. News came that Miltain was about to fall. Kilikash went south with all speed while the calm lasted, and rounded Bealsea with the Islandians to seaward and behind him, making no effort to win either Beal or Ardan. He ran into a region of stronger winds—it is rare that eastern Storn is ever calm. Skirting the barren coast south of Ailsea on June 10th, he saw the Islandian fleet bearing down before a strong southeast wind from rearwards. The fight began in a small gale that prevented the long oared ships from turning. Tor, whose plan it was to attack, had taken advantage of the elements to the utmost. Weatherly with the wind over the quarter, the three hundred Islandian ships could be handled easily. The Karain ships were much strung out; those ahead could not return at once. The Islandian ships each aimed to sheer off the oars of as many enemy vessels as possible before laying aboard. The Karain, manoeuvring to face their own foes, got into the roll of the sea. One after another they were crippled. Then the boarding began. The most crippled vessels were let go; many were swept upon the rocks. Those of the Karain who escaped among the rocks of Ailsea were hunted to death by the people of Storn.

The night promised a windless morrow. Tor decided not to risk another battle and in such airs as there were labored to seaward, hunting for wind and fog. In calm weather he would be no match for the beaked craft of Kilikash. The latter returned to Ailsea Island to restore his fleet so far as was possible. After a week he set out again, keeping his ships together. Meanwhile Tor had sailed for Stornsea and was ahead of Kilikash and to seaward, waiting and hoping for a southwest wind. Here luck failed. He was passed and the extraordinary thing is that his enemy did not know it, so far out to sea were the allies.

Kilikash put in at Storn Bay, and burnt the town. This, the first taste of war that the people of that nation had, was of importance later. It was an unfortunate move, for it enabled Tor to get to windward again. The Karain waited another week and then set out for Shores. This town they also burnt. The southwest winds were beginning. They determined to wait for a calm before seeking Islandia Bay. Two weeks passed. Raiding parties penetrated far into Niven and Alban. At last Kilikash decided the time was ripe to move. His ships kept well together, and the sea was smooth. Tor, in Selding Bay, prayed for wind, informed of his approach by signal fires. Kilikash, hugging the shore in a light mist, mistook Naba Point for the entrance to Islandia Bay. His fleet crowded into the corner of the coast to the west of that promontory. A fresh wind sprang up suddenly and Tor set sail. Kilikash was in the bad position of having to turn his line across the front of an enemy waiting to pounce, or to seek that enemy boldly against a heavy wind, or else to retreat opening his rear to the same sort of attack as had been his defeat before. He chose the second course and his ships made for Tor, who promptly took up the challenge. Had Kilikash been able to bring his ships forward in line abreast and not in an irregular mass tending to line ahead he might have won, but the mistake off Naba Point made this impossible. Bearing down on the van of his line in overwhelming force, Tor's ships, with plenty of wind to give them way, dodged the unwieldy beaks of the enemy heading into the wind, and as before crashed along the oars. This charge discouraged the Karain, and when it was over they were no match for their opponents. In the general melee that followed, many fought bravely, but the allies had bravery and skill both, and manageable ships against many that were disabled. It was a glorious, heroic fight with legends innumerable. It became soon a series of duels, two allied ships seeking to lay aboard one enemy and finish him before aid came. It lasted all night, and the next morning showed a sea covered with wreckage for miles, duels still going on, and such Karain ships as were not engaged making off to the eastward. This great and decisive victory was won on Juny 22nd. It completely broke the Karain sea power. Some two hundred and fifty ships were captured or destroyed and some twenty-five thousand men perished. On the allied side, fifty ships were lost and some three thousand lost their lives. Miltain was cleared, and eventually Carran. The queen was with her armies. She publicly announced at Madly on the day when the last rearguard of the Karain crossed the pass, that she was to marry Tor on the first day of the new year. It was a great moment. After seven years she had defeated her nation's greatest foe. All Islandia rejoiced.

Here we may speak of Alwina's compact with Tor, which was consummated by her marriage in Janvry. It was of far-reaching consequences and the wedding, which was one of its features, was largely a political matter; and yet, on the side of Tor at least, there was also a personal element. How far love and desire induced him to act is an insoluble problem. That it was of strong influence seems certain.

By building up an Islandian fleet the queen had been astute. The Winder vessels were no longer essential, and could almost have been dispensed with at the time of the compact. Not only had Islandia shown her power to do without them, but she had proved that, without her, Winder was in danger and that Winder, if too hostile, might suffer disaster. Tor, on marrying Alwina, gained more for his country than he lost. The incorporation of Winder into Islandia was the essential condition of the agreement. It meant to the people of that land the loss of their immunity from taxation and of their ship money, but it brought them equality in trade, the protection of brothers-in-arms, and a chance of seating their leading family on the throne. With much reduced bargaining power, they could scarcely complain of being overreached by their chief's compact.

Thus Alwina accomplished the dearest wish of her father, and for her people the addition of a seafaring folk as part of themselves. Tor, allowed to remain prince of Winder till his death, gained the woman he desired and kingship for his sons.

The only sufferer by the transaction was the doughty Marriner. He was sacrificed. It is not wholly to the Queen's credit that she made no special effort to reward him. He no longer was admiral of the Islandian fleet, second to none, but a subordinate of Tor's. This was too much for him and he retired to his valley facing the sea, Hoe Bay.

The wedding took place. The council ratified the queen's agreement, and on the day of marriage the necessary acts were done to incorporate Winder into Islandia.

There followed a few months of festivity and rejoicing. The queen was gayest of the gay in a gay court, but not for long. Having ousted the enemy, most were content, but not she, for early in Marth she set out with Tor on a journey through her country, including a visit to her cousin Dorn XI which resulted in a complete healing of the breach between their families. She also visited, for the first time in many years, her disgraced mother, who told her according to legend that her body was "Dorn", but the heart and head were of the accursed race of Alwin. But Alwina was concerned with other matters. She preached everywhere to an unwilling people the necessity of invasion. She made slow progress, but little by little convinced the intelligent that the only chance to win security was to crush the Karain beyond chance of recovery. More immediately profitable was her effort to consolidate the fleets of Islandia and Winder into a unified effective force. Her husband assisted her in this effort. Lastly, she journeyed to Storn, and by a judicious mixture of cajolery and threats disposed the people of that rocky rainy land to annexation.

She returned to The City in mid Som, and in Octen her first child, a daughter, was born. The opening of the next year saw Winder an integral part of Islandia and thither in Janvry the queen with her baby at her breast journeyed, and won the people to her, tactfully coming as the wife of their prince rather than as the powerful queen of a nation of which they were a small part. She continued her journeying to work up the warlike spirit, returning in the summer to The City.

The brilliant period of Islandian literature began at this time. Like Athens after the Persians and England after the Armada, an intense period of creativity began. Its tone at first was ardently patriotic, an inspiration traceable to Islandia's Gloriana far more closely than that of Elizabethan England to hers. Deming and Dury wrote stirring poems full of the epic war spirit in 1330, and stimulated many imitators.

On Janvry 1st the queen found herself ruler of all the lands south of the great range, with her dogs of war ready to loose. The army, under Strale, began to gather in Carran late in 1330. The fleet was already in rendezvous at Miltain.

Learning that the Karain in Mobono were fast preparing defences at the queen's command and without waiting till melting snow left open the roads of Miltain, in Febry, both moved. The campaign began badly. The Karain held the narrow passes along the sea, and the fleet was kept back by impossible storms. The queen, furious with delay, went forward to the front, and in Avrilis at Madly amid the army gave birth to her second child, another daughter. The child was premature by some time, and though it survived, it endangered its mother's life.

As soon as she could move she went to the front, and so inspired her army that in late Maya they broke the Karain lines and poured into the country. Fifty-six years before, Alwina's legendary great-grandfather had come this road and never returned. Such of his followers as had escaped remembered what they had seen. Except as slaves, no Islandians had ever entered Mobono. Nothing was known of it, except what rumor had to say and a distant view from the mountains to show.

The province thus entered caused extraordinary astonishment. It was populous and fertile beyond all expectations, but for all that it offered no resistance. The Islandians were suffered to reach the walls of its heart—Mobono—and the city was ill prepared to stand the siege which was at once begun.

It was apparent that the city was crowded, and that it was doomed unless food could come in. On the land side access was blocked, but to seaward the Karain fleet still moved out and in sailing north to unknown parts for grain. To cut those off required the Islandian fleet. It was slow in coming. The queen, with the army and suckling her second child, sent message after message to her husband. Finally, in Julian, he came and the situation at once changed. The Islandian army was suffering badly, with hordes of Demiji in turn investing it. Outside the harbor of Mobono, Tor fought his finest fight, proving that his delay was wise. Wind and weather was just as he would wish, and every ship was perfectly equipped and ready. The Karain fleet, only slightly inferior, was annihilated in a very short time with only slight loss. The city was now completely invested.

The city must have contained two hundred thousand persons of mixed blood. Many of the Islandian slaves there had forgotten their homes, but there were also many who prayed for deliverance. To rescue these people had been the hope of Alwina and her father, but to find any who preferred to stay was a rude surprise. Among these last was one of the wives of Kilikash, a woman of strong character. —in the defence of the palace she took a conspicuous part.

There was ill-feeling between the Winder manned fleet and the army, there were clashes in the streets and indescribable scenes. Alwina, meeting her husband, blamed him for the excess of his men and ordered him to take them away. There was evidently a sharp and terrible contest of wills, but Tor obeyed and in a few days the fleet withdrew and Tor went with them.

The queen's position was a terrible one. Now that Mobono was captured what was to be done with it? Neither she nor anyone in her suite were trained to govern a conquered province. She had an army straining for revenge in a seductive city amid a population as large within its environs as all Islandia. Not least, she had a young and sickly baby.

Against the desires of most of her counsellors, she ordered no general massacre. She even spared Kilikash for the present, nor did she ostensibly displace him. She in fact followed roughly the only precedent she had, an Islandian province, and keeping intact the machinery of the Karain state retained through it a control that would have been impossible if an Islandian replaced every Karain functionary.

The queen settled down in Mobono to work out her future policy—Karain must be made harmless and quiet, and the road to the mines must be kept open. For two years and a half the queen did not return to her own capital. In Janvy, 1332 and again in 1333 she met the National Council at Miltain. At the first meeting she obtained ratification for all she had done without great difficulty and with her successes still fresh in men's minds. Yet even then there were proponents of a policy of ruthlessness and massacre, and from a purely utilitarian point of view such a course seemed logical. But Alwina said characteristically, "There is no sucking the juice from an orange stamped under heel."

But it cannot be doubted that there were other reasons for Alwina's staying. One was her quarrel with Tor. There were other causes also—the capture of Mobono revealed another world known but dimly to the Islandians, the coastal cities to the north. Alwina's imagination was fired and later her ambition. There can be no doubt that this young queen, lonely because of her farsightedness and up to now so intensely practical, began to nourish dreams of an empire. There had already been breaks in the continuity of her good sense, evidenced by occasional wildness. The city where she dwelt was not conducive to reason, even to this day it is a strangely seductive place. What must it have been in its glory! A place of singers and dancers and its own weird erotic langor, poets, love and wine, it was something totally different to an Islandian. And the queen was surrounded by idolaters; many of her literary court had joined her. And not the least sinister influence was the son of Kilikash, Ahmid, a young man of great personal beauty, who, given more freedom than his father, doubtless laid deep plans with him.

The years that Alwina spent away from her capital, keeping her court at Mobono, truly started the literary and artistic movement of her time. Poets like Snetting were of a different order than Deming, a realistic school began to produce, and this movement led eventually in the next reign to the truly great work of the younger Bodwin. That the queen was the inspiration of much of this movement is clear. She encouraged the young men with every way in her power.

But the best that can be said for her is that she was far from wise. Those that admire her wish that there was certain proof that her behavior at Mobono was not as it seemed. The German historian Schlauter, who has given her period great study, believes the proof is uncontrovertable that she carried on liaisons with a number of men including Strale, young Mora, Deming, and even Ahmid, and others. But as sure as there is no proof that she did not misconduct herself there is equally no proof that she did. Yet it must be admitted that there is much against her. Most damning of all, because most sinister, is her relation with Ahmid. This man had connections in the west, in Kilik and elsewhere. He was anxious of course to reestablish his dynasty. It seems clear that he proposed to the queen a joint enterprise against all parts of the continent. She probably dallied with these ideas to a certain extent.

In the next year came the tragedy. Ahmid certainly made love to her, and undoubtedly desired her. On the 7th of Octen the queen's cries brought her attendants to her bedchamber, and when they arrived they found Strale lying murdered on the floor, the queen severely wounded, and Ahmid with a bloody knife. His guilt was undoubted, and when he was told he must die he committed suicide, and his father Kilikash, declaring all his hopes were gone, swallowed poison.

Alwina's fortunes were at a low ebb. Tor had astutely built up strong support in the capital. Many believed that Alwina was becoming a piece with her grandfather, great grandfather, and notorious mother. Talk of compelling her to abdicate was general, and it must be admitted Tor did not oppose it, perhaps playing the game to crush her only so far as he could safely go without crushing himself.

The queen showed her old ability at this crisis. Returning

to Islandia as soon as she had settled matters in Mobono, leaving her faithful friend Mora X and his eldest son in charge, she did not assume the guise of a penitent. Her appearance dispelled ugly rumors as to her condition— more beautiful than ever with the fire of power and long thoughts far ahead of her countrymen, she upbraided the council for its pusilanimity with regard to the war. She regained popular enthusiasm, and lastly she brought Tor to her begging for reconciliation. Alwina must have had an all but broken heart. She knew that her schemes must be put by; and she had no real love for Tor by this time, if ever.

The year was a quiet one. In Octen the queen bore a son and heir. Old breaches were closed. She had the consolation of seeing the last one of the tasks she had set herself on beginning her reign accomplished. Then abruptly all was changed, for due to the carelessness of an attendant the boy sickened and died. The blow was such that the queen never fully recovered. Her mourning and grief were so intense that even the dry official records of it burn. But though Alwina doubted her strength, she exposed herself to the risk of another child.

Her health was such that she left the city in Julian, and defying precedent almost religious, retired to a small chalet built for her in the sacred but dry, cool and healthy mountain air of the Frays; and here on Septen 22nd was born a son who was cared for by his mother alone and lived, although somewhat sickly, and ultimately proved that though his name was Tor his heart was his mother's.

Alwina's ill health continued, but a second son, who also survived, was born in Decen 1337. She now devoted herself to bringing up her children; her relations with her husband were friendly. That hard bargaining and astute Winderian was at last wholly given in to her spell, and Alwina, quite aware that she was not likely to live till her heir reached majority, spent much of her time in training Tor for the regency, and in preparing the way for his acceptance as such by the council.

She never left the Frays again. Her health rapidly declined. Her last year was spent in comparative peace, and in Decen she died in giving birth to a daughter, who subsequently married the grandson of Alwina's ancient foe Lord Dorn XI, the young prince's third cousin.

It may be wondered why so much time has been devoted to a single reign in so brief a narrative. It is partly because historic material is so abundant. Alwina's letters to Mora X are still preserved at Miltain in the possession of the descendant of their recipient, and among them are copies of many other papers of priceless value sent by her to him. The war poems of Deming and Dury are full of detail and fact. Snetting's account of Mora's voyage is not without much that bears on her whole reign. But most important of all, and far outmeasuring these, is the splendid history of her time by Bodwin the Younger. It is an account covering some two hundred pages mostly from first hand observation, for Bodwin was a soldier. It is accurate and restrained; to the psychologist interested in the character of the queen it may have faults, for little is discussed except public events—its style has that perfection for which Bodwin is so famous, and it contains descriptions of persons and events of a marvellous brilliancy.

It is not wholly because the amplitude of material tempts the historian that I have gone into Alwina's reign so much at length, but because of its great romance and interest. A mere girl forces her way to a throne denied by tradition to a woman, frees her country from the oppressors, extends its flag to other lands for the first time in its history, unites with it permanently and successfully two recalcitrant allies, and by her inspiring beauty and gallant conduct and direct influence brings into being a golden age of letters. Certainly such a woman and queen deserves a large place in Islandian history.

—Jean Perrier
The City
Islandia 1909

The Unicorn Masque

Ellen Kushner

I.

At the age of thirty-two, the queen was a dried rose. Although in her day she had numbered among the most valuable princesses on the marriage market, she had also been the most educated and the least beautiful. Contract after contract was dissolved before it could be consummated. Her younger sisters were married away to foreign powers, while she stayed at home to see her brother ascend the throne on their father's death, and descend it off the back of a rearing horse. The first five years of her reign had been marked by academic policies in council and dionysian splendors at court. It was in the dances, the gallant offerings of verse and song, that she found the attention and admiration denied her as a princess by all the marriage tokens courtesy had demanded be returned: the betrothal rings taken from her young hands, the portraits of foreign princes packed away.

After five years, though, the queen had begun to reconsider her state. Might the brilliant, posing revelry she delighted in be, not splendor, but merest frivolity? Frivolity lead to weakness—indeed, the mirror of history held it up as an early symptom of decay. It was true that she was surrounded by able counselors, but their wisdom would not live forever. She suddenly saw that she had been wrong to rush headlong into pleasure, leading the whole court with her as it was prone to do. So she curtailed the late-night revels that she might rise each morning at dawn to complete nine lines of translation before breakfast. Her constant entourage of beautiful, perfumed young men gave way to the ancient learned.

The court was amazed to find its favorite pastimes prohibited, its chiefest virtues in disgrace overnight. Its senior members took it in stride; they had lived through the rapid succession of three very different monarchs, and knew how to adapt. The country kept running much as before; only the fashions of whom to have to dinner changed: musicians were out, scholars were in. Soon books were replacing trinkets in the soft jeweled hands of courtiers. When the queen put off the gaudy gowns that had always outshone her, her faithful court apparelled itself with like sobriety. On this summer's royal progress through the north counties, though, the atmosphere relaxed as many of the younger set succumbed to bright and fanciful dress once more: time enough for drabness, they said, when school was called again in the fall.

Now the queen sat in her blue silk pavilion, shielded from the rays of the summer sun by three billowing walls weighted with her arms embroidered in gold. The fourth side was looped back, open to what breezes stirred the air. It was the queen's pleasure to keep this August's court on the broad summer lawns of her great lords' houses; there her retinue of nobles disported themselves at country pastimes while she assessed her lands and displayed her traditional right to beggar whom she chose in entertaining her. Despite her recent strictures, she continued to permit her liege lords to pay lavish tribute; they called her Divine Virgin, the Queen of Field and Grove, and presented musical masques, harvest fruits and their well-groomed children to her. It was one of these she awaited now: childless Lord Andreas' chosen heir, a youth reared abroad and newly come home to his guardian's estates. He was bound to be green; she only hoped he would not stammer, or trip.

They knew that he would not. There was less of chance involved than anyone could imagine in the young gentleman about to be presented to Her Grace. His noble patron put a final fret in the sober white frills around his neck, and stepped back for a look at their creation.

"Perfect," he wheezed, staring frankly at the poised and slender figure gilded like a confection by the shaft of sun coming through the mullion panes of the manor house.

The young man returned the look with a smile intended

to make the marrow of any one's bones run quicksilver, and said, "Your servant, sir." If not the smile, then surely the voice; perfect, perfect, infinitely precious with the sense that either could be shattered with the proper blow—if one were wise enough to see past the sterling perfection, and fool enough to want to destroy it.

"It is time," said the tall lean man who had always been there, standing in his dark robes amongst the shadows by the window. "He doesn't need to be fussed over, I've promised you that. And you've had all summer to admire him; now let be."

"Yess," breathed the fleshy lord, squeezing his fat, ringed fingers together in such sinister anticipation that the fair young man threw back his head and laughed. The tall man's eyes slid to his employer's, meeting unquenchable satisfaction there. This arrogance suited him: nothing had been left to chance.

He walked across the green lawns past the clusters of nobles knowing all eyes were on him. The silk of the pavilion fluttered fitfully in the hot summer air. Inside it the Queen sat riffling the pages of a book, formally oblivious to his approach until the bodyguard's pikes clashed together and apart to let the young man enter and kneel at her feet.

She was stunned at first by the blistering aureole over his bent head; then she realized that her eyes were only dazzled by the sun coming in the open tent-way, illuminating hair as light as mirrors.

He waited, head bowed before her, observing the court ways they had taught him with all their ancient formality, until he heard the queen say, "You are welcome." Then he raised his face to her.

The silk shaded her in a bath of color pure as cerulean moonlight. Slowly his eyes adjusted to distinguish her features. Her nose was sharp, her unpainted mouth small and pursed, like her father the king's. Narrow eyes of watery blue surveyed him under heavy half-moon lids. The jeweled clasps pinning her straight colorless hair flat on either side of her head only accentuated the harshness of her face. The only softness was in her cheeks, surprisingly full and round, and in the weakness of her chin. Against the sober, extravagent blue of her skirt, her pale hands, weighted with rings, restlessly toyed with a small book on her lap. Amber leather, stamped in gold. Quickly his eyes returned to his sovereign's face.

The queen caught her breath, then gave a small cough to cover it. She extended her hand for him to take; his limber fingers were smooth, with bones so fine she felt they might be hollow, like a bird's. The sculpted ridges of his lips touched the back of her hand, and then his eyes were again full on her.

"Sir, you are welcome," she said again; "I pray you rise and be seated."

He was modestly dressed in sober black, with white linen shirt ruffles crisp at wrist and throat. She watched him seat himself on a low stool across from her; his movements were lithe, his body as slender and tempered as wire.

He bore the queen's scrutiny calmly, with pride. He understood her expression, the cool reserve sheltering almost awed approval; understood and sympathized. He was flawless. Lord Pudge-Rings and his lean friend would have nothing but praise for him tonight.

"I am told," she said with pedantic formality, "that you spent many years abroad."

"Too many, madam, to please me." He smiled easily at her.

"You wished, then, to return?"

"Lady, it has been my dearest wish." Her eyes veiled slightly with reservation: she had a court full of men to spin her compliments. "Of course—" he laughed, his eyes dropping ruefully to his clasped hands—"one's dearest wish is always to go against one's elders, isn't it? They kept telling me how good it was for me to live abroad, so naturally I hated it." She nodded, thinking of all the hardships of duty. "My delicate health, they said, forbade travel, and my youth required stability." She could see them both, youth and recent illness, still in his face: the fine, girlish skin stretched over high-bred bones that had

not yet hardened into maturity. "So I studied." He looked
at her intently with eyes so blue that for a moment they
were all she saw in the pale sculptured face that held them
like jewels in a setting. "I resolved to do as much as I could
with whatever they gave me, so that—" He stopped abruptly, eyes downcast, his skin colored a delicate rose.
"Forgive me, Majesty. It cannot be of interest to Your
Grace what—"

"Study, sir," she said softly, "is always of greatest interest to me. Pray go on."

"I read, then," he said, equally softly. "And played the
lute. When they told me it might not be healthy for me to
be so much indoors, I took up riding, and the bow; and
spent hours at sword practice." He shifted in his seat, an
unconsciously graceful movement. If he could move that
way with a foil in his hands, he must be good.

"Do you plan to continue your studies now?"

"If I can get the books here. I have been through my
lord's library, it is woefully out of date. . . ."

She noticed his eyes fixed hungrily on her lap and
started, clutching the forgotten volume as she did so. The
queen smiled to realize what he had been staring at, and
held up the leather-bound book for him to see. "You must
look at this, then: my own presentation copy of Dunn's
new work on the movement of the heavens. It is only just
printed, few others will have it." She patted her skirt.
"Come, sit beside me and we shall read it." He rose and
settled again, like a dancer, at her feet. All she could see of
him now was the light sweep of hair, the dent of a smile
partly obscured by the arc of his cheek. "They are all
coming to the city now," she said eagerly: "the men of
science, the philosophers . . . I plan to lower the taxes on
printing . . . Ah, the country is all very well for quiet and
study, but you must come to my city for the books and the
minds . . . Now, then; here is the Preface."

He fixed his eyes on the page, printed with great carved
capitals and wood-cut illustrations, and tried not to stray to
the marginalia of her rounded fingertips and chewed-
looking thumb . . . . He knew nothing about Dunn, or

books on the heavens. He must study now to seem informed, and to remember it perfectly. He must be perfect. There was still so much to be learned.

Candlelight glowed late into the night in one room of Lord Andreas' manor. The queen's "simple country supper," with its eight simultaneous courses, five wines and attending jugglers and minstrels, had been cleared away hours ago from the great hall, and the court had gone to its well-deserved rest in the various chambers appointed. Only in this small room were tapers lit, their flames polishing the wood-paneled walls to an amber gloss. Despite the warmth of the night heavy curtains were drawn across the windows. It was unlikely that anyone would come wandering down this far corridor and see the light under the door.

The lord of the manor and his lean confederate sat at a round, taper-studded table as the delicate blond man rehearsed to them the story of his day. He struck pose after pose without being aware of it, concluding with one arm outstretched, each finger precisely curled as though to allure his audience; "And so tomorrow I bid you a sweet farewell, and join the royal progress on its way back to court!"

A poised stillness followed. It was broken by the rhythmic thud of flesh against flesh: the fat man was clapping. When echoes began to fill the room, he stopped.

"Excellent," he said. "She'll take you."

"Oh, yes." The melodious voice almost crowed its well-bred triumph. "We are not to be parted, Her Grace and I."

"Perfect!" the lord wheezed. Infected by his enthusiasm, the young man flourished a royal obeisance. "My humble duty to your lordship. And now, pardon me, gentlemen." The bow extended itself to the black-robed one. "I fear I must retire; the court rides out early tomorrow."

But the fat lord's hand snaked out before he could turn away. Fleshy, surprisingly strong fingers gripped his chin. "No. We do not pardon you."

He knew better than to flinch. He forced himself to meet the glinting, tiny eyes and say politely, "How may I serve your lordship?"

The hand tightened on his jaw. He could smell the remnants of dinner on the man's breath. "You will obey me," Lord Andreas said. "You do not leave until I dismiss you."

"Of course, sir." He made sure the light, willing smile touched his eyes as well as his mouth. But the strong fingers flung his face aside.

"Don't try your tricks on me!" his patron growled. He raised his velvet-clad arm again. The young man spun away from the blow, his hand automatically reaching for a dagger at his hip.

"You are unarmed," the tall man observed placidly from his seat at the table. "Excellent reflexes." He continued amicably, overriding the threat of violence as though he had not seen it, "I was admiring the bow you just made. Would you mind telling me where you learned it?"

The young man lowered his empty hands. A test, he thought; it had only been another test. Lord Andreas, silent now, had subsided into a chair. He steadied his breathing, and prepared the familiar answer. "Abroad, sir, I had tutors—"

"No." The lines of the man's lean face shifted to condescending mockery. "You learned it here, remember?"

"Don't tell me," the fat lord chimed in with interest, "that you're beginning to believe your own stories?"

He held his temper tightly in his clenched hands, letting its heat keep him from the chill of fear. "Forgive me," he said with icy good manners; "I didn't know—"

Their laughter pierced him, striking like hammer-blows inside his head.

"No," the lean man said. "Of course you didn't. You don't really believe all those stories you told the queen?"

"Of course not," he snapped. "I know what's real and what isn't."

"Of course you do." The man's long hand reached out to a taper set on the table near him. For a moment his fingers hovered over the flame as if about to bestow a benediction; then he pinched out the candleflame between two bony fingertips. "So do I." Smoke trailed up from the black wick, dissolving into darkness. "Who are you—really?"

He felt the world lunge away from him in a belly-wrench of blackness—he flung his hands forward, and caught the smooth wood of the table's edge.

"Oh, dear lord!" Lord Andreas' voice echoed in his head. "He's not going to faint, is he?"

"No, of course not." The man stood up, his black robes falling about him in folds of deeper blackness. The young man shrank from his approach. He did not want to be touched by anyone; he wanted only to be alone in perfect darkness, curled in upon himself like a seashell . . . But the other man was only holding out a chair to him. Mutely he sank into it.

"He's exhausted," the man said over his head to Andreas. "He wants to be alone."

"He'll be alone soon enough," Lord Andreas said. "Let him be quiet for once, and listen to me." He heaved his bulk up from the table, and stood before the younger man. "Give me your hand," Andreas told him. He held his right hand up and watched it tremble. "No," said his patron; "the other one." His left hand bore a gold signet ring. It seemed to sink into the flesh of Andreas' fingers as they handled it. The nobleman smiled grimly. "I had this made for you, the day you were born. Do you remember?"

He had to lick his lips before he could answer. "Yes."

"It is yours, and yours alone. Remember. Now," Lord Andreas said, settling back against the table. He kept the young man's hand in his. "I am going to give you the advice any patron would give his ward upon his departure for the royal court. But in your case, it is not mere words—it must be followed to the letter. Do you hear me?" He nodded. "First of all, you are not to touch wine or spirits on any account. It will be noted, but you ought to be enough

of a practiced liar by now to be able to make up excuses to
fit any occasion. You may gamble with dice or cards all you
like—I don't care how much money your run through, but
I expect you will win more than you lose. Dress well, but
not above your station: you're not to compete with the
great lords' sons. They will be impressed with your
swordsmanship—they ought to be!" his patron snorted.
"You're better than all of them. If one of them should pick
a quarrel for the pleasure of dueling with you, for god's
sake don't kill him. If you should be wounded, you know
you don't have to worry; just keep it covered until people
forget so they don't miss the scar." Andreas ran his thumb
over the smooth skin of the narrow wrist, which last week
had been torn by steel. "I think that's all . . . Oh, yes—the
usual warning, lest the ward's head be turned to in-
gratitude by the vices and splendors of the court: *We made
you, and we can unmake you.*" The heavy fingers met
sharply around the young man's hand. "Only in this case,
my dear, it is not an empty threat."

He pulled together his returning strength to smile coolly
up at the nobleman. "A threat indeed. I don't even know
how you made me; what precisely should I fear in being
unmade? I'm a better swordsman than any you could set
against me, and soon I shall have the favor of the crown. If
you d—"

The thin man interrupted the exchange with a mournful
sigh. "Bravado," he said. "You must have your little gestures. Appropriate, but scarcely wise." He touched the
candlewick with his bare finger, and the flame leapt again
into being, illuminating the harsh face from below.

The room was still, even the candle flames rose without
a flicker into the hot, dark air. The young man tasted sweat
on his upper lip, but did not move to wipe it away. "Ask
me," the lean man said. "Ask me again."

The silver-blue eyes fixed helpless on their creator.
"Who am I?"

"Yes . . ." Lord Andreas hissed in triumph, unable to
restrain himself from joining in. "Who are you? Where did
you come from? How did you gain all that expertise—with

the sword, the lute, your own smooth muscles? You have no memory of any life but this—you might not even be human." The fair head jerked upward, and Andreas laughed. "Does that worry you? Does it, my dear?"

The thin man's eyes burned like pale agates. "You must be one of those people who never remember their dreams. But that doesn't mean you never had them. Dream again, my lovely; dream again before you question the gift I gave you. . . ."

The younger man wanted to profess his dislike of riddles, and his distrust of dreams. But the tall one rose, and his shadow rose with him, long and black climbing the wall, along with the candleflame that became all he could see, a pillar of light. Out of it five fingers stretched, long and cool and dark, and touched his eyes, and he dreamed again—the old dream:

He was a woman, alone in a bare room weeping. It lasted only a moment, not enough time to know his name or face, or the cause of the tears; only the misery of being trapped by her own wishes, the four walls no refuge from what lay outside them when she herself was the room and the walls and the kernel of weakness and misery that refused to stop dreaming—

His hands were hot with tears. He opened his eyes to a world of indecipherable light; blinked, and sorted out the nimbus of each separate candle, and the white slashes of the two men's faces.

"It's all right now," the lean man said with alarming tenderness.

His eyes fell to his own hands, clasped on his lap. The gold ring on his forefinger glowed in a setting of tears like crystal. He turned his hand to see the light strike fire first from the tiny silver moon on one side, then from the ruby that was the sun . . . . In the center between them an etched figure danced, alone, one arm flung up toward the sun.

"Lazarus Merridon." He looked up, not sure which of them had addressed him. "Lazarus the Beggar," said the lean man. "Lazarus the New-Risen. A bit of local mythology. *Sol Meridionale:* brought forth at noon. If you're ever knighted you can use it as your motto."

"You see," said the nobleman; "you cannot fail us."

Lazarus rose to his feet, an elegant figure made all the more exquisite by the lineaments of exhaustion. Despite it all his voice was still bell-toned and honey-sweet. "And when I come to court," he asked, "what am I to do, besides gain a knighthood?"

"Anything you please, my dear," they said. "You cannot fail us."

II.

Against all previous expectation, the court's return to its seat in the capital that autumn was anything but dull. Little piles of silver were already passing from hand to jeweled hand, honoring strong speculation on the queen's newest study partner. No one could get quite near enough the strange beauty to discover the definite end of his charms; all that could be ascertained was that he did seem to understand whatever it was she was studying. He also proved to be a fine musician and an admirable dancer; and that was really what saved them all in the end from what had hitherto promised to be the most tedious winter in living memory—periods of mourning excepted, of course.

It was the autumn hunt that had suggested it to him, or possibly a bit of exotica from one of her books: after all, she couldn't possibly disapprove of a masque based on a classical theme, and the Hunt of the Unicorn was the subject of innumerable pages of commentary. Odds were ridiculously high that the masque would be approved even before he had played her any of the exquisite music he had composed, since the central role of the captivating Virgin could only be enacted by the court's own Sovereign Lady (*and only virgin,* the snigger went). No one even bothered to wager on who would be Unicorn, and so they lost an interesting gamble, for the composer demurred, and the role went to the young Earl Dumaine—a pretty enough dancer, but everyone knew she had tired of him last year.

On the night of the masque the great hall shone with a forest. Its pillars were wreathed in living greens, while flowery carpets hid the floor. The Master of Revels had outdone himself in fantastical trees of paper, canvas, wood, satin . . . he had wanted live birds, but it was suggested that they might interfere with the music, and possibly the dancers, so he had to make do with elaborate arrays of feathers, with little jeweled eyes peeping out between the leaves.

The sides of the room were thick with courtiers who were not in the performance. Rehearsals had been going on for weeks behind closed doors; except for the subject matter, occasional public bickerings that broke out over costumes and precedence, and the stray tune that would at times escape someone's lips, no one else knew anything about the contents of the masque. They waited in eager anticipation, admiring the decor. The musicians, splendidly decked out in silver and green, were already seated on a dais trimmed with ribbons and boughs. Among them was Lazarus Merridon, holding the lute he would play. His cool eyes swept the audience; then he nodded to the sackbut player, and the notes of an ornamented hunting-call sounded through the hall. Immediately the watching courtiers stopped their gossip-ridden fidgeting to fix their eyes on the center of the room.

First came the dance of the Lovers, then the dance of the Hunters. Then the queen stepped forth, robed in virgin white, her pale hair streaming loose about her, her light eyes bright with excitement. And the Unicorn pranced out, capered with his ivory horn, earning applause for his spectacular leaps, until he danced his way to the seated maiden and, on a burst of cymbals, laid his glowing horn in her lap . . . . Wildly enthused, the hunter-lords broke into unprogrammed shouting as they burst from the undergrowth to slay the unfortunate Earl, whose new silk doublet was actually slashed by a few of the spears. At the center of their dance of death sat the queen with hair unbound, her face flushed, her eyes glittering.

All the nimble of the court found themselves whirling and jumping to the final wild music of victory. The hall was streaked with spinning velvet, silk and satin, the sharp glints of blue, red, green, rainbow jewels flashing from hair and breast, belt and hat and dagger. . . .

Above them, on the musicians' dais, Lazarus Merridon sat playing the lute, and smiled. In his mind, weaving in and out through the wild and measured rhythms of strings and brass and timpani, sounded the voice of the nameless man: *It's all right now.*

Lord Thomas Berowne would have been one of the masquers, being the younger son of a duke and owning an admirable pair of legs himself; but he had only just returned from a foreign embassage on the day of the performance. In the course of the afternoon, however, he had acquired all the gossip to be had about its originator, and he watched the lutenist carefully that night. Lord Thomas had only a rudimentary, nobleman's knowledge of music, but he knew a great deal about courts; thus he was not surprised at the news that followed the next afternoon. Being an extremely well-liked young man, and well-connected, he got it before most others, and managed to be the first to seek out Lazarus Merridon to congratulate him on his success.

Lazarus Merridon smiled, noting the scatter of costly rings on the young lord's hands. "My lord is too generous, truly. Once the music was written, my part was all idleness, while others did the work."

Lord Thomas laughed, as though he'd made a joke. "Oh, the masque, of course! But your real achievement is the royal summons, you know."

Lazarus blinked. He had only just received the summons himself. God, what a place! "Her Majesty's retiring, yes," he said politely. "I shall be deeply honored to be in attendance tonight."

Lord Thomas smiled at this stiffness with cheerful amusement. "You're used to the ways of courts, I see. Never trust anyone who knows too much about you, or who acts too interested. But your own lines of information must not be very well set up yet: anyone here can tell you I'm harmless. My family's too rich to need to make trouble for anyone.'' His smile sought the musician's eyes. ''But I didn't come to gossip with you about the noble Berownes. I only wanted to pass on a little advice.'' Lord Thomas took his arm, walking familiarly with him down the gallery. It was an easy, comfortable hold. Lazarus tolerated it as he tolerated everything else the court had dealt him. ''You see . . .'' the young lord leaned his head of brown curls against the golden one—''I thought someone might as well tell you now. You're quite clearly the next royal favorite, and no one grudges you that—'' *Don't you?* Lazarus Merridon thought scornfully. ''—but you can't expect it to last, handsome stranger. It never does. You haven't been here long, you haven't seen the rest of them come and go the way some of us have.''

But, thought the stranger, *have any of you ever seen my like before, Lord Thomas?* A wry smile touched his lips; misinterpreting it Berowne said, ''Don't even consider it. The last one who tried to touch her was sent off to command a troop in the Northern Wars, and hasn't been heard of since.'' There was a tone to his voice that had been lacking before, a sternness underlying the friendly banter. Lazarus glanced at him, but saw only bland amiableness on the round pleasant face. He suddenly wished for an excuse to leave, to escape the company of this friendly man and his enquiring eyes. ''Oh, dear!'' Lord Thomas cried in mock distress. ''And have I managed to insult you, my silent Master Merridon?''

''Of course not, Lord Thomas.''

They stopped before a large diamondpane window. ''It would be unforgivably clumsy of me to insult a man I admire,'' said Berowne. The sun struck red lights off his hair as he stared out into the garden. ''I do, you know. Ever since you joined us on Progress—''

''Were you—?'' Lazarus began. There'd been so many of them then, each a name and a face and a title.

''Oh, you won't remember me,'' Thomas smiled easily,

turning from the window; "I noticed you, though—there was a quietness about you, an otherness, as though you came from very far away . . . you were raised abroad, weren't you?"

For a moment his repertory of lies froze on his tongue. "Abroad, yes . . ." Then he recovered his aplomb, saying ruefully, "I didn't think it showed so much."

Thomas laughed. "Insulting you again, am I? No, it doesn't show, not now. Not that it matters," he added cheerfully. "If I could play and sing as you do, I wouldn't care if I had two heads and a tail! But I haven't any talent, alas, only lots of expensive clothing . . . ."

Lazarus said, despite himself, "I'm not what—not as good as you think I am."

"Aren't you?" the nobleman asked seriously. "Then I should like to meet your master."

His fair skin gave him away. Thomas saw the flush bleed across the musician's face, and immediately was all contrition, nimbly complimenting him on his fashionably pale complexion and diverting the conversation to his unusual ring.

Lazarus' long slender fingers lay loosely in the other man's soft, well-cared-for ones while Thomas scrutinized the gold signet. "That's fine work. Sun, moon . . . is that a man or a woman there between them?"

"I don't know," he said softly.

"It's nice." Lord Thomas smiled, releasing his hand. "You must come see my new paintings sometime; not now, though; you're about to be attacked by some new admirers." Surely enough, a pair of eager courtiers were making their purposeful way down the gallery. "I daren't stand between you and glory, my dear sir; I might get crushed. Master Merridon, good day—and good luck."

"My Lord." Lazarus bowed briefly, but was interrupted by a hand on his arm. *"Thomas,"* the nobleman smiled. "If you think you can bring yourself to say it."

"Good day, Thomas." For an instant Lazarus met his eyes; then Berowne hurried off in the opposite direction as the two courtiers drew near.

He was relieved when evening came and he could withdraw from public attention to dress for the Retiring.

He arrived at the queen's apartments to find her sitting primly in her blue velvet chair, modestly wrapped in quilted satin and attending ladies. At the door he bowed, and again as he was bidden to enter; a third time before he approached, then he knelt to kiss her hand. When he rose, one of her women went back to brushing out her hair. It was long and fine, and clung to the brush like strands of cobweb. "Good evening, Lazarus," said the queen. She ignored the ministrations, smiling up at him with her pale, weak eyes. "Oh, please sit—there, in that chair; we're not so formal here at close of day. It is a time when I like the company of my friends."

He marveled at the thinness of her voice: one of the world's most powerful women, and she seemed as timid and brittle as a green girl. The fingers of one hand toyed with a golden tassel on her robe. Lazarus answered, "I am honored to be counted among them, Madam."

She leaned a little forward to focus her weak eyes on his face. "You *are* my friend. Your sweet voice and gentle music have lent grace to our court, and our studies together have given me great pleasure. Now I am able to give something to you." A small box was placed in her waiting hand. At a gesture from the queen he knelt before her. She lifted from the box a golden jewel glinting with gemstones, dripping with pearls. It was a unicorn, hung on a golden chain that splashed like water when she raised it. "Wear this for me," the queen said gravely, "in token of our friendship." He bent his head, and felt the heavy chain settle on his neck, weighting his shoulders. It was a princely gift.

Impulsively he twisted from his own finger a thin gold band set with a small ruby. "Madam, I have nothing so fine to offer in return. But if friendship will be content with tokens . . ."

The queen only stared at him.

"Have I offended, Madam?"

"No," she stammered; "no. It is a pretty ring. I—thank

you." But still she held it in her hand, as though she feared it might break. Gently then he rose, and knelt down at her side, lifting her blue-veined hand to slip his ring onto her forefinger. "There." He smiled up into her face, his eyes deepened to summer—sky blue in the candlelight. "Now I am ever at your Grace's hand."

When she blinked bright drops stood on her short color-less lashes. "Thank you." She swallowed.

A lady murmured something about retiring. "Yes," said the queen, her voice still thin, "it is late."

Lazarus Merridon rose and bowed. "Then good night, Majesty."

"Good night." As he backed from the Presence, she recollected herself. "Oh—Lazarus. You will come tomor-row night, please—and bring your lute."

The court's attentions were, if anything, worse the sec-ond day. On the fourth and fifth they slacked off; those who desired to make their interest known to him had done so, and now they waited to see whether he were truly in. He was, and the seventh day brought him no rest at all from the favor-seekers, and, worse yet, people with long-term goals trying to convince him that they were his friends. He sought refuge in his own rooms with orders to his servant to admit no one, and slept, deep muffled sleep with no dreams. Waking, he would sort through and return most of the gifts the courtiers had left, and dress for those dinners he could not avoid without seeming churlish. He dressed soberly, in tribute to his rank and to the queen's current tastes; the only gaudy thing about him was the unicorn jewel, which had been designed for show and not for taste.

He could, of course, do nothing for them but be graceful and witty at their tables, favoring them with what prestige his presence lent. The queen did not summon him to talk of court positions; she spoke of books and music and, recently, of the fears she harbored: of assassination, of her two sisters, married abroad to kings. "They never liked me—but how they would like my throne. . . . . My people love me, I know they do: they cheer as I pass by. But my younger sister always was a schemer—she seeks to suborn our loyal subjects to treason, for if I die her son inherits the throne . . . . she has spies, Lazarus . . . ." Then he would play the lute to her, as she lay back on many pillows in the great velvet bed of state, until she fell asleep, and her silent ladies blew the candles out.

He watched sourly for Thomas Berowne to come along with the rest of them, with more of his good advice and his friendly eyes; but the Duke's son was not among them— Too rich to need a favorite's favor, Lazarus told himself. When he encountered Lord Thomas about the palace, the young man only smiled pleasantly at him, and passed on.

The queen was more than usually melancholy, and did not wish to speak, so he sat and played to her while her ladies brushed and braided her hair for the night. She fretted under their care, turning her head so that her colorless hair escaped in cloud-snake wisps and had to be rebrushed, until she shook it out entirely and snapped to the hovering hands, "Be gone! I can attend myself."

The memories of the only other quarrels he had known made Lazarus nervous of this one; he kept his eyes on his fingers, his presence confined to the humming strings of the lute. Her ladies curtsied. They glanced at the gentle-man from long, lowered eyes, waiting for him to stop playing and take his leave. He remained oblivious to their looks, though not to the tension they engendered; at last he looked up, only to hear the queen command, "Let him stay." She raised her voice again in the face of their dumb opposition, but the effect was childish, not regal: "Let him stay, I say! He is a gentleman of my court, he will not harm his sovereign. There is a guard outside the door," she added dryly; "I shall scream if I need help."

He slid his conspirator's grin to her amid the flutter of skirts, good-nights and trailing sleeves. When the great door closed on the last of them he said, "Your grace is very tartar tonight."

"I meant to be," she pouted. "Let them learn to obey

me. I am their queen.''

"And mine," he smiled, taking the hand that bore his ring. "How shall I serve my sovereign tonight?"

She pressed his hand, or gripped it, then released it just as suddenly and rose to walk about the dark and lofty room. Tall tapers threw her shadows long against the walls; they crossed and recrossed each other so that the pacing lady peopled the room with smoky dancers. Lazarus waited for her to speak, but she only moved from object to object, picking things up and putting them down, a hairbrush, a mirror. . . . Her long robe of claret velvet dragged sluggishly after her across the polished floor. He picked some random liquid notes from his instrument, but the queen whirled with a tiny cry. He put the lute down gently, knowing that no matter how awkward he felt, his movements would still express nothing but fluid ease. Watching him seemed to calm her. She came and stood at his side, looking down at the soft-fringed head made golden by candlelight, and said softly, "Lazarus."

He looked up. Her eyes were full of tears. The queen's sad gaze fell to where her small fingers twisted his ring around and around on her left hand. "Will you serve me in all things?"

"In all things, Highness."

She shook her head, lips pressed tight. "Not in duty, please, not now." He put up one hand to stop her nervous twisting of the ring, and was amazed at the fierceness of her grip. He asked, "In friendship, then?"

She nodded, full-eyed, not trusting herself to speak.

"In friendship I will serve you all I can." He took both her hands, and rose to draw her gently toward her chair. "Sit down, now, and tell me what I can do." But with a little cry she broke his grasp and clasped him to her.

Under his chin he smelt the clean smell of her hair. He put his arms around her to ease her trembling, but it didn't seem to help. Her hands were little fists, clenched into the small of his back. He felt a tickle of whispered breath close to his neck: "Please. Don't laugh."

"No, Highness."

She drew back enough to view his face fully. "Oh," the queen said softly. He didn't move. Her shaking fingers came up; their tips brushed his lips, then traced the sculpted ridges carefully so that he smiled, and they ran over the new shape as well. She returned him a dewy smile; then slowly, somberly she raised her face, her weak eyes still wide. When her mouth touched his her body shuddered. He kept his still, although he wanted to smile under her lips' rigidness. His own were soft, pliant . . . she felt them so and slowly let her own relax to meld with them. But when his mouth responded to hers she stiffened, and would have pulled away if he had not stilled it again.

Now her hand traced his jaw, dreamily curled the shell of his ear, parted and smoothed his feather-light hair. One fingertip lightly brushed a delicately-veined eyelid, and arced along the slender wing of brow above it. His eyes were closed. Stiff-fingered she untied his collar to rest her touch on the base of his throat, where the pulse beat against translucent skin between the rising muscles.

The jet buttons of his doublet gave her some trouble; but when he lifted his arms to assist, her fingers froze until they withdrew. She unlaced his outer sheeves, and he felt the cool linen of his shirt hanging loose about his arms.

He was pure white and golden in the candlelight, almost too perfect to be real: gilded ivory, a confection . . . but his chest rose and fell with his breathing, deep and not so regular as it had been, the only sound in the still room. She kissed the soft mouth again, forcing it taut against her lips. She pressed her body to his, and her throat made a sound. "Highness," his quiet voice said into her hair, "shall I?"

Soft skin brushed her cheek as she nodded. Soon she stood with her feet in a pool of crimson velvet, and her white gown floated up over her head . . . He lifted her at last in his strong slender arms, without words marveling at her frailty, at his own infinite knowledge of her desires and his tender exaltation in them. He moved to her will, and his own thoughts made no difference as the unicorn jewel swung through the air, glittering in the candle flames.

Lord Thomas Berowne strolled down a long sunlit gallery of the palace, on his way to the library. In one hand he carried a scarlet rose: no matter the season, Berowne's wealth and desire kept him surrounded by flowers. Courtiers were clustered up and down the gallery in bunches, their voices hushed and excited. As he passed them people looked up, then resumed their conversation. Thomas lifted the delicate blossom to his nose. Suddenly there was silence at the other end of the hallway. It rippled out before the slender man approaching like some courtly spring tide. Lazarus Merridon walked with a breathtakingly careless grace, courteously answering isolated greetings, ignoring the buzz that grew behind him as he passed. When he reached Lord Thomas, though, he hesitated. The young lord smiled. "Congratulations," he said, and offered him the rose.

"I never thought," she said, lying in the curve of his arm in the dark, "that I would want to marry. Not once I was queen. And it doesn't matter that you are younger, and not of noble blood; I shall give you titles, and we will give my people an heir." She chuckled happily. "How my sister will be furious! There goes her hope of succession."

"You're not with child already!" he said, running his palm smoothly over her body.

She giggled. "No, silly man, how could I tell yet? But if we keep on like this, I will be. . . ."

The queen's chief lady was being rudely shaken. She peered through sleep-gummed lashes at the intruder, and made out the sharp, pale features of Master Lazarus Merridon, her lady's paramour.

"What time is it?"

"Midnight," he responded tersely. "Her Majesty's physician—you must fetch him at once!"

Lady Sophia pulled a dressing gown around her ample form; she was used to emergencies, and even to the ill manners of hysteria. "What is it?"

"I don't know!" He was dressed as scantily—as hastily

—as decency would allow. "I don't know, she is in pain—"

"Probably a touch of bad meat," Lady Sophia said comfortably. "Put your clothes on, Master Merridon, and go back to your own bed; I'll see to her Grace's comfort."

But for days thereafter her Grace knew no comfort. It was rumored that her physicians suspected poison. All her food was tasted, and certain investigations made, to no effect. Lazarus remained in her chamber, to sit by her side and play the lute and hold her hand. After a time her pain subsided into weakness, and he came again at night to give her joy.

"Lazarus, if I die. . ."

"Shh, shh, you won't die, you're getting better." But two days later, she woke up screaming again.

"Lazarus." He looked up. Thomas Berowne's hand lay on his shoulder, his eyes full of concern. "Lazarus, you can't sit here before her door all night like a dog. Her Grace is asleep, they say she's resting comfortably. Come up to my rooms." The eyes crinkled. "My dear father sent me a cask of old claret, I'd like you to help us empty it."

They had told him not to drink, Those Two. But what else had they done to him? What else had they told him? To hell with them and all their mysteries. Just once let him be—let him pretend to be a man like other men, and seek relief like others. Just once. He said, "I'll come."

Around Lord Thomas' polished table, faces were blurring. Lazarus Merridon dealt another round of cards. "Pentacles lead."

"Dammyou, Merridon," a lordling slurred, "you're as fresh as—a cucumber."

"I've been matching you cup for cup," said Lazarus mildly. "What do you bid?"

His head was quite clear. Alchohol, it seemed, had no effect on him. Winning a minor fortune from the cream of the junior nobility did only a little to console him.

"Merridon, put down your card!"

He was putting it down. It was down.

"Well, Merridon?"

What was their hurry?

"Go ahead, pick one."

"Lazarus," Thomas said sharply, "are you all right?"

Of course he was all right. He was fine.

"Lazarus?"

"I'm fine."

"No, you're pale."

"I'm perfectly all right," he said. Why were they all moving so quickly? He reached for his cup, watching the light gleaming on the ring on his hand, bright ruby claret at the bottom of the cup . . . . What was wrong with them all, were they nervous? Tom's mouth moved like hummingbird wings. "Hadn'tyou betterliedown?"

"I am fine," he said. "Look at my hand—" he held it out steadily, "and look at yours."

Earl Dumaine sloshed some claret into his cup. "Keep drinking, then."

"No," Tom said quickly. "You'd better go. You're utterly white. My man will see you to your rooms."

Lazarus lay on his bed, wide-eyed, watching the carved canopy above him. There really was nothing wrong; only it had taken a long time, walking back. When he blinked the canopy went into darkness, then reappeared. This was not drunkenness, this was something else. Those Two, they must have known this would happen. Why had they not told him? Wryly he thought, they could hardly have been afraid he'd not believe them. What did they want? What did they want of him? Fear was forming, a dark, slow tide at the back of his mind. He would give it no room for advancement. Now . . . what, so far, had he done? The masque, where the court had danced to his music— not enough . . . Gifts, favors he had received—not enough . . . He had lain with the queen of course; but she wasn't pregnant, and he doubted that she ever would be, by him: the genius of his black-robed creator could only extend so far. Why would they want him with her, if not to get her with child? Did they think if he wed her he would strive for their advancement?

The candle at his bedside had burned low. Numbly he realized that he had been thinking for over an hour. Too long. Am I dying? he thought suddenly. Am I poisoned? But none of the other card-players had been affected this way; they were just drunk. They might have drunk themselves into a stupor by now. He had heard that you could drink yourself to death. Drink could poison. But I feel fine, he thought, just slow. I cannot get drunk, I cannot be poisoned. . . .

He could not be poisoned. They had known this would happen, with wine, with any potent substance, and they had not told him. The queen was being poisoned, and he was immune. What poison had they taken together? But he had never reacted this way before. Of the poison they took together, he had never received his full share—It had come from him.

Lazarus Merridon turned slowly onto his side. It was ridiculous, a horrible notion. No one could do that, no one. It was unnatural, hideous, impossible. His candle flickered, guttered and went out. In the darkness he fell asleep.

"Master—." Lazarus jumped at the light touch on his arm. "I wouldn't have woken you, sir, but my lord sent orders the message was to be delivered at once."

It was breaking dawn. He sat up in bed and took the packet his man offered, and broke open the crimson wax that bore Andreas' seal. Several pieces of gold fell into his lap. They had been enclosed in a note from his patron:

> *My dear boy—*
>   *Your timing is abominable. Desist at once, and have the decency to wait until after the marriage, or you will make things very difficult for us. Remember: we made you. Do not fail us.*

He looked at the note without seeing it, jingling the gold his patron had sent in his other hand . . . . He had been right. Now there was nothing to do but to fail them.

The gold in his hand would see him out of the country; if he kept on the move he could live for nearly a year on it together with his winnings of last night; by then—God. His winnings. He had left them piled high on the table in Thomas Berowne's room.

Lazarus strode down the halls to Berowne's apartments. Light had just broken, only the palace servants were about. Lord Thomas' man protested that his master was not to be disturbed, but the pale gentleman brushed past him into the inner rooms.

Heavy curtains had been drawn over every possible source of light. Lazarus uncovered one window. He found the bed and pulled back its hangings. The curtain rings rattled on their rods, but the bed's occupant didn't stir.

"Thomas!"

Lord Thomas uncurled just enough to cast one eye up at his visitor. His head was rumpled and stubbled, and he stank of sour wine.

"Thomas, I need the money!"

"Who are you?" Lord Thomas managed to push out from some dimly-remembered area deep inside his throat.

"Lazarus Merridon; I need the money I won last night."

Thomas groaned, closed his eyes and listened to his head throb. "I put it somewhere. . . ."

Lazarus gripped his limp shoulder. "Please, Tom, it's important!"

"Where's the water?" Berowne croaked.

Lazarus cast about the room for it, and found an enamelled pitcher and basin. Tom took a swig from the pitcher and poured the rest over his head. He rose reluctantly and limped over to a cabinet, returned to his bedside for the key, and finally presented Lazarus with a knotted linen handkerchief heavy with gold.

"Thank you."

"Not at all," grunted Lord Thomas, sinking back as far as the edge of the bed. "Always delighted to oblige." He pressed his fingers into his eyes. "Now, would you mind telling me why you are calling for such fantastic wealth at this hour of night?"

"It's morning." Lazarus paced up and down the dusky room, nervously tossing the bundle in his hand. "I must ride home at once," he lied. "There was an urgent message from my guardian—"

"Does the queen know?"

"No." He shrugged brusquely. "She'll be all right now."

Tom's mouth opened and closed. "Will she?" he said quietly.

The fierceness of his visitor nearly knocked him over. "Yes! Yes, she will—Tom, you must believe me." The fair man clutched at Berowne's hand.

"Lazarus." Thomas looked at him. "What am I going to tell her?"

The silvery eyes darkened with tears. "I don't know," Lazarus whispered. "Tell her—I could not help it." He lifted the unicorn medal on his chest. "I have it still. I will send it before I come again. Can you tell her that?"

Lord Thomas closed his eyes. "Anything. Anything you like."

"Thank you." Berowne only barely heard the whispered words as he fell back within the bedcurtains. It was early yet. . . . He never missed the fullblown rose plucked from one of his crystal vases, that the queen found beside her on the pillow when she woke.

The Succubus

Its face is all fur,
It's kissing me
When I wake up.

It's panting,
It loves me,
How did it get in?

Shaped like a woman
Under the fur,
It has breasts.

It tries to speak
But can't,
Its fur is wet with tears.

—*John Alfred Taylor*

Ku Mei Li: A Chinese Ghost Story

M. Lucie Chin

On the western edge of the town of Soo Tzo, on the road to Nang Ching, there stood an inn which had once been a fine house. It commanded a magnificent view of the surrounding lands and was well known for the beauty and grace of its rooms. But it had not been well kept in recent years and, though still beautiful, had begun to show signs of neglect; for it was also known to be haunted.

Mun Yin Theu had never stayed at the inn, though he travelled that way often, but on this particular day a violent storm blew up and travel became slow and miserable. It was late afternoon when he came upon the inn and decided to stop for the day.

The storm was fierce and the inn quite full, but room was found for him and a bed was made up in the library. There was not time for a proper job of cleaning, and it was clear that the room had been shut up and unused, even for storage, for a very long time. But it would do.

He awoke in the middle of the night in a cold sweat. The rain still beat upon the roof and the air was hot and close and muggy. But Mun Yin Theu lay on his bed and shivered.

He found his baggage nearby and covered himself with spare garments but was still cold. He got up from his bed and searched the room but could find no drafts. It disturbed him greatly that he could not locate the source of his discomfort until he turned back to his bed and found a figure standing in his way.

It was the small, pale form of a woman, her face calm and lovely and sorrowful. Her hair was bound up in the style of a married woman of good station, and the brocade of her gown was rich and elegantly cut and stained all down the front with blood.

It was most unseemly for a woman of her position to be

found in a strange man's room, but the bloody dress was evidence of drastic deeds and Mun Yin Theu knew an opportunity to gain favor where it counted when he saw one. Once he had established that much, the means by which she had slipped into his room no longer bothered him.

"Madam," he said, bowing respectfully, "what tragedy has befallen you that you come seeking my aid?"

She did not reply but simply stood there, eyes downcast mournfully.

He addressed her again, and again she did not respond.

Thinking her stunned by the horror which had bloodied her gown, he reached out to touch the hem of her sleeve. But where his hand should have touched there was nothing, where it should have closed over a tiny, delicate wrist there was only illusion in the air.

Mun Yin Theu did not believe in ghosts, but seeing his hand pass cleanly through the apparition, he gasped and sprang back.

At last she raised her head and looked at him with eyes black as endless night, dead as the grave, and beneath her chin at the right side of her throat was a vicious, bloody slash of a wound. He had just time enough to see the wound, the streaming blood blackening the high collar of her gown, to realize that she held a bloody knife in her own right hand; just time enough to realize what she was . . . when the ghost vanished.

He sat on the edge of his bed, staring into the liquid night beyond the windows. The chill had vanished in the same instant as the ghostly lady, and the darkness wrapped itself about him like a great wet coat. Presently he lay down again and once more went to sleep.

A short time later he awoke again, and once more it was cold. Not as frigid as before. This time it was more like a cool breeze. It seemed to have direction and attracted his attention across the room toward the door.

She stood as before, head bowed, eyes downcast politely. Pale and fragile, she seemed to be made of the finest, sheerest silk and to glow with a soft, cool light, very faintly, just enough to separate her definitely from the shadows of the night.

For an instant she seemed to shimmer and twinkle as he sat up on his bed and took notice, and then she began to grow; becoming thinner and more pale til she seemed to fill the entire end of the room and finally, vanished completely, like smoke in the air. But this time the chill did not go away.

He sat in the dark once more waiting, and once again he felt the coolness stir and looked up to find her standing quite close. He could still see through her vaguely. It was unnerving, for even on this translucent apparition, the blood looked profoundly real.

"Lady," he said. "What do you wish of me?"

"Traveler," the ghost said in a small voice that sounded hollow and wavered slightly like an echo.

"Yes, madam, I am a traveler. I am a merchant and . . ."

"You are a man of Jung Tsee," she interrupted, naming his province.

"Yes," he said, "I am." He was amazed, but the workings of dreams can be quite strange, and surely this was a dream.

"You do not fear ghosts?" she said, raising her head. The gash in her throat was still there, but the blood had seemingly ceased to flow.

"I have never encountered a ghost before," Mun Yin Theu said. "I do not see that there is anything you could do to me that I should fear."

"You are a man of clear conscience, then," she said.

"Yes, I believe myself so."

"Traveler," she said again, and the voice seemed even thinner than before, "I have waited long for you. I had begun to believe there was none in the province of Jung Tsee with your courage and intelligence."

"You flatter me, lady," he said.

"Perhaps," she said, "but it is none-the-less true that I have waited many long and joyless years for one such as you. I am in need of your good will and assistance."

Mun Yin Theu was flattered beyond measure that his good will should be desired by one of such high rank, even if she *was* dead. But he had no idea of what help a ghost might need.

"My name in life was Ku Mei Li," the ghost said. "And this was once my house—after my husband died. But it was lost to greed and jealousy, as was my own life. I would avenge these wrongs to my ancestors and my husband's memory, and for this reason I beg your aid."

He sat upon his bed, hands on his knees and listened as the ghost told her story. The ghost did not sit but seemed to hover a short distance above the floor. It had the uncanny effect of seeming to be the most relaxed posture she could assume.

There was once a lady of wealthy family who was left a fine house and property by her late husband whom she had loved dearly. She was a virtuous woman, much respected by the community for her fidelity to her husband even in death, for she had taken a vow never to remarry.

The generosity of the bequest, however, attracted the envy of her brothers-in-law and their wives, and they began to spread rumors about her. Finally they openly accused her of having committed adultery with a man who had left the province and had her brought before the magistrate.

This magistrate was a powerful man and as corrupt an official as the district had seen in a long time. He took bribes from the family and the promise of more when the property was turned over to them, and they could lay their hands on the silks, spices, jewels and fine books in the estate.

The lady was presented before the magistrate and condemned for her shameful behavior; for betraying her vow of chastity, defiling her husband's memory and disgracing her ancestors. But because she was young and beautiful and desirable, and her estate was rich and the magistrate greedy, he offered to restore her good name and honor and condemn the evil in-laws if she would give herself to him as concubine.

She would gladly have given whatever material wealth he desired, but she had loved her husband genuinely and, no matter what might have been said, had not broken her vow and would not do so ever. The thought that, in spite of all she might do or say, this evil and lecherous man might possess the power to have his way with her in the end terrified her utterly, and that night, in her husband's beloved library, she had taken a knife and killed herself.

When the magistrate heard of this he flew into a rage. And when the family discovered that stores of wines and spices had been ruined and many of the rare silks and porcelains destroyed before she killed herself, the in-laws were afraid. But when they could not find so much as a trace of the family jewels, the magistrate, in a fit of vengeance, stripped the house of its remaining fine trappings and took the horses and livestock from the yard. He took for himself whatever he could carry and claimed large portions of ricelands in the name of the Emperor as income for the local government, proclaiming it to be just punishment for the family's heinous crime of driving their virtuous sister-in-law to kill herself.

The family was destitute, having only a little land and the house. Eventually they were reduced to innkeeping to provide an income and did fairly well til the rumors of the haunt in the old library began to spread. They locked the room up tight and continued to make a modest living over the years, though the presence of a ghost in the house kept them in reduced circumstances and assured that they would never again be wealthy.

"How may I assist you, lady?" Mun Yin Theu said humbly.

She told him the name of the magistrate, and he understood at once. He recognized the name of the man who had been governor of his own province for twenty years and had been no less corrupt in Jung Tsee than he had likely been anywhere else.

"I must journey to Jung Tsee if I am to have my peace at

last," she said. "I cannot make the journey alone for I do not know the way, and there are many obstacles in the material world which the dead cannot overcome.

"You journey now to Nang Ching," she said, once again correctly naming the place, "where you will stay for two months to do business. But upon your journey homeward, use this road again. When you pass this house, call my name aloud three times, and I will follow, though you will not see me. Call my name again when boarding or leaving a boat or passing over or under a bridge or through a gate. When you reach Jung Tsee I will appear to you again and tell you what to do.

"If you will agree to this I will reward you and make you a rich man, for I know the hiding place of the jewels my husband left."

It was an offer only a fool would refuse, and Mun Yin Theu, being no such fool, agreed immediately. After all, the ghost had no further need of such wealth. But before the ghost could depart, he asked one more thing as payment for his services.

"Were you alive, lady, I am sure you would refuse my request and correctly so, but it is partly for that reason that I ask it. Your constancy and virtue have won my admiration as well as your beauty, and since your chastity and honor are no longer at risk, I would bid you stay with me and be the lady of this house once more; forget that this is my bedroom for the night and treat me as you would a guest in your home. For I am too little used to the company of so lovely a lady and am loath to see it vanish into the night."

Ku Mei Li inclined her head modestly and folded her delicate hands. She stayed and sang poetry, some of it her husband's own, and told tales of the many people she had seen in her home in the years since it had become an inn, and sometime before dawn Mun Yin Theu fell asleep and did not see the lady vanish into the summer air.

When he awoke the next morning, the sun was already high in a cloudless sky and the puddles were drying up. In spite of how real it had all seemed during the night, in the daylight he found himself as much a disbeliever as ever.

But the vision of her was still strong and clear, and he congratulated himself on the vividness and beauty of his dream.

He gathered his baggage, but as he approached the door the tiles on the floor clattered loosely underfoot. He did not recall this being the case the night before when he had entered and left the room several times. Yet when he bent to examine them, he found that, indeed, the grouting had been scraped away and swept into a loose pile in the corner. He gave in to his curiosity then and lifted the tiles from the floor. Beneath a loose piece of sub-flooring was a small cavity into which had been set a small chest and several fat pouches. There he found gold and jade and opals and silver enough to supply dowries to half a dozen daughters, should he ever be burdened with so many. Or wealth enough to attract a wife with a sizeable dowry of her own. Being a man without land, this was far more wealth than he had ever dreamed he might possess and could, perhaps, provide the means to *acquire* a modest tract of land, if such should be found for sale in a civilized province.

All through the day he dreamed and planned of the many and various uses to which his new wealth might be put.

Business was good in Nang Ching and Mun Yin Theu prospered. He took a small house with two servants for his stay instead of the local inn as he had done in the past, and purchased new clothes. His obvious rise in circumstances did not go unnoticed by the men with whom he had done business over the years, and he was accorded a degree of respect and credibility which, when properly applied, enabled him to gain better prices and more advantageous bargaining positions.

It was a seductive experience, and as time went on he began to live higher and higher until he was once again due to return home. He bought himself a fine riding horse and two oxcarts and several more pack animals and loaded them with the goods acquired through business and all his new possessions and made ready to depart for Jung Tsee.

This also did not go unnoticed, and on the second day of his journey, the men he had hired to help transport his goods and household turned on him in the night and would have killed him had he not made off into the darkness on his new horse, leaving the others behind on foot with only the oxen and carts. He considered returning to the campsite and trying to drive them away, or following and trying to pick them off one at a time, but there were many of them, and he was weaponless and legal recourse was far too expensive now that all his possessions were gone. But he had his fine horse and the clothes on his back and even a few strings of cash in his pocket. If he were judicious about it, this would get him home where he could try to salvage some portion of his business and make a decent living again.

About noon the next day he came upon the inn where he had found the treasure which had caused him so much hard luck. It had been three months by the moon, and he had not thought much about the ghost since that night, though he often woke in the morning from a curious and poorly remembered dream with a strange sad longing for a proper wife and home and family.

At the inn he stopped to rest and water his horse and purchase a small meal, and afterward he wandered casually about the garden and through the cool house til he found the door to the library once more, but it was shut up tight and sealed.

He chided himself for behaving so foolishly, for it had been as much an awful dream as a beautiful one.

He paid for his meal and mounted his horse, but on an impulse he stopped at the front of the house and called out the name of Ku Mei Li. Much as he had expected, nothing happened, but he could not resist the urge and called again, louder, and then again louder still.

At the sound of his cry the door to the house was flung open and the innkeeper and his wife and son ran out, cursing and yelling.

"Be gone you foul and wicked wretch! You who calls the name of the dead—you curse us. You would ruin our house! Be gone!"

The innkeeper spat at him, and the wife and son and two servants in the side yard began to pick up stones and hurl them at him. They struck Mun Yin Theu on the legs and back and his horse on the flanks, and the animal bolted and fled with no urging from its rider.

"Be gone," they called after him. "You will not summon the dead to this place!"

The horse raced on and Mun Yin Theu clung to it with no thought to control its flight.

It was not possible. How could the name he had dreamed have been real? But the gems he had dreamed had been real. Why then should he not have been able to dream a real name? He still did not believe in ghosts. Nothing had happened at the inn when he called the name beyond the stoning, and there was nothing supernatural about that.

Yet when he went to sleep that night by a little fire at the side of the road, the night turned strangely cold from time to time, and he slept badly and dreamed a great deal.

With several days' journey still ahead and only the prospect of a poor and miserable homecoming before him, Mun Yin Theu set out the next day, weary in body as well as soul.

He slept in the open and took his meals at the market stalls of small villages that he passed to conserve his money and preserve some small illusion of the dignity and station his mount and attire still implied. To lodge at an inn and dine with the guests would have left him penniless at once, and to lodge with the peasants would have made him look a fool. So he did neither. No one noticed a traveler at the roadside, and his meals appeared to be the casual snacking of a shopper in the markets.

He passed several days in this manner and at last came to the river which marked the mid-point of his journey. He did not notice the two men on the bridge as he approached, but as the road curved out from behind a catalpa grove, he saw them standing at the foot of the bridge as though in conversation. They wore the shoddy dress of peasants, and one held a round straw hat in his hand. As he drew closer the conversation seemed to have grown into an argument, and they spoke to each other in quarrelsome tones with agitated gestures and paid no attention to his approach.

Standing together as they were in the middle of the road, they blocked access to the bridge, and when he was near enough, Mun Yin Theu called out to them, asking that they stand aside so he could pass.

They did not, however, and simply continued to argue. Mun Yin Theu looked for another way to cross the river, but it was wide and flowed swiftly. At the bank a boat was tied to the bridge. Not a large boat, but for all he could tell the object over which they quarreled.

He called out again, asking them to clear the path. This time they turned toward him but did not move out of the way.

"Stranger," one of them said to him. "Come, you must settle a dispute. My brother and I quarrel and cannot find an end to it."

Mun Yin Theu stopped before them, but something made him wary, and he did not dismount.

"Over what do you quarrel, here in the middle of this road in the middle of nowhere?" he asked, trying to maintain an aloofness of voice and posture to belie the fact that his fine clothes were becoming shabby from days and nights of constant wear and that his weariness was bone deep.

"It is here in this boat," the man said. "Come down and decide for us."

Instead, Mun Yin Theu stood in his stirrups, but he still had a poor vantage point and could make nothing out.

"I see nothing to quarrel over," he said.

There was a whisper of sound to his right, and as he turned that way, the round hat of the peasant came spinning through the air toward his head. It struck him just below the right ear as his horse shied and danced, and he lost his balance and fell sprawling to the ground, the wind knocked out of him. He struggled to get up, but one man wrestled him to the ground again while the other, the thrower of the hat, caught the horse.

The hand that had held the hat now possessed a knife and Mun Yin Theu knew the brigands meant to kill him if they could. He would struggle, but his breath was gone and so was most of his strength.

"Come, brother, quickly," said the man holding him. "Cut his throat. I would have his cash and fine coat as well as the horse."

But the horse was hard to control and suddenly spooked again, bolting away from the bridge, dragging its would-be thief several paces before he could stop it again. The man swore at the animal which had suddenly become utterly terrified. Then from behind him came a startled cry, but before he could turn and look, his arm was firmly in his brother's clutching grip. The man's face was ashen, and he babbled and pointed, and when his brother turned to look, he saw a terrible apparition.

Standing over Mun Yin Theu at the foot of the bridge, half the height of a tall tree and wispy thin as cloud, was the form of a woman; the blood on her knife and dress as vivid and real to the eye as her body was insubstantial. But where the head should have been there was only a bubbling, pulsing fountain of blood which flowed from her neck down over her shoulders and the front of her gown. The head, nestled snugly in the crook of her left arm, smiled at them, and laughed with a hollow whistling sound.

Then the apparition took its head firmly in both hands and placed it slightly askew, as though for lack of a mirror, upon its shoulders. The blood ceased to flow, but as it did so the thing laughed again and, wielding the knife slowly, stepped over the prone form of Mun Yin Theu and advanced upon the two men.

Screaming in terror, the brigands tumbled down the bank to their boat, using the knife to cut the rope. They huddled heads down in the bottom of the craft as the current took it swiftly out of sight around a bend.

A moment later the ghost of Ku Mei Li vanished also.

Mun Yin Theu could no longer believe he dreamed. He spent much of the afternoon tracking down the horse which had run off when the two men fled, and the bruises and sore muscles kept him firmly aware of reality with every step.

He had witnessed, open-eyed, all that had happened at the bridge. He knew that the knife and blood were but illusions, that the ghost could alter her appearance as she chose and that the weapon was as insubstantial as its bearer. He still could not understand what physical harm a ghost could inflict upon the corporeal world, but fear itself is a potent weapon. Because the highwaymen believed in the power of the ghost to do harm, the ghost possessed that power. They earned their own terror.

He found it strange and ironic that death had been the instrument to preserve his own life, and when he came upon the bridge again shortly before dusk, without the slightest hesitation he called the name of Ku Mei Li three times in a strong, clear voice and crossed the bridge.

"You could have been rid of me," the ghost said to him in his dream that night. "If you had crossed without calling me I could not have followed. I have been summoned away from my haunting place and would have been doomed to wander here in this strange land, lost, unavenged and without a path to guide me to the Land of the Dead.

"I have no kin in this place to light candles or burn offerings to my memory. None to pray for the peace of my soul. There is no rest for me til my beloved husband's shame is relieved."

"Do not despair, lady, I will not abandon you," he promised. Or at least he thought did. He seemed to remember that as part of the dream the next morning.

She came again the following night and spoke to him again in his sleep; giving him her thanks, telling of her husband and how she had loved him and he her, though she had been barren; and how he had, even as he lay dying, refused to find fault with her for the passing of his line to his younger brothers. She longed for that peace of mind in death which he had so abundantly provided in life. She missed him sorely and had hoped to find him again in the Land of the Dead. But duty burdened her soul and kept her from him.

"I know," he said aloud to his horse as he made ready to leave camp on his last day's ride home, "that I shall never find in this life as brave and constant a wife as Ku Mei Li. And I know that I shall always be a poor man for that. Even all the wealth she once gave me, the very silver with which I purchased you, my fine creature, could never gain me such a wife, for such qualities cannot be purchased; they are found in unexpected places and must be won."

A cool breeze drifted through the bamboo grove, and the horse danced and snorted. Mun Yin Theu smiled and mounted the horse, the last of his riches, and rode home.

That night, in his own house, upon his own bed, the ghost did not come to him in his sleep. Nor any other night for the next month. He was sorry and felt the absence keenly, but felt at the same time a sense of peace he had never known before. As he set about assessing the damage the past months had done to his financial circumstances, in fact he found he had become quite imperturbable. He was not destitute, but much time and hard work would be required to achieve once again a good living. Yet he did not feel the utter despair or anger he knew he would have felt even a few months ago. Instead, he sold what he had to: his small house, the fine horse; and set about his business once again.

At the end of a month, the magistrate Ahn Tring Yee returned from a visit to the mountains where he kept a home, and much to the surprise of Mun Yin Theu, the ghost appeared again one night. She stood in the road at the back of his shop, just beyond the gate. She shimmered into sight as he sat beside his small cooking fire at dusk in the small open shop yard. She was thin and pale, and he could not see her well but the blood on her gown was as awful as he remembered it.

"Lady Ku," he said. "I would offer my humble hospitality if you could but partake. The time has been long, and I did not expect to see you again. What is it you wish of me?"

"It is time," she said. "Ahn Tring Yee has returned to the city, and I have waited. Tomorrow night there is a banquet at his hall. Musicians and jugglers and acrobats have been summoned, and there will be much merriment and confusion. I would humbly beg one more favor of you, kind sir, but I have no more wealth to grant you in return."

"It is enough, lady. It was fate and my own foolishness which cost me what you gave in good faith, not knowing that I would ever return to guide you.

"Tell me what you wish, for this business is not yet done for me, either. And then, perhaps . . ." He hesitated. He believed in his heart all that he had said, yet he had to ask this one more thing. "Stay with me this evening, and sing and tell stories as you did that one night before."

"Yes," she said. "I will do this if you bid me enter."

Suddenly Mun Yin Theu understood why the ghost had been so totally absent from his life for the past month. When he had entered his home, and later, when he moved into the little shop, he had not called her. She could not pass his gate nor could she pass his door. He sat in his yard and softly called her name three times. He thought he saw the fleeting flicker of a smile on the lovely face, and the form grew brighter and hovered near the fire and stayed.

On the evening of the banquet Mun Yin Theu disguised himself as a juggler and entered the house of Ahn Tring Yee in the company of actors and musicians and storytellers and dancers. It was easy and yet it was not. He had no trouble concealing himself among the entertainers and escaping notice. But when he reached the gate he was surrounded by a mob of people. He softly called the name of Ku Mei Li three times as he was crowded forward. If he had balked he would have been noticed. As it was, the gateman asked whom it was he sought, and he lied saying it was his sister who carried his juggler's tools. He did not dare call again and hurried on through the gate.

Once inside he discarded his juggler's gear lest he be asked to perform and made himself out to be a lackey, hanging around the fringes of the performers, but he could not get near the house itself or into it. He feared that at last, at the moment which had counted most, he had failed her.

As twilight fell, lamps were lit and two large pots of fire stood flanking the dais upon which Ahn Tring Yee sat with his two honored guests. He presented them with lavish foods and elaborate entertainments, none of which drew the least bit of Mun Yin Theu's attention. He searched the faces of he crowd repeatedly but could not find her. She was most likely invisible, he was sure, but that only left him with no recourse but to wonder, so he indulged his human frailty and searched.

As the meal ended and the acrobats were replaced by dancers, he thought he caught a bit of a glimmer, a shimmering of light at the edge of his vision. But the wavering light from the fires played tricks on his eyes. He turned to see the dancing girls taking their positions before the dais, fans open, heads bowed; and among them there was one who was slim and pale and more beautiful to his eye than all the rest.

She was also one too many, though at first he did not notice this. But as the dance progressed, she moved outside the symmetry of its patterns for she had placed herself squarely in front of the ensemble. No one else seemed to notice the departure from form, either, and the musicians plied their trades and the girls danced.

The magistrate was more inclined toward this type of entertainment than most of what had gone before, and his attention was captured immediately. He eyed the young women before him with satisfaction, but his gaze rested longest and most often on the one in front. Though Ku Mei Li danced well enough and seemed to know the common steps, her dance was a sensuous thing, fitting the music but only vaguely related to the movements of the other dancers. It was clearly meant to entice, and this it did although no one seemed amazed or attracted but Mun Yin Theu and Ahn Tring Yee.

The magistrate smiled and chuckled and nodded to his neighbors, but they only looked at him strangely behind his back.

Mun Yin Theu edged around the dais for a better view and perhaps a word caught on the breeze.

"There is something . . ." the magistrate said, "something about that one which brings back memories of youth."

The man on his left chuckled. "Wine," he said, "and a stirring of the blood always bring back such memories."

"They may be old and dim for you," Ahn Tring Yee said, "but I need not think back so far for memories of *that* kind. I may be old but I am still fit for those kinds of sport.

"No, it is *someone* she reminds me of."

"Which?" said the man on his left.

"The one in front," the magistrate said. "Lovely child. Like a flower waiting to be plucked. Would one of you fancy her for the night?"

"Perhaps," said the guest on his right. "They are all lovely, but I do not know which one you think so special. They change places so quickly my old eye does not know which to follow."

"The one in the front, of course," Ahn Tring Yee said pointing, a bit annoyed. "She stands alone before the rest and shamelessly flirts with her fan. See? See there? She does not dance so well, but that is a small price to pay for all the rest. I suspect she dances well enough, indeed, for her master in a dark room."

The two guests exchanged glances, and while Ahn Tring Yee was absorbed in his watching, the one on the right reached over and took his wine cup, sipping from it slightly. He put it back, shook his head and looked baffled.

"I wish I could remember," Ahn Tring Yee muttered,

". . . who . . ."

Ku Mei Li's fan fluttered and flashed. Her body undulated under the slim dance costume. As she stepped and turned and bent to the music, she moved closer to the magistrate's dais. Her fan hovered before her face but above the rim her eyes brazenly sought those of the magistrate, and when they found him, he saw in them the endless depths of blackness like a starless night.

He shivered and tried to look away but each time he glanced back she captured his gaze again.

"Who," he muttered, disturbed. "Why should I feel I know you, child? Are you my own?"

"No," came the answer, and he was shocked to hear it. She could not have heard him muttering to himself at such a distance, above the music. Startled, he sat back in his chair as she stepped closer and lowered her gaze, bowing her head above the open fan. She had stopped dancing, and Mun Yin Theu realized that no one saw her but the magistrate Ahn Tring Yee and himself. The two men on the dais and most of the other guests watched Ahn Tring Yee's abrupt, exaggerated movements carefully, but he did not seem to notice that their attention was on him rather than this brash and shameless young woman.

"Who are you?" he demanded. "I forbid you to come closer. How dare you behave so?"

She began to sway gently before him.

"My name is Ku Mei Li," she said. "Perhaps you remember me, perhaps not . . ."

"No!" he said. "I do not."

"I will help you recall," she said, eyes still downcast demurely. "I was a young widow in the town of Soo Tzo."

"Soo Tzo!" he blustered. "Soo Tzo was twenty years ago. You are but a child, barely that old now."

The two guests who flanked him had grown alarmed at his ravings and summoned the servants, but Ahn Tring Yee was not aware of them.

"Yes," the dancer said behind her fan, "you are correct. Think, Ahn Tring Yee. Think of the family of Ku, and you will remember."

At that she snapped the fan shut and instantly it became a dagger. Ahn Tring Yee lurched back in his chair, pointing, and his two guests jumped from their seats and moved away from him. The dancing and music stopped but Ku Mei Li continued to sway, coming closer. Her eyes sought his and as they did so she raised her head. Suddenly upon the smooth, white throat a great wound appeared like a red blossom and the knife was bloody and the blood pulsed from the slash in her neck and flowed down her shoulder and arm and the front of her gown.

"No!" he screamed, trying to push himself deeper into the chair. "It cannot be!"

"What, Governor?" the guest on the left asked, summoning the courage to venture close enough to touch the man's arm. "What cannot be?"

"You are dead!" Ahn Tring Yee protested, ignoring him.

"I?" the man said, taken aback. To speak of a man's death while he was still alive and well was to wish a curse upon him, and the guest fled the dais again, this time in anger.

"Yes," Ku Mei Li said. Her voice made a gurgling sound now as she spoke. "I am dead, and well you should recall."

The ghost began to turn and dance more freely now and as she stooped and spun about, blood flew in all directions, reddening the tiles of the courtyard and spattering the garments of Ahn Tring Yee who leapt from his seat, brushing at his clothing, and took refuge behind his chair. Two servants ran up and tried to calm him, but he would not be calmed. They took him gently by the arms but he pushed them away with cries and curses and never took his eyes from the apparition.

"Once you desired me, Ahn Tring Yee. You said if I gave my body to you, you would restore the honor of my husband's good name. I have waited long to find you, magistrate, and as I hear you speak, you would still have this body which is no longer whole in flesh and bone. I give it to you now. Would that please you?"

Her dance returned to a swaying rhythm. The dagger vanished, and she took her head in both hands and lifted it from her shoulders, holding it toward the magistrate at arm's length.

"Here, come, I offer you these lips to kiss."

Ahn Tring Yee was transfixed. His hands gripped the back of the chair, and he stared straight ahead, seemingly at nothing. Mun Yin Theu was also transfixed. The horror and fascination of what he knew no human eyes could see but his own and those of the magistrate compelled him and drew him closer to the scene.

The head floated free of the hands and hovered in the air smiling as the body continued to dance and turn and blood flooded the tiles.

"These arms to hold you, these hands to caress you . . ." she crooned, and the sleeves fell limp at the sockets of her shoulders, the arms drifted free and came at the magistrate, hands stroking air, fingers curling and beckoning.

The guests and servants stood about, coaxing and calming, trying to persuade the suddenly crazed man into the quiet refuge of his home and the safety of an opiated sleep.

When the arms departed their body and reached for him, Ahn Tring Yee screamed and lurched from the dais. Tripping in his haste, he fell almost at the feet of Mun Yin Theu. All now convinced that the magistrate has lost his mind, two large servants, at the direction of the senior of Ahn Tring Yee's guests, took him by the arms and guided him with gentle force toward the entrance of his house, where he could be confined to his room until someone in authority could decide what to do.

"Magistrate!" the floating head of Ku Mei Li called after him. "I have offered you but a small part of myself. The rest would give you pleasure, too." And the headless, armless body, sleeves flapping, blood flying, ran across the yard toward Ahn Tring Yee who screamed again and struggled in the grip of his servants as they dragged him toward the doorway.

Immediately, Mun Yin Theu saw what he must do to

discharge his duty to the ghost of Ku Mei Li.

"Magistrate!" he called. "What do you see that frightens you so?"

"Her!" Ahn Tring Yee yelled, struggling to point. "The woman! Stop her!"

"What woman? Who is she?"

"Ku Mei Li!" he yelled. "Ku Mei Li!"

As he spoke the words the body vanished, blood and all. The arms disappeared and the head laughed once, shimmered, and was gone.

"What?" Mun Yin Theu called out from the fringes of the crowd. "What was her name?"

"Ku Mei Li." The magistrate moaned the name a third and final time as the servants carried him through the doorway and closed it firmly behind them.

The screaming stopped shortly before dawn. The servants, thinking he had fainted or exhausted himself into sleep, entered and found he had hanged himself with a silk sash from a beam.

Mun Yin Theu went about his business quietly and patiently and built a good living for himself, but he never married. From time to time in the first couple of years after the death of Ahn Tring Yee, he would stop and quietly speak aloud the name of Ku Mei Li three times before crossing bridges or passing through gateways or doors, but she never answered him. The coolness of breezes which touched him was not the same as the chill touch of the presence of the dead, and, though he still dreamed of her often, she was not present in the dreams as she had once been.

In his old age he passed once more a night at the inn in Soo Tzo and heard the owner tell of the day in his childhood memory when his father and grandfather had been visited by a magician who had, in repayment for their great kindness and hospitality, exorcised the ghost of a long dead relative from the house. Calling her by name, he had taken her ghost as his concubine and ridden off into the sky on a dragon. The haunt dispelled, the family had lived well and prospered ever since.

Mun Yin Theu had laughed at the end of the tale and gotten up and retired to the bed he had insisted they make for him in the library. And that night, for the first time in years, the old man dreamed of Ku Mei Li and knew she had found the way to her beloved husband and dwelt in contentment in the Land of the Dead.

Tatuana's Tale

Miguel Angèl Asturias

Translated by Patricia Emigh and Frank MacShane

Father Almond Tree, with his pale pink beard, was one of the priests who were so richly dressed that the white men touched them to see if they were made of gold. He knew the secret of medicinal plants, the language of the gods that spoke through translucent obsidian, and he could read the hieroglyphics of the stars.

One day he appeared in the forest, without being planted, as though brought there by spirits. He was so tall he prodded the clouds, he measured the years by the moons he saw, and was already old when he came from the Garden of Tulan.

On the full moon of Owl-Fish (one of the twenty months of the four-hundred-day year), Father Almond Tree divided his soul among the four roads. These led to the four quarters of the sky: the black quarter, the Sorcerer Night; the green quarter, Spring Storm; the red quarter, Tropical Ecstasy; the white quarter, Promise of New Lands.

"O Road! Little Road!" said a dove to White Road, but White Road did not listen. The dove wanted Father Almond Tree's soul so that it would cure its dreams. Doves and children both suffer from dreams.

"O Road! Little Road!" said a heart to Red Road, but Red Road did not listen. The heart wanted to distract Red Road so it would forget Father Almond Tree's soul. Hearts, like thieves, don't return what others leave behind.

"O Road! Little Road!" said a vine trellis to Green Road, but Green Road did not listen. It wanted the Father's soul to get back some of the leaves and shade it had squandered.

How many moons have the roads been traveling?

The fastest, Black Road, whom no one spoke to along the way, entered the city, crossed the plaza and went to the merchants' quarter, where it gave Father Almond Tree's soul to the Merchant of Priceless Jewels in exchange for a little rest.

It was the hour of white cats. They prowled back and forth through the streets. Wonder of rosebushes! The clouds looked like laundry strung across the sky.

When Father Almond Tree found out what Black Road had done, he once again took on human form, shedding his tree-like shape in a small stream that appeared like an almond blossom beneath the crimson moon. Then he left for the city.

He reached the valley after a day's travel, just at evening time when the flocks are driven home. The shepherds were dumfounded by this man in a green cloak and pale pink beard. They thought he was an apparition and answered his questions in monosyllables.

Once in the city, he made his way to the western part of town. Men and women were standing around the public fountains. The water made a kissing sound as it filled their pitchers. Following the shadows to the merchants' quarter, he found that part of his soul Black Road had sold. The Merchant of Priceless Jewels kept it in a crystal box with gold locks. He went up to the Merchant, who was smoking in a corner, and offered him two thousand pounds of pearls for the piece of soul.

The Merchant smiled at the Father's absurd suggestion. Two thousand pounds of pearls? No, his jewels were priceless.

Father Almond Tree increased his offer. He would give him emeralds, big as kernels of corn, fifty acres of them, enough to make a lake.

The Merchant smiled again. A lake of emeralds? No, his jewels were priceless.

He would give him amulets, deer's eyes that bring rain, feathers to keep storms away, marijuana to mix with his tobacco.

The Merchant refused.

He would give him enough precious stones to build a fairy-tale palace in the middle of the emerald lake!

The Merchant still refused. His jewels were priceless—

why go on talking about it? Besides, he planned to exchange this piece of soul for the most beautiful slave in the slave market.

It was useless for Father Almond Tree to keep on making offers and show how much he wanted to get his soul back. Merchants have no hearts.

A thread of tobacco smoke separated reality from dream, black cats from white cats, the Merchant from his strange customer. As he left, Father Almond Tree banged his sandals against the doorway to rid himself of the cursed dust of the house.

After a year of four hundred days, the Merchant was returning across the mountains with the slave he had bought with Father Almond Tree's soul. He was accompanied by a flower bird who turned honey into hyacinths, and by a retinue of thirty servants on horseback.

The slave was naked. Her long black hair, wrapped in a single braid like a snake, fell across her breasts and down to her legs. The Merchant was dressed in gold and his shoulders were covered with a cape woven from goat hair. His thirty servants on horseback stretched out behind like figures in a dream.

"You've no idea," said the Merchant to the slave, reining in his horse alongside hers, "what your life will be like in the city! Your house will be a palace, and all my servants will be at your call, including me, if you like." His face was half lit by the sun. "There," he continued, "everything will be yours. Do you know I refused a lake of emeralds for the piece of soul I exchanged for you? We'll lie all day in a hammock and have nothing to do but listen to a wise old woman tell stories. She knows my fate and says that it rests in a gigantic hand. She'll tell your fortune as well, if you ask her."

The slave turned to look at the countryside. It was a landscape of muted blues, growing dimmer in the distance. The trees on either side formed so fanciful a design it might have appeared on a woman's shawl. The sky was calm, and the birds seemed to be flying asleep, winglessly. In the granite silence, the panting of the horses as they went uphill sounded human.

Suddenly, huge solitary raindrops began to spatter the road. On the slopes below, shepherds shouted as they gathered their frightened flocks. The horses stepped up their pace to find shelter, but there wasn't enough time. The wind rose, lashing the clouds and ripping through the forest until it reached the valley, which vanished from sight under blankets of mist, while the first lightning bolts lit up the countryside like the flashes of a mad photographer.

As the horses stampeded, fleeing in fear, reins broken, legs flying, manes tangled in the wind and ears pressed back, the Merchant's horse stumbled and threw the man to the foot of a tree which at that instant, split by lightning, wrapped its roots about him like a hand snatching up a stone and hurled him into the ravine.

Meanwhile Father Almond Tree, who had remained in the city, wandered the streets like a madman, frightening children, going through garbage, talking to donkeys, oxen and stray dogs, which, like men, are all sad-eyed animals.

"How many moons have the roads been traveling?" he asked from door to door, but the people were dumfounded by this man in a green cloak and pale pink beard, and they slammed them shut without answering as though they'd seen a specter.

At length Father Almond Tree stopped at the door of the Merchant of Priceless Jewels and spoke to the slave, who alone had survived the storm.

"How many moons have the roads been traveling?"

The answer which began to form froze on her lips. Father Almond Tree was silent. It was the full moon of Owl-Fish. In silence their eyes caressed each other's faces like two lovers who have met after a long separation.

They were interrupted by raucous shouts. They were arrested in the name of God and the King, he as a warlock and she as his accomplice. Surrounded by crosses and swords, they were taken to prison, Father Almond Tree with his pale pink beard and green cloak, the slave displaying flesh so firm it seemed to be made of gold.

Seven months later, they were condemned to be

burned alive in the Plaza Mayor. On the eve of the execution, Father Almond Tree tattooed a little boat on the slave's arm with his fingernail.

"Tatuana, by means of this tattoo," he said, "you will be able to flee whenever you are in danger. I want you to be as free as my spirit. Trace this little boat on a wall, on the ground, in the air, wherever you wish. Then close your eyes, climb aboard and go . . .

"Go, my spirit is stronger than a clay idol.

"My spirit is sweeter than the honey gathered by bees sipping from the honeysuckle.

"As my spirit, you'll become invisible."

At once, Tatuana did what Father Almond Tree said: she drew a little boat, closed her eyes, and , as she got in, the boat began to move. So she escaped from prison and death.

On the following morning, day of the execution, the guards found in the cell only a withered tree, whose few almond blossoms still retained their pale pink color.

Overheard on a Saltmarsh

Nymph, nymph, what are your beads?
Green glass, goblin. Why do you stare at them?
Give them me.
          No.
Give them me. *Give them me.*
                 No.

Then I will howl all night in the reeds,
Lie in the mud and howl for them.

Goblin, why do you love them so?

They are better than stars or water,
Better than voices of winds that sing,
Better than any man's fair daughter,
Your green glass beads on a silver ring.

Hush I stole them out of the moon.

Give me your beads, I desire them.
             No.

I will howl in a deep lagoon
For your green glass beads, I love them so.
Give them me. Give them.
          No.

—Harold Monro

Tales of Houdini

Rudy Rucker

Houdini is broke. The vaudeville circuit is dead, ditto big-city stage. Mel Rabstein from Pathé News phones him up looking for a feature.

"Two G advance plus three points gross after turn-around."

"You're on."

The idea is to get a priest, a rabbi and a judge to be on camera with Houdini in all the big scenes. It'll be feature-length and play in the Loew's chain. All Houdini knows for sure is that there'll be escapes, bad ones, with no warnings.

It starts at four in the morning, July 8, 1948. They bust into Houdini's home in Levittown. He lives there with his crippled Mom. Opening shot of priest and rabbi kicking the door down. Close on their thick-soled black shoes. Available light. The footage is grainy, jerky, can't-help-it cinema-verité. It's all true.

The judge has a little bucket of melted wax, and they seal up Houdini's eyes and ears and nose-holes. The dark mysterioso face is covered over and over before he fully awakes, relaxing into the events, leaving dreams of pursuit. Houdini is ready. They wrap him up in Ace bandages and surgical tape, a mummy, a White Owl cigar.

Eddie Machotka, the Pathé cameraman, time-lapses the drive out to the airstrip. He shoots a frame every ten seconds so the half-hour drive only takes two minutes on screen. Dark, the wrong angles, but still convincing. There's *no cuts*. In the back of the Packard, on the laps of the priest, judge and rabbi, lies Houdini, a white loaf crusty with tape, twitching in condensed time.

The car pulls right onto the airstrip, next to a B-29 bomber. Eddie hops out and films the three holy witnesses unloading Houdini. Pan over the plane. "The Dirty Lady," is lettered up near the nose.

The Dirty Lady! And it's not crop-dusters or reservists flying it, daddyo, it's Johnny Gallio and his Flying A-Holes! Forget it! Johnny G., the most decorated WWII Pacific combat ace, flying, with Slick Tires Jones navigating, and no less a man than Moanin' Max Moscowitz in back.

Johnny G. jumps down out of the cockpit, not too fast, not too slow, just cool flight-jacket Johnny. Moanin' Max and Slick Tires lean out the bomb-bay hatch, grinning and ready to roll.

The judge pulls out a turnip pocket-watch. The camera zooms in and out, 4:50 AM, the sky is getting light.

Houdini? He doesn't know they're handing him into the bomb-bay of The Dirty Lady. He can't even hear or see or smell. But he's at peace, glad to have all this out in the open, glad to have it *really happen.*

Everyone gets in the plane. Bad camera-motion as Eddie climbs in. Then a shot of Houdini, long and white, worming around like an insect larva. He's snugged right down in the bomb-cradle with Moanin' Max leaning over him like some wild worker ant.

The engines fire up with a hoarse roar. The priest and the rabbi sit and talk. Black clothes, white faces, gray teeth.

"Do you have any food?" the priest asks. He's powerfully built, young, with thin blonde hair. One hell of a Notre Dame linebacker under those robes.

The rabbi is a little fellow with a fedora and a black beard. He's got a Franz Kafka mouth, all tics and teeth. "It's my understanding that we'll breakfast in the terminal after the release."

The priest is getting two hundred for this, the rabbi three. He has a bigger name. If the rushes work out they'll be witnessing the other escapes as well.

It's not a big plane, really, and no matter which way Eddie points the camera there's always a white piece of Houdini in the frame. Up front you can see Johnny G. in profile, handsome Johnny not looking too good. There's sweat beads on his long upper lip, booze sweat. Peace is coming hard to Johnny.

"Just spiral her on up," Slick Tires says softly. "Like a

bed-spring, Johnny."

Out the portholes you can see the angled horizon sweep by, until they hit the high mattress of clouds. Max watches an altimeter, grinning and showing his teeth. They punch out of the clouds, into high slanting sunlight. Johnny holds to the helix. . .he'd go up forever if no one said stop . . . but now it's high enough.

"Bombs away!" Slick Tires calls back. The priest crosses himself and Moanin' Max pulls the release handle. Shot of white-wrapped Houdini in the coffin-like bomb-cradle. The bottom falls out, and the long form falls slowly, weightlessly at first. Then the slipstream catches one end, and he begins to tumble, dark white against the bright white of the clouds below.

Eddie holds the shot as long as he can. There's a big egg-shaped cloud down there, with Houdini falling to-wards it. Houdini begins to unwrap himself, you can see the bandages trailing him, whipping back and forth like a long flagellum, then *thip* he's spermed his way into that rounded white cloud.

On the way back to the airstrip, Eddie and the sound-man go around the plane asking everyone if they think Houdini'll make it.

"I certainly hope so," the rabbi.

"I have no idea," the priest, hungry for his breakfast.

"There's just no way," Moanin' Max. "He'll impact at two hundred miles per."

"Everyone dies," Johnny G.

"In his position I expect I'd try to drogue-chute the bandages," Slick Tires.

"It's a conundrum," the judge.

The clouds drizzle and the plane throws up great sheets of water when it lands. Eddie films them getting out and filing into the small terminal, deserted except . . .

Across the room, with his back to them, a man in pyjamas is playing pin-ball. Cigar-smoke. Someone calls to him, and he turns, Houdini.

Houdini brings his mother to see the rushes. Everyone

except her loves it. She's very upset, though, and tears at her hair. Lots of it comes out, lots of white old hair on the floor next to her wheelchair.

Back at home Houdini gets down on his knees and begs and begs until she gives him permission to finish the movie. Rabstein at Pathé figures two more stunts will do it.

"No more magic after that," Houdini promises. "I'll use the money to open us a little music shop."

"Dear boy."

For the second stunt they fly Houdini and his Mom out to Seattle. Rabstein wants to use the old lady for reaction shots. Pathé sets the two of them up in a boarding house, leaving the time and nature of the escape indeterminate.

Eddie Machotka sticks pretty close, filming bits of their long strolls down by the docks. Houdini eating a Dungeness crab. His Mom buying taffy. Houdini getting her a wig.

Four figures in black slickers slip down from a fishing boat. Perhaps Houdini hears their footfalls, but he doesn't deign to turn. Then they're upon him: The priest, the judge, the rabbi, and this time a doctor as well—could be Rex Morgan.

While the old lady screams and screams, the doctor knocks Houdini out with a big injection of sodium pentathol. The great escape artist doesn't resist, just watches and smiles till he fades. The old lady bashes the doctor with her purse before the priest and rabbi get her and Houdini bundled onto the fishing boat.

On the boat it's Johnny G. and the A-Holes again. Johnny can fly anything, even a boat. His eyes are blood-shot and all over the place, but Slick Tires guides him out of the harbor and down the Puget Sound to a logging river. Takes a couple of hours, but Eddie time-lapses it all . . . Houdini lying in half of a hollowed-out log and the doc shooting him up every so often.

Finally they get to a sort of mill-pond with a few logs in it. Moanin' Max and the judge have a tub of plaster mixed up, and they pour it in around Houdini. They tape over his head-holes, except for the mouth, which gets a breathing tube. What they do is to seal him up inside a big log, with the breathing-tube sticking out disguised as a branch-stub. Houdini is unconscious and locked inside the log by a plaster-of-paris filling . . . sort of like a worm dead inside a Twinkie. The priest and the rabbi and the judge and the doctor heave the log overboard.

It splashes, rolls, and mingles with the other logs waiting to get sawed up. There's ten logs now, and you can't tell for sure which is the one with Houdini in it. The saw is running, and the conveyor belt snags the first log.

Shot of the logs bumping around. In the foreground, Houdini's Mom is pulling the hair out of her wig. Big SKAAAAAZZZT sound of the first log getting cut up. You can see the saw up there in the background, a giant rip-saw cutting the log right down the middle.

SKAAAZZZZT! SKAAAAZZZZZT! SKAAAZZZZT! The splinters fly. One by one the logs are hooked and dragged up to the saw. You want to look away, but you can't . . . just waiting to see blood and used food come flying out. SKAAAZZZZT!

Johnny G. drinks something from a silver hip-flask. His lips move silently. Curses? Prayers? SKAAAZZZZT! Moanin' Max's nervous horse-face sweats and grins. Houdini's Mom has the wig plucked right down to the hair-net. SKAAAAZZZZZT! Slick Tires's eyes are big and white as hard-boiled eggs. He helps himself to Johnny's flask. SKAAAZZT! The priest mops his forehead and the rabbi . . . SKNAKCHUNKFWEEEEE!!!

Plaster dust flies from the ninth log. It falls in two, revealing only a negative of Houdini's body. An empty mold! They all scramble onto the mill dock, camera panning around, looking for the great man. Where is he?

Over the shouts and cheers you can hear the juke-box in the mill-hands' cafeteria. The Andrews Sisters. And in there's . . . Houdini, tapping his foot and eating a cheeseburger.

"Only one more escape," Houdini promises, "And

then we'll get that music shop."

"I'm so frightened, Harry," his bald Mom says. "If only they'd give you some warning."

"They have, this time. Piece of cake. We're flying out to Nevada."

"I just hope you stay away from those show-girls."

The priest and the rabbi and the judge and the doctor are all there, and this time a scientist, too. A low-ceilinged concrete room with slits for windows. Houdini is dressed in a black rubber wet-suit, doing card-tricks.

The scientist, who's a dead ringer for Albert Einstein, speaks briefly over the telephone and nods to the doctor. The doctor smiles handsomely into the camera, then handcuffs Houdini and helps him into a cylindrical tank of water. Refrigeration coils cool it down, and before long they've got Houdini frozen solid inside a huge cake of ice.

The priest and the rabbi knock down the sides of the tank, and there's Houdini like a big ice firecracker with his head sticking out for a fuse. Outside is a truck with a hydraulic lift. Johnny G. and the A-Holes are in it, and they load Houdini in back. The ice gets covered with pads to keep it from melting in the hot desert sun.

Two miles off, you can see a spindly test-tower with a little room on top. This is an atom-bomb test-range, out in some godforsaken desert in the middle of Nevada. Eddie Machotka rides the truck with Houdini and the A-Holes.

Shot of the slender tower looming overhead, the obscene bomb-bulge at the top. God only knows what strings Rabstein had to pull to get Pathé in on this.

There's a cylindrical hole in the ground right under the tower, right at ground zero, and they slip the frozen Houdini in there. His head, flush with the ground, grins at them like a peyote cactus. They drive back to the bunker, fast.

Eddie films it all in real-time, no cuts. Houdini's Mom is in the bunker, of course, plucking a lapful of wigs. The scientist hands her some dice.

"Just to give him fighting chance, ve von't detonate until

you are rolling a two. Is called snake-eyes, yes?"

Close on her face, frantic with worry. As slowly as possible, she rattles the dice and spills them onto the floor.

Snake-eyes!

Before anyone else can react, the scientist has pushed the button, a merry twinkle in his faraway eyes. The sudden light filters into the bunker, shading all the blacks up to gray. The shock-wave hits next, and the judge collapses, possibly from heart-attack. The roar goes on and on. The crowded faces turn this way and that.

Then it's over, and the noise is gone, gone except for . . . an insistent *honking,* right outside the bunker. The scientist un-dogs the door and they all look out, Eddie shooting over their shoulders.

It's *Houdini!* Yes! In a white convertible with a breast-heavy show-girl!

"Give me my money!" he shouts. "And color me gone!"

Oh! My Name is John Wellington Wells

Oh! my name is John Wellington Wells—
I'm a dealer in magic and spells,
  In blessings and curses,
  And ever-filled purses,
In prophesies, witches, and knells!
If you want a proud foe to 'make tracks'—
If you'd melt a rich uncle in wax—
  You've but to look in
  On our resident Djinn,
Number seventy, Simmery Axe.

We've a first class assortment of magic;
  And for raising a posthumous shade
With effects that are comic or tragic,
  There's no cheaper house in the trade.
Love-philtre—we've quantities of it;
  And for knowledge if anyone burns,
We keep an extremely small prophet, a prophet
  Who brings us unbounded returns:
    For he can prophesy
    With a wink of his eye,
    Peep with security
    Into futurity,
    Sum up your history,
    Clear up a mystery,
    Humor proclivity
    For a nativity.
    With mirrors so magical,
    Tetrapods tragical,
    Bogies spectacular,
    Answers oracular,
    Facts astronomical,
    Solemn or comical,
    And, if you, want it, he
  Makes a reduction on taking a quantity!
              Oh!
If anyone anything lacks,
He'll find it all ready in stacks,
  If he'll only look in
  On the resident Djinn,
Number seventy, Simmery Axe!

W. S. Gilbert

Elric at the End of Time

Michael Moorcock

1. In Which Mrs. Persson Detects An Above Average Degree of Chaos In the Megaflow

RETURNING FROM CHINA to London and the Spring of 1936, Una Persson found an unfamiliar quality of pathos in most of the friends she had last seen, as far as she recalled, during the Blitz on her way back from 1970. Then they had been desperately hearty: It was a comfort to understand that the condition was not permanent. Here, at present, Pierrot ruled and she felt she possessed a better grip on her power. This was, she admitted with shame, her favourite moral climate for it encouraged in her an enormously gratifying sense of spiritual superiority: the advantage of having been born, originally, into a later and probably more sophisticated age: The 1960s. Some women, she reflected, were forced to have children in order to enjoy this pleasure.

But she was uneasy, so she reported to the local Time Centre and the bearded, sullen features of Sergeant Alvarez who welcomed her in white, apologising for the fact that he had himself only just that morning left the Lower Devonian and had not had time to change.

"It's the megaflow, as you guessed," he told her, operating toggles to reveal his crazy display systems. "We've lost control."

"We never really had it." She lit a Sherman's and shook her long hair back over the headrest of the swivel chair, opening her military overcoat and loosening her webbing. "Is it worse than usual?"

"Much." He sipped cold coffee from his battered silver mug. "It cuts through every plane we can pick up—a rogue current swerving through the dimensions. Something of a twister."

"Jerry?"

"He's dormant. We checked. But it's like him, certainly. Most probably another aspect."

"Oh, sod." Una straightened her shoulders.

"That's what I thought," said Alvarez. "Someone's going to have to do a spot of rubato." He studied a screen. It was Greek to Una. For a moment a pattern formed. Alvarez made a note. "Yes. It can either be fixed at the nadir or the zenith. It's too late to try anywhere in between. I think it's up to you, Mrs P."

She got to her feet. "Where's the zenith."

"The End of Time."

"Well," she said, "that's something."

She opened her bag and made sure of her jar of instant coffee. It was the one thing she couldn't get at the End of Time.

"Sorry," said Alvarez, glad that the expert had been there and that he could remain behind.

"It's just as well," she said. "This period's no good for my moral well-being. I'll be off, then."

"Someone's got to." Alvarez failed to seem sympathetic. "It's Chaos out there."

"You don't have to tell me."

She entered the make-shift chamber and was on her way to the End of Time.

2. In Which The Eternal Champion Finds Himself at the End of Time.

ELRIC OF MELNIBONE shook a bone-white fist at the greedy, glaring stars—the eyes of all those men whose souls he had stolen to sustain his own enfeebled body. He looked down. Though it seemed he stood on something solid, there was only more blackness falling away below him. It was as if he hung at the centre of the universe. And here, too, were staring points of yellow light. Was he to be judged?

His half-sentient runesword, Stormbringer, in its scabbard on his left hip, murmured like a nervous dog.

He had been on his way to Imrryr, to his home, to reclaim his kingdom from his cousin Yyrkoon; sailing from the Isle of the Purple Towns where he had guested with Count Smiorgan Baldhead. Magic winds had caught the Filkharian trader as she crossed the unnamed waters between the Vilmirian peninsula and the Isle of Melnibone. She had been borne into the Dragon Sea and thence to The Sorcerer's Isle, so-called because that barren place had once been the home of Cran Liret, the Thief of Spells, a wizard infamous for his borrowings, who had, at length, been dispatched by those he sought to rival. But much residual magic had been left behind. Certain spells had come into the keeping of the Krettii, a tribe of near-brutes who had migrated to the island from the region of The Silent Land less than fifty years before. Their shaman, one Grrodd Ybene Eenr, had made unthinking use of devices buried by the dying sorcerer as the spells of his peers sucked life and sanity from him. Elric had dealt with more than one clever wizard, but never with so mindless a power. His battle had been long and exhausting and had required the sacrifice of most of the Filkharians as well as the entire tribe of Krettii. His sorcery had become increasingly desperate. Sprite fought sprite, devil fell upon devil, in planes both physical and astral, all around the region of The Sorcerer's Isle. Eventually Elric had mounted a massive summoning against the allies of Grrodd Ybene Eenr with the result that the shaman had been at last overwhelmed and his remains scattered in Limbo. But Elric, captured by his own monstrous magickings, had followed his enemy and now he stood in the Void, crying out into apalling silence, hearing his words only in his skull:

"Arioch! Arioch! Aid me!"

But his patron Duke of Hell was absent. He could not exist here. He could not, for once, even hear his favourite protege.

"Arioch! Repay my loyalty! I have given you blood and souls!"

He did not breath. His heart had stopped. All his movements were sluggish.

The eyes looked down at him. They looked up at him. Were they glad? Did they rejoice in his terror?

"Arioch!"

He yearned for a reply. He would have wept, but no tears would come. His body was cold; less than dead, yet not alive. A fear was in him greater than any fear he had known before.

"Oh, Arioch! Aid me!"

He forced his right hand towards the pulsing pommel of Stormbringer which, alone, still possessed energy. The hilt of the sword was warm to his touch and, as slowly he folded his fingers around it, it seemed to swell in his fist and propel his arm upwards so that he did not draw the sword. Rather the sword forced his limbs into motion. And now it challenged the void, glowing with black fire, singing its high, gleeful battle-song.

"Our destinies are intertwined, Stormbringer," said Elric. "Bring us from this place, or those destinies shall never be fulfilled."

Stormbringer swung like the needle of a compass and Elric's unfeeling arm was wrenched round to go with it. In eight directions the sword swung, as if to the eight points of Chaos. It was questing—like a hound sniffing a trail. Then a yell sounded from within the strange metal of the blade; a distant cry of delight, it seemed to Elric. The sound one would hear if one stood above a valley listening to children playing far below.

Elric knew that Stormbringer had sensed a plane they might reach. Not necessarily their own, but one which would accept them. And, as a drowning mariner must yearn for the most inhospitable rock rather than no rock at all, Elric yearned for that plane.

"Stormbringer. Take us there!"

The sword hesitated. It moaned. It was suspicious.

"Take us there!" whispered the albino to his runesword.

The sword struck back and forth, up and down, as if it battled invisible enemies. Elric scarcely kept his grip on it. It seemed that Stormbringer was frightened of the world it had detected and sought to drive it back but the act of seeking had in itself set them both in motion. Already Elric could feel himself being drawn through the darkness, towards something he could see very dimly beyond the myriad eyes, as dawn reveals clouds undetected in the night sky.

Elric thought he saw the shapes of crags, pointed and crazy. He thought he saw water, flat and ice-blue. The stars faded and there was snow beneath his feet, mountains all around him, a huge, blazing sun overhead—and above that another landscape, a desert, as a magic mirror might reflect the contrasting character of he who peered into it—a desert, quite as real as the snowy peaks in which he crouched, sword in hand, waiting for one of these landscapes to fade so that he might establish, to a degree, his bearings. Evidently two planes had intersected.

But the landscape overhead did not fade. He could look up and see sand, mountains, vegetation, a sky which met his own sky at a point half-way along the curve of the huge sun—and blended with it. He looked about him. Snowy peaks in all directions. Above—desert everywhere. He felt dizzy, found that he was staring downward, reaching to cup some of the snow in his hand. It was ordinary snow, though it seemed reluctant to melt in contact with his flesh.

"This is a world of Chaos," he muttered. "It obeys no natural laws." His voice seemed loud, amplified by the peaks, perhaps. "That is why you did not want to come here. This is the world of powerful rivals."

Stormbringer was silent, as if all its energy were spent. But Elric did not sheath the blade. He began to trudge through the snow toward what seemed to be an abyss. Every so often he glanced upward, but the desert overhead had not faded; sun and sky remained the same. He wondered if he walked around the surface of a miniature world, that if he continued to go forward he would eventually reach the point where the two landscapes met. He wondered if this were not some punishment wished upon him by his untrustworthy allies of Chaos. Perhaps he must choose between death in the snow or death in the desert.

He reached the edge of the abyss and looked down.

The walls of the abyss fell for all of five feet before reaching a floor of gold and silver squares which stretched for perhaps another seven feet before they reached the far wall, where the landscape continued—snow and crags— uninterrupted.

"This is undoubtably where Chaos rules," said the Prince of Melniboné. He studied the smooth, chequered floor. It reflected parts of the snowy terrain and the desert world above it. It reflected the crimson-eyed albino who peered down at it, his features drawn in bewilderment and tiredness.

"I am at their mercy," said Elric. "They play with me. But I shall resist them, even as they destroy me." And some of his wild, careless spirit came back to him as he prepared to lower himself onto the chequered floor and cross to the opposite bank.

He was half-way over when he heard a grunting sound in the distance and a beast appeared, its paws slithering uncertainly on the smooth surface, its seven savage eyes glaring in all directions as if it sought the instigator of its terrible indignity.

And, at last, all seven eyes focused on Elric and the beast opened a mouth in which row upon row of thin, vicious teeth were arranged, and uttered a growl of unmistakeable resentment.

Elric raised his sword. "Back, creature of Chaos. You threaten the Prince of Melniboné!"

The beast was already propelling itself towards him. Elric flung his body to one side, aiming a blow with the sword as he did so, succeeding only in making a thin incision in the monster's heavily muscled hind leg. It shrieked and began to turn.

"Back!"

Elric's voice was the brave, thin squeak of a lemming attacked by a hawk. He drove at the thing's snout with Stormbringer. The sword was heavy. It had spent all its energy and there was no more to give. Elric wondered why he, himself, did not weaken. Possibly the laws of nature

were entirely abolished in the Realm of Chaos. He struck
and drew blood. The beast paused, more in astonishment
than fear.

Then it opened its jaws, pushed its back legs against the
snowy bank, and shot towards the albino who tried to
dodge it, lost his footing, and fell, sprawling backwards, on
the gold and silver surface.

3. In Which Una Persson Discovers An Unexpected Snag

THE GIGANTIC BEETLE, rainbow carapace glittering,
turned as if into the wind which blew from the distant
mountains, its thick, flashing wings beating rapidly as it
bore its single passenger over the queer landscape.

On its back Mrs. Persson checked the instruments on
her wrist. Ever since Man had begun to travel in time it had
become necessary for the League to develop techniques
to compensate for the fluctuations and disruptions in the
space-time continua; perpetually monitoring the chrono-
flow and megaflow. She pursed her lips. She had picked
up the signal. She made the semi-sentient beetle swing a
degree or two SSE and head directly for the mountains.
She was in some sort of enclosed (but vast) environment.
These mountains, as well as everything surrounding them,
lay in the territory most utilised by the gloomy, natural-
born Werther de Goethe, poet and romantic, solitary
seeker after truth in a world no longer differentiating between the degrees of reality. He would not remember her,
she knew, because, as far as Werther was concerned, they
had not met yet. He had not even, if Una were correct,
experienced his adventure with Mistress Christia, the Everlasting Concubine. A story on which she had dined out
more than once, in duller eras.

The mountains drew closer. From here it was possible to
see the entire arrangement (a creation of Werther's very
much in character): a desert landscape, a central sun, and,
inverted above it, winter mountains. Werther strove to
make statements, like so many naïve artists before him, by

presenting simple contrasts: The World is Bleak/The World is Cold/Barren Am I As I Grow Old/Tomorrow I Die, Entombed In Cold/For Silver My Poor Soul Was Sold—she remembered he was perhaps the worst poet she had encountered in an eternity of meetings with bad poets. He had taught himself to read and write in old, old English so that he might carve those words on one of his many abandoned tombs (half his time was spent in composing obituaries for himself). Like so many others he seemed to equate self-pity with artistic inspiration. In an earlier age he might have discovered his public and become quite rich (self-pity passing for passion in the popular understanding). Sometimes she regretted the passing of Wheldrake, so long ago, so far away, in a universe bearing scarcely any resemblances to those in which she normally operated.

She brought her wavering mind back to the problem. The beetle dipped and circled over the desert, but there was no sight of her quarry.

She was about to abandon the search when she heard a faint roaring overhead and she looked up to see another characteristic motif of Werther's—a gold and silver chessboard on which, upside down, a monstrous dog-like creature was bearing down on a tiny white-haired man dressed in the most abominable taste Una had seen for some time.

She directed the aircar upwards and then, reversing the machine as she entered the opposing gravity, downwards to where the barbarically costumed swordsman was about to be eaten by the beast.

"Shoo!" cried Una commandingly.

The beast raised a befuddled head.

"Shoo."

It licked lips and returned its seven-eyed gaze to the albino, who was now on his knees, using his large sword to steady himself as he climbed to his feet.

The jaws opened wider and wider. The pale man prepared, shakily, to defend himself.

Una directed the aircar at the beast's unkempt head.

The great beetle connected with a loud crack. The monster's eyes widened in dismay. It yelped. It sat on its haunches and began to slide away, its claws making an unpleasant noise in the gold and silver tiles.

Una landed the aircar and gestured for the stranger to enter. She noticed with distaste that he was a somewhat unhealthy looking albino with gaunt features, exaggeratedly large and slanting eyes, ears that were virtually pointed, and glaring, half-mad red orbs.

And yet, undoubtedly, it was her quarry and there was nothing for it but to be polite.

"Do, please, get in," she said. "I am here to rescue you."

"Shaarmraaam torjistoo quellahm vyeearrr," said the stranger in an accent that seemed to Una to be vaguely Scottish.

"Damn," she said, "that's all we need." She had been anxious to approach the albino in private, before one of the denizens of the End of Time could arrive and select him for a menagerie, but now she regretted that Werther or perhaps Lord Jagged were not here, for she realised that she needed one of their translation pills, those tiny tablets which could 'engineer' the brain to understand a new language. By a fluke—or perhaps because of her presence here so often—the people at the End of Time currently spoke formal early twentieth century English.

The albino—who wore a kind of tartan divided kilt, knee-length boots, a blue and white jerkin, a green cloak and a silver breastplate, with a variety of leather belts and metal buckles here and there upon his person—was vehemently refusing her offer of a lift. He raised the sword before him as he backed away, slipped once, reached the bank, scrambled through snow and disappeared behind a rock.

Mrs Persson sighed and put the car into motion again.

4. In Which The Prince of Melniboné Encounters Further Terrors

XIOMBARG HERSELF, THOUGHT Elric as he slid beneath the snows into the cave. Well, he would have no dealings with the Queen of Chaos; not until he was forced to do so.

The cave was large. In the thin light from the gap above his head he could not see far. He wondered whether to return to the surface or risk going deeper into the cave. There was always the hope that he would find another way out. He was attempting to recall some rune that would aid him, but all he knew depended either upon the aid of elementals who did not exist on this plane, or upon the Lords of Chaos themselves—and they were unlikely to come to his assistance in their own Realm. He was marooned here: the single mouse in a world of cats.

Almost unconsciously he found himself moving downwards, realising that the cave had become a tunnel. He was feeling hungry but, apart from the monster and the woman in the magical carriage, had seen no sign of life. Even the cavern did not seem entirely natural.

It widened; there was phosphorescent light. He realised that the walls were of transparent crystal and, behind the walls, were all manner of artefacts. He saw crowns, sceptres and chains of precious jewels; cabinets of complicated carving; weapons of strangely turned metal; armour, clothing, artefacts whose use he could not guess—and food. There were sweetmeats, fruits, flans and pies, all out of reach.

Elric groaned. This was torment. Perhaps deliberately planned torment. A thousand voices whispered to him in a beautiful, alien language:

"*Bie-meee . . . Bie-meee . . .*" the voices murmured. "*Baa-gen, baa-gen . . .*"

They seemed to be promising every delight, if only he could pass through the walls; but they were of transparent quartz, lit from within. He raised Stormbringer, half-tempted to try to break down the barrier, but he knew that even his sword was, at its most powerful, incapable of destroying the magic of Chaos.

He paused, gaping with astonishment at a group of

small dogs which looked at him with large brown eyes, tongues lolling, and jumped up at him.

"*O, Nee Tubbens!*" intoned one of the voices.

"Gods!" screamed Elric. "This torture is too much!" He swung his body this way and that, threatening with his sword, but the voices continued to murmur and promise, displaying their riches but never allowing him to touch.

The albino panted. His crimson eyes glared about him. "You would drive me insane, eh? Well, Elric of Melniboné has witnessed more frightful threats than this. You will need to do more if you would destroy his mind!"

And he ran through the whispering passages, looking to neither his right nor his left, until, quite suddenly, he had run into blazing daylight and stood staring down into pale infinity—a blue and endless void.

He looked up. And he screamed.

Overhead were the gentle hills and dales of a rural landscape, with rivers, grazing cattle, woods and cottages. He expected to fall, headlong, but he did not. He was on the brink of the abyss. The cliff-face of red sandstone fell immediately below and then was the tranquil void. He looked back:

"*Baa-gen . . . O, Nee Tubbens . . .*"

A bitter smile played about the albino's bloodless lips as, decisively, he sheathed his sword.

"Well, then," he said. "Let them do their worst!"

And, laughing, he launched himself over the brink of the cliff.

5. In Which Werther de Goethe Makes A Wonderful Discovery

WITH A GESTURE of quiet pride, Werther de Gothe indicated his gigantic skull.

"It is very large, Werther," said Mistress Christia, the Everlasting Concubine, turning a power ring to adjust the shade of her eyes so that they perfectly matched the sky.

"It is monstrous," said Werther modestly. "It reminds us all of the Inevitable Night."

"Who was that?" enquired golden-haired Gaf the Horse in Tears, at present studying ancient legendry. "Sir Lew Grady?"

"I mean Death," Werther told him, "which overwhelms us all."

"Well, not us," pointed out the Duke of Queens, as usual a trifle literal minded. "Because we're immortal, as you know."

Werther offered him a sad, pitying look and sighed briefly. "Retain your delusions, if you will."

Mistress Christia stroked the gloomy Werther's long, dark locks. "There, there," she said. "We have compensations, Werther."

"Without Death," intoned the Last Romantic, "there is no point to Life."

As usual, they could not follow him, but they nodded gravely and politely.

"The skull," continued Werther, stroking the side of his air-car (which was in the shape of a large flying reptile) to make it circle and head for the left eye-socket, "is a Symbol not only of our Mortality, but also of our Fruitless Ambitions."

"Fruit?" Bishop Castle, drowsing at the rear of the vehicle, became interested. His hobby was currently orchards. "Less? My pine-trees, you know, are proving a problem. The apples are much smaller than I was led to believe."

"The skull is lovely," said Mistress Christia with valiant enthusiasm. "Well, now that we have seen it . . ."

"The outward shell," Werther told her. "It is what it hides which is more important. Man's Foolish Yearnings are all encompassed therein. His Greed, his Need for the Impossible, the Heat of his Passions, the Coldness which must Finally Overtake him. Through this eye-socket you will encounter a little invention of my own called The Bargain Basement of the Mind . . ."

He broke off in astonishment.

On the top edge of the eye-socket a tiny figure had emerged.

"What's that?" enquired the Duke of Queens, craning his head back. "A random thought?"

"It is not mine at all!"

The figure launched itself into the sky and seemed to fly, with flailing limbs, towards the sun.

Werther frowned, watching the tiny man disappear. "The gravity field is reversed there," he said absently, "in order to make the most of the paradox, you understand. There is a snowscape, a desert . . ." But he was much more interested in the newcomer. "How do you think he got into my skull?"

"At least he's enjoying himself. He seems to be laughing." Mistress Christia bent an ear towards the thin sound, which grew fainter and fainter at first, but became louder again. "He's coming back."

Werther nodded. "Yes. The field's no longer reversed." He touched a power ring.

The laughter stopped and became a yell of rage. The figure hurtled down on them. It had a sword in one white hand and its red eyes blazed.

Hastily, Werther stroked another ring. The stranger tumbled into the bottom of the aircar and lay there panting, cursing and groaning.

"How wonderful!" cried Werther. "Oh, this is a traveller from some rich, romantic past. Look at him! What else could he be? What a prize!"

The stranger rose to his feet and raised the sword high above his head, defying the amazed and delighted passengers as he screamed at the top of his voice:

"Heeshgeegrowinaz!"

"Good afternoon," said Mistress Christia. She reached in her purse for a translation pill and found one. "I wonder if you would care to swallow this—it's quite harmless . . ."

"Yakooom, oom glallio," said the albino contemptuously.

"Aha," said Mistress Christia. "Well, just as you please."

The Duke of Queens pointed towards the other socket.

A huge, whirring beetle came sailing from it. In its back was someone he recognised with pleasure. "Mrs. Persson!"

Una brought her aircar alongside.

"Is he in your charge?" asked Werther with undisguised disappointment. "If so, I could offer you . . ."

"I'm afraid he means a lot to me," she said.

"From your own age?" Mistress Christia also recognised Una. She still offered the translation pill in the palm of her hand. "He seems a mite suspicious of us."

"I'd noticed," said Una. "It would be useful if he would accept the pill. However, if he will not, one of us . . ."

"I would be happy," offered the generous Duke of Queens. He tugged at his green and gold beard. "Werther de Goethe, Mrs. Persson."

"Perhaps I had better," said Una nodding to Werther. The only problem with translation pills was that they did their job so thoroughly. You could speak the language perfectly, but you could speak no other.

Werther was, for once, positive. "Let's all take a pill," he suggested.

Everyone at the End of Time carried translation pills, in case of meeting a visitor from Space or the Past.

Mistress Christia handed hers to Una and found another. They swallowed.

"Creatures of Chaos," said the newcomer with cool dignity, "I demand that you release me. You cannot hold a mortal in this way, not unless he has struck a bargain with you. And no bargain was struck which would bring me to the Realm of Chaos."

"It's actually more orderly than you'd think," said Werther apologetically. "Your first experience, you see, was the world of my skull, which was deliberately muddled in that I meant to show what Confusion was the Mind of Man . . ."

"May I introduce Mistress Christia, the Everlasting Concubine," said the Duke of Queens, on his best manners. "This is Mrs. Persson. Bishop Castle. Gaf the Horse in Tears. Werther de Goethe—your unwitting host—and I am the Duke of Queens. We welcome you to our world.

Your name, sir . . . ?"

"You must know me, my lord duke," said Elric. "For I am Elric of Melniboné, Emperor by Right of Birth, Inheritor of the Ruby Throne, Bearer of the Actorios, Wielder of the Black Sword . . ."

"Indeed!" said Werther de Goethe. In a whispered aside to Mrs. Persson: "What a marvellous scowl! What a noble sneer!"

"You are an important personage in your world, then?" said Mistress Christia, fluttering the eyelashes she had just extended by half an inch. "Perhaps you would allow me . . ."

"I think he wishes to be returned to his home," said Mrs. Persson hastily.

"Returned?" Werther was astonished. "But the Morphail Effect! It is impossible."

"Not in this case, I think," she said. "For if he is not returned there is no telling the fluctuations which will take place throughout the dimensions . . ."

They could not follow her, but they accepted her tone.

"Aye," said Elric darkly, "return me to my realm, so that I may fulfill my own doom-laden destiny . . ."

Werther looked upon the albino with affectionate delight. "Aha! A fellow spirit! I, too, have a doom-laden destiny."

"I doubt it is as doom-laden as mine." Elric peered moodily back at the skull as the two air cars fled away towards a gentle horizon where exotic trees bloomed.

"Well," said Werther with an effort, "perhaps it is not, though I assure you . . ."

"I have looked upon hell-born horror," said Elric, "and communicated with the very Gods of the Uttermost Darkness. I have seen things which would turn other men's minds to useless jelly . . ."

"Jelly?" interrupted Bishop Castle. "Do you, in your time, have any expertise with, for instance, blackbird trees?"

"Your words are meaningless," Elric told him, glowering. "Why do you torment me so, my lords? I did not ask to visit your world. I belong in the world of men, in the Young Kingdoms, where I seek my weird. Why, I have but lately experienced adventures . . ."

"I do think we have one of those bores," murmured Bishop Castle to the Duke of Queens, "so common amongst time-travellers. They all believe themselves unique."

But the Duke of Queens refused to be drawn. He had developed a liking for the frowning albino. Gaf the Horse in Tears was also plainly impressed, for he had fashioned his own features into a rough likeness of Elric's. The Prince of Melniboné pretended insouciance, but it was evident to Una that he was frightened. She tried to calm him.

"People here at the End of Time . . ." she began.

"No soft words, my lady." A cynical smile played about the albino's lips. "I know you for that great unholy temptress, Queen of the Swords, Xiombarg herself."

"I assure you, I am as human as you, sir . . ."

"Human? I, human? I am not human, madam—though I be a mortal, 'tis true. I am of older blood, the blood of the Bright Empire itself, the blood of R'lin K'ren A'a which Cran Liret mocked, not understanding what it was he laughed at. Aye, though forced to summon aid from Chaos, I made no bargain to become a slave in your realm . . ."

"I assure you—um—your majesty," said Una, "that we had not meant to insult you and your presence here was no doing of ours. I am, as it happens, a stranger here myself. I came especially to see you, to help you escape . . ."

"Ha!" said the albino. "I have heard such words before. You would lure me into some worse trap than this. Tell me, where is Duke Arioch? He, at least, I owe some alliegance to."

"We have no one of that name," apologised Mistress Christia. She enquired of Gaf, who knew everyone. "No time-traveller?"

"None." Gaf studied Elric's eyes and made a small

adjustment to his own. He sat back, satisfied.

Elric shuddered and turned away mumbling.

"You are very welcome here," said Werther. "I cannot tell you how glad I am to meet one as essentially morbid and self-pitying as myself!"

Elric did not seem flattered.

"What can we do to make you feel at home?" asked Mistress Christia. She had changed her hair to a rather glossy blue in the hope, perhaps, that Elric would find it more attractive. "Is there anything you need?"

"Need? Aye. Peace of mind. Knowledge of my true destiny. A quiet place where I can be with Cymoril, whom I love."

"What does this Cymoril look like?" Mistress Christia became just a trifle over-eager.

"She is the most beautiful creature in the universe," said Elric.

"It isn't very much to go on," said Mistress Christia. "If you could imagine a picture, perhaps? There are devices in the old cities which could visualise your thoughts. We could go there. I should be happy to fill in for her, as it were . . ."

"What? You offer me a simulacrum? Do you not think I should detect such witchery at once? Ah, this is loathsome! Slay me, if you will, or continue the torment. I'll listen no longer!"

They were floating, now, between high cliffs. On a ledge far below a group of time-travellers pointed up at them. One waved desperately.

"You've offended him, Mistress Christia," said Werther pettishly. "You don't understand how sensitive he is."

"Yes I do." She was aggrieved. "I was only being sympathetic."

"Sympathy!" Elric rubbed at his long, somewhat pointed jaw. "Ha! What do I want with sympathy?"

"I never heard anyone who wanted it more." Mistress Christia was kind. "You're like a little boy, really, aren't you?"

"Compared to the ancient Lords of Chaos, I am a child,

aye. But my blood is old and cold, the blood of decaying Melniboné, as well you know." And with a hugh sigh the albino seated himself at the far end of the car and rested his head on his fist. "Well? What is your pleasure, my lords and ladies of Hell?"

"It is your pleasure we are anxious to achieve," Werther told him. "Is there anything at all we can do? Some environment we can manufacture? What are you used to?"

"Used to? I am used to the crack of leathery dragon wings in the sweet, sharp air of the early dawn. I am used to the sound of red battle, the drumming of hooves on bloody earth, the screams of the dying, the yells of the victorious. I am used to warring against demons and monsters, sorcerers and ghouls. I have sailed on magic ships and fought hand to hand with reptilian savages. I have encountered the Jade Man himself. I have fought side by side with the elementals, who are my allies. I have battled black evil . . ."

"Well," said Werther, "that's something to go on, at any rate. I'm sure we can . . ."

"Lord Elric won't be staying," began Una Persson politely. "You see—these fluctuations in the megaflow—not to mention his own destiny . . . He should not be here, at all, Werther."

"Nonsense!" Werther flung a black velvet arm about the stiff shoulders of his new friend. "It is evident that our destinies are one. Lord Elric is as grief-haunted as myself!"

"How can you know what it is to be haunted by grief . . . ?" murmured the albino. His face was half-buried in Werther's generous sleeve.

Mrs. Persson controlled herself. She rose from Werther's aircar and made for her own. "Well," she said, "I must be off. I hope to see you later, everybody."

They sang out their farewells.

Una Persson turned her beetle westward, towards Castle Canaria, the home of her old friend Lord Jagged.

She needed help and advice.

6. In Which Elric of Melniboné Resists the Temptations of the Chaos Lords

ELRIC REFLECTED ON the subtle way in which laughing Lords of Chaos had captured him. Apparently, he was merely a guest and quite free to wander where he would in their Realm. Actually, he was in their power as much as if they had chained him, for he could not flee this flying dragon and they had already demonstrated their enormous magical gifts in subtle ways, primarily with their shapechanging. Only the one who called himself Werther de Goethe (plainly a leader in the heirarchy of Chaos) still had the face and clothing he had worn when first encountered.

It was evident that this realm obeyed no natural laws, that it was mutable according to the whims of its powerful inhabitants. They could destroy him with a breath and had, subtly enough, given him evidence of that fact. How could he possibly escape such danger? By calling upon the Lords of Law for aid? But he owed them no loyalty and they, doubtless, regarded him as their enemy. But if he were to transfer his allegiance to Law . . .

These thoughts and more continued to engage him, while his captors chatted easily in the ancient High Speech of Melniboné, itself a version of the very language of Chaos. It was one of the other ways in which they revealed themselves for what they were. He fingered his rune-sword, wondering if it would be possible to slay such a lord and steal his energy, giving himself enough power for a little while to hurl himself back to his own sphere . . .

The one called Lord Werther was leaning over the side of the beast-vessel. "Oh, come and see, Elric. Look!"

Reluctantly, the albino moved to where Werther peered and pointed.

The entire landscape was filled with a monstrous battle. Creatures of all kinds and all combinations tore at one another with huge teeth and claws. Shapeless things slithered and hopped; giants, naked but for helmets and greaves, slashed at these beasts with great broadswords and axes, but were borne down. Flame and black smoke drifted everywhere. There was a smell. The stink of blood?

"What do you miss most?" asked the female. She pressed a soft body against him. He pretended not to be aware of it. He knew what magic flesh could hide on a she-witch.

"I miss peace," said Elric, almost to himself, "and I miss war. For in battle I find a kind of peace . . ."

"Very good!" Bishop Castle applauded. "You are beginning to learn our ways. You will soon become one of our best conversationalists."

Elric touched the hilt of Stormbringer, hoping to feel it grow warm and vibrant under his hand, but it was still, impotent in the Realm of Chaos. He uttered a heavy sigh.

"You are an adventurer, then, in your own world?" said the Duke of Queens. He was bluff. He had changed his beard to an ordinary sort of black and was wearing a scarlet costume; quilted doublet and tight-fitting hose, with a blue and white ruff, an elaborately feathered hat on his head. "I, too, am something of a vagabond. As far, of course, as it is possible to be here. A buccaneer, of sorts. That is, my actions are in the main bolder than those of my fellows. More spectacular. Vulgar. Like yourself, sir. I admire your costume."

Elric knew that this Duke of Hell was referring to the fact that he affected the costume of the southern barbarian, that he did not wear the more restrained colours and more cleverly wrought silks and metals of his own folk. He gave tit for tat this time. He bowed.

"Thank you, sir. Your own clothes rival mine."

"Do you think so?" The hell-lord pretended pleasure. If Elric had not known better, the creature would seem to be swelling with pride.

"Look!" cried Werther again. "Look, Lord Elric—we are attacked!"

Elric whirled.

From below were rising oddly-wrought vessels—something like ships, but with huge round wheels at their sides, like the wheels of water-clocks he had seen once in Pikarayd. Coloured smoke issued from chimneys mounted on their decks which swarmed with huge birds dressed in human clothing. The birds had multi-coloured plumage, curved beaks, and they held swords in their claws, while on their heads were strangely shaped black hats on which were blazed skulls with crossed bones beneath.

"Heave to!" squawked the birds. "Or we'll put a shot across your bowels!"

"What can they be?" cried Bishop Castle.

"Parrots," said Werther de Goethe soberly. "Otherwise known as the hawks of the sea. And they mean us no good."

Mistress Christia blinked.

"Don't you mean pirates, dear?"

Elric took a firm grip on his sword. Some of the words the Chaos Lords used were absolutely meaningless to him. But whether the attacking creatures were of their own conception, or whether they were true enemies of his captors, Elric prepared to do bloody battle. His spirits improved. At least here was something substantial to fight.

7. *In Which Mrs. Persson Becomes Anxious About the Future of the Universe*

LORD JAGGED OF Canaria was nowhere to be found. His huge castle, of gold and yellow spires, an embellished replica of Kings Cross Station, was populated entirely by his quaint robots, whom Jagged found at once more mysterious and more trustworthy than android or human servants, for they could answer only according to a limited programme.

Una suspected that Jagged was, himself, upon some mission, for he, too, was a member of the League of Temporal Adventurers. But she needed aid. Somehow she had to return Elric to his own dimensions without creating further disruptions in the fabric of Time and

Space. The Conjunction was not due yet and, if things got any worse, might never come. So many plans depended on the Conjunction of the Million Spheres that she could not risk its failure. But she could not reveal too much either to Elric or his hosts. As a Guild member she was sworn to the utmost and indeed necessary secrecy. Even here at the End of Time there were certain laws which could be disobeyed only at enormous risk. Words alone were dangerous when they described ideas concerning the nature of Time.

She racked her brains. She considered seeking out Jherek Carnelian, but then remembered that he had scarcely begun to understand his own destiny. Besides, there were certain similarities between Jherek and Elric which she could only sense at present. It would be best to go cautiously there.

She decided that she had no choice. She must return to the Time Centre and see if they could detect Lord Jagged for her.

She brought the necessary co-ordinates together in her mind and concentrated. For a moment all memories, all sense of identity left her.

Sergeant Alvarez was beside himself. His screens were no longer completely without form. Instead, peculiar shapes could be seen in the arrangements of lines. Una thought she saw faces, beasts, landscapes. That had never occurred before. The instruments, at least, had remained sane, even as they recorded insanity.

"It's getting worse," said Alvarez. "You've hardly any Time left. What there is, I've managed to borrow for you. Did you contact the rogue?"

She nodded. "Yes. But getting him to return . . . I want you to find Jagged."

"Jagged? Are you sure?"

"It's our only chance, I think."

Alvarez sighed and bent a tense back over his controls.

8. In Which Elric and Werther Fight Side By Side Against Almost Overwhelming Odds

SOMEWHERE, IT SEEMED to Elric, as he parried and thrust at the attacking bird-monsters, rich and rousing music played. It must be a delusion, brought on by battle-madness. Blood and feathers covered the carriage. He saw the one called Christia carried off screaming. Bishop Castle had disappeared. Gaf had gone. Only the three of them, shoulder to shoulder, continued to fight. What was disconcerting to Elric was that Werther and the Duke of Queens bore swords absolutely identical to Stormbringer. Perhaps they were the legendary Brothers of the Black Sword, said to reside in Chaos?

He was forced to admit to himself that he experienced a sense of comradeship with these two, who were braver than most in defending themselves against such dreadful, unlikely monsters—perhaps some creation of their own which had turned against them.

Having captured the Lady Christia, the birds began to return to their own craft.

"We must rescue her!" cried Werther as the flying ships began to retreat. "Quickly! In pursuit!"

"Should we not seek reinforcements?" asked Elric, further impressed by the courage of this Chaos Lord.

"No time!" cried the Duke of Queens. "After them!"

Werther shouted to his vessel. "Follow those ships!"

The vessel did not move.

"It has an enchantment on it," said Werther. "We are stranded! Ah, and I loved her so much!"

Elric became suspicious again. Werther had shown no signs, previously, of any affection for the female.

"You loved her?"

"From a distance," Werther explained. "Duke of Queens, what can we do? Those parrots will ransom her savagely and mishandle her objects of virtue!"

"Dastardly poltroons!" roared the huge Duke.

Elric could make little sense of this exchange. It dawned on him, then, that he could still hear the rousing music. He looked below. On some sort of dais in the middle of the bizarre landscape a large group of musicians was assembled. They played on, apparently oblivious of what happened above. This was truly a world dominated by Chaos.

Their ship began slowly to fall towards the band. It lurched. Elric gasped and clung to the side as they struck yielding ground and bumped to a halt.

The Duke of Queens, apparently elated, was already scrambling overboard. "There! We can follow on those mounts."

Tethered near the dais was a herd of creatures bearing some slight resemblance to horses but in a variety of dazzling, metallic colours, with horns and bony ridges on their backs. Saddles and bridles of alien workmanship showed that they were domestic beasts, doubtless belonging to the musicians.

"They will want some payment from us, surely," said Elric, as they hurried towards the horses.

"Ah, true!" Werther reached into a purse at his belt and drew forth a handful of jewels. Casually he flung them towards the musicians and climbed into the saddle of the nearest beast. Elric and the Duke of Queens followed his example. Then Werther, with a whoop, was off in the direction in which the bird-monsters had gone.

The landscape of this world of Chaos changed rapidly as they rode. They galloped through forests of crystalline trees, over fields of glowing flowers, leapt rivers the colour of blood and the consistency of mercury, and their tireless mounts maintained a headlong pace which never faltered. Through clouds of boiling gas which wept, through rain, through snow, through intolerable heat, through shallow lakes in which oddly fashioned fish wriggled and gasped, until at last a range of mountains came in sight.

"There!" panted Werther, pointing with his own rune-sword. "Their lair. Oh, the fiends! How can we climb such smooth cliffs?"

It was true that the base of the cliffs rose some hundred feet before they became suddenly ragged, like the rotting teeth of the beggars of Nadsokor. They were of dusky, purple obsidian and so smooth as to reflect the faces of the three adventurers who stared at them in despair.

It was Elric who saw the steps cut into the side of the cliff.

"These will take us up some of the way, at least."

"It could be a trap," said the Duke of Queens. He, too, seemed to be relishing the opportunity to take action. Although a Lord of Chaos there was something about him that made Elric respond to a fellow spirit.

"Let them trap us," said Elric laconically. "We have our swords."

With a wild laugh, Werther de Goethe was the first to swing himself from his saddle and run towards the steps, leaping up them almost as if he had the power of flight. Elric and the Duke of Queens followed more slowly.

Their feet slipping in the narrow spaces not meant for mortals to climb, ever aware of the dizzying drop on their left, the three came at last to the top of the cliff and stood clinging to sharp crags, staring across a plain at a crazy castle rising into the clouds before them.

"Their stronghold," said Werther.

"What are these creatures?" Elric asked. "Why do they attack you? Why do they capture the Lady Christia?"

"They nurse an abiding hatred for us," explained the Duke of Queens, and looked expectantly at Werther, who added:

"This was their world before it became ours."

"And before it became theirs," said the Duke of Queens, "it was the world of the Yargtroon."

"The Yargtroon?" Elric frowned.

"They dispossessed the bodiless vampire goat-folk of Kla," explained Werther. "Who, in turn, destroyed—or thought they destroyed—the Grash-Tu-Xem, a race of Old Ones older than any Old Ones except the Elder Old Ones of Ancient Thriss."

"Older, even than Chaos?" asked Elric.

"Oh, far older," said Werther.

"It's almost completely collapsed, it's so old," added the Duke of Queens.

Elric was baffled. "Thriss?"

"Chaos," said the duke.

Elric let a thin smile play about his lips. "You still mock me, my lord. The power of Chaos is the greatest there is, only equalled by the power of Law."

"Oh, certainly," agreed the Duke of Queens.

Elric became suspicious again. "Do you play with me, my lord?"

"Well, naturally, we try to please our guests . . ."

Werther interrupted. "Yonder doomy edifice holds the one I love. Somewhere within its walls she is incarcerated, while ghouls taunt at her and devils threaten."

"The bird-monsters . . . ?" began Elric.

"Chimerae," said the Duke of Queens. "You saw only one of the shapes they assume."

Elric understood this. "Aha!"

"But how can we enter it?" Werther spoke almost to himself.

"We must wait until nightfall," said Elric, "and enter under the cover of darkness."

"Nightfall?" Werther brightened.

Suddenly they were in utter darkness.

Somewhere the Duke of Queens lost his footing and fell with a muffled curse.

9. *In Which Mrs. Persson At Last Makes Contact With Her Old Friend*

THEY STOOD TOGETHER beneath the striped awning of the tent while a short distance away armoured men, mounted on armoured horses, jousted, were injured or died. The two members wore appropriate costumes for the period. Lord Jagged looked handsome in his surcoat and mail, but Una Persson merely looked uncomfortable in her wimple and kirtle.

"I can't leave just now," he was saying. "I am laying the foundations for a very important development."

"Which will come to nothing unless Elric is returned," she said.

A knight with a broken-lance thundered past, covering them in dust.

"Well played Sir Holger!" called Lord Jagged. "An ancestor of mine, you know," he told her.

"You will not be able to recognise the world of the End of Time when you return, if this is allowed to continue," she said.

"It's always difficult, isn't it?" But he was listening to her now.

"These disruptions could as easily affect us and leave us stranded," she added. "We would lose any freedom we have gained."

He bit into a pomegranite and offered it to her. "You can only get these in this area. Did you know? Impossible to find in England. In the thirteenth century, at any rate. The idea of freedom is such a nebulous one, isn't it? Most of the time when angry people are speaking of 'freedom' what they are actually asking for is much simpler—respect. Do those in authority or those with power ever really respect those who do not have power?" He paused. "Or do they mean 'power' and not 'freedom'. Or are they the same . . . ?"

"Really, Jagged, this is no time for self-indulgence."

He looked about him. "There's little else to do in the Middle East in the thirteenth century, I assure you, accept eat pomegranites and philosophise . . ."

"You must come back to the End of Time."

He wiped his handsome chin. "Your urgency," he said, "worries me, Una. These matters should be handled with delicacy—slowly . . ."

"The entire fabric will collapse unless he is returned to his own dimension. He is an important factor in the whole plan."

"Well, yes, I understand that."

"He is, in one sense at least, your protègé."

"I know. But not my responsibility."

"You must help," she said.

There was a loud bang and a crash.

A splinter flew into Mrs. Persson's eye.

"Oh, zounds!" she said.

10. In Which The Castle Is Assaulted And The Plot Thickened.

A MOON HAD appeared above the spires of the castle which seemed to Elric to have changed its shape since he had first seen it. He meant to ask his companions for an explanation, but at present they were all sworn to silence as they crept nearer. From within the castle burst light, emanating from guttering brands stuck into brackets on the walls. There was laughter, noise of feasting. Hidden behind a rock they peered through one large window and inspected the scene within.

The entire hall was full of men wearing identical costumes. They had black skull caps, loose white blouses and trousers, black shoes. Their eyebrows were black in dead white faces, even paler than Elric's, and they had bright red lips.

"Aha," whispered Werther, "the parrots are celebrating their victory. Soon they will be too drunk to know what is happening to them."

"Parrots?" said Elric. "What is that word?"

"Pierrots, he means," said the Duke of Queens. "Don't you, Werther?" There were evidently certain words which did not translate easily into the High Speech of Melniboné.

"Ssh," said the Last Romantic, "they will capture us and torture us to death if they detect our presence."

They worked their way around the castle. It was guarded at intervals by gigantic warriors whom Elric at first mistook for statues, save that, when he looked closely, he could see them breathing very slowly. They were unarmed, but their fists and feet were disproportionately large and could crush any intruder they detected.

"They are sluggish, by the look of them," said Elric. "If we are quick, we can run beneath them and enter the castle before they realise it. Let me try first. If I succeed, you follow."

Werther clapped his new comrade on the back. "Very well."

Elric waited until the nearest guard halted and spread his huge feet apart, then he dashed forward, scuttling like an insect between the giant's legs and flinging himself through a dimly lit window. He found himself in some sort of store-room. He had not been seen, though the guard cocked his ear for half a moment before resuming his pace.

Elric looked cautiously out and signalled to his companions. The Duke of Queens waited for the guard to stop again, then he, too, made for the window and joined Elric. He was panting and grinning. "This is wonderful," he said.

Elric admired his spirit. There was no doubt that the guard could crush any of them to a pulp, even if (as still nagged at his brain) this was all some sort of complicated illusion.

Another dash, and Werther was with them.

Cautiously Elric opened the door of the store-room. They looked onto a deserted landing. They crossed the landing and looked over a balustrade. They had expected to see another hall, but instead there was a miniature lake on which floated the most beautiful miniature ship, all mother-of-pearl, brass and ebony, with golden sails and silver masts. Surrounding this ship were mermaids and mermen bearing trays of exotic food (reminding Elric how hungry he still was) which they fed to the ship's only passenger, Mistress Christia.

"She is under an enchantment," said Elric. "They beguile her with illusions so that she will not wish to come with us even if we do rescue her. Do you know no counter-spells?"

Werther thought for a moment. Then he shook his head.

"You must be very minor Lords of Chaos," said Elric, biting his lower lip.

From the lake, Mistress Christia giggled and drew one of the mermaids towards her. "Come here, my pretty piscine!"

"Mistress Christia," hissed Werther de Goethe.

"Oh!" The captive widened her eyes (which were now both large and blue). "At last!"

"You wish to be rescued?" said Elric.

"Rescued? Only by you, most alluring of albinoes!"

Elric hardened his features. "I am not the one who loves you, madam."

"What? I am loved? By whom? By you, Duke of Queens?"

"Sshh," said Elric. "The demons will hear us."

"Oh, of course," said Mistress Christia gravely, and fell silent for a second. "I'll get rid of all this, shall I?"

And she touched one of her rings.

Ship, lake and merfolk were gone. She lay on silken cushions, attended by monkeys.

"Sorcery!" said Elric. "If she has such power, then why—?"

"It is limited," explained Werther. "Merely to such tricks."

"Quite," said Mistress Christia.

Elric glared at them. "You surround me with illusions. You make me think I am aiding you, when really . . ."

"No, no!" cried Wether. "I assure you, Lord Elric, you have our greatest respect—well, mine at least—we are only attempting to—"

There was a roar from the gallery above. Rank upon rank of grinning demons looked down upon them. They were armed to the teeth.

"Hurry!" The Duke of Queens leapt to the cushions and seized Mistress Christia, flinging her over his shoulder. "We can never defeat so many!"

The demons were already rushing down the circular staircase. Elric, still not certain whether his new friends deceived him or not, made a decision. He called to the Duke of Queens. "Get her from the castle. We'll keep them from you for a few moments, at least." He could not help himself. He behaved impulsively.

The Duke in Queens, sword in one hand, Mistress Christia over the other shoulder, ran into a narrow passage. Elric and Werther stood together as the demons rushed down on them. Blade met blade. There was an unbearable shrilling of steel mingled with the cacklings and shrieks of the demons as they gnashed their teeth and rolled their eyes and slashed at the pair with swords, knives and axes. But worst of all was the smell. The dreadful smell of burning flesh which filled the air and threatened to choke Elric. It came from the demons. The smell of Hell. He did his best to cover his nostrils as he fought, certain that the smell must overwhelm him before the swords. Above him was a set of metal rungs fixed into the stones, leading high into a kind of chimney. As a pause came he pointed upward to Werther, who understood him. For a moment they managed to drive the demons back. Werther jumped onto Elric's shoulders (again displaying a strange lightness) and reached down to haul the albino after him.

While the demons wailed and cackled below, they began to climb the chimney.

They climbed for nearly fifty feet before they found themselves in a small, round room whose windows looked out over the purple crags and, beyond them, to a scene of bleak rocky pavements pitted with holes, like some vast, unlikely cheese.

And there, rolling over this relatively flat landscape, in full daylight (for the sun had risen), was the Duke of Queens in a carriage of brass and wood, studded with jewels, and drawn by two bovine creatures which looked to Elric as if they might be the fabulous oxen of mythology who had drawn the war-chariot of his ancestors to do battle with the emerging nations of mankind.

Mistress Christia was beside the Duke of Queens. They seemed to be waiting for Elric and Werther.

"It's impossible," said the albino. "We could not get out of this tower, let alone across those crags. I wonder how they managed to move so quickly and so far. And where did the chariot itself come from?"

"Stolen, no doubt, from the demons," said Werther. "See, there are wings here." He indicated a heap of feathers in the corner of the room. "We can use those."

"What wizardry is this?" said Elric. "Man cannot fly on bird wings."

"With the appropriate spell he can," said Werther. "I am not that well versed in the magic arts, of course, but let me see . . ." He picked up one set of wings. They were soft and glinted with subtle, rainbow colours. He placed them on Elric's back, murmuring his spell:

Oh, for the wings, for the wings of a dove,
To carry me to the one I love . . .

"There!" He was very pleased with himself. Elric moved his shoulders and his wings began to flap. "Excellent! Off you go, Elric. I'll join you in a moment."

Elric hesitated, then saw the head of the first demon emerging from the hole in the floor. He jumped to the window ledge and leapt into space. The wings sustained him. Against all logic he flew smoothly towards the waiting chariot and, behind him, came Werther de Goethe. At the windows of the tower the demons crowded, shaking fists and weapons as their prey escaped them.

Elric landed rather awkwardly beside the chariot and was helped aboard by the Duke of Queens. Werther joined them, dropping expertly amongst them. He removed the wings from the albino's back and nodded to the Duke of Queens who yelled at the oxen, cracking his whip as they began to move.

Mistress Christia flung her arms about Elric's neck. "What courage! What resourcefulness!" she breathed. "Without you, I should now be ruined!"

Elric sheathed Stormbringer. "We all three worked together for your rescue, madam." Gently he removed her arms. Courteously he bowed and leaned against the far side of the chariot as it bumped and hurtled over the peculiar rocky surface.

"Swifter! Swifter!" called the Duke of Queens casting urgent looks backward. "We are followed!"

From the disappearing tower there now poured a host

of flying, gibbering things. One again the creatures had changed shape and had assumed the form of striped, winged cats, all glaring eyes, fangs and extended claws.

The rock became viscous, clogging the wheels of the chariot, as they reached what appeared to be a silvery road, flowing between the high trees of an alien forest already touched by a weird twilight.

The first of the flying cats caught up with them, slashing.

Elric drew Stormbringer and cut back. The beast roared in pain, blood streaming from its severed leg, its wings flapping in Elric's face as it hovered and attempted to snap at the sword.

The chariot rolled faster, through the forest to green fields touched by the moon. The days were short, it seemed, in this part of Chaos. A path stretched skyward. The Duke of Queens drove the chariot straight up it, heading for the moon itself.

The moon grew larger and larger and still the demons pursued them, but they could not fly as fast as the chariot which went so swiftly that sorcery must surely speed it. Now they could only be heard in the darkness behind and the silver moon was huge.

"There!" called Werther. "There is safety!"

On they raced until the moon was reached, the oxen leaping in their traces, galloping over the gleaming surface to where a white palace awaited them.

"Sanctuary," said the Duke of Queens. And he laughed a wild, full laugh of sheer joy.

The palace was like ivory, carved and wrought by a million hands, every inch covered with delicate designs.

Elric wondered. "Where is this place?" he asked. "Does it lie outside the Realm of Chaos?"

Werther seemed non-plussed. "You mean our world?"

"Aye."

"It is still part of our world," said the Duke of Queens. "Is the palace to your liking?" asked Werther.

"It is lovely."

"A trifle pale for my own taste," said the Last Romantic.

"It was Mistress Christia's idea."

"You built this?" the albino turned to the woman. "When?"

"Just now." She seemed surprised.

Elric nodded. "Aha. It is within the power of Chaos to create whatever whims it pleases."

The chariot crossed a white drawbridge and entered a white courtyard. In it grew white flowers. They dismounted and entered a huge hall, white as bone, in which red lights glowed. Again Elric began to suspect mockery, but the faces of the Chaos lords showed only pleasure. He realised that he was dizzy with hunger and weariness, as he had been ever since he had been flung into this terrible world where no shape was constant, no idea permanent.

"Are you hungry?" asked Mistress Christia.

He nodded. And suddenly the room was filled by a long table on which all kinds of food were heaped—and every thing, meats and fruits and vegetables, was white.

Elric moved to take the seat she indicated and he put some of the food on a silver plate and he touched it to his lips and he tasted it. It was delicious. Forgetting suspicion, he began to eat heartily, trying not to consider the colourless quality of the meal. Werther and the Duke of Queens also took some food, but it seemed they ate only from politeness. Werther glanced up at the faraway roof. "What a wonderful tomb this would make," he said. "Your imagination improves, Mistress Christia."

"Is this your domain?" asked Elric. "The moon?"

"Oh, no," she said. "It was all made for the occasion."

"Occasion?"

"For your adventure," she said. Then she fell silent.

Elric became grave. "Those demons? They were not your enemies. They belong to you!"

"Belong?" said Mistress Christia. She shook her head.

Elric frowned and pushed back his plate. "I am, however, most certainly your captive." He stood up and paced the white floor. "Will you not return me to my own plane?"

"You would come back almost immediately," said

Werther de Goethe. "It is called the Morphail Effect. And if
you did not come here, you would yet remain in your own
future. It is in the nature of Time."

"This is nonsense," said Elric. "I have left my own realm
before and returned—though admittedly memory becomes weak, as with dreams poorly recalled."

"No man can go back in Time," said the Duke of
Queens. "Ask Brannart Morphail."

"He, too, is a Lord of Chaos?"

"If you like. He is a colleague."

"Could he not return me to my realm? He sounds a
clever being."

"He could not and he would not," said Mistress Christia. "Haven't you enjoyed your experiences here so far?"

"Enjoyed?" Elric was astonished. "Madam, I think . . .
Well, what has happened this day is not what we mortals
would call 'enjoyment'."

"But you *seemed* to be enjoying yourself," said the
Duke of Queens in some disappointment. "Didn't he,
Werther?"

"You were much more cheerful through the whole
episode," agreed the Last Romantic. "Particularly when
we were fighting the demons."

"As with many time-travellers who suffer from anx-
ieties," said Mistress Christia, "you appeared to relax
when you had something immediate to capture your attention . . ."

Elric refused to listen. This was clever Chaos talk, meant
to deceive him and take his mind from his chief concern.

"If I was any help to you," he began, "I am, of
course . . ."

"He isn't very grateful." Mistress Christia pouted.

Elric felt madness creeping nearer again. He calmed
himself.

"I thank you for the food, madam. Now, I would sleep."

"Sleep?" she was disconcerted. "Oh! Of course. Yes. A
bedroom?"

"If you have such a thing."

"As many as you like." She moved a stone on one of

her rings. The walls seemed to draw back to show bed-chamber after bedchamber, in all manner of styles, with beds of every shape and fashion. Elric controlled his temper. He bowed, thanked her, said goodnight to the two lords and made for the nearest bed.

As he closed the door behind him, he thought he heard Werther de Goethe say: "We must try to think of a better entertainment for him when he wakes up."

11. In Which Mrs. Persson Witnesses The First Sign Of The Megaflow's Disintegration

IN CASTLE CANARIA Lord Jagged unrolled his antique charts. He had had them drawn for him by a baffled astrologer in 1590. They were one of his many affectations. At the moment, however, they were of considerably greater use than Alvarez's electronics.

While he used a wrist computer to check his figures, Una Persson looked out of the window of Castle Canaria and wondered who had invented this particular landscape. A green and orange sun cast sickening light over herds of grazing beasts who resembled, from this distance at any rate, nothing so much as gigantic human hands. In the middle of the scene was raised some kind of building in the shape of a vast helmet, vaguely Greek in conception. Beyond that was a low, grey moon. She turned away.

"I must admit," said Lord Jagged, "that I had not understood the extent . . ."

"Exactly," she said.

"You must forgive me. A certain amount of amnesia—euphoria, perhaps?—always comes over one in these very remote periods."

"Quite."

He looked up from the charts. "We've a few hours at most."

Her smile was thin, her nod barely perceptible.

While she made the most of having told him so, Lord Jagged frowned, turned a power ring and produced an already lit pipe which he placed thoughtfully in his mouth, taking it out again almost immediately. "That wasn't Dunhill Standard Medium." He laid the pipe aside.

There came a loud buzzing noise from the window. The scene outside was disintegrating as if melting on glass. An eery golden light spread everywhere, flooding from an apex of deeper gold, as if forming a funnel.

"That's a rupture," said Lord Jagged. His voice was tense. He put his arm about her shoulders. "I've never seen anything of the size before."

Rushing towards them along the funnel of light there came an entire city of turrets and towers and minarets in a wide variety of pastel colours. It was set into a saucer-shaped base which was almost certainly several miles in circumference.

For a moment the city seemed to retreat. The golden light faded. The city remained, some distance away, swaying a little as if on a gentle tide, a couple of thousand feet above the ground, the grey moon below it.

"That's what I call megaflow distortion," said Una Persson in that inappropriately facetious tone adopted by those who are deeply frightened.

"I recognise the period." Jagged drew a telescope from his robes. "Second Candlemaker's Empire, mainly based in Arcturus. This is a village by their standards. After all, Earth was merely a rural park during that time." He retreated into academe, his own response to fear.

Una craned her head. "Isn't that some sort of vehicle heading towards the city. From the moon—good heavens, they've spotted it already. Are they going to try to put the whole thing into a menagerie?"

Jagged had the advantage of the telescope. "I think not." He handed her the instrument.

Through it she saw a scarlet and black chariot borne by what seemed to be some form of flying fairground horses. In the chariot, armed to the teeth with lances, bows, spears, swords, axes, morningstars, maces and almost every other barbaric hand-weapon, clad in quasi-mythological armour, were Werther de Goethe, the Duke of Queens and Elric of Melniboné.

"They're attacking it!" she said faintly. "What will happen when the two groups intersect?"

"Three groups," he pointed out. "Untangling that in a few hours is going to be even harder."

"And if we fail?"

He shrugged. "We might just as well give ourselves up to the biggest chronoquake the universe has ever experienced."

"You're exaggerating," she said.

"Why not? Everyone else is."

12. The Attack On The Citadel Of The Skies

"MELNIBONÉ! MELNIBONÉ!" CRIED the albino as the chariot circled over the spires and turrets of the city. They saw startled faces below. Strange engines were being dragged through the narrow streets.

"Surrender!" Elric demanded.

"I do not think they can understand us," said the Duke of Queens. "What a find, eh? A whole city from the past!"

Werther had been reluctant to embark on an adventure not of his own creation, but Elric, realising that here at last was a chance of escape, had been anxious to begin. The Duke of Queens had, in an instant, aided the albino by producing costumes, weapons, transport. Within minutes of the city's appearance, they had been on their way.

Exactly why Elric wished to attack the city, Werther could not make out, unless it was some test of the Melnibonéan's to see if his companions were true allies or merely pretending to have befriended him. Werther was learning a great deal from Elric, much more than he had ever learned from Mongrove, whose ideas of angst were only marginally less notional than Werther's own.

A broad, flat blue ray beamed from the city. It singed one wheel of the chariot.

"Ha! They make sorcerous weapons," said Elric. "Well, my friends. Let us see you counter with your own power."

Werther obediently imitated the blue ray and sent it back from his fingers, slicing the tops off several towers. The Duke of Queens typically let loose a different coloured ray from each of his extended ten fingers and bored a hole all the way through the bottom of the city so that fields could be seen below. He was pleased with the effect.

"This is the power of the Gods of Chaos!" cried Elric, a familiar elation filling him as the blood of old Melniboné was fired. "Surrender!"

"Why do you want them to surrender?" asked the Duke of Queens in some disappointment.

"Their city evidently has the power to fly through the dimensions. If I become its lord I can force it to return to my own plane," said Elric reasonably.

"The Morphail Effect. . ." began Werther, but realised he was spoiling the spirit of the game. "Sorry."

The blue ray came again, but puttered out and faded before it reached them.

"Their power is gone!" cried Elric. "Your sorcery defeats them, my lords. Let us land and demand they honour us as their new rulers."

With a sigh, Werther ordered the chariot to set down in the largest square. Here they waited until a few of the citizens began to arrive, cautious and angry, but evidently in no mood to give any further resistance.

Elric addressed them. "It was necessary to attack and conquer you, for I must return to my own Realm, there to fulfill my great destiny. If you will take me to Melniboné, I will demand nothing further from you."

"One of us really ought to take a translation pill," said Werther. "These people probably have no idea where they are."

A meaningless babble came from the citizens. Elric frowned. "They understand not the High Speech," he said. "I will try to Common Tongue." He spoke in a language neither Werther, the Duke of Queens nor the citizens of this settlement could understand.

He began to show signs of frustration. He drew his sword Stormbringer. "By the Black Sword, know that I am

Elric, last of the royal line of Melniboné! You must obey me. Is there none here who understands the High Speech?"

Then, from the crowd, stepped a being far taller than the others. He was dressed in robes of dark blue and deepest scarlet and his face was haughty, beautiful and full of evil.

"I speak the High Tongue," he said.

Werther and the Duke of Queens were non-plussed. This was no one they recognised.

Elric gestured. "You are the ruler of the city?"

"Call me that, if you will."

"Your name?"

"I am known by many names. And you know me, Elric of Melniboné, for I am your lord and your friend."

"Ah," said Elric lowering his sword, "this is the greatest deception of them all. I am a fool."

"Merely a mortal," said the newcomer, his voice soft, amused and full of a subtle arrogance. "Are these the renegades who helped you?"

"Renegades?" said Werther. "Who are you, sir?"

"You should know me, rogue lords. You aid a mortal and defy your brothers of Chaos."

"Eh?" said the Duke of Queens. "I haven't got a brother."

The stranger ignored him. "Demigods who thought that by helping this mortal they could threaten the power of the Greater Ones."

"So you did aid me against your own," said Elric. "Oh, my friends!"

"And they shall be punished!"

Werther began: "We regret any damage to your city. After all, you were not invited . . ."

The Duke of Queens was laughing. "Who are you? What disguise is this?"

"Know me for your master." The eyes of the stranger glowed with myriad fires. "Know me for Arioch, Duke of Hell!"

"Arioch!" Elric became filled with a strange joy. "Arioch! I called upon thee and was not answered!"

"I was not in this Realm," said the Duke of Hell. "I was forced to be absent. And while I was gone, fools thought to displace me."

"I really cannot follow all this," said the Duke of Queens. He set aside his mace. "I must confess I become a trifle bored sir. If you will excuse me."

"You will not escape me." Arioch lifted a languid hand and the Duke of Queens was frozen to the ground, unable to move anything save his eyes.

"You are interfering, sir, with a perfectly—" Werther too was struck dumb and paralysed.

But Elric refused to quail. "Lord Arioch, I have given you blood and souls. You owe me . . ."

"I owe you nothing, Elric of Melniboné. Nothing I do not choose to owe. You are my slave . . ."

"No," said Elric. "I serve you. There are old bonds. But you cannot control me, Lord Arioch, for I have a power within me which you fear. It is the power of my very mortality."

The Duke of Hell shrugged. "You will remain in the Realm of Chaos forever. Your mortality will avail you little here."

"You need me in my own Realm, to be your agent. That, too, I know, Lord Arioch."

The handsome head lowered a fraction as if Arioch considered this. The beautiful lips smiled. "Aye, Elric. It is true that I need you to do my work. For the moment it is impossible for the Lords of Chaos to interfere directly in the world of mortals, for we should threaten our own existence. The rate of entropy would increase beyond even our control. The day has not yet come when Law and Chaos must decide the issue once and for all. But it will come soon enough for you, Elric."

"And my sword will be at your service, Lord Arioch."

"Will it, Elric?"

Elric was surprised by this doubting tone. He had always served Chaos, as his ancestors had. "Why should I turn against you? Law has no attractions for one such as Elric of Melniboné."

The Duke of Hell was silent.

"And there is the bargain," added Elric. "Return me to my own Realm, Lord Arioch, so that I might keep it."

Arioch sighed. "I am reluctant."

"I demand it," bravely said the albino.

"Oho!" Arioch was amused. "Well, mortal, I'll reward your courage and I'll punish your insolence. The reward will be that you are returned from whence you came, before you called on Chaos in your battle with that pathetic wizard. The punishment is that you will recall every incident that occurred since then—but only in your dreams. You will be haunted by the puzzle for the rest of your life—and you will never for a moment be able to express what mystifies you."

Elric smiled. "I am already haunted by a curse of that kind, my lord."

"Be that as it may, I have made my decision."

"I accept it," said the albino, and he sheathed his sword, Stormbringer.

"Then come with me," said Arioch, Duke of Hell. And he drifted forward, took Elric by the arm, and lifted them both high into the sky, floating over distorted scenes, half-formed dream—worlds, the whims of the Lords of Chaos, until they came to a gigantic rock shaped like a skull. And through one of the eye-sockets Lord Arioch bore Elric of Melniboné. And down strange corridors that whispered and displayed all manner of treasures. And up into a landscape, a desert in which grew many strange plants, while overhead could be seen a land of snow and mountains, equally alien. And from his robes Arioch of Hell produced a wand and he bade Elric take hold of the wand, which was hot to the touch and glittered, and he placed his own slender hand at the other end, and he murmured words which Elric could not understand and together they began to fade from the landscape, into the darkness of limbo where many eyes accused them, to an island in a grey and storm-tossed sea; an island littered with destruction and with the dead.

Then Arioch, Duke of Hell, laughed a little and vanished, leaving the Prince of Melniboné sprawled amongst corpses and ruins while heavy rain beat down upon him.

And in the scabbard at Elric's side, Stormbringer stirred and murmured once more.

13. In Which There Is A Small Celebration At The End Of Time

WERTHER DE GOETHE and the Duke of Queens blinked their eyes and found that they could move their heads. They stood in a large, pleasant room full of charts and ancient instruments. Mistress Christia was there, too.

Una Persson was smiling as she watched golden light fade from the sky. The city had disappeared, hardly any the worse for its experience. She had managed to save the two friends without a great deal of fuss, for the citizens had still been bewildered by what had happened to them. Because of the megaflow distortion, the Morphail Effect would not manifest itself. They would never understand where they had been or what had actually happened.

"Who on earth was that fellow who turned up?" asked the Duke of Queens. "Some friend of yours, Mrs. Persson? He's certainly no sportsman."

"Oh, I wouldn't agree. You could call him the ultimate sportsman," she said. "I am acquainted with him, as a matter of fact."

"It's not Jagged in disguise is it?" said Mistress Christia who did not really know what had gone on. "This is Jagged's castle—but where is Jagged?"

"You are aware how mysterious he is," Una answered. "I happened to be here when I saw that Werther and the Duke were in trouble in the city and was able to be of help."

Werther scowled (a very good copy of Elric's own scowl). "Well, it isn't good enough."

"It was a jolly adventure while it lasted, you must admit," said the Duke of Queens.

"It wasn't meant to be jolly," said Werther. "It was

meant to be significant."

"Ah."

Lord Jagged entered the room. He wore his familiar yellow robes. "How pleasant," he said. "When did all of you arrive?"

"I have been here for some time," Mrs. Persson explained, "but Werther and the Duke of Queens . . ."

"Just got here," explained the Duke. "I hope we're not intruding. Only we had a slight mishap and Mrs. Persson was good enough . . ."

"Always delighted," said the insincere lord. "Would you care to see my new—?"

"I'm on my way home," said the Duke of Queens. "I just stopped by. Mrs. Persson will explain."

"I, too," said Werther suspiciously, "am on my way back."

"Very well. Goodbye."

Werther summoned an aircar, a restrained figure of death, in rags with a sickle, who picked the three up in his hand and bore them towards a bleak horizon.

It was only days later; when he went to visit Mongrove to tell him of his adventures and solicit his friend's advice, that Werther realised he was still speaking High Melnibonéan. Some nagging thought remained with him for a long while after that. It concerned Lord Jagged, but he could not quite work out what was involved.

After this incident there were no further disruptions at the End of Time until the beginning of the story concerning Jherek Carnelian and Miss Amelia Underwood.

14. *In Which Elric of Melniboné Recovers From a Variety of Enchantments and Becomes Determined to Return to the Dreaming City*

ELRIC WAS AWAKENED by the rain on his face. Wearily he peered around him. To left and right there were only the dismembered corpses of the dead, the Krettii and the Filkharian sailors destroyed during his battle with the half-brute who had somehow gained so much sorcerous power. He shook his milk-white hair and he raised crimson eyes to the grey, boiling sky.

It seemed that Arioch had aided him, after all. The sorcerer was destroyed and he, Elric, remained alive. He recalled the sweet, bantering tones of his patron demon. Familiar tones, yet he could not remember what the words had been.

He dragged himself over the dead and waded through the shallows towards the Filkharian ship which still had some of its crew. They were, by now, anxious to head out into open sea again rather than face any more terrors on Sorcerer's Isle.

He was determined to see Cymoril, whom he loved, to regain his throne from Yyrkoon, his cousin . . .

15. In Which A Brief Reunion Takes Place At The Time Centre

WITH THE MANUSCRIPT of Colonel Pyat's rather dangerous volume of memoirs safely back in her briefcase, Una Persson decided that it was the right moment to check into ıe Time Centre. Alvarez should be on duty again and his instruments should be registering any minor imbalances result'ı ʒ from the episode concerning the gloomy albino.

Alvarez was not alone. Lord Jagged was there, in a disreputable Norfolk jacket and smoking a battered briar. He had evidently been holidaying in Victorian England. He was pleased to see her.

Alvarez ran his gear through all functions. "Sweet and neat," he said. "It hasn't been as good since I don't know when. We've you to thank for that, Mrs P."

She was modest.

"Certainly not. Jagged was the one. Your disguise was wonderful, Jagged. How did you manage to imitate that character so thoroughly? It convinced Elric. He really thought you were whatever it was—a Chaos Duke?"

Jagged waved a modest hand.

"I mean," said Una, "it's almost as if you *were* this fellow 'Arioch' . . ."

But Lord Jagged only puffed on his pipe and smiled a secret and superior smile.

Song of Amergin

Restored from medieval Irish and Welsh variants

I am a stag: *of seven tines,*
I am a flood: *across a plain,*
I am a wind: *on a deep lake,*
I am a tear: *the Sun lets fall,*
I am a hawk: *above the cliff,*
I am a thorn: *beneath the nail,*
I am a wonder: *among flowers,*
I am a wizard: *who but I*
Sets the cool head aflame with smoke?

I am a spear: *that roars for blood,*
I am a salmon: *in a pool,*
I am a lure: *from paradise,*
I am a hill: *where poets walk,*
I am a boar: *renowned and red,*
I am a breaker: *threatening doom,*
I am a tide: *that drags to death,*
I am an infant: *who but I*
Peeps from the unhewn dolmen arch?

I am the womb: *of every holt,*
I am the blaze: *on every hill,*
I am the queen: *of every hive,*
I am the shield: *for every head,*
I am the grave: *of every hope.*

—*Robert Graves*

Viriconium Knights

M. John Harrison

The bravos of the High City whistle to one another all night
as they go about their grim factional games among the
derelict observatories and abandoned fortifications at
Lowth. Sometimes desultory and distant, sometimes
shockingly close at hand, these shrill exchanges—short,
preemptory blasts interspersed with the protracted, wailing responses which always seem to end on an interroga-
tive note—form the basis of a complicated language. You
wake suddenly to their echo in the leaden hours before
dawn. When you go to the window the street below is
empty. You may hear running footsteps, or an urgent sigh.
After a minute or two the whistles move away in the
direction of the Tinmarket or the Margarethestrasse. Next
morning some minor lordling is discovered in the gutter
with his throat cut, and all you are left with is the impression of a secret war, a lethal patience, a quiet maneuvring
in the dark.

The children of the Quarter pretend to understand these
signals. They know the names of all the most desperate
men in the city. In the mornings on their way to the Lycee
on Simeonstrasse they scrutinise every lined, exhausted
face, every meal-coloured cloak, every man with a sword
and soft shoes who swaggers past on the Boulevard
Aussman.

"There goes Antic Horn," they whisper, "master of the
Blue Anemone Philosophical Association." And: "Last
night Osgerby Practal killed two of the Queen's men right
underneath my window. He did it with his knife—like
this!—and then whistled the 'found and killed' of the
Locust Clan . . ."

If you had followed the whistles one raw evening in
December some years after the War of the Two Queens,
they would have led you to an infamous cobbled yard

behind the inn called 'The Dryad's Saddle' at the junction of rue Miromesnil and Salt Pie Lane. The sun had gone down an hour before, under three bars of ragged orange cloud. Wet snow had been falling since. Smoke and steam drifted from the inn in the light of a half open door, there was a sharp smell in the air, compounded of embrocation, saveloys and burning coal. The yard was crowded on three sides with men whose woollen cloaks were dyed at the hem the colour of dried blood, men who stood with the braced instep affected only by swordsmen and dancers. They were quiet and intent, and for the most ignored the laughter that came from the inn.

Long ago someone had set four wooden posts into the yard. Blackened and still, capped with snow, they formed a square fifteen or twenty feet on a side. Half a dozen apprentices were at work to clear the square, using long-handled brooms to sweep away the slush and blunted trowels to chip at the hardened ridges of ice left by the previous day's encounters.

(By day these lads sell sugared anemones in the Rivelin Market. They run errands for the card sharps. But in the afternoon their eyes become distant, thoughtful, excited: and at night they put on their loose, girlish woolen jackets and tight leather breeches to become the handlers and nurses of the men who wear the meal-coloured cloaks. What are we to make of them? They are thin and ill-fed, but so devout. They walk with a light tread. Even their masters do not understand them.)

A grey-haired man sat on a stool among the members of his faction while two apprentices prepared him. They had taken off his cloak and his mail shirt, and strapped up his right wrist with a wide leather thong. They had pulled back the hair from his heavy face and fastened it with an ornamental steel clasp. Now they were rubbing embrocation into his stiff shoulder muscles. He ignored them, staring emptily at the combat square where the blackened posts waited for him like corpses pulled out of a bog. He showed no sign that he felt the cold, though his bare arms, covered in thick old scars, were purple with it. Once he inserted two fingers beneath the strapping on his wrist to make sure it was tight enough. His sword was propped up against his knees. Idly he pushed the point of it down between two cobblestones and began to lever them apart.

One of the apprentices leaned forward and whispered something in his ear. For a moment it appeared he wouldn't answer. Then he cleared his throat as if he had not spoken to anybody for a long time.

"I've never heard of him," he said. "And anyway, why should I be frightened of some stripling from Mynned?"

The boy smiled calmly down at him.

"I will always follow you, Practal. Even if he cuts your legs off."

Suddenly, without turning round or even moving his head, Practal reached up and grabbed the boy's thin forearm.

"If he kills me you'll run off with the first poseur who comes in here wearing soft shoes and a cloak of the right colour!"

"No," said the boy.

Practal held his arm a moment longer then gave a short laugh. "More fool you," he said, but he seemed to be satisfied. He went back to prising at the loose cobblestones.

A few minutes later the Queen's man came into the yard from the inn, surrounded by the courtiers in yellow velvet cloaks who had escorted him down from Mynned. Practal studied them briefly and spat on the cobbles. The inn was quiet now. From its half-open door a few latecomers watched, placing bets in low voices while smoke moved slowly in the light and warmth behind them.

The Queen's man ignored Practal. He walked round the combat square, kicking vaguely at each wooden post as he came to it and staring about as if he had forgotten something. He was a tall youth with big, mad-looking eyes and hair which had been cut and dyed so that it stuck up from his head like a crest of scarlet spines. He had on a pale green cloak with an orange lightning flash embroidered on the back; when he took it off the crowd could see that instead of a mail shirt he was wearing a chenille blouse. Practal's faction laughed and pointed. He gazed blankly at them, then with an awkward motion pulled the blouse off and tore it in half. This seemed to annoy the courtiers, who moved away from him and stood in a line along the fourth side of the yard. His chest was thin and white, his back long and hollow. A greenish handkerchief was knotted round his throat. He had as many scars as Practal.

Practal said loudly, "He's a weak-looking thing, then. I wonder why he bothered to come here!"

The Queen's man must have heard this, but he went on lurching randomly about, chewing on something he had in his mouth. Then he scratched his queer coxcomb violently, knelt down, and rummaged through his discarded garments until he came up with a ceramic sheath about a foot long. When the crowd saw this there was some excited betting, most of it against Practal; Practal's faction looked uneasy. Hissing through his teeth as if he was soothing a horse, the Queen's man jerked the power-knife out of its sheath and made a few clumsy passes with it. It gave off a dreary, lethal buzzing noise and a cloud of pale motes which wobbled away into the wet air like drugged moths; and as it went it left a sharp line of light behind it in the gloom.

Osgerby Practal shrugged.

"He will need long arms to use that thing," he said.

Someone called out the rules of the fight. As soon as one of the combatants was cut, he had lost. If either of them stepped outside the square he would be judged as having given in. Practal paid no attention. The Queen's man nodded interestedly as each point was made then walked off smiling and whistling.

Practal, who had some experience of mixed fights, kept his sword back out of the way of the power-knife: partly to reduce the risk of having it chopped in half, partly so that his opponent would be encouraged to come to him. The boy adopted an odd, flat-footed stance, and after a few seconds of wary circling began to breathe heavily through his open mouth. Suddenly the power-knife streaked out between them, fizzing and spitting like a firework. Practal stepped sideways and let it pass. Before the boy could regain his balance, Practal had hit him on the top of the head with the flat of his sword. The boy reeled back with a grunt and fell against one of the corner posts, biting his underlip and blinking.

The courtiers clicked their tongues impatiently.

"Come out of that corner and show us a fight!" suggested someone from Practal's faction. There was laughter.

The boy spoke for the first time. "Go home and look between your wife's legs, comrade," he said. "I think I left something there last night."

This answer amused the crowd further. He grinned round at them. Practal moved in very quickly and hit him very hard at the angle between his shoulder and neck, again with the flat of the blade. The power-knife fell out of his numbed hand and started to eat its way into the cobbles an inch from his foot, making a dull droning noise. He stood there looking down at it and rubbing his neck.

Practal rested the point of his sword against the boy's diaphragm. But the boy refused to look at him: instead he went on massaging his neck and staring over the heads of the crowd at the door of 'The Dryad's Saddle' as if he had the idea of going in there for a drink.

Practal lowered the sword and said to the crowd, "If I kill him too quickly you will give me a reputation for murdering children. We will have a rest."

He returned to his stool and sat down with his back to his opponent. His apprentices wiped his face with a towel, murmuring in low voices, and gave him a dented flask from which to wet his mouth. He held it up. "Do you want to share this?" he called over his shoulder.

"No thanks," said the boy. "Afterwards I can drink it all."

There was more laughter. Practal jumped to his feet, knocking over the stool and spilling the wine. "Fair enough then!" he shouted, his face red. "Come on!" But for a moment nothing happened. The boy had begun to hack with his heel at a ridge of hard old ice the apprentices had left sticking to the cobbles in the centre of the square. The power-knife, held negligently close to his right leg, flickered and sent up whitish motes which floated above the crowd giving off a sickly smell. The boy seemed worried. He kicked repeatedly at the ice, and when he couldn't get it to shift, took an uncertain pace or two forward.

"This square has been badly prepared," he said.

The courtiers shifted irritably. The crowd jeered.

"I don't care about that," said Practal and threw himself at the boy, driving him back with a sustained and very positive attack, whirling the sword in an impressive figure of eight so that it flashed and shone in the light from the inn door. Practal's faction cheered and waved their arms. The boy retreated unsteadily and when his foot caught the ridge of ice in the centre of the square, fell over with a cry. Practal raised the sword and brought it down hard. The boy smiled. He moved his head quickly out of the way and with a clang the blade buried itself between two cobblestones. Even as Practal tried to lever it clear the boy reached round behind his legs and cut the tendons at the back of his knee.

Practal let go of the sword and staggered about the square with his mouth open, holding the backs of his legs. The boy got up and followed him about until he collapsed, then knelt down and put his face close to Practal's to make sure he was listening. "My name is Ignace Retz," he said quietly. Practal bit the cobbles. The boy raised his voice so that the crowd could hear. "My name is Ignace Retz, and I daresay you will remember it."

"Kill me," said Practal.

Ignace Retz shook his head. A groan went through the crowd. Retz walked over to the apprentice who was holding Practal's mail shirt and meal-coloured cloak. "I will need a new shirt and cloak," he said, "so that these fine people are not tempted to laugh at me again." After he had taken the clothes, to which he was entitled under the rules of the combat, he returned the power-knife to its ceramic sheath, handling it more warily than he had done in the heat of the fight. He looked tired. One of the courtiers touched him on the arm and said coldly, "It is time to go back to the High City."

Retz bowed his head.

As he was walking towards the inn door, with the mail shirt rolled up into a heavy ball under one arm and the cloak slung loosely round his shoulders, Practal's apprentice came up and stood in his way, shouting, "Practal was the better man!"

Retz looked down at him and nodded.

"So he was."

The apprentice began to weep. "The Locust Clan will not allow you to live for this!" he said wildly.

"I don't suppose they will," said Ignace Retz.

He rubbed his neck. The courtiers hurried him out. Behind him the crowd had gone quiet. As yet, no bets were being paid out.

Mammy Vooley held a cold and disheartening court. She had been old when the Northmen brought her to the city after the War of the Two Queens. Her body was like a long ivory pole about which they had draped the faded purple gown of her predecessor. On it was supported a very small head which looked as if it had been partly scalped, partly burned, and partly starved to death in a cage suspended above the Gabelline Gate. One of her eyes was missing. She sat on an old carved wooden throne with iron wheels, in the middle of a tall whitewashed room that had five windows. Nobody knew where she had come from, not even the Northmen whose queen she had replaced. Her intelligence never diminished. At night the servants heard her singing in a thin whining voice, in some language none of them knew, as she sat among the ancient sculptures and broken machines that were the city's heritage.

Ignace Retz was ushered in to see her by the same courtiers who had led him down to the fight. They bowed to Mammy Vooley and pushed him forward, no longer bothering to disguise the contempt they felt for him.

Mammy Vooley smiled at them. She extended her hand and drew Retz down close to her bald head. She stared anxiously into his face, running her fingers over his upper arms, his jaw, his scarlet crest. She examined the bruise Practal had left on his neck. As soon as she had reassured herself he had come to no harm she pushed him away.

"Has my champion been successful in defending my honour?" she asked. When she spoke dim blue lights came on behind the windows, dim blue faces which seemed to repeat quietly whatever she said. "Is the man dead?"

Immediately Retz saw that he had made a mistake. He could have killed Practal, and now he wished he had. He wondered if she had been told already. He knew that whatever he said the courtiers would tell her the truth, but to avoid having to answer the question himself he threw Practal's mail shirt on the floor at her feet.

"I bring you his shirt, ma'am," he said.

She looked at him expressionlessly. A cold silence filled the room. Bubbles went up from the mouths of the faces in the windows. From behind him Retz heard someone say, "We are afraid the man is not dead, your majesty. Retz fought a lazy match and then hamstrung him by a crude trick. We do not understand why. His instructions were clear."

Retz laughed dangerously.

"It was not a crude trick," he said. "It was a clever one. Some day I will find a trick like that for you."

Mammy Vooley sat like a heap of sticks, her single eye directed at the ceiling.

After a moment she seemed to shrug. "It will be enough," she said remotely. "But in future you must kill them, you must always kill them. I want them killed." And her mottled hand came out again from under the folds of her robe, where tiny flakes of whitewash and damp plaster had settled like the dust in the convoluted leaves of a foreign plant. "Now give me the weapon back until the next time."

Retz massaged the side of his neck. The power-knife

had left some sort of poisonous residue inside his bones, some grey vibration which made him feel leaden and nauseated. He was afraid of Mammy Vooley and even more afraid of the dead, bluish faces in the windows; he was afraid of the courtiers as they passed to and fro behind him, whispering together. But he had made so many enemies down in the Low City that tonight he must persuade her to let him keep the knife. To gain time he went down on one knee. Then he remembered something he had heard in a popular play, 'The War with the Great Beetles'.

"Ma'am," he said urgently, "let me serve you further! To the south and east lie those broad wastes which threaten to swallow up Viriconium. New empires are there to be carved out, new treasures dug up! Only give me this knife, a horse, and few men, and I will adventure there on your behalf!"

When tegeus-Cromis, desperate swordsman of 'The War with the Great Beetles' had petitioned Queen Methvet Nian in this manner, she had sent him promptly (albeit with a wan, prophetic smile) on the journey which was to lead to his defeat of the Iron Dwarf, and thence to the acquisition of immense power. Mammy Vooley only stared into space and whispered, "What are you talking about? All the empires of the world are mine already."

For a second Retz forgot his predicament, so real was his desire for that treasure which lies abandoned amid the corrupt marshes and foundering, sloth-haunted cities of the south. The clarity and anguish of his own hallucination had astonished him.

"Then what will you give me for my services?" he demanded bitterly. "It is not as if I have failed you."

Mammy Vooley laughed.

"I will give you Osgerby Practal's mail shirt," she said, "since you have spurned the clothes I dressed you in. Now—quickly!—return me the weapon. It is not for you. It is only to defend my honour as you well know. It must be returned after the combat."

Retz embraced Mammy Vooley's thin, oddly-articulated legs and tried to put his head in her lap. He closed his eyes. He felt the courtiers pull him away. Though he kicked out vigorously they soon stripped him of the meal-coloured cloak—exclaiming in disgust at the whiteness of his thin body—and found the ceramic sheath strapped under his arm. He thought of what would happen to him when the Locust Clan caught him, defenceless, somewhere among the ruins at Lowth or down by the Isle of Dogs where his mother lived. "My lady," he begged, "lend me the knife. I will be in need of it before dawn . . ." But Mammy Vooley would not speak to him. With a shriek of despair he threw off the courtiers and pulled the knife out. Leprous white motes floated in the cold room. The bones of his arm turned to paste.

"This is all I ever got from you," he heard himself say. "And here is how I give it you back, Mammy Vooley!"

With a quick sweep of the knife he cut off the hand she had raised to dismiss him. She stared at the end of her arm and then at Retz: her face seemed to be swimming up toward him through dark water, anxious, one-eyed, unable to understand what he had done to her.

Retz clapped his hands to his head.

He threw down the weapon, grabbed up his belongings, and—while the courtiers were still milling about in fear and confusion, dabbing numbly at their yellow cloaks where Mammy Vooley's blood had spattered them—ran moaning out of the palace. Behind him all the dim blue lips in the throne room windows opened and closed agitatedly, like disturbed pond life.

Outside on the Proton Way he fell down quivering in the slushy snow and vomited his heart up. He lay there thinking, Two years ago I was nothing; then I became the Queen's champion and a great fighter; now they will hunt me down and I will be nothing again. He stayed there for twenty minutes. No-one came after him. It was very dark. When he had calmed down, and the real despair of his position had revealed itself to him, he put on Osgerby Practal's clothes and went into the Low City, where he walked about rather aimlessly until he came to a place he knew called 'The Bistro Californium'. He sat there drinking lemon gin until the whistling began and his fear drove him out on to the streets again.

It was the last hour before dawn, and a binding frost had turned the rutted snow to ice. Retz stepped through an archway in an alley somewhere near Line Mass Quays and found himself in a deep narrow courtyard where the bulging housefronts were held apart by huge balks of timber. The bottom of this crumbling well was bitterly cold and full of a darkness unaffected by day or night; it was littered with broken pottery and other rubbish. Retz shuddered. Three sides of the courtyard had casement windows; the fourth was a blank, soot-streaked cliff studded with rusty iron bolts; high up he could see a small square of moonlit sky. For the time being he had thrown his pursuers off the scent. He had last heard them quartering the streets down by the canal. He assured himself briefly that he was alone and sat down in a doorway to wait for first light. He wrapped his woollen cloak round him.

A low whistle sounded next to his very ear. He leapt to his feet with a scream of fear and began to beat on the door of the house.

"Help!" he cried. "Murder!"

He heard quiet ironic laughter behind him in the dark.

Affiliates of the Locust Clan had driven him out of the Artists Quarter and into Lowth. There on the familiar hill he had recognised with mounting panic the squawks, shrieks and low plaintive whistles of a dozen other factions, among them Anax-Hermax's High City Mohocks, the Feverfew Anschluss with their preternaturally drawn-out 'we are all met', the Yellow Paper Men and the Fifth of September—even the haughty mercenaries of the Blue Anemone. They had waited for him, their natural rivalries suppressed. They had made the night sound like the inside of an aviary. Then they had harried him to and fro across Lowth in the sleety cold until his lungs ached, showing themselves only to keep him moving, edging him steadily

towards the High City, the palace: and Mammy Vooley.
He believed they would not attack him in a private house;
or in daylight, if he could survive until then.

"Help!" he shouted. "Please help!"

Suddenly one of the casements above him flew open
and a head appeared, cocked alertly on one side. Retz
waved his arms. "Murder!" The window slammed shut
again. He moaned and battered harder at the door, while
behind him the piercing whistles of the Yellow Paper Men
filled the courtyard. When he looked up, the timber balks
were swarming with figures silhouetted against the sky.
They wanted him out of the yard and into the city again.
Someone plucked at his shoulder, whispering. When he
struck out whoever was there cut him lightly across the
back of the hand. A moment later the door opened and he
fell through it into a dimly-lit hall where an old man in a
deep blue robe waited for him with a candle.

At the top of some stairs behind the heavy baize curtain
at the end of the hall there was a large room with stone
floor and plastered white walls, kept above the freezing
point by a pan of glowing charcoal. It was furnished with
heavy wooden chairs, a sideboard of a great age, and a
lectern in the shape of an eagle whose outspread wings
supported an old book. Along one wall hung a tapestry,
ragged and out of keeping with the rest of the room, which
was that of an abbot, a judge, or a retired soldier. The old
man made Retz sit in one of the chairs and held the candle
up so that he could examine Retz's spiky scarlet screst,
which he had evidently mistaken for the result of a head
wound.

After a moment he sighed impatiently.

"Just so," he said.

"Sir," said Retz, squinting up at him, "are you a doctor?" And: "Sir, you are holding the candle so that I cannot
see you."

This was not quite true. If he moved his head he could
make out an emaciated yellow face, long and intelligent-
looking, the thin skin stretched over the bones like wax

paper over a lamp.

"So I am," said the old man. "Are you hungry?" Without waiting for an answer he went to the window and looked out. "Well, you have outwitted the other wolves and will live another day. Wait here." And he left the room.

Retz passed his hands wearily over his eyes. His nausea abated, the sweat dried in the hollow of his back, the whistles of the Yellow Paper Men moved off east toward the canal and eventually died away. After a few minutes he got up and warmed himself over the charcoal pan, spreading his fingers over it then rubbing the palms of his hands together mechanically while he stared at the lectern in the middle of the room. It was made of good steel, and he wondered how much it might fetch in the pawn shops of the Margarethestrasse. His breath steamed in the cold air. Who was the old man? His furniture was expensive. When he comes back, Retz thought, I will ask him for his protection. Perhaps he will give me the eagle so that I can buy a horse and leave the city. An old man like him could easily afford that. Retz examined the porcelain plates on the sideboard. He stared at the tapestry. Large parts of it were so decayed he could not understand what they were meant to show; but in one corner he could make out a hill, and the steep path which wound up it between stones and the roots of old trees. It made him feel uncomfortable and lonely.

When the old man returned he was carrying a tray with a pie and some bread on it. Two or three cats followed him into the room, looking up at him expectantly in the brown, wavering light of the candle. He found Retz in front of the tapestry.

"Come away from there!" he said sharply.

"Sir," said Retz, bowing low, "you saved my life. Tell me how I can serve you."

"I would not want a murderer for a servant," replied the old man.

Retz bit his underlip angrily. He turned his back, sat down, and began to stuff bread into his mouth. "If you lived out there you would act like me!" he said indistinctly. "What else is there?"

"I have lived in this city for more years than I can remember," said the old man. "I have murdered no-one."

At this there was a longish silence. The old man sat with his chin on his chest and appeared lost in thought. The charcoal pan ticked as it cooled; a draught caught the tapestry so that it billowed like a torn net curtain in the Boulevard Aussman; the cats scratched about furtively in the shadows behind the chairs. Ignace Retz ate, drank, wiped his mouth: he ate more and wiped his mouth again. When he was sure the old man wasn't watching him he boldly appraised the steel eagle. Once, on the pretext of going to the window, he even got up and touched it.

"What horror we are all faced with daily!" exclaimed the old man suddenly.

He sighed.

"I have heard the cafe philosophers say: 'the world is so old that the substance of reality no longer knows quite what it ought to be. The original template is lost. History repeats over and again this one city and a few frightful events—not rigidly, but in a shadowy, tentative fashion, as if it understands nothing else but would like to learn.' "

"The world is the world," said Ignace Retz. "Whatever they say."

"Look at the tapestry," said the old man.

Retz looked. The design he had made out earlier, with its mountain path and stunted yew trees, was more extensive than he had thought. In it a bald man was depicted trudging up the path. Above him in the air hung a large bird. Beyond that, more mountains and valleys went away to the horizon. No stitching could be seen. The whole was worked very carefully and realistically, so that Retz felt that he was looking through a window. The man on the path had skin of a yellowish colour, and his cloak was blue. He leaned on his staff as if he was out of breath. Without warning he turned round and stared out of the tapestry at Retz. As he did so the tapestry rippled in a cold draught, giving off a damp smell, and the whole scene vanished.

Retz began to tremble. In the distance he heard the old man say, "There is no need to be frightened."

"It is alive," Retz whispered. "Mammy Vooley—" But before he could say what he meant another scene had presented itself.

It was dawn in Viriconium. The sky was a bowl of cloud with a litharge stain at its edge. Rain fell on the Proton Way where, supported by a hundred pillars of black stone, it spiralled up toward the palace. Halfway along this bleak ancient sweep of road two or three figures in glowing scarlet armour stood watching a man fight with a vulture made of metal. The man's face was terribly cut; blood and rain made a dark mantle on his shoulders as he knelt there on the road; but he was winning. Soon he rose tiredly to his feet and threw the bird down in front of the watchers, who turned away and would not acknowledge him. He stared out of the tapestry. His cheeks hung open where the bird had pecked him; he was old and grey-haired and his eyes were full of regret. His lips moved and he disappeared.

"It was me!" cried Ignace Retz. "Was it me?"

"There have been many Viriconiums," said the old man. "Watch the tapestry."

Two men with rusty swords stumbled across a high moor. A long way behind them came a dwarf wearing mechanical iron stilts. His head was laid open with a wound. They waited for him to catch up, but he fell behind again almost immediately. He blundered into a rowan tree and went off in the wrong direction. One of the men, who looked like Ignace Retz, had a dead bird swinging from his belt. He stared dispiritedly out of the tapestry at the real Retz, took the bird in one hand, and raised it high in the air by its neck. As he made this gesture the dwarf passed in front of him, his stilts leaking unhealthy white gasses. They forded a stream together, and all three of them vanished into the distance where a city waited on a hill.

After that, men fought one another in the shadow of a cliff, while above them on the eroded skyline patrolled huge iridescent beetles. A fever-stricken explorer with de-

spairing eyes sat in a cart and allowed himself to be pulled
along slowly by an animal like a tall white sloth, until they
came to the edge of a pool in a flooded city. Lizards circled
endlessly a pile of corpses in the desert.

Eventually Retz grew used to seeing himself at the
centre of these events, although he was sometimes surprised by the way he looked. But the last scene was too
much for him.

He seemed to be looking through a tall, arched window,
around the stone mullions of which twined the stems of an
ornamental rose. The thorns and flowers of the rose
framed a room where curtains of silver light drifted like rain
between enigmatic columns. The floor of the room was
made of cinnabar crystal and in the centre of it had been
set a simple throne. Standing by the throne, two albino
lions couchant at her feet, was a slender woman in a velvet
gown. Her eyes were a deep, sympathetic violet colour,
her hair the russet of autumn leaves. On her long fingers
she wore ten identical rings, and before her stood a knight
whose glowing scarlet armour was partly covered by a
black and silver cloak. His head was bowed. His hands
were white. At his side he wore a steel sword.

Retz heard the woman say clearly, "I give you these
things, Lord tegeus-Cromis, because I trust you. I would
even give you a power knife if I had one. Go to the south
and win great treasure for us all."

Out of the tapestry drifted the scent of roses on a warm
evening. There was the gentle sound of falling water, and
somewhere a single line of melody repeated over and over
again on a stringed instrument. The knight in the scarlet
armour took his queen's hand and kissed it. He turned to
look out of the window and wave as if someone he knew
was passing. His black hair was parted in the middle to
frame the transfigured face of Ignace Retz. He smiled.
Behind him the queen was smiling. The whole scene
vanished, leaving a smell of damp, and all that could be
seen through the rents in the cloth was the plaster on the
wall.

Ignace Retz rubbed his eyes furiously. He jumped up, pulled the old man out of his chair, clutched him by the upper arm and dragged him up to the tapestry.

"Those last things!" he demanded. "Have they really happened?"

"All queens are not Mammy Vooley," said the old man, as if he had won an argument. "All knights are not Ignace Retz. They have happened, or will."

"Make it show me again."

"I cannot. I am a caretaker. I cannot compel."

Retz pushed him away with such violence that he fell against the sideboard and knocked the tray off it. The cats ran excitedly about, picking up pieces of food in their mouths.

"I must not believe this!" cried Retz. He pulled the tapestry off the wall and examined it intently, as if he hoped to see himself moving there. When it remained mere cloth he threw it on the floor and kicked at it. "How could I live my life if I believed this?" he asked himself. He turned back to the old man, took him by the shoulders and shook him. "What did you want to show me this for? How can I be content with this ghastly city now?"

"You need not live as you do," said the old man. "We make the world we live in."

Retz threw him aside. He hit his head on the sideboard, gave a curious angry groan and was still. He did not seem to be dead. For some minutes Retz lurched distractedly to and fro between the window and the wall where the tapestry had been, repeating, "How can I live? How can I live!" Then he rushed over to the lectern and tried to wrench the steel eagle off it. It would be daylight by now, out in the city; they would be coughing and warming their hands by the naphtha flares in the Tinmarket. He would have few hours in which to sell the bird, get a horse and a knife, and leave before the bravos began hunting him again. He would go out of the Haunted Gate on his horse, and go south, and never see the place again.

The bird moved. At first he thought it was simply coming

loose from the plinth of black wood on which it was set. Then he felt a sharp pain in the palm of his left hand, and when he looked down the thing was alive and struggling powerfully in his grip. It cocked its head, stared up at him out of a cold, violent eye. It got one wing free, then the other, and redoubled its efforts. He managed to hold on to it for a second or two longer, then, crying out in revulsion and panic, he let go and staggered back shaking his lacerated hands. He fell over something on the floor and found himself staring into the old man's stunned china blue eyes.

"Get out of my house!" shouted the old man. "I've had enough of you!"

The bird meanwhile rose triumphantly into the air and flapped round the room, battering its wings against the walls and shrieking, while coppery reflections flared off its plumage and the cats crouched terrified underneath the furniture.

"Help me!" appealed Retz. "The eagle is alive!" But the old man, lying on the floor as if paralysed, set his lips and would only answer, "You have brought it on yourself."

Retz stood up and tried to cross the room to the door at the head of the stairs. The bird, which had been obsessively attacking its own shadow on the wall, promptly fastened itself over his face, striking at his eyes and tearing with its talons at his neck and upper chest. He screamed. He pulled it off him and dashed it against the base of the wall, where it fluttered about in a disoriented fashion for a moment before making off after one of the cats. Retz watched it appalled, then clapped his hands to his bleeding face and blundered out of the room, down the narrow staircase, and out into the courtyard again. He slammed the door behind him.

It was still dark.

Sitting on the doorstep Retz felt his neck cautiously to determine the extent of his injuries. He shuddered. They were not shallow. Above him he could still hear the trapped bird shrieking and beating its wings. If it escaped it would find him. As soon as he had stopped bleeding he backed shakily away across the courtyard and passed through the àrch into a place he did not know.

He was on a wide, open avenue flanked by ruined buildings and heaps of rubble. Meaningless trenches had been dug across it here and there, and desultory fires burned on every side. Dust covered the broken chestnut trees and uprooted railings. Although there was no sign at all of dawn, the sky somehow managed to throw a curious blue light over everything. Behind him the walled court-yard now stood on its own like a kind of blank rectangular tower. He thought he was still looking at the old man's tapestry; he thought there might have been some sort of war in the night with Mammy Vooley's devastating weapons; he didn't know what to think. He started to walk nervously in the direction of the canal, then run. He ran for a long time but could not find it. Acres of shattered roof tiles made a musical scraping sound under his feet. If he looked back he could still see the tower; but it got smaller and smaller, and in the end he forgot where to look for it.

All through that long night he had no idea where he was, but he felt as if he must be on a high plateau, windy and covered completely with the dust and rubble of this un-familiar city. The wind stung the wounds the bird had given him. The dust pattered and rained against the fallen walls. Once he heard some kind of music coming from a distant house—the febrile beating of a large flat drum, the reedy, fitful whine of something like a clarinet—but when he approached the place it was silent again, and he be-came frightened.

Later a human voice from the ruins quite near him made a long drawn out *ou lou lou lou*, and was answered immediately from far off by a howl like a dog's. He fled from it between the long mounds of rubble, and for a while hid in the gutted shell of a cathedral-like building. After he had been there for about an hour several indistinct figures appeared outside and began to dig silently and energeti-cally in the road. Suddenly, though, they were disturbed; they all looked up together at something Retz couldn't see, and ran off with their spades. While this was going on he heard feet scraping around him in the bluish dark. There was a deep sigh. *Ou lou lou* sounded, shockingly close, and he was alone again. They had examined him, who-ever they were, and found him of no interest.

Towards dawn he left the building to look at the trench they had dug in the road. It was shallow, abortive, already filling up with grey sand. About a mile away he found a dead man, hidden by a corner of masonry that stood a little over waist high.

Retz knelt down and studied him curiously.

He lay as if he had fallen heavily whilst running away from someone, his limbs all askew and one arm evidently broken. He was heavily built, dressed in a loose white shirt and black moleskin trousers tied up below the knees with red string. He had on a fish's head mask, a thing like a salmon with blubbery lips, lugubrious popping eyes, and crest of stiff spines, worn in such a way that if he had been standing upright the fish would have been staring glassily into the sky. Green ribbons were tied round his upper arms to flutter and rustle in the wind. Beside him where he had dropped it lay a power-knife from which there rose, as it burned its way into the rubble, a steady stream of poison-ous yellow motes.

They had taken off his boots. His naked white feet were decorated with blue tattoos which went this way and that like veins.

Retz stared thoughtfully down at him. He climbed on to the wall and looked carefully both ways along the empty road. Whatever place the old man and the bird had con-signed him to, it would have its Mammy Vooley. He would have to fit in. It was in his nature. Ten minutes later he emerged from behind the wall dressed in the dead man's clothes. They were too large, and he had some trouble with the fish's head, which stank inside: but he had tied on the red string and the ribbons: and he had the knife. By the time he had finished all this dawn had come at last, a lid of brownish cloud tilted back at its eastern rim on streaks of yellow and emerald green, revealing a steep hill he had not previously seen. It was topped with towers, old fortifica-

tions, and the copper domes of ancient observatories. Retz
set off in the direction the trench-diggers had taken.
'Shroggs Royd' announced the plaques at the corners of
the demolished streets: 'Ouled Nail'. Then: 'rue Sepile'.

That afternoon there was a dry storm. Particles of dust
flew about under a leaden sky.

The Magician

William Kotzwinkle

The magician stood in the alley outside the cabaret, breathing the night air. Under the light of the stage door sat his wife, sewing a silver button on his evening jacket. A sturdy, buxom woman, she cut the thread with her strong teeth, then stood and held the jacket out.

The magician turned and stepped toward her lightly, a magician's walk, pointed-toed across the stones, through the mist rolling in from the river, as a ship edging out to sea sounded its mournful horn.

"The horns of Tibet," said the magician. "You hear them down the mountain passes, invoking the Buddha."

"Yes, darling," said his wife, holding out his jacket, smiling patiently.

The night is hypnosis, he thought, not daring to look in her eyes, for he would go tumbling into them. From within the cabaret came the sound of a trumpet; in the stage doorway his wife's eyes were wickedly bright, and he could not resist.

"Please, darling," she said, for he hadn't much time before his act, but she let him fall, until she could feel him inside her, rummaging around in her old loves, her flown and tattered past. What a strange one he was, always exploring around inside her with those eyes of his, peering into the dear dead days of a woman. It was bizarre play, but she let him, for some men demanded much more, and it was more painful in the giving. That was the way of the waterfront, where strange men came ashore. Into their arms she'd fallen, for she loved a sea story, and their dark songs. But then along he'd come, the top-hatted magic one, and she had said so here you are at last, which was all a magician needed, some portentous note to thrill him for an age or two. So they'd married, and he was still looking around inside her, and he has plenty more to see, she thought, before he grows tired.

She broke the spell, waving his jacket at him. He turned gracefully, plunging his arms into the sleeves, noticing at the same moment a wandering couple coming out of the mist on the avenue—an elderly man in evening dress, singing to himself, on his arm a young woman in high-collared cape, with her hair cut short, like a boy. As the lights of the cabaret appeared to them, the young girl began to plead, "Oh, may we stop here? They have a magic show!"

"Yes, yes," said the old fellow, continuing on, in deep tremolo, his song, *"O du Liebe meiner Liebe . . ."*

The magician watched them move out of the lamplight and pass under the awning of the cabaret.

"Yes," said the magician's wife, handing him his top hat, "she's very beautiful."

"Now, my dear," said the magician with a laugh, "you know me better than that." He tapped his hat and kissed her on the forehead. Women were so quick to suspect a man it made one blush. "Come, old girl," he said, giving her his arm, "I feel a good show brewing."

The dancing girls kicked their bare legs in the glow of the footlights, scattering balloons over the smoky stage, then disappeared into the wings amid applause and the rattle of dishes. Three drunken pit musicians struck up a tinny fanfare; one of the dancing girls returned, holding a gilt-edged sign bearing the magician's legend.

His wife kissed him on the cheek and he made his entrance, coming out onto the stage from the wings. Removing his white gloves and top hat, he signaled to the light bridge.

A spotlight swept through the audience, illuminating the tables, and at the magician's direction stopped amid a setting of sparkling wine goblets and dessert dishes, on the table of an elderly man in evening dress. His companion, a young woman, tried to withdraw from the smoky beam. The magician came to the edge of the stage.

"Please," he said, holding out his hand, "will you assist

me?"

Seeing the girl's reluctance, the audience began to clap. Her escort helped her from her seat. She walked toward the stage, smiling nervously. In her short-cropped hair and cape she looked like a beautiful schoolboy.

The hypnosis began slowly; the magician asked her questions, relaxing her with small talk, at the same time flashing in her face the brilliant stone from his ring, playing its reflection over her eyes like a miniature spotlight.

They stood in the middle of the stage, he smiling confidently, she looking fearfully into his fierce, piercing fox-eyes. She would not let herself be hypnotized, that was that, she would resist.

He stepped closer to her, touching her wrist lightly with his fingers. Her face was purple in the spotlight, her dark eyes like windows, and he could not resist slipping through them, into her hidden dimension.

The center of his forehead tingling, he passed through the delicate veil; there was her youth and its tender longing, there her childhood and its delight, here her infancy in white, and finally the darkness of the womb in which she had slept. He started to surface, then saw a light in the darkness, and he plunged through this still more delicate veil, into her most secret self. Down he went, through the gloomy ruins, where her antique past was kept, and long-dead shadows chased.

Standing still as a stone on the stage, the young woman heard distant voices, as if calling across the water. Something had happened, a magic show, how odd she felt, as if in a dream.

Through the labyrinth he tracked, into the depths of her soul, where her spirit was hidden away in its meditation. As in the rooms of a museum, he passed the relics of her former lives—a nun's veil, a gladiator's net, a beggar's tin cup.

Suddenly a figure appeared, a priestess, highborn, by

the sea, of luminous and beautiful body, in the hallway of a temple hauntingly familiar to him. In gold-braided sandals and a necklace of shells she walked by the sea and he who walked beside her . . .

The young woman and the magician stood motionless on the smoke-filled stage, she floating on the waves of the trance, he agasp with a recollection.

"I loved you on Atlantis," he said with trembling voice.

Instantly the waves enveloped her, her mind swam, she was under. There was a city with waving banners. She stood inside an ocean shell and felt the water on her feet. How sweet it was upon the beach and he who danced upon the waves . . .

No, he thought, pulling back from her, but he could not stop his descent, for they were ancient lovers.

A thousand lives have I loved you, she said, seeing clearly in the mirror of her heart the chain of their love.

Struggling in the tidal wave, he turned to the audience. "Now, ladies and gentlemen, tonight I would like to perform for you a most daring feat of magic!" With trembling hands, he lifted the girl and placed her between two chairs. She lay stretched out in the air, stiff as a board.

She saw now, worlds were tucked within worlds, memory was vast. She came down a river and there on its banks she saw him dancing in a loose gown. She lay in the river on stones as omens reared in the sky—a procession of elephants in gold harness, and he, dancing, brown-skinned, an African prince.

"Now then," said the magician, snapping his fingers, "bring on the box." He held to the edge of a chair, trying to pull himself together.

Two of the dancing girls came out, carrying a large wooden box, which they placed between a pair of sawhorses.

"The subject is in deep trance," said the magician, raising one of her arms in the air, where it remained motionless, until he lowered it again. He noticed her eyes fluttering, and through the brief slits he saw the Orient, shining. So, he had beheaded the Boss of Tu Shin for her, and, he saw this quite clearly, placed the head on a pole in the Boss's garden.

Covered in fans, she saw in a mirror pool, sparkling, the eastern world. Oh yes, elegantly had she performed, serving the warrior. Then, changing, she was gone. The snow-capped mountains melted and she was in the lowland. Sitting in the door of a temple, legs folded, was a yogi, thin as paper, eyes flashing in exaltation. Devastated by his gaze, she surrendered and became him.

"As you will notice, ladies and gentlemen—" The magician lifted the lid, his forehead pounding. So he had loved her there, too, in the incense of Benares the sacred city, in the seventy-nine positions. "—the box is empty."

He worked the lid, with shaking hands. The stage was covered in visions. In the center was a beating heart from which civilizations were streaming. Upon the Mayan cliffs he saw a priest in gold robes lower his knife into a virgin, naked on an altar of stone.

"Ladies and gentlemen, I hope you will notice—" He turned the box upside down. "—no false bottom, no escape hatch."

The temple of the sun crumbled, was covered by the jungle, faded into the earth. The priest vanished, only to emerge again from the beating heart, into the court of the virgin, now a Syrian Queen, and it was she who bestowed upon him the high honor of her favored circle. With great ceremony and the blowing of trumpets was he castrated.

"Now, ladies and gentlemen," he said, wiping the sweat from his brow, "you will observe the teeth of this saw are sharp as a razor." He brushed the air in front of his eyes, fighting through the cobwebs of memory: In the last century, he had left a townhouse in top hat and evening cape, swinging a silver-headed cane. Following the opera, drawn by the moontide, he retired to a brothel to escape the rain, and there in the parlor she sat, laughing darkly, clad in beads. *Let me take you away,* he said, and *no,* she said, removing her beads, *it is impossible.*

"Very well," said the magician, "a piece of magic rarely seen west of Morocco." He picked her up, laid her in the box. Just so, long ago, in the shadow of the Sphinx, had he tucked her away, into the pyramid.

Upward she rose, with brilliant birds, to their paradise, where she reclined on a couch in the heaven of her lover. *It is for the secret of your illusions that I love you,* she said, as they floated through triangles.

She heard the music of the conch horn, bells, and he, on a platform, thousand-eyed, revealed himself to her as he truly was, and he was, in fact, invisible. *No,* she said, *I must have you,* and there, she saw to her relief, he was the swan and she his lake. *These, my true regions,* he whispered, and became the lotus floating, then the toad.

". . . this perilous operation, learned in Cairo . . ." He closed the lid, sat on the box. Glancing backstage through the curtains and cables, he saw his wife, smiling at him from the wings. Yes, he thought, I'm in a bit of a mess. Sweating coldly, he looked down at the box, inside of which his subject lay sleeping.

And who am I? she asked, dissolving into this life, that life, here, there, palaces and so forth, and then, satisfied that she was eternal, she relaxed, recognizing from the heights: She was no one.

He began to saw.

She heard the slow beating of a drum, saw the jungle, wild plumage. Her body covered in gold fur, she beheld him seated across from her, in the door of a mountain cave, licking his great paw, ferocious, her king, winking at her.

"It is not often I perform this feat for fear of arrest," said the magician. "However, since we are at the end of town . . ." The teeth ripped through the box and sawdust flew in the air.

Back, back, she was gone, more was coming. They were clumsy dragons, loving in lost swamps. His long neck, green skin, ponderable his tail, and her strange egg: The night was pterodactyl, sharp-beaked, she was afraid. Somewhere, she thought, I was a girl.

"I will now ask the gentleman in the front row, that is right, you sir, to come up and examine the depth of the incision I have made in this box." The magician leaned confidently on the box, inside of which the saw was deeply inserted.

The camel will take us away, he whispered, and turning, she saw a kneeling sad-eyed beast. Lifting her silken robe, white, embroidered with dragons, she climbed up to the cab atop the camel's back, where sat the magician, smiling, clad in the cloak of the desert. Slowly the beast stood and walked, like the rocking of waves.

"Very well, my good man," said the magician, "if you are satisfied that no chicanery is being offered here, I shall proceed."

Across the night sand they rode, beneath the lonely heavens, he silent, she in prayer, until they came to an oasis, around which a fierce tribe had gathered, and he was their chief. She descended amid the animals and the oil lamps. Attended by his other wives, she was taken into an arabesque tent. A rug was spread, pillows, their dinner, dates, wine. She listened to voices outside their tent talking of battle and it thrilled her.

"Observe: The torso is separated from the legs."

She was his tenth wife, bore him a son, lived a life of precious price in Bagdad, died an old woman, was buried in a jeweled ebony box. Death was dark and impossible, the coffin opened. He stood over it, in a faded tuxedo, beckoning to her. "You're back," he said.

She stepped out, weakly, onto the smoky stage. People were clapping dully. The room was spinning. She fell into his arms. "Never leave me," she whispered.

He bowed, took her by the hand. The stage was bending. Her legs were trembling and she could not feel her feet. Slowly, he led her toward the stairs. Yes, she thought, he's taking me away.

"Goodbye," he said. The spotlight blinded her. She turned away and saw behind him on the stage a piece of scenery—a balcony window above a courtyard. She stared down a pathway in the painted garden, to the sea, and the white sail of a passing ship. "Take me away," she said.

"Impossible," he said, his face pale and drawn.

She turned to the stairs with trepidation, for they were moving, as if alive. "I thought I was a young girl," she said, warily placing her foot on the top step. "I am an ancient woman."

He released her hand, and turning to the audience, bowed once again, then withdrew across the stage into the wings.

Music began. She descended the stairs. Girls with painted faces came out behind her on the stage, covered in balloons. She stepped carefully onto the floor of the cabaret, which appeared to be tilted on its side. Someone was at her elbow, with his arm around her waist. "Well, my dear," asked her elderly escort, "how did you like being sawed in half?"

A stagehand carried the box into the wings. The magician carried it the rest of the way, into the dressing room, where his wife sat, reading a paper. Beside her in a chair, a child was sleeping.

"How tired you look," she said. "Are you all right?"

"Yes, of course," he said, removing his tie.

She helped him off with his cape and jacket and packed

his tuxedo and their other belongings in the magic box.
They left by the stage door and walked through the alley-
way, the magician carrying the box, his wife holding their
sleeping child on her shoulder.

A carriage came up the avenue and the magician hailed
it. "To the railway station," he said, handing the box up to
the driver.

They climbed into the carriage, sank into the leather
seats. The magician stared out the window, toward the
river lights. His wife, settling the child in her lap, saw the old
gentleman and the girl coming out of the cabaret. "The fog
seems to be lifting," she said, drawing her shawl around
the child.

The driver cracked his whip. The carriage pulled away,
into the night.

Sea Change

C. J. Cherryh

They had come to Fingalsey from elsewhere, and the sea did not love them. It could have been that their ill luck followed them from that elsewhere, but however that might have been (later generations did not remember) ill luck was on them here.

It was a gray village next to the barren rocks of which it was made. There might have been color in Fingalsey once, but sea wind had scoured the timbers of the doors and windows and salt mist had corroded them into grooved writhing channels, and somber gray lichens clung to the stones of the village as much as they blotched the living rocks of the island, the one peak which was the heart and height of this barren sweep. Fingalsey was dull and color-less even to the black goats which grazed the heights and to the weathered black boats hull-up on its beach. It agreed not at all with the sea and sky when the sun shone in a blue heaven; and agreed well when, more often than not, the cold mists settled or cloud scudded and hostile waves beat at the rocks. They netted from those rocks on such days, the people of Fingalsey, in their drab home-spun, culled shellfish in the shallows, slung at birds, herded their meager goats—with fear set out in their little boats to risk the tides and the rocks—knowing their luck, that the sea hated them.

It had voices, this sea. It murmured and complained constantly to the shore. It roared and wailed in storm. It took lives, and souls, and broke boats and gnawed at the shore.

But Malley went down to it one day, wandered from childbed and walked down by the rocks one spring. She was the first who went gladly—having given life, took an end of it: hugged the sea to her breast and gave herself to it in turn . . . a fine fair spring day, that Malley died, and left a life behind.

The father—the child had none, unless the rumors were true, and Malley who loved the sea had consorted there with Minyk's-son, who drowned the month before, whose boat was broken and who never came home again. *An unlucky child,* the women in the village whispered of the redhaired babe Malley left. *Dead father, dead mother. The sea's child. Ill luck's daughter.*

Hush! hissed the Widow, Malley's mother, rocking the babe in her arms; and such was the look in the Widow's sad eyes that there was no arguing.

The whispers which died slowly in Fingalsey—did die: the child grew fair, hair red as evening sun, eyes blue as the rare clear skies. The sun danced about her as she played, and the wind played pranks. She was all the gaiety, all the colors that Fingalsey was not, all the laughter they had never had—the first of three hearty, healthy children of that exceptional year; and first of years of bright-cheeked children, in years of calmer winds and full bellies. The boats went out and came home again safe. The sea brought up fish and shellfish. The goats grew sleek and fat on grass that throve in mild summers.

Fingalsey's child, they called her now, Mila the Widow's granddaughter, the luck, brought of the gift the sea was given, summer and brightness. Before her, before Malley went to the sea, the dead had almost outnumbered the living in Fingalsey . . . the quiet, sunken graves of the dead high up the hill, a graveyard overgrazed by goats and drowned when the rains came . . . the level, empty graves of the unfound dead, the lost ones, the unhallowed, which the sea took and did not return—the cairns of gray, lichened stone which marked these empty places had become a village reduced in scale, tenantless, doorless houses on the hill's unhallowed side, above the rocks where the sea gnawed hungrily in storm, where goats wandered conscienceless.

But in these years healthy children played there, and grew, and in spring found flowers blooming among the forgotten cairns, grass and brush grown high. There was laughter in Fingalsey, and new nets hung among the racks by seaside. Houses once giving way to time, empty and with roofs sagging—were lived-in and thriving, filled with new marriages and new babies.

Came the summers one by one, sixteen of them. The sea's child became a fair young girl and her two year-mates fair youths. Mila tended the Widow's goats (and from that time the herd thrived amazingly, and the Widow prospered, in milk and good white cheeses). She waded the calm pools below the cairns culling shellfish with her age-mates, netting what fish ventured within her reach, laughing and giving away what she and the Widow had beyond their needs.

Her year-mates grew tall, twin brothers, Ciag and Marik Tyl's-sons. They were dark as Mila was bright, of dark parents and loving. The luck that was Mila's they shared, so that when their aging father found the sea too strenuous they took out the boat and the nets together, fared out recklessly and with unfailing fortune. The sea played games with them, and they laughed and dared it.

They shared boat, shared nets, shared house, shared table.

One thing at last they did not share, and that was the Widow's redhaired granddaughter.

Inevitably they must love her. All Fingalsey loved her. Fingalsey hearts soared to hear her singing, merry trills and cheerful tunes of her own making. Young men's eyes burned to see her walking, a flash of white and gold and sunset on the hillside paths, among the black goats, or running down the trail to the sea, skipping from the curling tide and laughing at the old gray demon, making nothing of his bluster and his threats.

They loved. That was, after all, as Mila expected, having had nothing but love—having expected nothing else all her life. In such abundance, she did not know the degrees and qualities of love, knew nothing of selfishness, nothing of want or of things out of reach.

Marik surprised her on the high path, as she was bringing the goats home—he waited to give her gifts, the best of the catch they had gotten, carried in a seagrass basket . . . but then, he had given her gifts all his life, and she had given him as many—a perfect shell, a prized piece of wood the sea had shaped: whatever Mila had, she gave away again. She smiled at him and gave her hands when he reached, and gave her lips when he kissed—but differently this time: she gazed at him after with flushed delight.

"I love you," he said. She knew this was true: she never doubted; and that this love was forever, she never doubted that either, or why else was the Widow the Widow, solitary? That was the only shadow on her happiness, to think in that moment on the Widow, her loneliness, having lost husband, lost daughter, black-clad forever.

"I love *you*," she said, because she always had . . . but she had never reckoned who it would be out of all the folk she loved that she would become the Widow for, if luck should turn. Marik kissed her again and would have done more than kissed, but the Widow had counseled Mila some things, and she would not. She fled, blushing with confusion.

And met Ciag coming up the self-same path.

Marik came hastening down behind, with a basket of forgotten fish on his arm, *seaward* running. She stopped. Marik did, in hot consternation. Ciag had stopped first of all, his face gone stark and grim.

No words were spoken, no move made, but for the white gulls which screamed to the winds aloft, the rustle of the grass and the dull murmur of the sea which was never absent, day or night, from the ears and the minds of Fingalsey.

Mila went quite pale, and skipped by on the shoulder of the hill, fled faster—gone from innocence, for suddenly she perceived a hurt inevitable, and something beyond mending.

Ciag came the next day, waiting beside the Widow's door in the morning. He had brought his own gift, a garland of daisies and primroses. He offered it with the merry flourish with which he had offered her a thousand gifts. He was skilled at weaving garlands as he was nets and cords and all such things—slighter than his brother Marik and quicker. She did not mean to take it, but so brightly and so quickly he offered it to her hands, that her hands reached on their own; and when they had touched the flowers they touched his hands. His fingers closed on hers, and his eyes were full of grief.

"I love you," he said, "too."

"I love you," she whispered, for she found it true. It had always been true: her two year-brothers, her dearest friends, the other portions of her soul. But she pushed the flowers back at him.

He thrust them a second time at her, laughing as if it meant nothing. "But they have to be for you," he said. "I made them for you. Who else?"

She put them on, but she would not let him kiss her, though he tried. She fled from the Widow's door to the midst of the street. . . and stopped, for there stood Marik.

She had not remembered the fishes. She had left them in Marik's hand on the hillside, running from him. But she wore Ciag's garland. There was anger on Marik's brow.

She fled them both, running, as far as the goats' pen . . . she let them forth, snatched up her staff, walked in their midst, flowerdecked, up the hillside, away from them both. All that day she found no song to sing for her charges, not then or coming home.

The brothers both met her that evening, each with a basket holding one great fish, as alike as rivalry could make them. She laughed at that and took the gifts; but there was hardness in Ciag's eyes and deep wounding in Marik's— her laughter died, when she looked into Marik's face. She still wore the flowers, day-faded and limp about her neck. She took Marik's gift first now, held it closer in her arm; took Ciag's basket and hardly looked at it. Then Marik's face lost some of its wounded look; and Ciag's bore a deeper shadow.

Mila fled away inside the Widow's house, and that evening had appetite for neither gift.

Every day after that they gifted her, both laughing, as if they had discovered amusement in their plight. Then the knot bound up in Mila's heart loosed: she took every gift and laughed with them when they laughed, walked with them both—but not separately—waded with them among the pools and shared goat's-cheese with them when they scanted their fishing and their own parents to be with her. She sang again, and laughed, but sometimes the songs died away into hollowness when she was alone, and sometimes the laughter was difficult—because she knew that someday she had to choose, that someday the both of them would not be with her, but one alone.

One gray fall day, with the storms beating at the shore and all minds numbed by the vast sound, it was Marik who found her, in that gray mist, by the boats which huddled like plain dark stones, hull-up along the shore, by the nets which hung ghostly and dripping in the fog.

"I have no gift today," he said.

She smiled at him all the same, shrugged, stood numb and cold while he took her hand, numb until she thought how she had waited for this time. Her eyes gave him yes, and drifted high toward the hill.

He would go now. He tugged on her hand.

"Tomorrow morning," she said, counting on another day of fog, and pulled her hand away.

He was there, before the dawning, perhaps all the night. She walked up the hill in the dark, having slipped out of her warm bed in the Widow's house, having flung on her skirt and shawl—barefoot over the wet ground and the cold rocks, up the far shoulder of the hill, among the cairns, that side furtherest from the sight of the village. The sea crashed at the foot of the hill, drowning all small sounds. The fog occasionally became leaden droplets. A shadow waited for her among the waist-high cairns.

What if it should be Ciag? she thought in fear, and knew

by that fear which brother she chose, and that she had long since chosen. It was not Ciag: she knew Marik's stature, tall and strong—knew the touch of his calloused hands, his warmth, looked into his face in the dark and came into his shadowy arms as into a haven safe and longed-for.

He spoke her name—Mila, Mila, over and over, like a song. She kissed him silent and stayed still a time, where she wanted to be.

"What of Ciag?" she asked then sadly. "What of him?"

"What of Ciag?" he echoed in a hard-edged voice.

"He'll be alone," she said. "I want him for my friend, Marik." She felt Marik's body within her arms breathe out a sigh as if he had feared all his life and gave up fear forever.

"He'll mend in time. He'll hold our children and sit by our fire and forget his temper. He's my brother. He'll forgive."

"Shall I marry you?" she asked.

"Will you?"

She would. She nodded against him, kissed him, full of warmth. "But don't tell Ciag. I will." She thought that this was right, though it was the bravest thing she had ever thought to do.

"I will," said Marik.

That was a claim she gladly gave place to.

There was no sound there but the sea. The sun rose on them twined in each other, and rose more quickly, more treacherously quickly than they would have believed, sunk as they were in love. There was the dull roar of sea and wind, wind to take the fog; there was the night and suddenly light; and they hastened back, going separate paths, different directions to the village in headlong flight. The light grew as the wind and sun stripped away the mist, so that it was possible to tell color. The traitor goats were bleating in their pens, and Mila could see below the hill a figure waiting.

Marik's trail led down first: she saw him reach that place and pause; saw the two youths stare at each other face to face. She shrank down against the rocks, not wanting to be seen, not daring—waited there, cold and shivering while the light grew and the village stirred to life—until she realized to her distress that with people awake there was no hope of coming unseen back to the village.

She walked back up the hill and down again by yet another trail. When anxious searchers found her, she was walking along the rocks below the cairns, her feet quite chilled, her skirts made a pocket, full of shellfish. "I couldn't sleep," she told the grim-faced men and women who had turned out searching for her. Beyond their faces she saw—her heart stopped—Marik and Ciag both, faces hard and not at all bewildered by her behavior. Other faces among the crowd grew frowns, suspecting; the youngest stayed puzzled.

She must walk past Ciag and Marik both in returning to the village among her would-be rescuers—must hug the Widow when she had dumped her shellfish at the porch; and the Widow held her back then and looked at her in the eyes—looked deep and wisely, as if she knew something of her shame.

So did others. There were whispers in the village that day, whispers from which she had been safe all her life till now—whispers which blamed her, and both brothers. The brothers glowered and said nothing. There was a fight by the nets, and Agil's eldest son had a broken tooth and Ciag a gashed hand, both the brothers against the three strong sons of Agil.

The girls and women whispered too, more viciously. The Widow held her peace, waiting, perhaps, on Mila to speak, which Mila would not, could not. Mila took the goats up the hill the next morning and sat frowning at the ground and staring out at the sea, which was gray as the skies were gray, and bristling with the roughness of winter winds.

Gifts resumed on the morrow, both brothers in full view of the village. That turned the gossip to amazement, and in some hearts, to bitter jealousy, because Marik and Ciag were the handsomest and richest young men in the village, and deeply, forlornly, the young girls had had hope of one or the other of them. *Witchery,* they whispered at their mending, hating Mila. And the women recalled drowned mother, drowned father, and bastardy. *The sea's bastard,* rumors ran the louder. *Ill luck,* Agil's eldest son murmured among the young men, to salve the hurt of his broken tooth; and Agil himself repeated it in council, until the whole village was miserable.

Mila wept, and waited for Marik to do something. The look in Ciag's eyes these days was unbearable; and she imagined that Marik might after all have talked to him. Perhaps it was now for her to refuse Ciag's gifts, but she did not know.

The sea roughened, shivering in winter, and the waves came high up the shore. The slighter boats did not launch at all. The brothers went out day by day, defying the waves, giving the best they caught—poor in this season— to Mila, neglecting their own parents, who walked sorrowful and shamed amid the gossip of the village.

On a certain day, storm boded, and no boats put out at all. The men huddled in the hall, mourning over the weather.

But Marik went down to the boats and stared out at the sea; and Ciag joined him there. "Will you go out?" Ciag asked: he spoke little to Marik, because he was bitter with his brother, who had told him the truth: let Mila refuse me herself, Ciag had said; and because he loved Ciag, Marik was caught between. Now—*"Dare* you go?" Ciag asked again; and Marik felt the sting of challenge, which of them was the better man, which of them dared more for Mila's gift.

"Aye," Marik answered, and set his shoulder to the boat. The two of them heaved her out, ignoring the black cloud which lay in the east of Fingalsey. Marik went for his reasons, that his pride was stung; and Ciag went for his, which were dark and bitter—while the sea sang with voices long unheard on Fingalsey.

That was dawning. By noon, there was dire foreboding in the village, because there was one boat out, and they all knew whose. By afternoon the rain had begun, and winds drove the waves higher, sending white breakers against the rocks at Fingal's Head.

Evening came, and folk gathered at the brothers' door, in the wind and driving rain, to bestow their pity on the brothers' heartsick parents. But the Widow did not come, while Mila—Mila huddled between the houses and against the wall, and listened to the gossip of the gathered crowd, shivering in rain and lightning.

Then, in full dark, a walker came up the shore, amid the howling of the wind-racked sea—a man dark and draggled and reeling with exhaustion, from across the Head.

Mila ran first to meet him, caught his icy arms and looked into Ciag's haggard white face. "Marik?" she asked, striking him to the heart. His eyes took on a wild look.

"Drowned," he said.

The villagers closed about, parents seized on Ciag, who flinched from their arms and their eyes, who babbled a tale of a great swelling wave and a struggle to fight the currents which drove their boat. The wind howled over his voice. The rain drove down; and they bore him shuddering and sobbing toward his parents' house and hearth—"Mila?" he asked. "Mila?"

"Send for Mila," his father said.

But Mila had run from out the village and down the shore in the night and the drenching wind, by paths she knew in the dark, along the rocks, in the crash of spray.

There was a place the currents brought all wrecks and flotsam, the finest shells, and once, in the old, unlucky days, the bodies the sea was willing to give back—a place where fanged rocks broke the waves and the sea swirled back into a recess of calmer water. Mila fled there, among rocks awash with spray and the fangs backspilling white torrents under the lightnings.

There, beached, on its side, lay the brothers' boat.

She reached it, looked inside, ran her hands over the undamaged wood, her heart broken by sudden surmise. The seas crashed in her ears, her eyes were blurred with salt spray and tears. She looked outward, where the crags called the Teeth broke the white spray—looked over her shoulder villageward, for far away on the wind came voices hailing her: the villages hailing her, she reckoned—and then not, for these voices sang, rising and falling in the wind, and one of them she knew.

"Marik?"

She stepped out into the sea, struggled amid the surge and the wrack, knee-deep, hip-deep, battered by the waves. She found that recess where dead men beached, hating what she came to find, and bound to find it. The voices wailed—low and human ones among them, the villagers certainly, seeking her, wanting her back. She struggled the harder in the surge, drenched in cold rain and the colder breakers of the sea, her feet faltering on rocks which tore numb flesh.

She found him, in the lightnings and the heaving of the waves, a drifting white figure, face-down. She cried aloud and fought toward him, her skirts swept by the sea. She was no longer cold. The sea caressed and did not bruise. The rain enveloped her like a veil of ice. She was numb with grief.

He was naked—surely he had cast off every hindrance to try to breast the waves; but the currents were treacherous here and the rocks were cruel and sharp. He had struggled to live, and Ciag had lost him—but not lost the boat, *not* the precious boat, the boat which brought Ciag home. She reached Marik's body, thrown to and fro by the surge which swept him too, his white limbs loose, his dark hair that spread in the water like weed—she held her dead close and wept, hearing the singing of the wind.

The body moved gently to the rocking waves, moved—suddenly with will and life, writhed over in her arms, head turning. The eyes were dark and vast in Marik's face; the streaming hair flowed with the currents; the skin was white and no less cold. Dead arms enfolded her, dead lips parted to kiss, and the teeth were razor-sharp, a mouth ribbed and cool and tasting of kelp and sun-warmed sea.

"Mila!" she heard call distantly.

Lips clung, teeth pierced, and all the green thunder of the sea roared through her veins. Lips clingingly parted, and cold arms fell away, lithe white body arched to cleave the surge, to flash away with a pale glimmering among the black waves, lost at once in darkness and depths.

Other voices whispered, murmured. Hands touched her feet, her legs beneath the water, fingers tugged at her skirts; voices sang—and touch and voices vanished together at the next outward surge of the waves.

"Mila!" Ciag's hoarse voice cried, from somewhere up on the rocks above. Other voices joined his: "Mila!" and rocks crashed and bounded down into the pools with white splashes, from Ciag's reckless course downhill. He floundered out to her, embraced her in hot arms, carried her from the tidepool, himself yielded to the hands of the young men who had dared follow him. Other hands lifted Mila, carried her and him to solid land, chafed her cold flesh and his. Seaweed was tangled about her, and blood and the taste of the sea was on her lips. She shut her eyes to the gray and the dark and saw only sunwarmed green.

They carried her back to the Widow's house. She lay listlessly beneath many blankets, sipped at soup the Widow poured between her unresisting lips, turned her face from Ciag when he knelt by her bed and pressed her hand. A succession of staring faces that night—Ciag's always—and the Widow's—voices which whispered about her, and she could not hear; but she had heard such whispers before and cared nothing for them.

Then the storm passed and the day came, gray and cold. She rose up from her bed against the Widow's protest, walked out into the village. The place was deserted: all of them were up the hill at the making of Marik's—empty—cairn, among the others, on the hill's unhallowed left. She walked up the path and watched them at their work. Others moved away, but Ciag came and took her listless hand.

She gazed at the cairns; and Ciag softly lied—how Marik had been thrown from the boat when they came in among the rocks, how he had tried to save his brother. Mila turned on Ciag a face open and heartless, and drew back her hand, walked away down by the sea, in the roar of the rocks and the peace.

Ciag came down to her and dragged her back by the hand, while all the villagers stared and muttered—brother against brother, and the evil plain to see.

Mila came back and stood silent, went back to the village when they went, and surrendered to the Widow's care. She ate, listlessly, listlessly lay abed at evening; but when night came full and the Widow slept, she rose up and slipped out again in her shift, in the bitter cold, to walk along the shore, the lefthand way, below the cairns. She walked by the sea's edge in the tide pools, sat on a stone, gazing out to sea, and the waters, liquid black, reflected a pallid moon.

So Ciag found her at dawn, and desperately took her hand. She turned on him a soulless smile and pulled away. Perhaps it was the place that daunted him. He stood. She walked away singing, but not the songs she had once sung—loose and tuneless, her singing now, like the sea.

Villagers shied from her path. Barelimbed in her white shift she walked beside the boats and the nets. The Widow brought her a black shawl, brought her into the house, fed her and warmed her and dressed her in widow's black. Mila stroked her own red hair and sat drowsing until the warmth wearied her. Then she remembered the goats and went out again, but someone else had taken them to pasture.

She walked, singing her wild, wordless tune, and the winds played merrily among her black skirts, the fringes of her shawl, the strands of her bright hair. She hummed to herself, and fished by the rocks, and at times saw Ciag following. She ran finally, lightly eluding him—sat high among the cairns, among the black goats. The child watching them fled, leaving the place, and her.

Ciag came, spoke to her madly, forlornly, and she stared through him, walked away, leaving the goats to stray where they would.

"Mila!" he cried, as he had cried that night.

She walked among the cairns and back down to the shore, and so to the village, among the hull-up boats, singing to herself, listening to the sea.

There was, that day, a second drowning: Agil's eldest son, fishing off the rocks, and no body washed ashore. Another cairn rose on the leftward side.

And on the day after that, Agil's grieving wife drowned herself, so that there was another.

All the while the stones went into place on the hilltop there was the faint fair singing that was Mila, off along the rocks. The villagers did not speak of it—or of Ciag, absent from them. The luck had gone from Fingalsey, and they knew it.

Ciag knew, and kept his lonely boat near the shore, on the fair days when he went out alone. It rocked, at times, out of time with wind and waves. Motions touched it which chilled his heart. Ripples passed round it, and splashes sounded when his back was turned.

Untroubled, Mila walked the shore, walked the hills, sat among the cairns—by twilight walked the shore, when the last boats had come in.

He was there by night—he—the white shape beneath the darkling green: she bent low above the waters, reached fingers to pallor which might have been her own image, which vanished with the breaking of the surface. Bubbles swirled on the eddies, broke, vanished, the white shape gone, like a dream.

So all the days passed, one to the next. Only Ciag brought her gifts, his poor catches, from which she walked away, distractedly—and wherever she walked in the village the children shied away and the goats looked at her from wise slit eyes over the bars of the pen.

"I'll marry her," Ciag said to the Widow, as if that settled things.

"Ask her," the Widow said, staring at him from eyes wise as the black goats'.

He did, and Mila stared through him and stirred the pot she had been set to stir, for she did such simple tasks for the Widow, moving without thought.

"She will not," the Widow said.

From that day Ciag grew desperate, spying on her when she would walk by the sea, never far from her—until all the village whispered in fear, not alone of her, but of Ciag. The winter winds blew and the waters heaved: no one ventured to sea, but two children drowned shell-hunting among the rocks, when the high surge ripped at the land. Storm drove at them, a great black wall of cloud coming far across the sea, and the mourning village shut its doors, its dead unfound, at twilight.

The wind came. The waves crashed on the shore for hours before the gale, and battered at the land. Boats which had always been safe were torn loose and threatened, and young men ran to save them.

Mila walked, along the shore. The rail had broken at the goats' pen. The beasts scampered free, on this side and on that of her, and up the hill, to huddle shivering and bleating among the cairns, staring after her, on the path which led to Fingal's Head, to the Teeth, and the sea.

The air was full of spray. The waves thundered and streamed white off the rocks. She walked a dream, in which the cold was warmth, the night was clear, the curtains of wind-borne spray caressed her and desired. The voices in the sea sang siren-songs, male and female choruses. Her feet found the remembered rocks, her blinded eyes sought wraiths in the surge and the backspill. Knee-deep, hip-deep, tuggings of the surge at her skirts, and the voices singing.

She fell down into the green thunder, a stinging flood into lungs and eyes and ears until the sea was all. Gentle hands reached out for her, pale limbs flashed, and *he* wrapped her close in his arms and bore her down.

There was no more pain. Cold arms and dark eyes, hair adrift like seaweed, and the beauty of him, the pale, chill beauty—she began to move, swifter, surer, pacing him, with a twisting torrent of pale bodies spiraling about them both in the green waters—large, deep eyes, delicate, jointed lips, and razor teeth that sparkled like shards of ice, hair flowing like torrents of shadow and pallor, dark and bright, mingling, as hers with his. Familiar faces, child-faces and old faces and faces she had never seen—father and drowned mother and kindred, all the lost souls of Fingalsey. . . .

And he—holding her fast. She laughed, and swept the currents, one with them and with him, her large eyes seeing the sea as she had never dreamed it, heart swelling with what she had never felt. She joined the song, loving the cold and the power of it.

She was there—at dawn Ciag found her pale, naked body face down among the rocks, her red hair flowing about her like some strange anemone. "Help," he cried to the villagers who lined the cliff in the foggy dawn. "Help me!"—because she was far out among the rocks, and her dead weight filled his arms.

But the Widow walked away, and his mother and his father, casting down their torches like falling stars, trailing smoke and fire into the sea; and one by one the others did so, deserting him, and her.

Ciag wept. He had loved her. He clung to her in the sea. The roar filled his ears, the white spray breaking on the Teeth hit the wind and drenched him even here.

Something touched him, beneath the water. Not the current, but small tuggings at his clothes, nips at his ankles when he must catch his balance in the water. He refused to let her go, held to her, struggled waist-deep in the surge.

She turned in his arms; white arms reached and enfolded, vast eyes stared into his, sea-dark; lips touched his, chill, and teeth razory-fine—a taste of sun and sea . . .

All the green depths—parted from him. The slim white body arched away, scattering drops of sea, a glimmering in the dark waters swifter than sight.

The voices laughed in the wind, and the taste lingered,

blood and sea-wrack.

"Brother," one called.

He followed.

The Prince and
the Serving Girl "(#2)

Contributors' Notes

Poet, teacher, broadcaster, surrealist, social protestor, and career diplomat (long his country's ambassador to France), Guatemalan novelist MIGUEL ANGEL ASTURIAS (1899–1974) won the 1967 Nobel Prize for Literature, and the 1966 Lenin Peace Prize. Mixing ardent nationalism with native myth, Asturias' fantasies bring the pantheon of Mayan gods, devils and wizards into confrontation against Guatemala's conquerors and oppressors. Notable books include *The Legends of Guatemala*, *The Bejewelled Boy*, *Men of Maize*, and *Mulata*.

Winner of the Hugo Award and the John W. Campbell Memorial Award, C. J. CHERRYH's science fiction and science fantasy novels deftly evoke truly alien cultures and languages. Of "Sea Change" she writes: "the inspiration came from the Celtic coasts, the isolation I felt in all the settlements whose faces are set towards the sea—where the elements have a face and substance, and the seasons bring only cyclic change. Myths grow in such places, where human beings touch a presence larger than humankind, and the sounds of the waves never cease. Motion strikes against the immoveable, sea against the land; and humankind sit poised between". Cherryh's novels include *The Gate of Ivrel*, *Sunfall* and *Ealdwood*.

M. LUCIE CHIN has a B.F.A. in painting, has held "the predict-able series of weird jobs artists and writers seem prone to", and exhibits her photographs regularly in galleries in New York and other cities. She lives currently in New York where she has a view of the Hudson River and Palisades from her typewriter and a dear friend named Portia who is "half Russian blue, half Brand X, and all cat". Chin's fantasies are derived from Chinese tradition, although "they are not retellings of two thousand year old tales but new stories from the old material which are true to the behavior and thoughts of the Chinese from a Westerner's frame of reference. There is a great deal of material within the mythos which is rich in traditions and ideas almost analogous to Western thinking, but which seems to have taken one or two small steps to the side—and which has been greatly ignored. I find this unfortu-nate. Not just in terms of Chinese and Oriental mythologies but in terms of all the vast amounts of unusual, strange and exotic material out there just waiting for someone to realize that fantasy does not *end* with Merlin or St. George".

JOHN CROWLEY came to New York City from the Midwest in 1964, and earned his living in films and television. He now makes his home in the Berkshire Hills of New England. Crowley is the author of *The Deep, Beasts,* and *Engine Summer.* His latest novel, *Little, Big,* is an immense and unusual magical tale of contemporary fantasy.

GILLIAN FITZGERALD makes her publishing debut with "Poo-ka's Bridge". "Storytelling is a dying art, something I did not realize until I became a school librarian. Many of these children had never been told a story! This was at odds with my own experience. I grew up in an Irish household (four generations under the same roof); the oral tradition was alive and well in the Connelly/FitzGerald family. With this background, it is only natural that my stories grow out of the Irish folk tradition and are meant to be read aloud".

Author of *On Moral Fiction,* a controversial critique of modern literature, several aspects of JOHN GARDNER's opus are of special interest to fantasy readers. A reknown medievalist, Gardner's scholarly work ranges from *The Life and Times of Chaucer* to translations of the alliterative Morte Arthure and the works of the Gawain poet. His children's fairy tale books include *Dragon, Dragon, King of the Hummingbirds,* and *A Child's Bestiary.* Gardner, who has variously stated his writing influences as Chaucer, Melville, and Walt Disney, is recipient of awards including the National Institute of Arts and Letters award, 1975, and the National Book Critics Book Circle award, 1976. Gardner's adult fiction includes *Freddy's Book, Grendel, In The Suicide Mountains, Jason and Medeia* (epic blank verse), *The King's Indian, October Light* and *The Sunlight Dialogues.*

SIR WILLIAM SCHWENK GILBERT (1836–1911) is best remembered for his classic light comic operas, written in collaboration with composer Arthur Sullivan, such as *The Pirates of Penzance, H.M.S. Pinafore,* and *The Mikado.*

ROBERT GRAVES, pre-eminent British poet, novelist and critic, is also author of *The White Goddess: A Historical Grammer of Poetic Myth.* "English poetic education should, really, begin not with *Canterbury Tales,* not with *The Odyssey,* not even with *Genisis,* but with *The Song of Amergin,* an ancient Celtic calendar-alphabet . . . which briefly summarizes the prime poetic myth". According to Celtic tradition, Amergin of the Fair Knee was the chief druid of the Milesians who came to Ireland to make war on the Tuatha de Danann. Amergin was the first to land; placing his foot on Irish soil, he is said to have burst into this prophetic song.

NICHOLAS STUART GRAY (1922–1981), a Highland Scot, began writing in his nursery and grew up to become a respected actor, director, children's playwright, and fantasist. His works include *The Seventh Swan, Mainly in Moonlight,* and *The Edge of Evening.*

M. JOHN HARRISON is a British mountaineer and writer of science fiction, mainstream fiction, and fantasy. "Viriconium Knights" is set in the world of his critically acclaimed novels *The Pastel City* and *Storm of Wings*. "The best fantasy is *terra incognita*. The reader is first lured into it and then abandoned. If he doesn't enjoy his subsequent bewilderment he should be reading *Which Car?* instead". Harrison currently makes his home in the north of England.

WILLIAM KOTZWINKLE has been described by *The New York Times* as "the fabulist, the gifted bard, the natural storyteller", and by *Playboy* as "strange, illusive, irridescent . . . Elephants, magicians, dreamers dance through young Kotzwinkle's fantasy world". Kotzwinkle's work includes *Dr. Rat* (winner of the World Fantasy Award), *Fata Morgana, Herr Nightingale and the Satin Woman,* and *Jack in the Box.* Kotzwinkle also writes children's fiction.

ELLEN KUSHNER lives on Manhattan's upper west side, in a building festooned with gargoyles. Lutenist, Renaissance scholar, collector and performer of folksongs and madrigals, she has edited fantasy and science fiction at Ace Books and at Pocket Books, and is editor of the fantasy anthology *Basilisk.* About "Unicorn Masque" she writes: "This is a Renaissance fantasy. In dress and manners it is set in an alternate sixteenth century England (except for the poison, which is patently high Jacobean). Most 'high fantasy' written these days is Medieval in setting and outlook: stone keeps are guarded with no fear of cannon; economy and loyalties are feudal. Great attention is paid to the construction of a universe in which man is only one element: equally important are the workings of magic and all the details that make the imagined world real to the reader. The Renaissance man, on the other hand, saw himself as a microcosm; in him was the sum of all creation. Its writers were fascinated with the questions of human responsibilities and individual identities. In 'The Unicorn Masque' are no wonders or marvels greater than the protagonist himself . . ." She notes that William Shakespeare and Dorothy Dunnette provided the inspiration for this story.

URSULA K. LE GUIN's honors include multiple recognitions by science fiction's Hugo and Nebula awards, the Horn Book Award, the Newbury Medal, and the National Book Award (for juvenile literature); her essays about fantasy are collected as *Languages of the Night*. In defining the difference between science fiction and fantasy in *Parabola,* she writes: "with the shift from the outside to the inside, from the object to the subject, things begin to slip and change. We fall down rabbit holes where the laws of gravity do not apply at all and no equations can save us . . . the original and instinctive movement of fantasy is, of course, inward . . .". In addition to non-fiction and mainstream works, Le Guin's lyric, humanistic sf should interest fantasy readers. Le Guin's fantasy includes *A Wizard of Earthsea, The Tombs of Atuan,* and *The Farthest Shore.* Le Guin is the daughter of writer Theodora Kroeber (*Ishi in Two Worlds*) and anthropologist Dr. Alfred Kroeber, and lives with her family in the American Northwest.

GABRIEL GARCÍA MÁRQUEZ was born in an isolated tropical region of Colombia, but has lived most of his life in Mexico, Venezuela, Paris, and Spain. His fiction, such as the international bestselling novels *One Hundred Years of Solitude,* and *The Autumn of the Patriarch,* have earned García Márquez a reputation as a modern master of literature.

"His life was a mixture of fantasy and practicality" reads *The Oxford Companion*'s biographical note on poet HAROLD MONRO (1879–1932). Monro, a major salon figure in 20th Century English verse, published numerous poetry magazines, while his Poetry Bookshop was a haven for British metaphysical poets.

An influential editor of strong esthetic conviction and occasional blues and rock performer, Nebula award winner MICHAEL MOORCOCK's popular and acclaimed fiction ranges from main-stream novels to comic suspense to science fiction, displaying a stylistic command from glib barbarian swords-&-sorcery through a literary spectrum to non-linear prose montage. A bibliog-rapher's bane, Moorcock's pure fantasy novels alone are far too numerous to list here. The six volume heroic adventures of Elric, a trilogy and two related books about the "Dancers at the End of Time", and the evocative romance *Gloriana* should be of special interest to readers of "Elric at the End of Time", and a convincing demonstration of Moorcock's versatility.

PAT MURPHY is employed as a science writer at SeaWorld, an oceanarium park in California, where she writes about the ocean and its inhabitants. "Some famous person—I don't recall who—said that the truth exists, falsehood we must invent. I don't agree. When I'm writing, I invent or discover one form of truth . . . I write about people. But I subscribe to a broader view than most folks do. The category includes aliens, animals, ghosts, spirits—and, of course, silkies".

ANDREW J. OFFUTT is perhaps best known for his popular swordswinging, swashbuckling adventure novels in the tradition of Robert E. Howard. The prose poem "Little Boy Waiting at the Edge of the Darkwood" shows a more delicately moody side of Offutt's fantasy.

New Yorker editor ALASTAIR REID, a Scots poet and essayist, is one of the major translators of Spanish-language authors cred-ited with bringing the work of writers like Jorge Luis Borges to American audiences. His fantasy prose includes *Fairwater* and *Allth*; best known of Mr. Reid's poetry volumes is *Oddments Inklings Omens Moments*.

RUDY RUCKER, born in Louisville, Kentucky, has written three rather wild science fiction novels, *White Light, Software,* and *Spacetime Donuts,* as well as works of scientific nonfiction. He holds a Ph.D. in Mathematical Logic, and has lectured on the Philosophy of Mathematics at Oxford and Heidelberg; he has been an underground cartoonist, has discussed infinity with Kurt Gôdel (if not with M.C. Escher and J. S. Bach), and is the great-great-great grandson of philosopher Georg Wilhelm Friedrich Hegel. "*Fantasy* is fervid description of some alternative universe, generally one which has more magic than ours. *Magic* I take to be meaningful constellations of events which are not time-like trees of cause and effect. On a pre-conscious level we fantasize constantly. Fantasy is a type of activity, not a subject matter. Fantasy is a tool for finding out what things mean . . . I made up 'Tales of Houdini' by telling them out loud one time in Germany driving from Heidelberg to Speyer—we had this horrible tiny 1972 German Ford with three kids wedged in the back . . ."

JESSICA AMANDA SALMONSON is the author of *The Tomoe Gozen Saga,* stern and elegant fantasy based on Japanese legendry and the women *samauri* of Japanese history. She is also the World Fantasy Award winning editor of *Amazons,* an anthology of feminist heroic fantasy—a second volume is forthcoming. Salmonson currently makes her home in the outskirts of Seattle in an old house with fruit trees that she shares with illustrator Wendy Adrian Schultz.

MASAO TAKIGUCHI was born in Seoul, Korea in 1919. She has published three books of poetry, and is known to American audiences primarily through the pages of *TransPacific.* She received the first Muroo Prize for her work in 1960.

JOHN ALFRED TAYLOR was born in Missouri in 1931. Taylor was "exposed to Oz books and E. R. Burroughs' Mars stories before I was old enough to know better, so enjoy writing science fiction and horror stories when not in the mood for poetry; though still believe 'A Poem a Day Keeps the Madhouse Away' ". Taylor's poetry has been widely published; "The Succubus" comes from the pages of *TransPacific*.

ANTANAS VAIČIULAITIS was born in Vilkaviskis, Lithuania, studied in Kaunas and Paris, and began publishing fiction while still a student. He worked as a teacher, magazine editor, diplomat, and translator. During World War II he emigrated to the U.S. and taught French at several colleges; he has worked closely with the Voice of America and was the editor of the magazine *Aidai*. As well as a writer of superb fiction, he is an anthologist, literary critic, and has translated the works of several French Catholic authors.

EVANGELINE WALTON began publishing fantasy with *The Virgin and the Swine* (later retitled *The Island of the Mighty*) in 1936—the fourth branch in her brilliant Mabinogion tetralogy (the other three volumes being *Prince of Annwn, the Children of Llyr*, and *The Song of Rhiannon*). These four novels draw on the four branches of the Welsh National Epic, the Mabinogi, recreating the myth in prose form. "The Judgement of St. Ives" draws upon Breton myth; a forthcoming, and eagerly awaited, novel, applies the same storytelling magic to Greek mythology. Walton currently makes her home in the American Southwest.

AUSTIN TAPPAN WRIGHT, (1883–1931), was a Boston lawyer and teacher; *Islandia*, a classic of American fiction, was a life-long project of his and did not see publication until after his death. The novel as published is approximately one third of its original length, and comprises only a part of the wealth of Islandian material. The novel has been in print since 1942, and has attracted a wide underground audience. Other material includes the Perrier *History*, fables, verse, maps, charts, and diverse information concerning the country and people of Islandia.

Tappan Wright King notes: "Sylvia Wright Mitarachí, the author's eldest daughter and my favorite aunt, died in May of this year, while completing a biography of another strong, independent woman, her great-aunt Melusina Fay Peirce, an early feminist. It was Sylvia who edited *Islandia* by a third to publishable length, and handled correspondence and negotiations on the work for nearly four decades. It is my hope that this first publication of unpublished Islandia material may serve as a small memorial of her years of service to Austin Wright's unique vision."

JANNY WURTS is a painter, illustrates professionally, plays the bagpipes, trains and rides horses, is an experienced sailor—from catamarans to windsurfers, composes multi-track synthesizer music, has traveled throughout Europe, Russia and Africa, saw the total eclipse of the sun off Mauritania in 1973, has crewed on 2000 mile Atlantic sailing runs, tested plankton for the National Science Institute, is experienced at canoeing, kayaking, rock-climbing, archery and silversmithery . . . and is 27 years old. This is her first published story; a novel is forthcoming from Ace. Wurts currently lives on the farm of author/naturalist Daniel P. Mannix "where a normal day can include everything from wrestling a 10-foot boa whose mouth has to be checked for fungus to chasing the chickens off the easel". Of "The Renders" she says: "to my mind, fantasy becomes compelling through its links with reality. The deeds of powerful wizards, swashbuckling heros, or firebreathing dragons, no matter how imaginatively contrived, are not convincing if their actions and settings are not logically consistent, and soundly based on true experience".

1923 Nobel Laureate for Literature, the Irish poet, dramatist and occultist WILLIAM BUTLER YEATS (1865–1939) is widely considered one of the finest poets of the English language. Yeats' deep, mystical involvement with Celtic myth is apparent to even the casual reader. Further, Yeats was an ardent collector and collator of Faery stories from the Irish oral tradition, and a central figure in the re-discovery of Irish legend, through such books as *Irish Fairy and Folk Tales,* and *The Celtic Twilight.* " 'Have you ever seen a fairy or such like?' I asked an old man in County Sligo. 'Amn't I annoyed with them', was the answer".

JANE YOLEN is the author of over sixty books, most of them published for young people but with the timelessness of good fantasy that makes them truly ageless. "The stories that touch us—child and adult—deeply, like our myths, are crafted visions, shaped dreams . . . not the smaller dreams that you and I have each night, rehearsals of things to come or anticipation/dread turned into symbols, but the larger dreams of all humankind". Yolen lives on a farm in New England with her husband and children. Her latest work is, *Touch Magic: Fantasy, Faerie and Folklore in the Literature of Children.*

Elsewhere....

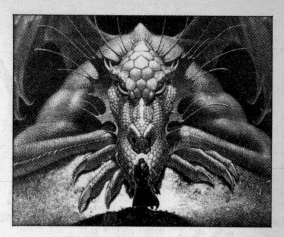

A DRAGON'S DOZEN

Thirteen authors and thirteen illustrators join to bring
you dragons, in all their bright and terrible variety. Among them:

GEORGE R.R. MARTIN & ALICIA AUSTIN

A child whose body is never warm
finds an ally in a dragon made of ice...

MICHAEL BISHOP & VAL LAKEY

A dragon lies coiled inside a teacher's heart...

JANE YOLEN & TERRI WINDLING

A boy steals a dragon and trains it for the cockfights...

ROGER ZELAZNY & GEOFFREY DARROW

A knight goes into business with an enterprising dragon...

AND MORE...

The dragons come to you at any hour of day or night.
And their eyes are always shining.

**DRAGONS
OF
LIGHT**

**Edited
by
ORSON
SCOTT
CARD**

ACE
SCIENCE
FICTION

0-441
16633-4
275

BASILISK

THE CROWNED DRAGON, WHOSE
GLANCE CONVEYED A CERTAIN IMMORTALITY.

BASILISK:

A collection of stories of timeless fantasy: the ancient and lasting themes of shape-shifting, the quest for the fatal beast, deadly wizardry, perilous bargains...by some of the modern masters of the field:

URSULA K. LE GUIN

ALAN GARNER

M. JOHN HARRISON

NICHOLAS STUART GRAY

BASILISK:

Come touch the enduring, the eternal enchantment of the fisherman who married a seal-woman, the enchantress whose surest enemy was her own cruel desires, the wizard whose love for a traitor brought him to the edge of fire....

EDITED BY
ELLEN KUSHNER

ACE
SCIENCE
FICTION

0-441
04820-X
225

ONCE THERE WAS MAGIC IN THE WORLD....

Unlimited magic, enough magic for every wizard's son who ever wished to cast a spell. But the "mana," the power that makes the magic and fuels the spells, is drying up, a natural resource wasted by centuries of careless and short-sighted magicians.

In **The Magic Goes Away** master fantasist Larry Niven chronicled the end of an age, and the beginning of a new world where steel and muscle rule. In this eagerly awaited sequel, Larry Niven has invited Poul Anderson, Steve Barnes, Mildred Downey Broxon, Dean Ing and Fred Saberhagen into his world to tap the hidden reserves of mana and uncover the forgotten places of power. All is not lost. The magic *may* return.

THE MAGIC MAY RETURN

Illustrated by Hugo winner Alicia Austin

ACE SCIENCE FICTION

0-441 51548-7 695

EDITED BY LARRY NIVEN